"Deftly plays with for[...]
you into a labyrinth[...]
RIAN HUGHES

"Thomas Ligotti goes cyberpunk by way of *House of Leaves* in *Basilisk*, a compulsive, ambitious, audacious book that will worm into your head much like the viruses it details. It's the kind of book that takes over your life and leaves you afraid to be with your own brain. Damn you, Matt Wixey."
PAUL TREMBLAY, *New York Times* **bestselling author of** *Horror Movie* **and** *A Head Full of Ghosts*

"One doesn't read *Basilisk*. This book must be dismantled like a bomb. A hacker's *House of Leaves*, a Nabokovian bio-weapon, a piece of cypherpunk folklore, this found footage mindphuck is pure red-pilled adrenaline."
CLAY McLEOD CHAPMAN, **author of** *Wake Up and Open Your Eyes*

"*Basilisk* possesses everything I look for in weird, boundary-pushing, disorienting horror fiction. Disturbing, intricately complex and utterly maddening, this novel seems so impossible and yet completely inevitable at the same time. A remarkable literary achievement. This book feels dangerous to touch, let alone read."
ERIC LAROCCA, **author of** *Things Have Gotten Worse Since We Last Spoke*

:HELLO FRIEND
who are you
:HELLO FRIEND
01110111 01100101
01100101 00100000
I SEE YOU. COME JOIN US. PLAY OUR GAME.

BASILISK

MATT WIXEY

hf4Do[redacted]A73+8M·Y
CWUOp1KN37[redacted]
Z9aoF8w6QDbmNUh2N1FMk
S4AVT4z4WSrjFq2rVoelu
[redacted]8z1MDFA
EjT[redacted]
09prPtcrgQHL[redacted]
[redacted]qzn2wsgpqPRj
DBEa8jG4XN127HUnG[redacted]

TITAN BOOKS

Basilisk
Print edition ISBN: 9781803367354
E-book edition ISBN: 9781803367361

Published by Titan Books
A division of Titan Publishing Group Ltd
144 Southwark Street, London SE1 0UP
www.titanbooks.com

First edition: July 2025
10 9 8 7 6 5 4 3 2 1

Extract from *Neuromancer* (1984)
© William Gibson reproduced with
kind permission.
Extract from *Stewart Lee's Comedy
Vehicle* © Stewart Lee reproduced
with kind permission.
Extract from the Elk Cloner code
© Richard Skrenta reproduced
with kind permission.
Extract from the Spot the Fed contest
rules by DEF CON and the Dark Tangent
reproduced with kind permission.
"Brain-virus" by Avinash Meetoo,
used under CC by 2.5.
Extract from *The Hitchhiker's Guide to
the Galaxy* (1979) © Douglas Adams
reproduced with kind permission.

Every effort has been made to source
and contact copyright holders and those
requiring likeness approvals. If any
omissions do occur, the publisher will be
happy to give full credit in subsequent
reprints and editions.

This is a work of fiction. All of the
characters, organizations, and events
portrayed in this novel are either
products of the author's imagination or
are used fictitiously. Any resemblance
to actual persons, living or dead
(except for satirical purposes), is
entirely coincidental.

A CIP catalogue record for this title is
available from the British Library.

EU RP (for authorities only)
eucomply OÜ, Pärnu mnt. 139b-14,
11317 Tallinn, Estonia
hello@eucompliancepartner.com,
+3375690241

Printed and bound by CPI Group Ltd,
Croydon, CR0 4YY.

*For Mousey and Nay Nay, who
keep me safe from basilisks.*

For James, who fights his with courage.

And for Anisha, as promised.

FOREWORD

What you are about to read was sent to me in July 2023, from an anonymous email account. It arrived as an attachment, with no message. I have been unable to verify most of its content, and all attempts to identify and communicate with the sender of the document have failed. I presume it is fiction, although it is possible that some names, locations, and other details have been changed or falsified to prevent verification. Having reached out to various colleagues, it does not appear that it has been sent to anyone else – or if it has, those recipients haven't come forward.

I have no idea why it was sent to me, although one explanation may be that I am a security professional and have presented research at a number of security conferences, so I therefore have something of a public profile in the field (some of my work is cited, directly and indirectly, in the document). Still, I am unable to account for why I was singled out specifically.

The document is complex, and strange, and contains some unusual ideas, some of which touch on my own research. Because of – or perhaps despite – this, I decided it deserves a larger audience. I toyed with the idea of simply making the document publicly available, but was concerned that doing so would encourage modifications and subsequent misinterpretations. As such, I approached a literary agent, who has assisted me in securing a publisher and making the document available as a traditionally bound book.

It has not been edited or modified in any way, beyond cosmetic changes required for formatting and typesetting. No text has been redacted (other than text which already was), deleted, or added. Any hyperlinks within the document have been expanded so that readers can access them. I have many thoughts about this document, and have extensively researched what I can, but have resisted the temptation to add my own analysis or commentary to it (as time goes on, and if there is a sufficient audience, I may release an annotated version). The text is therefore presented as I received it, so that you can encounter it as I did – with fascination, wariness and trepidation.

Matt Wixey, November 2024

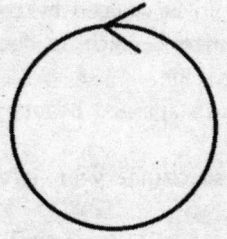

Ceci n'est pas un livre.

1. Access to computers - and anything which might teach you something about the way the world works - should be unlimited and total. Always yield to the Hands-On Imperative!
2. All information should be free.
3. Mistrust authority - promote decentralization.
4. Hackers should be judged by their hacking, not bogus criteria such as degrees, age, race, or position.
5. You can create art and beauty on a computer.
6. Computers can change your life for the better.

> \- Steven Levy, *Hackers: Heroes of the Computer Revolution* (1984)

Tell me how you want to die, and I'll tell you who you are.

> \- E.M. Cioran, *Tears and Saints* (1937)

Music to hack people by: https://open.spotify.com/playlist/4qrIiSODtOpFJbeawZSnpR 😎

HELLO FRIEND!

THE WEBSTER PAPER ❶

Holly Soames ①
04/11/2019 08:34

         ✕

Authored by Alexandra WEBSTER dob 06/10/1995 F. Deceased.

This document was recovered from WEBSTER's laptop (KD/01, CW/01) after her death. Due to its contents Counter Terrorism Cyber Operations was tasked with conducting a preliminary assessment on 04/11/2019. As requested, investigative opportunities have been appended as per scope (below) and recommendations and conclusions will be attached at the end of the document. The report reference is DPRT156721334/19.

Scope of assessment:
- Initial CT Cyber review of document re reported 'cyberweapon' and explanation of technical terms for the benefit of the senior management team

Assess veracity and feasibility of content
- Identify investigative opportunities pertaining to this and to closed SCD1 investigation into murder of Otto SALAS (see HRT34842202/19. SCD1 Homicide Command investigation, closed)
- Identify investigative opportunities pertaining to LVMPD investigation into MISPER Jay MORTON (see MERLIN 457585738/18, x-ref in HOLMES)
- Identify investigative opportunities pertaining to subject 'THE HELMSMAN' (pars NK)

Note that some of the investigative opportunities identified throughout are being actively pursued while others have yet to be actioned. This document will be updated with further information as it becomes available (further comments have been added to the copies of 'THE HELMSMAN TEXTS' embedded in this document, although these await full technical assessment by Innovation/R&D and some elements will require assessment by specialists). DPRT156721334/19 contains full list of actions and statuses as well as descriptions of persons of interest.

Some technical terms have been explained in comments where WEBSTER has provided insufficient detail and where relevant to the above aims.

        Reply | **Resolve** |

1: WE ARE FUCKED
c. FEBRUARY 2019 ❶

Elizabeth Sandifer writes, "Let us assume that we are fucked." ❷

A year ago I would have said that was fair, insofar as it applied to all of us, collectively and somewhat vaguely, but I now know that it applies to me, personally, and very specifically. It applied to Jay❸ when he walked out into that desert under a sea of indifferent stars. And, because you are reading this, it now applies to you.

Here we are then, both of us. Both fucked. First of all, I hope you see some solidarity in that.

We can, at least, look forward to being fucked in a wholly novel and unexpected fashion. May you be fucked in interesting ways, as the Chinese proverb has it.* There are already so many means by which to die; it's almost refreshing to learn that one's demise may come about from something new.

I remember visiting a friend of mine, who was reading medicine, at university. During a lull in the conversation I picked up one of her brick-like textbooks on diseases, and as I leafed through that dry catalogue of decay and despair – my casual interest turning first

---

* Fun fact: "May you live in interesting times" is probably not a Chinese proverb, as the internet would have you believe. According to Fred Shapiro in *The Yale Book of Quotations* (2006), the closest known Chinese saying is: "Better to be a dog in days of peace than a human in times of war!" But then one John Francis Davis adds to this that the Chinese "by adherence to a steady, quiet system … proceed without confusion, and bad men have nothing to gain." I'm not sure that last one is true. My experience over the last year or so has shown that the status quo can be something that bad people will quite desperately try to maintain – violently, if necessary.

13

to shock and then outright horror – I was astonished that I wasn't dead already, and more so that anyone ever lived past thirty. By some miracle we continually evade most of the innumerable things that would kill us. And yet we're all about to be fucked anyway, by something entirely novel. Another page in my friend's already weighty book, pushed in right at the end, just when we thought we might have a chance.

It hardly seems fair – but then, as my father used to say: "Write a letter, Alex; see who cares."

So. On learning that we are fucked, three questions present themselves: *What am I being fucked by? Who is responsible for the fucking? And can I ameliorate the situation so that I am fucked as minimally as possible, and ideally not at all?*

I won't keep you in suspense: the answers to the first two questions are: the basilisk,❶ and The Helmsman.❷

As for the third, that may depend on you, but I very much suspect that the answer is: 'no fucking way'. That is to say, no, you can't escape this, any more than you can escape being damaged by cell mutations or murdered by a sudden brain aneurysm – any more than the earth can dodge an asteroid. But I'll get to that.

Which brings me to my next point: if we are fucked, jointly and individually, and if that state of fuckedness is almost certainly inevitable, then I can at least attempt to shed some light on the nature of the fucking. You won't be unconscious of the irony that if you are in possession of this document you probably know more about it than most people already (which is why you, like me, are fucked), but I doubt you know enough.

* * *

When I think about this thing I'm writing (I'm hesitant to call it a book, and absolutely refuse to call it a story), I sometimes console myself by couching it, at least

Holly Soames①
22/11/2019 04:29
See c4 of 'The Helmsman Texts' (THT) for definition.

Holly Soames②
04/11/2019 09:01
No trace.

internally, as a valiant endeavour. A Quixotic, Pyrrhic struggle, a stone tossed blindly at Goliath. There is that optic to it, in that if it ever finds its way into the public domain I will almost certainly not be around to see it. And of course, for a hacker, there is nothing more emblematic of our crusading, abstract world than staring down a nameless and faceless foe. The Man, the G, the abyss. Who wouldn't want to believe that their legacy is a record of righteous indignation, a note of resistance to inspire those rebels who will pick up my sword when I can no longer bear its weight? I write this, I tell myself, so that you will not be as afraid as I have been, because terror cannot survive knowledge.*

All this is heavily infused with ego, obviously, however wonderful it might sound – and the truth is that my cause may not actually be noble or fearless at all. I can't help but think that more than anything else it is a confession – one I'm writing to occupy myself while waiting to die, with the sole intention that people don't blame me.

* * *

I once saw an interview with a man who'd been shot where he explained what the experience was like. The thing that struck me most was his description of an odd, painless tranquillity after the shot but before the pain – a physiological defence mechanism inducing a tiny delay between stimulation and response. You may have experienced it on a smaller scale with something as insignificant as stubbing your toe or burning your finger – a brief time where you cannot feel the sensation but know, helplessly and completely, that it is on its way.

This thing I'm writing, whatever I call it, is being written in that moment. Between Jay's disappearance

---

* Although, of course, The Helmsman's entire point is that knowledge brings its own terror.

(death, OK, death❶ – I'll try to be honest with you from now on) and whatever is waiting for me, patient and still, not too far down the line.

Hey – have laptop, will write a letter, see who cares. I won't let the optics concern me, because it's not my concern. You're in the best place to judge whether what I'm saying is the work of a fearless soldier of light fighting dark forces or the snivelling of a guilt-ridden coward. Or both. I'm just here to tell you what happened, and you can make up your own damn mind.

So long as you understand that, either way, we're fucked.

∗   ∗   ∗

If I *am* writing this in a moment it feels like a long one. Once the Las Vegas police and the National Park Service had finished their less-than-exhaustive search❷ for Jay,* I came back to London and quit my job. I tried to make it work for a while, and to give my colleagues their due so did they. Richard,❸ the CEO, even offered me a week of discretionary bereavement leave – which, given his previous standards of parsimony, was astonishingly generous.

I spent that week poring over what Jay and I had

---

* Not being an expert in either the field of law enforcement or the process of searching for missing people, I may be biased or misinformed, but it appeared to me that the authorities expected to find a body relatively quickly, and when one failed to surface they shrugged their shoulders. Perhaps they were reluctant to look more closely for fear of finding even more bodies; I'm told the deserts outside Las Vegas are notorious for the number of corpses underneath their sands. Either way, after four days, the authorities could no longer justify the expenditure or resources and stopped the search. Jay has still not been found. A police officer took me to one side and told me that as Jay had no history of mental illness and appeared lucid and rational when last seen, he may have decided of his own free will to disappear. Eoin didn't believe that, and neither do I. Needless to say, the authorities paid little attention to Eoin's account of The Helmsman and why we believed he, or ▓▓▓▓ ▓▓▓▓▓▓▓▓▓▓▓▓▓▓, were responsible for Jay's disappearance.

Holly Soames①
04/11/2019 10:12
No suggestion from MERLIN report or LVMPD report that MORTON is deceased.

Holly Soames②
04/11/2019 10:28
LVMPD did not appear to deviate from their SOP for MISPERS.

Holly Soames③
04/11/2019 10:29
Richard BANKS. Suggest re-interviewing to corroborate some of the events in this document.

come to call, between ourselves, *The Helmsman Texts*, looking for any sign or reason that would explain – well, let's be honest, any of it – and found nothing, just as I had always done before. When I returned to Cybotage everything else felt smaller and much less important. I looked at Richard and Nina and Omar and Kevin and Ronnie, and realised I barely knew them – that in comparison to the game, they barely mattered. I didn't know how to *talk* to them anymore, except about Jay, and they didn't want to listen to that.

I understand why, but to not talk about him was a deceit I couldn't fathom. Cybotage was the place where Jay had been Jay, more than he had been anyone anywhere else. No matter how much easier it might make things, you can't purge someone from a place to which they belonged, because people leave traces of themselves, however smudged or indistinct. Jay was everywhere in that office. There was such presence in his absence.

I'm not angry with them; grief is a hard thing to navigate with anyone, let alone colleagues, so I made it easier on everyone and resigned. Richard asked me to stay, but I shook my head and then his hand, and left Cybotage for the last time, less than a year after my first day.

Some security career I'd had: worked on a few engagements, solved some puzzles, travelled to a conference, and got my friend killed.

On the plus side, there's a chance – a tiny, outside, *infinitesimal* chance – that I might just save the world.

But let's park that for now.

* * *

A couple of weeks after leaving I realised I was brassic. I'm not bad with money, no worse than I am with anything else, but it simply hadn't occurred to me that there wouldn't be any more cash coming in, until that cash dwindled to almost nothing. I had enough for a month's rent – maybe two, if I rationed food – but if I'm honest, my main concern was this document, which I first decided to write following that strange journey into the desert, and which has since occupied my thoughts almost entirely.

No one was going to pay me to write it, unfortunately, so I applied for a job at a small secondary school❶ about forty minutes from my flat.❷

My degree in Computer Science was recent enough to be relevant, and Richard had given me a reference far better than my eight months of experience probably merited. So, at the age of twenty-three, I found myself saying goodbye to one career before it had really begun, and beginning another.

The pay is obviously nowhere near what I was earning at Cybotage, but that's to be expected; I no longer perform witchcraft, subverting software and injecting poison payloads to find weaknesses in large corporate networks. Now I reset passwords for kids who reek of Lynx and Oxy pads, and who regard me with half fear and half sneer. Sometimes I help teachers with the projectors, something they always have trouble with. Once in a while my new boss, Milo,❸ lets me roll out Group Policy updates. That's always an exciting day.

Milo doesn't like hackers, no matter that I was on the ethical side of the profession – I think he worries that one day I'll decide to take down the school network just for shits and gigs – and neither is he the friend and boss that Jay was, but he's OK. Fifty-ish, balding, walks as though one of his legs is made out of wood (it isn't, I checked). He's got a hoarse, barking sort of laugh and a way of squinting one eye at people when they ask him a question. If it wasn't for the polo shirts and chinos he'd make an excellent pirate. Perhaps he moonlights, I don't know.

And he's right to be suspicious, because not so long

ago I'd have been so fucking bored with this job that I *would* have entertained myself by poking holes in the school's infrastructure and putting malware on the system for the lulz. But now, of course, there's this, and it's quite enough effort to hack together what happened without actually hacking into the bargain.

So as my skills rust away, I make enough money to survive and to write. I go to the school, I come home, I microwave a ready meal and eat it at my desk, and then I start what I have come to think of as my real work: revisiting a nightmare. I unpack, and repack, the knowledge that we are all totally, excruciatingly, thoroughly – well, you know the score by now.

*   *   *

Every time I read the news I see something that might be linked. A man who worked in threat intelligence❶ in San Francisco, for instance, is missing. He's been gone for seven days now. 'Fears grow for missing tech worker', the headlines say.❷

But I can't know for sure, and this is part of the problem: tying cause to effect, motive to action, is almost impossible. Another example: earlier today, I spent forty-seven minutes staring at the screen and not writing, because I thought I could discern very slight fluctuations in the brightness, changes which repeated in a rhythmic pattern suggestive of encoded communications. Such behaviour would indicate an attempt to exfiltrate information or convey a message, like an air-gap bypass;❸ it put me in mind of a few of the exhibits on The Tour, Jay's museum of the dark arts, which he showed me when I first joined. Or the numbers station, the first stage of The Helmsman's game. And I wondered if someone was trying to covertly communicate something to me. It is exactly the sort of thing The Rearguard❹ would have done.

But after forty-seven minutes of attempting to

Holly Soame❶
04/11/2019 1:33
Threat intelligence (TI) = Sub-discipline of cyber security which involves tracking hackers and their techniques and tools.

Holly Soames❷
06/11/2019 08:03
No trace of any articles with this headline.

Holly Soames❸
04/11/2019 11:59
Hacking technique which uses light, sound, etc. to leak information from air-gapped (physically separated) computers.

Holly Soames❹
04/11/2019 12:02
No trace.

transcribe the message using several encoding schemes – Morse, Manchester, coded mark inversion, all the usual suspects – I pulled myself together and realised that there was no pattern at all, just an HDMI cable that needed replacing. This is what The Helmsman has stolen from me: my ability to discern signal from noise. And what has he left in its place? A fascination with the grotesque, an obsession with the worst of ourselves.

Today, for example, I read about engineering students who were asked to design a hypothetical blood pipeline❶ for transporting blood between two cities for an assessment. The students, excited to be faced with such an unusual challenge, created their designs. They determined the optimal route and materials. They factored in structure, fluid mechanics and the risk of rust. They worked hard on this. They put *effort* into it.

When their designs were submitted the professor told them they had all failed. Not a single one of them had asked what the pipe was for, or whose blood would be running through it. I can imagine The Helmsman laughing his head off at that.

We have been fucking ourselves so well, in so many ways, for so long, that there hardly seems to be a need for someone to come up with a new method. And yet I find myself writing this, and you find yourself reading it.

✳   ✳   ✳

The Helmsman's game, or at least mine and Jay's version of it, is no longer active. I check the links every day, hoping that it might have finally come back to life, but all the components are gone, and the email address no longer sends its auto-responses with their peculiar attachments, so there is no way you will be able to receive *The Helmsman Texts* the way Jay and I did. But you need to read them to understand all this, so I've included all the spewings we received from

Holly Soames①
04/11/2019 13:01
Likely this 2009 article by Gideon LEVY: 'And there lie the bodies' in Haaretz: https://www.haaretz.com/2009-01-04/ty-article/and-there-lie-the-bodies/0000017f-df31-d856-a37f-fff1e5bc0000.

that deranged and brilliant mind – and whatever else The Helmsman may be, he is brilliant – within this document at the appropriate points.

The fact that the game has disappeared may be a positive development, indicating the game is over, or it may be more ominous: the game may have simply moved to another stage. Given what The Helmsman says in his fifth chapter I suspect it is the latter, but it may just be that ███████████████████ are doing their work well;❶ if I can say anything charitable about them at all, it's that they strike me as 'people' who take a great deal of professional pride in their work.

The only person who knows I am writing this is Otto,❷ and even he doesn't know what exactly it is, other than a vague understanding that it's an account of what happened to a friend who went missing. He believes I am doing it to process my grief – which is at least partially true – so he lets me get on with it. He has no idea that I'm also doing it to try and save the world, and I don't think he would believe me if I told him. In any case, I won't tell him – I won't tell *anyone* – because of what ███████████████ made me do in the desert. And I will not be put in that position again, not for anyone. Ever.

It's a shame, because given that Otto is a history teacher, of a sort, he would probably be quite helpful, and the prospect of sewing together disparate pieces of a mystery might hold some allure for him. Then again, I have a strong suspicion that he wouldn't be able to process any of it – not Fairlop Waters, and certainly not ████████████████. He would think I am making it up, or he would leave, or both.

Because Otto is kind and gentle and easy-going. Otto likes panel shows and action films and 90s music. Otto only reads nonfiction. On holidays Otto likes to stay within the grounds of his hotel. Otto doesn't play games. Otto is all surface, with no dark tangents or sharp

Holly Soames①
04/11/2019 14:47
WEBSTER repeatedly alleges that '██████████ ██████' (no trace) deliberately remove and/or obfuscate content from the internet, particularly that relating to players of the 'game'. Suggest listing all examples in this document and dip-sampling with social media/ site providers to ascertain the reason(s) the profiles, posts, videos, articles, etc. were removed.

Holly Soames②
04/11/2019 14:58
Otto SALAS dob 09/08/1989 M. Deceased.

edges. He reminds me of a hollow sphere in that way; everything that can be inspected is right there, available, on the surface. I like that about him. I don't ever have to worry about any hidden cunning or creativity, and I'm glad, because I have had enough of those things.

More than anything I like the fact that Otto knows nothing about computers. He has a laptop, and a smartphone, and a Google Home, but he has no clue how they work, and no curiosity about how they could be compromised❶ or weaponised. He thinks Incognito mode will protect him from malware. He believes he is completely safe because he has an antivirus program – which he *paid* for – and he has only the haziest idea of what I used to do for a living.

I asked him once if he was worried about being hacked, and in his open brown herbivore's eyes there was a surprise, almost a distress, at the unwelcome intrusion of such a thought – as though I'd suggested doing something indecent or illegal.

"Why on earth would anyone want to hack *me*?" he said. "I'm not interesting enough."

The truth is that his lack of curiosity about what I'm writing is probably not a bad thing for either of us.

Otto is a supply teacher, and currently filling in at the school for a teacher who's off long-term sick. We met a week or so after I started, when he came to the IT room to ask for a website to be unblocked. His degree was in history, and he has ambitions to write a textbook on post-war Japan; occasionally he pores over and makes notes in a huge tome entitled *Embracing Defeat*. This, to me, seems rather on-the-nose, but I haven't remarked on it aloud because he wouldn't get it.

We are sleeping together, which is vanilla but pleasant. He asks me what I want. On Saturdays we go to second-hand bookshops and try out new branches of chain restaurants.

He's supportive – distantly – of my writing,

Holly Soames①
04/11/2019 15:16
In its security sense, i.e. breached/attacked.

although he occasionally expresses concerns that I am spending too much time on it (and, by implication, not enough on him). "Your hobby," he calls it.

It's as good a word as any.

* * *

This document will not claim to be, nor hold, an answer. If you are a hacker you have probably already internalised the two truths it contains: my crime is curiosity❶ and satisfaction is a lie.

Holly Soames①
04/11/2019 15:20
'The Conscience of a Hacker' by THE MENTOR (1986) in Phrack. See http://phrack.org/issues/7/3.html.

Uncertainty is what has always appealed to me. I am happy, or at least as happy as I can be, when the cat is both alive and dead. There is nothing more tedious or disappointing than a mystery solved. If life has a meaning (and it is not forty-two), then it is to be found only in the search for answers. If I find solace in anything, it is that there is no conceivable end to this search. I do not exist in certainty, only in potential. I can't see you and I will probably never meet you. But I hope you, like me, find some comfort in questions, and in the cold and endless multitudes they may spawn within you.

This document is no different: it is a series of questions, most related to the fact that we are fucked. A series of questions with no answers, and what could be a nobler reason to write it than that? What could be a more fitting tribute to Jay? What hacker could ask for a better eulogy?

* * *

But this document also constitutes a responsibility.

And that responsibility is now yours, because, by fair means or foul you have somehow ended up reading it. That may be because I have finally finished it, or, more likely, because something has happened to me: I have become infected, or ███████████████ have decided I'm too much of a risk to keep alive. It

23

doesn't matter, if I'm honest. The important thing is that *you hold this document in your hands*. And there's no getting around it: this means you are at risk. But you have to keep going. You have to show this to people. Do not keep it to yourself.

You may assume, as Sandifer does, as I do, that we are fucked.

But an assumption is all it is. It could be wrong. You could prove it wrong.

Thank you.

In memory of Jay 'brix' Morton, 1985–2018

2: HACKING, FOLKLORE, AND THE GAME
c. FEBRUARY—MARCH 2019 / FEBRUARY—MARCH 2018

To be a hacker is to dance to hidden tunes. But more than that, it is to rewrite the song and repurpose the instruments. Make a piano sound like a guitar; disguise a vuvuzela as a clarinet to get it past security; redesign a flute so that it produces the flatulent bellow of a tuba. All because we can.

We don't just hear a melody, we compose it.

When you're a hacker no music is unplayable. Any instrument or style can be mastered, so long as you have the drive to understand it. That's what moves us beyond all else: the urge to take things apart, learn how they work, and reshape them. Legend has it that the term 'hacker' originated at MIT, to describe those students who came up with particularly innovative or interesting solutions to creating model trainsets.❶

It means finding surprising answers to problems – sometimes, problems nobody has yet thought to ask – and posing questions of your own.

Criminal hackers, sometimes known as 'black hats' after a trope in old Western films❷ take a vicious pride in destruction, in the creation of exploits and malware and their damaging effects. They find exhilaration in senseless devastation and the acquisition of money through criminal enterprise, immersed in their heaving little worlds of malice.

Jay, like me, was a hacker, not a criminal. He hated black hats with a passion, although he admired some of the skills they demonstrated (as evidenced by his curation of The Tour), but our obsession with The

Holly Soames①
04/11/2019 15:27
For reference, see Steven LEVY's 2014 WIRED article: wired.com/2014/11/the-tech-model-railroad-club/ (Steven Levy, 2014).

Holly Soames②
04/11/2019 15:31
e.g. *The Old West in Fact and Film: History versus Hollywood* (Jeremy AGNEW, 2012).

Helmsman's game arose from our shared disease of curiosity. That, and nothing else.

We just had to know.

* * *

I joined Cybotage, a small information security outfit – one of those firms inaccurately described as 'agile' in marketing bumf and accurately defined as 'fucking chaos' by the actual staff – in February 2018, a few months after graduating from university, as a junior penetration tester.❶

Cybotage was based on the first floor of a red-brick office building in East London called Gants House.❷

On the floor above us was a DVLA test centre, so we became inured to the sight of people sweating over copies of *The Highway Code* in reception, and the screams of delight and moans of anguish as candidates learnt their results. Sometimes, over a ciggy at the back of the building, the DVLA staff would tell us stories. My favourite was the one involving a short, scrawny, acne-ridden seventeen-year-old kid who, upon getting into the car with his examiner, donned green sunglasses, reclined his seat, put one hand on top of the wheel, and said, "Let's roll, motherfucker." I wonder where that kid is now.

Gants House backed on to a railway line, and you'd regularly hear the shocking scream of a train as it barrelled past outside, making the floors and walls vibrate and our mugs jump and shudder on the desks. When the weather turned warmer Richard refused to let us turn on the air con because he believed it would make too much of a dent in the firm's already meagre coffers – so we kept the windows open and flinched on cue, every twenty minutes.

The penetration testing team was small – only four of us: Jay, Nina, Kevin❸ and myself – and there

Holly Soames①
05/11/2019 08:26
CTF = Capture The Flag. Competitive wargames for hackers involving simulated scenarios.

Holly Soames②
05/11/2019 08:44
Slang for hacking and experimenting with telecommunications systems and equipment, particularly public telephone networks. Popular from the 1970s until the 1990s, now considered 'old school.'

Holly Soames③
05/11/2019 08:52
The cypherpunks were a loose collective of scientists, mathematicians and programmers – including Timothy MAY, John GILMORE, Adam BACK, Matt BLAZE, Jude MILHON, Eric HUGHES and Julian ASSANGE – who referred to themselves as 'crypto-anarchists'. They believed that cryptography could enable the upheaval of various societal structures and concepts and thus bring about a completely private and anonymous world. See 'A cypherpunk's manifesto' by Eric HUGHES (1993) https://www.activism.net/cypherpunk/manifesto.html.

Holly Soames④
06/11/2019 11:46
No trace of any posts by this alias on the forums of which I'm aware.

were two other small teams which dealt with threat intelligence and incident response. Jay was the team leader, a veteran pentester who had been involved in the hacking community since his teens. I'd heard about him during my degree, and had read some of his blogs after applying for the position. He was big 'in the scene', as we say – presenting research at prominent conferences, participating in CTFs,❶ and regularly releasing new tools and code. Jay knew the history of hacking inside out, from phreaking❷ and cypherpunks❸ to cryptocurrencies and ransomware. And he ruled Cybotage, more or less, for all that Richard was ostensibly in charge. A raised eyebrow from Jay could torpedo a proposal; a single email could shift a strategy. He could have easily secured a senior position at one of the corporate firms, but I think he preferred to be a big fish in a tiny pond. When I googled him before starting at Cybotage, his name and nick, 'brix', were spoken with respect in all the forums❹ that mattered. I didn't meet him at my interview – Richard and Nina had led it – but I did on my first day.

And I hated him.

* * *

Sophie, a tall woman with large grey eyes and a soft voice, led my induction, such as it was. She ushered me around the little office to meet everyone, and we ended our tour at the tiny kitchen where Jay was reading something on his phone and eating a sandwich. He was dressed in what I would come to think of as his uniform: black baseball cap, black jeans, white t-shirt hanging loose on his thin frame. He didn't look up as we came in.

"This is Alex," Sophie said to him. "Your new pentester."

Jay turned to us. His lips – shaped in a languid curve, like an archer's bow – twisted slightly into a brief smile as we shook hands. His eyes flickered over my face, and then, out of nowhere, he said:

"What's your favourite vulnerability?"

I blinked. "Sorry, what?"

"Jay," Sophie said gently. "It's her first day."

Jay waited, watched.

The question *had* thrown me. I'd become interested in security at university, although my degree had barely covered the subject, and I'd done some playing around at home with test rigs and vulnerable VMs❶ and so on – but a favourite vulnerability? *Is this a test?* I thought wildly. *Is he expecting something original, something highly exotic?* I struggled for a second or two to think of something impressive, dredging my memory, until something eventually bobbed to the surface and I snatched at it.

"Er, probably MS08-067?"❷

There was a pause.

"Seriously?"

"I haven't really looked at many—"

"What is it you like about it?"

"Jay," Sophie said again. "She's been interviewed already."

"Yeah, by Nina and Richard," Jay said. "Not me." His eyes were still on me. "Why do you want to be a hacker?"

I'd been asked this at my interview, and I had an answer ready. I can't remember if it was what I truly believed at the time, or if I'd cynically tried to predict what my interviewers would like to hear. Knowing myself, it was probably the latter.

"I want to help organisations improve their security and make society safer by finding vulnerabilities and helping to mitigate them," I said in a rush, the words stacking up and collapsing into each other. Even to my ears it sounded mealy-mouthed.

Jay waited a few seconds, as though expecting

Holly Soames①
05/11/2019 09:07
VM = virtual machine.

Holly Soames②
05/11/2019 09:09
A critical vulnerability from 2008 affecting Microsoft's SMB (Server Message Block) protocol. Well-known in the security industry and often used as a learning exercise for people new to the field.

more, his smile slowly dying, before turning back to his phone and taking a bite out of his sandwich.

"Great," he said through a mouthful of bread. Disappointed. "Cool. Look forward to working with you."

It *had* been a test, and I had failed. Sophie gave me a slack sort of smile, raised her eyebrows in sympathy, and led me back to my desk.

Our world can be wonderful; it attracts minds which can do and think things nobody thought possible. But it also draws the worst: the intolerant, the insecure. After that first encounter, I placed Jay firmly in the second camp. He was a talented misanthrope, I decided, one who saw others as inferior and unworthy of his time and attention. Later, as I got to know him better, I realised that was how he was with everyone: awkward, combative, as though everything had to be challenged. It wasn't personal, it was just who he was, and what made him a good hacker. He would have been dismayed to learn that it made others uncomfortable. It was simply how he processed information: absorb it, understand it, streamline it, and then precisely exploit the gaps and weaknesses he had identified. It wasn't a character flaw, I suppose I mean, although it could certainly come across that way.

At the time, though, I made a mental note to try and steer clear of him as much as I possibly could.

* * *

Naturally that was difficult in such a small team, and a couple of weeks later I found myself partnered with him for five days in Basingstoke for my first ever client engagement, an internal infrastructure test at an insurance company. ❶

We would work from their office, connect our testing laptops to their internal network, and probe for vulnerabilities before writing up our findings in a report.

Holly Soamesⓘ
05/11/2019 09:33
Believe this to be
BARLOW HEALTH,
16 CHAPEL ROAD,
RG22 5TX.

29

On the first day, the client contact (Colin,**❶** I think his name was; most of our clients' IT people seemed to be called Colin) met us in reception. After he'd briefed us – me spending most of the time trying to look as though I understood what was going on – we got a flimsy plastic cup of cheap coffee each from the vending machines, the material so thin it felt like it was warping with the heat of the liquid, and set up our laptops at two adjoining desks in the corner of the large open-plan office.

"Know what you're doing?" Jay asked.

"Well, I've done some stuff at home," I said, "on a testing rig, which I—"

I stopped myself. *Don't blather. Show him you belong here.*

"Yes," I said.

"Know how to do a SYN**❷** scan?"

"Yes."

"Get started, then," Jay said. "Whatever subnet you're on at the moment."

I nodded again and kicked off the scan. I remember wanting, stupidly, to impress him. Find something juicy as fast as possible. Get domain admin**❸** in the first hour, show him I wasn't some lame noob**❹** who could barely run Metasploit. **❺**

Ridiculous, isn't it, the hoops we feel we have to jump through? The proof we think we need to provide.

Something caught my eye in the scan results and I leant forwards. I hadn't been aware of Jay watching me, but he must have been, because he said casually: "Found something?"

"Maybe," I said, trying to keep the excitement out of my voice. "A Linux box. It's open on 21, 80, 443.**❻** Looks like it's running some sort of weird distro."**❼**

"So what's the plan?" Jay said.

I thought back to those late nights at university hacking Vulnhub**❽** VMs.

Holly Soames①
05/11/2019 09:49
Was not interviewed as part of SCD1's investigation. Suggest doing so. Full name not known.

Holly Soames②
05/11/2019 10:32
A type of scan to identify live hosts on a network.

Holly Soames③
05/11/2019 10:32
i.e. control of the whole network.

Holly Soames④
05/11/2019 10:33
noob or n00b = newbie.

Holly Soames⑤
05/11/2019 10:41
An open-source modular exploit/attack framework

Holly Soames⑥
05/11/2019 10:42
Ports open on the machine for various services. In this case 21 = FTP (File Transfer Protocol), 80 = HTTP (webserver), 443 = HTTPS (secure webserver).

Holly Soames⑦
05/11/2019 10:43
Distro = distribution i.e. the type of Linux operating system.

Holly Soames⑧
05/11/2019 10:46
An online repository of deliberately vulnerable virtual machines, used by security researchers and hackers to practise attack techniques.

Holly Soames①
05/11/2019 10:49
i.e. gather
information on the
target for possible
vulnerabilities and
access opportunities.

Holly Soames②
05/11/2019 11:03
Vulnerability scanner
for webservers.

Holly Soames③
05/11/2019 11:05
Telnet = remote
command-line
interface. Insecure
and now largely
replaced by SSH
(Secure Shell).

"Enumerate❶ it, look at the running services, see if there are any known exploits for them."

"Cool. Off you go." There was something in his voice which should have made me stop right there, but I couldn't. I was thrilled that barely half an hour into my very first test I'd already found something noteworthy. I immediately started running all manner of things with little thought to any strategy. Brute forcing the FTP server; Nikto❷ for the web services; Metasploit scans; googling for exploits.

But over the next ninety minutes, every single thing I threw at that box bounced off it. Every scan or attack produced absolutely nothing of value, and my shoulders began to slump.

Jay said nothing until it was almost lunchtime. "Any luck?"

"No," I said, my voice tight with frustration.

Jay typed something on his laptop. "Scan it again." I did, and the box was now open on port 23. Telnet.❸

"And again," he said, now typing something else, and the Telnet server had disappeared. There was a strange expression on his face, something I couldn't quite read. At the time it seemed like pity.

"It's *my* machine, rookie," he said. "You're scanning *my* machine."

I should have laughed it off; looking back, it is funny, the sort of anecdote many pentesters might tell against themselves in the bar after a conference. And I was a junior tester, on my first engagement; it was an easy mistake to make. I should have been kinder to myself, and I had no reason to feel embarrassed.

But a voice in my head swore and hissed: *you should have taken half a second to think about it, you fucking idiot. You've made yourself look* stupid.

And that word. Those two syllables, sagging with the weight of the scorn they implied.

Rookie.

It wasn't quite as bad as 'noob', but it was close.

From that point on Jay looked over my shoulder to make sure I was typing the right commands and accurately interpreting the results. When I did, he offered no praise or comment. When I made a mistake, I could hear a bored, supercilious smile in his voice as he corrected me.

I clenched my fists and waited for the day to be over.

* * *

When I got back to my little studio flat that night, I lay in bed and stared at the ceiling until the muted grey light of dawn told me it was time to get dressed and return to Basingstoke. I groaned, dreading it. I *knew* cyber security was where I belonged, but the problem was convincing anyone else. I'd envisioned doing so on this engagement by flexing my skills, cracking the network in record time, and forcing Jay to re-examine his initial assessment of me. To have had that wonderful vision so brutally stripped away, on the first day of the job, was devastating.

The next day I said nothing to Jay unless he asked me a direct question, and I answered with the minimum number of words possible, without embellishment or elaboration. I no longer trusted myself not to say something stupid.

The day passed without incident, but on the third morning we made some progress – Jay coming up with all the ideas, me executing them under his supervision – to the point where, just before lunch, we acquired a low-privileged shell❶ on someone's machine in the office.

An hour or so later, I made my second mistake.

* * *

On previous days we'd eaten lunch together in the insurance company's canteen, both of us spending the hour reading our phones in silence. But on the

Holly Soames①
05/11/2019 11:23
i.e. they had access to it from their laptops, but not admin access.

32

third day I told Jay I wanted to finish up an e-learning package on my work laptop during the break. He shrugged and left me to it. And as the office was one of those places where everybody traipses off for lunch at the same time, I was alone.

I connected to the shell. My chance at redemption, I reasoned, was for me to present Jay with local administrator access, if not full domain administrator privileges. The shell we had was useful, but a reverse Meterpreter❶ shell would be more so; it would enable me to load all sorts of tools and modules that I'd read about during those long hours studying blogs and tutorials, and I could perhaps leverage those to escalate my privileges. I spun up a payload on my testing laptop, and used the shell to upload it to the user's machine.

But there was no connection to my Meterpreter listener,❷ and then the shell itself stopped responding to commands. I restarted it, and then restarted my own machine, feeling the first lurch of panic. I realised that I had somehow fucked up our shell, and then something much worse happened: a bald man in a navy polo-shirt whom I hadn't seen before came into the office, unplugged one of the employee's computers, and took it away.

Oh, shit, I thought.

* * *

When Jay returned he tried to connect to the shell, and muttered under his breath when it didn't work. I felt him looking at me and was ready to plead ignorance, but before he could say anything an unsmiling Colin approached our desks, a sheet of paper in his hand.

"A word. Now, please."

Jay shot me another look. I didn't trust myself to return it, but instead got up and followed them both to a conference room. Each footstep required a colossal effort, but I barely felt my soles touch the carpet.

Holly Soames① **05/11/2019 11:58** A Metasploit payload which provides an interactive shell with which to launch further attacks.

Holly Soames② **05/11/2019 13:24** A tool which is set up to receive connections from a Meterpreter payload.

I'm afraid I can't remember much about Colin. I have only a vague impression of a somewhat frog-like face which seemed to stretch unnaturally, as though his flesh was elastic. He may have been wearing a plaid shirt, although I could well be confusing him with one of the other dozen Colins at various Cybotage clients.[*]

"I have an analyst," this particular Colin said, clasping his hands together, "who is unable to meet a very tight – and very important – deadline, because his computer has been taken away for examination. It seems as though, at lunchtime today, his machine was infected with malware." His tone was calm, even pleasant, but I looked down at his hands and saw the knuckles were white.

"I see," Jay said carefully.

"In the last ten minutes, I've had the CISO❶ on one line demanding that we check the entire network for signs of compromise, and a very angry Sales Director on the other, who is concerned that we are going to miss a deadline and lose a client. A very big client. Both of them want an update immediately. Before I give it to them, I thought I would ask if there was any chance that trained, qualified pentesters – *expensive* pentesters – would ever be so *stupid* as to upload a plain, signatured payload❷ to a user's computer. Particularly as the scope of this engagement specifically precludes putting malicious binaries❸ on users' machines."

In the flustered fumble of my thoughts following this speech, one thing was clear: I had made myself and Jay – and by extension Cybotage – look like rank amateurs. Best outcome: I would get a bollocking, from both the client and Jay, and probably from Richard too, and be benched for the next few engagements, doing

[*] Perhaps Colins naturally gravitate to IT, seeking employment in a field with a reputation as dry and unexciting as their names, or perhaps it is just confirmation bias on my part. Someone should do a study.

Holly Soames①
05/11/2019 13:32
CISO = Chief Information Security Officer.

Holly Soames②
05/11/2019 13:45
Plain Meterpreter payloads are signatured by most antivirus products. WEBSTER evidently forgot to encrypt or obfuscate the payload she uploaded, resulting in the machine being flagged and quarantined.

Holly Soames③
05/11/2019 13:48
i.e. executable programs.

Holly Soames①
05/11/2019 14:03
'External
infrastructure' i.e.
testing those parts
of a network exposed
on the internet.

admin or running crappy automated external inf tests ❶ back at Gants House. No hacking, no imagination, just pointing and clicking and jumping as the trains shrieked through the station outside. Jay would wonder if his team was the right place for me. The worst: we would lose the client, have to waive the engagement fee, and I'd be gently told that perhaps this wasn't working out.

Jay looked at me again, and this time I forced myself to make eye contact. He seemed to be waiting for something, and I turned to Colin, my face burning. Phrases were forming in my head already, phrases like *really really sorry* and *first engagement* and *it will never happen again*. Colin met my gaze, waiting for the confession.

Jay cleared his throat and spoke.

"That was me."

I stared at him.

"I see," Colin said.

"We had a shell on that machine, and I must have copied the wrong binary over. Completely my fault."

"Right."

"It's not ideal."

"No."

"But at least your analyst can get his computer back."

"You appreciate that from the perspective of the business, as Head of IT, I'm to blame for this."

"Yes."

"But I will make sure that in the event of any loss we'll be holding your company accountable."

"I understand that."

"I will, of course, have to inform your CEO of this incident."

"Of course," Jay said. "And I'm sure he'll be open to discussing the final invoice."

Colin grunted. "You can find your own way back to your desks. I've got calls to make."

He stood and opened the door for us to leave.

When Jay and I got back to our corner of the office, I thought about trying to explain, but all I could manage was a very small: "Sorry."

He scratched his chin and swung his chair away from me, towards his own laptop.

We didn't speak another word to each other all day.

* * *

On the train back to London that evening, he did say something. He said ten words that are burnt into my memory. I can still remember everything about the moment he said them: their cadence, the way lights rushed past the black windows, the warmth from the heater underneath the table.

"Next time, just ask me. It's alright not to know."

"OK," I said. I knew I was about to cry, but rather than toss me any worthless words of comfort, Jay stayed silent and looked out of the window at the dark fields, and offered me the gift of letting me cry in silence.

It's alright not to know.

How I wish I'd listened.

Oh, Jay.

* * *

I've been thinking about The Tour. I can't quite remember when I first saw it, but it would have been shortly before that first engagement at Basingstoke, which means it was also before Jay and I found The Helmsman's game, and the first chapter of *The Helmsman Texts*. The *Texts* would have been a good addition to The Tour, even its star exhibit. Certainly, everything else on there now seems humdrum in comparison.

The Tour was a museum and an initiation, a collection of objects which served as an introduction for new Cybotage recruits into the attributes and qualities of the best hackers. 'The Tour' was far too grand a name for a small portion of the office sectioned off by three bulletin boards, but to us *rookies*, so inexperienced and new to security, it hummed with magic.

Inside the space demarcated by the boards were two desks pushed together, and on the desks were the exhibits themselves. When I close my eyes, I can still see them, artefacts of thought and cunning jostling for space, some hanging precariously over the edge of the tables.

At the centre was Jay's pride and joy: a working laser microphone❶ consisting of an infrared laser module on a small tripod, and a photodiode listener.

"One of the things you learn in this job," Jay told me, stroking the tiny listener fondly, "is that *everything* is data. Ons and offs, 1s and 0s. Light, sound, text. Any of them can be transformed into any other." *Hacking is alchemy*, he was saying. *These are the secrets you will learn.*

The laser microphone had been used by a threat actor group to eavesdrop on boardroom conversations at an energy company from a hotel across the road. They'd left in a hurry, Jay said; by the time the police❷ arrived the attackers and their laptops were gone, but the laser microphone – partially disassembled, as though they'd been in the middle of packing it up when they realised they had run out of time – remained. Cybotage was hired by the energy company to do a post-incident review, and Jay had managed to acquire the microphone from the police after offering to make a generous donation to the Police Orphans Fund.❶ At least, that's what he told us – for all I know he built it himself and the tale was something he'd fabricated to impress naïve new joiners like me.

Next to the laser microphone was a USB stick with a specially designed circuit that would fry the hard drive❷ of any computer it was inserted into. This was one of Nina's favourites; she was always keen on the destructive side of things.

Then there was a cable which looked like a simple USB charger but could be used to steal data❸ by plugging it into a laptop, and a Raspberry Pi❹ with a 4G module disguised as a power strip, intended to be used as a 'drop box' – a device attached to a company's internal network by a bribed employee or a hacker who socially engineered their way in – which could then be connected to remotely in order to access the network from afar.

And one of the more creative devices was an infrared cloner, which could capture and imitate any infrared signal.

Holly Soames①
18/11/2019 15:42
Enquiries reveal no donations from MORTON.

Holly Soames②
05/11/2019 14:54
Probably USBKill (https://usbkill.com) or similar device.

Holly Soames③
05/11/2019 15:01
Known as 'juice jacking' e.g. https://o.mg.lol.

Holly Soames④
05/11/2019 15:09
A small single-board computer often used by hobbyists.

The hacker who had inspired this exhibit had been using it in a particularly amusing way, by combining it with an open-source audio recognition code library. Apparently his wife was a huge fan of *Gilmore Girls* and had the show playing in the background almost constantly, which he hated. So he produced an audio fingerprint of the theme song, and wrote a Python script so that his laptop would continuously monitor the microphone. When the theme song was detected, a signal was sent to the infrared cloning device, which then transmitted the 'power off' signal for the television, previously captured from the remote. In other words, whenever *Gilmore Girls* started in his flat, the TV turned itself off.❶ Puerile, yes, but that hack was part of a presentation❷ which would later come in handy during the first of The Helmsman's puzzles.

All of these items had been obtained by Jay over a period of years. Some were commercially available, others were one-off proofs-of-concept that Jay had constructed himself or obtained from acquaintances, usually after offering some of his own research products in trade – and some had (supposedly) been acquired from law enforcement investigations.❸

Finally, a sizeable portion of the desk space was allocated to a shoebox containing a jumble of floppy discs, CDs, and USB sticks: Jay's malware collection.

"My petri dishes," Jay said, picking them up and letting them fall through his hands like water, his face alight with fascination. "A different virus on each one, all the way back to the eighties. *History.*"

By looking at the pathogens sitting quietly in that vivarium you could trace the very evolution of malware as a discipline. Some were so old that the operating systems and vulnerabilities they targeted were long-dead. They were the equivalent of ancient paleoviruses found deep in permafrost – once deadly and feared, now dormant. Others had not so long ago crippled the internet, and if released now could still cause carnage. They captivated us. Each had taken its author hours, weeks, even years, to create. Long evenings spent perfecting the dark art of weaponised code, long days spent in thought turned to the shadowy and nefarious practice of evading defences. There was craft, and love, in those dead things.

The sheer diversity and plurality of the collection was enthralling: RATs, and worms, and ransomware, oh my; keyloggers and crypto-miners and memory scrapers; destructive malware and espionage malware and trolling❷ malware. Armoured polymorphs which changed their own code to evade detection; viruses laden with anti-debugger techniques to trick malware analysts; trojans which had once been used to form colossal armies of infected zombie machines; malware born of wars and rivalries and collaborations and uneasy shifting alliances. Malware born of creativity and imagination. "My crime is that of curiosity," says the hacker manifesto.❸ "Information wants to be free,"❹ we say. Writing new worlds: beauty in the baud, poetry in the program, the sublime in the software. Even in the clinical violence of a virus there can be a grace, a mastery, an aesthetic.

Holly Soames①
06/11/2019 08:04
RATs = Remote Access Tools/ Trojans. Worms = self-replicating malware. Keyloggers = malware which records keystrokes. Crypto-miners = malware which hijacks a computer's resources to generate cryptocurrency for the attacker. Memory scrapers = malware which covertly searches RAM for sensitive information.

Holly Soames③
06/11/2019 08:23
See earlier comment re. this phrase.

Holly Soames④
06/11/2019 08:25
See Steven LEVY, https://medium. com/backchannel/ the-definitive-story- of-information- wants-to-be-free- a8d95427641c#. y7dΩamvr3 (2014).

Holly Soames②
06/11/2019 08:13

Usually synonymous with harassment, referring to the intentional use of abuse and insults in order to provoke or exacerbate arguments and inflict emotional damage (background: Yimin CHEN's '"Being a butt while on the internet": Perceptions of what is and isn't internet trolling' (2015)). In security, however, the term has a more nuanced meaning. It can also refer to deliberately misunderstanding or misinterpreting online discourse, sowing bait, misdirecting conversations, or performing some other act of sophistry to generate amusement. It is also used as a catch-all term for any form of intentionally generated annoyance. For a primer on trolling, see Matt JOYCE's 'The art of trolling' (2012 DEF CON talk).

Reply   Resolve

I should point out that we never used any exhibit on The Tour for our engagements. They were simply part of a shrine to the arts we practised and worked against, a museum for people fascinated and repulsed by their field. I imagine virologists and microbiologists and parasitologists feel the same way when they inspect the elegant, alien murderers writhing beneath their microscopes.

So, in one respect, *The Helmsman Texts* – even The Helmsman's weapon – would make an entirely apposite addition to The Tour, representing as they do a pinnacle of thought and ingenuity.

But to add them would be sacrilege. The artefacts on The Tour, whilst malicious, were viewed by us with a strange sort of affection, because their motives, uses and design were located so firmly within our understanding and so concretely within our discipline.

They were completely unlike anything produced by The Helmsman.

* * *

If I am short of money these days, I am at least rich in dreams. It's the one thing I have had no shortage of since Jay's disappearance: I dream every night, without fail. My dreams are not, as you might expect, about The Helmsman, or Jay walking into the desert, or Sarah Mayers. ❶ They are not about ▓▓▓▓▓▓▓▓ ▓▓▓▓▓▓, the 'freaks', as The Rearguard called them, born and raised in the Uncanny Valley – not even the one who terrified me the most, the smiling blonde woman who chased us down a seemingly endless Vegas hotel corridor and sat with me on desert rocks.

Instead I dream about the snake, and the last evening of the Basingstoke engagement, when I spoke to The Helmsman for the first time.

* * *

We, or should I say Jay, got a shell on another machine, and on the fifth afternoon obtained local administrator access through a misconfigured service that let us launch cmd.exe with elevated privileges. And then we ran out of time; the engagement was over. We spent the last couple of hours putting together our findings and writing up our notes, ready to draft the report the following week.

"I'll stay and finish up, if you want," I said to Jay, as the clock ticked past five and the employees began to file out. "You can go."

One thing I always liked about Jay was that explanations were superfluous. He saw my offer for the apology it was and accepted it without discussion.

"Don't stay too late," he said. "And don't do anything on the network."

"Learnt my lesson," I said.

Jay gathered his things and started towards the exit. "You've got the conn, rookie," he called over his shoulder. "Stay out of trouble." And he was gone.

I leant back in my chair and stretched, alone in the office. There wasn't much left to do, if I recall correctly, only cropping screenshots and collating some of the scan outputs. It would only take twenty minutes, and I reasoned that I could take my time; leaving later than usual would allow me to avoid the Friday evening rush at the train station. I was looking forward to a seat in the warm and doing the *Evening Standard* sudoku on the forty-minute journey back to London.

I decided I'd get myself a cup of coffee from the vending machine before I started, and stood up, looking out on to the rest of the office and the banks of dead black screens.

Then one of them came to life.

I frowned and went over to it. Whoever sat there had logged out for the night, like everyone else, and the machine had gone to sleep. Until, that is, something had woken it.

I peered at the screen, assuming the machine had rebooted itself to install an update or something of that nature, but there was nothing to see except the normal Windows login display.

I shrugged to myself, and was about to resume my trip to the coffee machine when the screen on the next desk lit up. And the one next to that. And another, and another, until every single monitor glowed. I started, and then laughed at myself.

It's someone from IT, you bell-end. Automatic updates, scheduled for Friday evening when nobody stays late.

But, severely chastened by my experience earlier in the week, I didn't see any reason to let it go, just in case. I'd be conscientious and check – and if it turned out to be nothing, no one would ever have to know how easily I'd shat not one but several bricks.

From the credentials we'd gathered over the course of the week, I picked a set at random and logged into one of the machines with PsExec. ❶ Once I had access, I ran a command to list logged-on users. The account I was using appeared, as expected, as a console session. And above it was another account, logged in over RDP. ❷

There you go then, moron. It's Colin's lot, remoting in to do whatever they need to do. Nothing to worry about.

Perhaps I might have left it there, and perhaps my life, all our lives, would have been very different, but I didn't. Instead I looked at the account name for the RDP session, and froze.

The account name was 4b3rr4710n. 'Aberration.' ❸

A hacker's nick.

The network was being compromised.

I closed the PsExec session, breathing fast, and started another on a new host with new credentials. Again I saw the account I was using, and again there was a second account logged in – but the name was different this time. LOOKONTHEDESKTOP. ❹

Without stopping to think about it I changed my working directory to the desktop, listed the contents, and surprised myself by having the presence of mind to start taking screenshots.

```
C:\Users\jstedson\Desktop>dir
dir
Volume in drive C is Windows
Volume Serial Number is D6B8-1068

Directory of C:\Users\jstedson\Desktop

28/01/2018   17:12    <DIR>          .
28/01/2018   17:12    <DIR>          ..
17/12/2017   13:03    <DIR>          2017
28/01/2018   17:12              15   HELLOFRIEND.txt
29/07/2017   09:27           4,547   JUL17reports.xlsx
28/01/2018   16:51              21   Microsoft
04/10/2016   06:02           2,359   MicrosoftEdge.lnk
15/05/2017   11:04    <DIR>          Personal
15/05/2017   10:51    <DIR>          Reports
              4 File(s)          2,404 bytes
              5 Dir(s)  48,218,353,664 bytes free
```

I read the HELLOFRIEND.txt file:

```
C:\Users\jstedson\Desktop>type HELLOFRIEND.txt
type HELLOFRIEND.txt
HELLO FRIEND
```

Up to that point I had done all the right things, and if I had stopped there and gone no further I probably would have received praise for my quick thinking. I may have even helped to restore Cybotage's damaged reputation with the client, and my similarly damaged reputation with Jay. And I promise you, I took my phone out, ready to call him – but I couldn't prise my eyes away from those words.

I have written and rewritten this paragraph several times in an attempt to articulate what was going through my mind, but the best I can come up with is this: *something in those words called out to me.*

As if deep within a dream, I put my phone down and added a line to the file.

```
C:\Users\jstedson\Desktop>echo who are you >>
HELLOFRIEND.txt
echo who are you >> HELLOFRIEND.txt
```

When I read the file again, *someone had replied.*

```
C:\Users\jstedson\Desktop>type HELLOFRIEND.txt
type HELLOFRIEND.txt
HELLO FRIEND
who are you
YOU WILL SEE THE PRETTIEST THINGS
```

I responded, and again there was a reply, longer this time:

```
why are you on this network
ONCE A RABBIT SANG A SONG ABOUT A SNARE
YOU WILL SING SONGS TOO!
SING SUCH PRETTY SONGS
SING AND SO MANY OTHER THINGS!
YOU COULD PROBABLY FLY IF YOU WANTED TO
```

The words crawled across the screen and squirmed in my vision.

```
Im screencapping all this
WHY THEY
WHY THEY AND NOT YOU
I SEE YOU I SEE YOU I SEE YOU I SEE YOU I SEE YOU
```

I looked around wildly upon reading that last line – even went to the window and peered out – but the office was as deserted as it had been since Jay had left. Outside, it was already dark and the only movement was the winter-stripped trees shifting stiffly in the wind, lit by the car park's brilliant white lights.

I went back to my desk and checked the file again. There was more.

```
COME JOIN US PLAY OUR GAME!
youtube.com/watch?v=uynSIw4-Euc
COME JOIN US PLAY OUR GAME!
youtube.com/watch?v=uynSIw4-Euc
COME JOIN US PLAY OUR GAME!
youtube.com/watch?v=uynSIw4-Euc
```

```
```

I wrote back, and received one final response.

```
get off the network now
OK BYE BYE
SEND FLAG TO THISISTHEBASILISK@GMAIL.COM
ALL BEST,
THE HELMSMAN
```

When I read the file a final time there was nothing there – only my own words, echoed back at me:

```
C:\Users\jstedson\Desktop>type HELLOFRIEND.txt
type HELLOFRIEND.txt
who are you?
```

I checked, but my account was the only one still logged into the machine. And as I looked up there was a flickering and all the monitors in the office turned black as the computers rebooted.

Whoever the hackers were, they had gone.

I watched the YouTube video,❶ and then, feeling more lost than I ever had before, I finally picked up my phone and called Jay.

Holly Soames①
06/11/2019 11:18
No trace of this or the email address. Consider RIPA subs.

*   *   *

It's those lines of text, irrational and insistently cheerful, that I see in my dreams now. I hear the voice on the video, too, but I'll come to that.

Jay was waiting on the platform at Basingstoke when I called, and asked what was wrong, but I just said I needed him to come back. I would like to say that this was because I was so agitated, but I promised you I'd be honest. The truth is that I kept it to myself because if I had told him everything then and there, he would have called Colin, and the IR.❷ team at Cybotage, and I didn't want that to happen. Because I was *curious*. I was *intrigued*. I was no longer sure the client had been breached – not really. I knew what those messages meant, and I knew what I wanted to do.

We are fucked, and the fact of our being fucked

Holly Soames②
06/11/2019 11:21
IR = Incident Response, i.e. those who investigate breaches which have been committed and try to remove malware, find the entry point, etc., by forensically examining compromised systems.

may be, in the final analysis, ultimately attributable to external forces – but all too often it is we who fuck ourselves first, and hardest.

* * *

The video is no longer on YouTube, of course (like the rest of the game, it has probably been removed by ▮▮▮▮▮▮▮▮▮▮▮▮▮▮▮▮▮▮ or someone working with or for them), but I downloaded it at the time, and I have uploaded a recording❶ of the audio here: https://soundcloud.com/andrea-walker-229812176/vigenere-numbers-station-recording/s-OYwRbFxYixm?si=63e0ff78e5aa4755858359d61b097aab – the audio is the only relevant part of it, there's no 'video' as such. But since the game is no longer operational, you won't get a response from the email address (which I presume is also the doing of ▮▮▮▮▮▮▮▮▮▮▮▮▮▮▮▮▮) – believe me, I've tried.

I watched that video over and over again while I waited for Jay. It was entitled: 'VIGENERE❷ NUMBERS STATION❸ RECORDING', uploaded by a user called Dev Null.❹ The audio, which plays over a still image of a derelict radio tower somewhere in a forest, begins with a burst of static, followed by a rapid blur of voices and music as whoever is operating the

Holly Soames①
06/11/2019 11:32
Run past forensics, download and exhibit.

Holly Soames②
06/11/2019 11:52
No trace.

Holly Soames③
06/11/2019 13:39
Shortwave broadcasts of music and numbers at set frequencies at set times. Likely maintained and run by security services to provide instructions to operational officers. Example: https://priyom.org/media/247818/e3.mp3 (Simon Mason, date unknown, priyom.org). For further background see this BBC article by Olivia SORREL-DEJERINE: 'The secret world of the "numbers stations"'. (2014): bbc.co.uk/news/magazine-24910397. Various number stations are indexed at priyom.org, although there is no trace of the one described here. It is likely fictional.

Holly Soames④
06/11/2019 14:17   ✕

No trace. DEV NULL is a reference to /dev/null, a virtual null device on Linux operating systems. It discards anything written or piped to it. It has been a common pseudonym in the security community for some time, along with the derivation Dave NULL. e.g. *Spam Wars: Our Last, Best Chance to Defeat Spammers, Scammers and Hackers* by Danny GOODMAN in 2004.

Reply   **Resolve**

radio slides up and down the frequencies. After a few more seconds of static is a recording of 'Three Blind Mice'. The music is synthetic, like chiptune, and the pitch varies considerably.

A woman's voice, stilted and robotic, reads out a series of numbers. This goes on for some time, and is followed by a long, digital buzzing, like a data transmission. Everything is then repeated in reverse, and the recording ends with a whine, a howl of static and a happy, garbled, almost unintelligible voice – perhaps The Helmsman himself❶ – shouting, "Hello friends!"*

This is what I hear on a loop when I dream – staccato numbers devoid of emotion; a warped rendition of 'Three Blind Mice'; a loud and joyful voice almost lost in static. Over and over.

See how they run. See how they run.

But at the time, all I knew was that somewhere within that video was a flag,❷ and I wanted it.

* * *

Jay was not delighted to be back in the office on a Friday evening.

"What is it?" he said, dropping his rucksack to the floor and fixing me with a glare that suggested any headway I may have made with him in the last couple of days was under serious threat. "What have you done?"

I bridled a little at this. "I haven't done *anything*. Look."

I showed him the screenshots, told him what had happened, and played the video. We watched it together in the empty office, and when it had finished Jay pulled out his phone.

Holly Soames①
06/11/2019 14:28
Biometrics opportunity re. voice identification? Run past forensics/ Innovation.

Holly Soames②
06/11/2019 14:40
A flag is usually the objective of a CTF – a word, sentence or random value which is only obtainable when the player has completed the challenge. It is used as proof that they have succeeded.

---

* Why The Helmsman selected this particular piece of lore for his first puzzle, I don't know. Perhaps he was fascinated, as I am, by the possibility that some numbers stations are 'Dead Hand' systems – that is, if they ever stop broadcasting, nuclear missiles may be launched at pre-arranged targets. Of course, if that happens, we'll all be fucked in an entirely unsurprising manner.

"Wait," I said. "Wait a minute."

"I have to call Colin."

"But they're gone now. They were here for less than five minutes, I told you that."

"So? Nothing to stop them coming back," Jay said, putting the phone to his ear. "They might have been on the network for months."

I heard the line ringing, and I reached out gently to touch the hand holding the phone – held it in my own, and lowered it. Jay didn't resist as I tapped the phone's screen and ended the call. He looked at me with uncertainty, an indecision which I found immensely appealing. Perhaps, for reasons beyond the limited understanding I have of my own psychology, I am attracted to doubt. I saw none of the solid, almost lazy sense of self-confidence Jay usually projected. For the first time in his professional life he was facing something outside his experience, and I felt a strange sense of affinity with him because of it. We were each as clueless as the other.

"What are you doing?" he said distantly.

"Didn't you read what they wrote? It's not a compromise. It's a game."

* * *

Like any field, cyber security has its folklore, much of it concerning pranks, games and stories. The Max Headroom Incident❶, as an example of the former, has reached almost mythical status. In 1987, hackers breached a Chicago television network's broadcast system, interrupting a rerun of an old *Doctor Who* episode to transmit footage of an unknown man wearing a rubber mask of the satirical character Max Headroom while ranting, singing, moaning, and screaming cryptic nonsense in a digitally altered voice. At one point an unknown associate spanks his naked arse with a fly-swatter. The people responsible have

Holly Soames①
06/11/2019 15:07
A well-known incident in the security community. Footage of it is available at youtube.com/watch?v=jjeUuakHsLw (Kenny Triton, 2012). For further background see this 2013 Motherboard VICE article by Chris KNITTEL, 'The mystery of the creepiest television hack' archived at: web.archive.org/web/20140918011433/http://motherboard.vice.com/read/head-room-hacker. See also an academic essay by Mary TANDER, 'I just made a giant master-piece: The ethics of disruptive performance art and the Max Headroom Incident' in Innovations in Art and Theatre (2002).

never been identified, and in both this and the fact that the incident hinged on a compromise, there is a clear parallel with the beginning of The Helmsman's game.

Cicada 3301, ❶ too, has a certain resemblance to the game, as a multi-stage puzzle run by an anonymous group. The first Cicada challenge was posted on a public forum and solving it led to further puzzles, which required not just knowledge of steganography and hacking but also of literature, music, the occult and numerology. Those who reached the final stages were not made aware of who the group were – only contacted and told that they should start working on technical projects for the good of the world. Commentators have speculated it may have been a game, or a recruitment drive by an intelligence agency or a cult, but the organisers have never been identified, and the purpose of the game remains unknown.

Holly Soames①
06/11/2019 15:33
For background see 'Cicada: Solving the Web's deepest mystery' (2015) by David KUSHNER in Rolling Stone: rollingstone.com/culture/culture-news/cicada-solving-the-webs-deepest-mystery-84394/.

> Hello.
>
> Epiphany is upon you. Your pilgrimage has begun. Enlightenment awaits.
>
> Good luck.
>
> 3301

* * *

There are stories everywhere. Some are well-known, others require you to wander among the internet's dusty library shelves of abandoned pages and dead links to find them. Creepypasta. ❶ The SCP Foundation. ❷ The Mariana Trench (rumoured to be a distinct, and deeper, part of the dark web).* Slender Man. The Wyoming Incident. Candle Cove. Jeff the Killer. The Russian Sleep Experiment. Ted the Caver, ❸ all the way back in 2001. Strictly, in terms of their content, internet-based stories are no more or less scary than those told around campfires (my favourite was the one about the gang who would drive around at night with their head-lights off, and follow any vehicle which flashed them as a courtesy, in order to kill the occupants; there was something about its ardent nihilism that gripped me).

But internet-based stories often blur the ontological boundaries between reality and fiction in a way that traditional urban legends seldom do, particularly with ARGs. ❹ In fact, the rise of ARGs (along with so-called

* This is bullshit, obviously, a term thrown around to confuse and bait noobs, in the same way that Australians will sometimes mutter darkly about the threat of vicious and carnivorous 'drop bears' in the presence of tourists.

'internet mysteries' – Unfavorable Semicircle, mortis. com,❶ etc.) suggests that a writer with a story feels that they have to distort ontological boundaries – and create a sense of disturbing, inexplicable mystery – in order to reach audiences who not only demand but expect that level of narrative complexity and ambiguity. So it seemed entirely credible to me that those baffling words on jstedson's desktop, and the numbers station video, were the start of a sort of creepypasta ARG story – a form of marketing, recruitment, or entertainment – or a game like Cicada 3301, or, like the Max Headroom Incident, a random and fucked-up prank.

Strange, perhaps, but ultimately harmless.

* * *

"It's still a compromise."

"It's a puzzle, and we should solve it," I said. "Don't you want to know what comes next?"

"Alex. We *can't*."

"Do you seriously think a real threat actor would behave like this?"

"I don't care. They've broken the law."

"We could be the first people to crack it," I said, speaking quickly. "We could write about it. A con❷ talk, publish a paper, blogs,❸ whatever. Jay, this could be *huge*."

He said nothing, so I switched tack. "I am a criminal," I said. "My crime is..."

"Curiosity," Jay finished, surprised. "'The Conscience of a Hacker.'❹ You know about that?"

He took off his cap and ran a hand through his hair. "You know it's probably just a skiddie❺ trolling us, right?" he said, but I saw the shine of interest in his eyes and knew I'd won.

"If it is we'll just forget it," I said. "No one has to know."

I played the video again and started taking notes.

"You're doing it now? Why can't you work on it at home?"

"Are you going to help me or not?"

Jay was quiet for a very long time. I can see him now, as he was then, wavering, hesitating at the same junction we all come to in this field at one time or another, his face solemn and still.

It's alright not to know.

He looked at his watch, then took off his coat and sat down next to me.

"Fuck it," he said, the devil in his grin. "Let's play."

---

* Jay kept a fairly active security blog – of course ▮▮▮▮▮▮▮▮▮▮▮ took it down ages ago, along with recordings of his talks, which is a loss for the security community in general, as well as me personally – containing all the articles on his research, tutorials and other minutiae of offensive security. He had an interest in the off-centre and esoteric – as you might have guessed from the exhibits on The Tour – and never missed a chance for self-promotion, although perhaps that's uncharitable. It was more that he never missed a chance to share something cool with other people. He genuinely got a kick out of it, even though he had a fear of public speaking. "I hate being on stage," he told me once, when I was at his and Eoin's house. "I can't stand it."

3: SEE HOW THEY RUN
c. MARCH–APRIL 2019 / FEBRUARY–MARCH 2018

I'm back at the Cybotage office, and it's late at night. A fox shrieks in the distance. The overhead fluorescents are off, but the chilled glow of the streetlights outside casts synthetic moonlight over the desks and chairs. The building shivers as a train hurtles by, and the thunder of its rhythmic vibrations rise up through the floors and into my body. My bones shake. Bad vibrations.

Don't forget that this is a choice.

I'm sitting at my old desk, and in front of me is a large, thick snake in the process of consuming itself. It forms a ring, an ouroboros.❶ The serpent swallows its tail, its body coiling and curling, thumping against the desk in obscene convulsions of agony or ecstasy. Its jaws stretch further to engulf itself, inch by inch, and I turn away, unable to look. I don't want to see what happens when it gets to the head because I can't imagine it.

Someone is standing behind me, and I know that it's one of ▓▓▓▓▓▓▓▓▓▓▓▓▓▓▓▓▓▓ – the misshapen child from Fairlop Waters, maybe, or the smiling blonde woman – and I know they are there to make me see it. And I have to, because I have no totem with me now. I am unguarded, naked, defenceless. This is the thing which has stalked me all this time, waiting to enfold me in pale and too-long arms.

This is what you wanted.

I feel a pressure on both sides of my head: hands, forcing me to watch. The snake glares at me with its crazed reptilian eyes and gulps down another inch. Its body undulates in enthralling, inconceivable ways.

Holly Soames①
22/11/2019 14:33
A snake eating its own tail. This seems to be an important symbol to THE HELMSMAN (and later to WEBSTER) and a crude image of it appears at the start of each chapter in THT. Limited research conducted into the subject indicates that the symbol originates from an ancient Egyptian funerary text called The Book of Gates (see 'The Egyptian Ouroboros: An iconological and theological study,' a 2015 PhD dissertation by Dana Michael REEMES). Erik HORNUNG, in Conceptions of God in Egypt: The One and the Many (1982), says that it represents formless disorder, encircling reality.

54

Holly Soames①
07/11/2019 10:24
See article 'The
Ouroboros and the
unity of matter in
alchemy: A study
in origins' by Harry
J. SHEPPARD
(1962). Note that the
basilisk also has
some relevance to
alchemy, although
it's not clear if there
are any further links.

Holly Soames②
07/11/2019 10:37
See 'The Ouroboros
(Part 2): Towards
an intersubjective-
heuristic method
for ecopsychology
research' by David
KEY and Margaret
KERR (2011).

Holly Soames③
07/11/2019 10:39
OS = operating
system.

In alchemy❶ the ouroboros is a symbol of the all-as-one: eternity and seasons and life. Alchemists sought to break free of the cycle of life and death and to live forever. Jung thought the ouroboros represented the assimilation of the opposite.❷

Physician, devour thyself.

* * *

The little IT office I share with Milo at the school is more a storage cupboard than anything else. A couple of worn school desks have been squeezed into it, although I can't quite work out how this feat was accomplished.

Each desk has a cheap armless swivel chair behind it, and a battered laptop on top. On Milo's is an additional monitor – bulky and archaic, with only a VGA port (I sometimes tell Milo, "The secret is to bang the rocks together," but, disappointingly for someone who works in IT, he doesn't get the reference). Lining the walls are old servers, copies of antique software (including Windows 95, the whole OS❸ on a crooked tower of floppy discs), and an antique network diagram which Milo doesn't need because it's all in his head, and which I don't use because I can figure it out if I need to.

We were sitting there this morning, the school's heating ramped up to full throttle against the cold, the radiator gurgling, our little desk lamps glowing, and I was thinking how lucky I am to have this job. It requires almost no mental energy – allowing me to save myself for writing – and I can stay warm on days like today. There is no danger, true, and no risk, but I have lost enough.

There was a knock at the door. Milo folded up his newspaper – a local rag he often brings in from home, the *Redbridge Herald* – and, the office being so small, opened the door without having to fully haul himself to his feet.

Otto stood in the doorway beaming at us, while we squinted stupidly at him, blinded by the sudden and unwelcome intrusion of fluorescent light from the corridor.

"The cave people of IT!" he said. "Sorry to disturb your slumbers."

Milo rolled his eyes and returned to his newspaper, unfolding it with a crinkling flourish. Otto winked at me.

"Mr Salas," I said. "Forgotten your password again?"

"Nope!" he said cheerfully. "I changed it to something more memorable. It's—"

"La la la la la," I sang, fingers in my ears. "Remember what we talked about? Shouting out your passwords makes Milo sad."

Milo grunted absently.

"Right, right," Otto said. "Sorry. Anyway, I definitely won't forget it from now on, because I've written it on a Post-it Note and stuck it to my laptop."

"You're trying to antagonise me, aren't you? You're doing it deliberately. You must be."

"Am I— am I not supposed to write my password down?"

"Troll."

"I don't know what that means."

"Of course you don't." I gestured at the corner of the IT office, where Milo and I kept a little kettle and an overflowing pot of teabags and coffee sachets filched from the staff room. "Got a free period? Coffee?"

Otto leant against the doorframe, looking embarrassed.

"Actually, I wanted to ask you something."

"Projector problems, is it?"

"No, nothing like that." He glanced at Milo, who was reading his newspaper and occasionally turning the page with a loud crackle. "We can talk later. If you're busy."

"No, go on. You've intrigued me."

He cleared his throat. "I wondered if you'd fancy

a midweek outing? Tomorrow. A play, the one I told you about. *King of Fleas.*❶ Been sold-out for ages, but I managed to get a couple of tickets. What do you reckon?"

"Oh." I didn't say anything else, but he must have seen my face. I write on weekdays; he knew this. That's always been the understanding. Weekdays and Sundays are mine, Saturdays are ours.

"You don't have to," he went on hurriedly. "I can get a refund. It's just that we said we really wanted to see it, and there aren't any tickets for Saturdays, so I thought..."

I remembered the conversation he was referring to distinctly. *He* was the one who had wanted to see *King of Fleas*, because it was about post-war Japan. I'd expressed mild interest, if that.

"Actually, we *are* a bit busy at the moment," I said. "Talk about it later?"

He looked around, taking in the cup of coffee I'd just made and the newspaper Milo was resolutely ploughing through.

"A night off wouldn't hurt you."

"Otto," I said. "*Later.*"

"I just meant—"

"I know what you meant."

On Otto's good-natured face – and it *is* a good-natured face, I have always been a good judge of character that way – was puzzlement and pain. I've seen these things so often in myself that it's no effort to recognise them in others.

"I'm trying to take your mind off things. That's all. It'll be fun. Healthy."

There was the rustle of another page being turned, and underneath it the silence of someone listening very intently.

"Milo, would you excuse us? Just for a minute?" I said.

Milo sighed, pulled himself upright, and began to shuffle out of the room. It was a long process, because he had to turn sideways to fit through the gap between the desks, and his gammy leg kept catching, and Otto had to move out of the way to let him through the small doorway.

"You really want to do this now?" I said, when Milo had finally left.

"I— OK, I promised myself I wasn't going to say this, but—"

"But here you are, about to say it anyway."

"I think you're spending too much time thinking about someone who's long gone."

"We agreed weekdays—"

"If you're still this upset over someone who left months ago, then—"

"He didn't *leave!*"

A silence.

"Whatever it was," Otto said, "I'm here *now*. And I get that writing down what happened is something you think you need to do, I really do, but Alex, do you— I mean, do you have any idea what it's like to tell people that I can't see my girlfriend on weekdays?"

"So don't tell them."

"Yes, but—"

"You're seeing me now, aren't you?"

"You know that's not the same thing, and if Mr Bellings gets better, we—"

"Can't make the play," I said, looking at my laptop. "Sorry. Maybe next time."

"You know, maybe you should speak to someone. Someone who can help you process this. I don't think you're handling it very well on your own."

"Does it look," I said, "like I give a shit about what you think?"

His mouth opened, and then he left without another word.

After a while I slammed my fist down on the desk so hard it left a bruise.

Needless to say, we never went to see the play.

* * *

Later, I picked up Milo's paper, and buried deep inside the middle pages was a tiny article:

Thursday, 24 April 2019

Computer expert took own life

A local computer security expert took his own life after a sudden stress-induced breakdown, East London coroner Nadia Aidan concluded today, recording a verdict of suicide.

Shane Carson, 37, was found dead in his Ilford home on 5 November last year. He was not known to local mental health services, but his colleagues reported he had seemed tired and distant in the days leading up to his death.

He is survived by his wife, Lorena, and their two children. ❶

Holly Soames①
07/11/2019 11:19
No trace of article in print or online form. Refers to Shane CARSON dob 11/03/1981 M. Deceased.

I read this several times, then took the pair of scissors from the pot of stationery on Milo's desk. I carefully snipped out the article, folded it gently, and put it in the inside pocket of my jacket, over my heart.

* * *

The Helmsman's game is the story of a weapon, and at the end is the weapon itself, aimed squarely at the player (and as you'll see, it was never just Jay and me; others have played too, although it's impossible to say how many). It's an intricate and beautifully made puzzle-box with a loaded gun inside, rigged to blow your head off when you open it. But, unlike a gun, one of the most significant obstacles to understanding the nature of this weapon is that its effects – symptoms, if you like – seem to be inconsistent, both in the form they take or in the time required for them to present themselves. This makes it difficult to attribute reports of deaths or injuries to The Helmsman, or to convince others that these incidents might be linked in any way. This is probably why no one, including relatives of the victims, has reported any connection to The Helmsman or his game, at least not in anything I've come across.

I've thought about trying to tell someone myself – a journalist, perhaps – but, aside from the risk it would pose to them, I don't think there's the slightest chance they'd take it seriously. Like a near-death experience or a religious epiphany (assuming they're not the same thing), The Helmsman's game is something you have to go through yourself to believe, although obviously one of my hopes in writing this document is that that will change. But I know how I'd come across to any respectable reporter: a crazed conspiracy theorist, surrounded by jars of well-matured urine and walls covered in untidy paranoid scrawls, only a few dubious discoveries away from that most ignominious item of headwear, the tinfoil hat.

To most people, the world is an assortment of violent, random events, and I would be accused of perceiving patterns and correlations in the chaos which do not exist. Correlation, after all, does not always mean causation, although I have always wondered at that phrase.* This is one perspective.

But here is another: can't everything be linked? Can't the all be the one? Couldn't we all be complicit in a chain reaction which we are powerless to stop or even discern?

---

*At university, one of my professors told us that the homicide rate in some cities correlates positively with sales of ice cream, but that does not mean that one is the result of the other. The common factor, the explanation goes, is summer, when more ice cream is purchased and the temperature is higher, which drives more people to murder ❶ (although there are alternative explanations which shouldn't be overlooked: perhaps murderers like to cool down with a 99 after the deed, or perhaps people flip out when all the good lollies have been sold and only those fucking awful Fruit Pastille ones are left).

Holly Soames①
18/11/2019 22:40
VALIS, by Philip K.
DICK, 1981. Note
that WEBSTER does
not finish the quote:
"Another sentence
exists, another
series of words, that
could heal you. If
you're lucky you will
get the second, but
you can be certain of
getting the first."

Holly Soames②
22/11/2019 03:17
Paraphrased in c3
THT, and appears in
a TANNHAUSER play
in c4 THT.

Holly Soames③
07/11/2019 13:42
e.g. 'Every ROSE has
its thorn: The dark
art of Remote Online
Social Engineering',
a 2018 Black Hat
USA talk which
cites psychological
research on this
topic. Note also in
the presentation the
comments about
police officers.

Holly Soames④
07/11/2019 13:47
David WEBSTER
dob 17/01/1965 M.
Deceased.

Holly Soames⑤
07/11/2019 13:58
Clara WEBSTER
nee FANNING dob
21/11/1968 F. Not
interviewed by SCD1
as part of their
investigation.

Philip K Dick wrote, *There exists, for every person, a sentence – a series of words – which has the power to destroy them.* ❶

Quite apart from being an interesting parallel to The Helmsman's weapon (and something he references himself in *The Helmsman Texts*), ❷ it also makes me think of what I said to Jay that evening, and whether, completely unbeknownst to me and without any intention of doing so, I destroyed him then and there, several months before he actually died.

Are you going to help me or not?

If this is a confession, then one of the sins I am seeking absolution for must be this.

I try to be kinder, to both myself and the person I was, but the truth is that I am an expert at deception and manipulation. People are always easier to exploit than machines. We are so good at it. We lie to each other habitually, compulsively, and yet we suck at knowing when we are being lied to. ❸

Is it any wonder we are fucked?

* * *

When I think about that evening in Basingstoke, I'm reminded of my father. ❹ Ever the eclectic weirdo, he owned a collection of typewriters. He was an amateur creative writer as well; having read some of his work after he died, I was pleased to find he wasn't bad, although he never achieved much recognition. What little success he did have he attributed to his typewriters.

He kept them in his study, in a large metal cabinet with glass doors. Each time the postman arrived with a large and heavily wrapped box, which happened two or three times a year, my mother ❺ would roll her eyes and tell my father, "Put the filthy bloody thing in your office so it doesn't clutter up the house."

In the sanctity of his study, where I'd often visit him, he'd look at the cabinet or whatever machine happened to be on his desk at that moment, and say, "There's something wonderful about using a typewriter, Alex." He waxed lyrical about the sensation of fingertips on keytops, forcing typeslugs to physically imprint ink into the fibres of paper. The cheerful ding of the bell as it reached the end of the line, the rasp of the carriage returning.

One day – it must have been in 2012 or so – I asked him why he was so fascinated with obsolete technology. As a 'digital native' – a term which felt quaint even then – I couldn't wrap my head around it. To my mind, a computer performed all the functions a typewriter could, and better, and more.

He smiled, resting his palm against the side of his latest acquisition, a huge squat beast from the 1940s that reminded me of Paul Sheldon's machine in *Misery*.

"This thing you call obsolete," he said, "was made before I was born, and it'll be here after I'm dead. It'll outlast you, too. Can you say that about a laptop?"

I shrugged. "But you can write on a laptop *now*."

He pressed a key on the typewriter. A typebar rose, smacked the platen, and fell back, with the short efficient snap of a gunshot. Then he tapped a key on the laptop open at the edge of his desk, and it made a muted little *thunk*.

"When you understand those two sounds," he said, "you'll get it."

I didn't get it, and still don't, but I have come to learn that everyone has their irrational obsessions, and I should be the last person to criticise someone for theirs, especially when my own has proved to be so destructive.

The reason The Helmsman's first puzzle reminds me of my father's typewriter collection is that there was one which was a complete anomaly, and therefore the only one which ever really interested me: a Smith Corona Classic 12, ❶ an odd, boxy machine from the 1970s. It had cost him a significant amount because it

Holly Soames①
07/11/2019 14:05
https://
typewriterdatabase.
com/197x-smith-
corona-classic-
12-valpar.5574.
typewriter

was a rare variant, and very odd. Unlike virtually every other typewriter ever made, and unlike most Classic 12s, there was no line bell or touch control. The margins were not adjustable, and there was no margin release. The bar for setting tabs was not connected to anything and there was no shift key. Most peculiar of all, instead of a full keyboard it had only one row, comprising ten Greek letters in a mix of upper and lowercase.

"It's a mystery!" my father would say proudly whenever he showed it to anyone. "Nobody knows what it's for – not even the people who used to work at Smith Corona."

Some collectors speculated that it was for inserting mathematical symbols into theses or papers, but there was neither an integral symbol nor an epsilon. Others suggested that it was used for typing the names of college fraternities and sororities, like Phi Beta Kappa, but it was missing several common letters used in those names: kappa, lambda, psi and gamma. And what's more, those names are always in uppercase – so why the lowercase letters?

Some said the Greek Classic 12s were the result of a factory error, or the work of some disturbed troll who had produced them as a long-term practical joke – the mechanical equivalent of the Max Headroom Incident, I suppose. And other, more sinister explanations abounded amongst the very small but fervently vocal crossover of typewriter enthusiasts and conspiracy theorists, such as the typewriters having been used for psychical research as part of the MKUltra programme, or specially made for secret societies.

My dad loved his Classic 12 for its rarity. I loved it for its lack of sanity. All other typewriters had a ruthlessly functional structure. You could see exactly how everything worked if you just put enough time into studying the relevant repair manuals. But that Classic 12 went out of its way, in the most bizarre way, to defy logic.

The mystery was alive for over thirty years, and may have continued indefinitely until an amateur collector bought one and found it came with a strip of card❶ containing various combinations of Greek letters above a numbered scale from 1–10, and a copyright notice for Valpar Corp, 1974.

Holly Soames①
07/11/2019 14:22
See https://typewriterdatabase.com/197x-smith-corona-classic-12-valpar.1469.typewriter

Within a few hours a puzzle that had endured for almost three decades was neatly solved. The Valpar Corporation apparently performed cognitive testing and vocational assessments, and the modified Classic 12 was used, along with the card, for pattern recognition and typing ability, as part of an assessment which also involved mail sorting, filing and book-keeping.

When my father found out about this, shortly before he died of the slow cancer which, even when he had started his collection, was probably making its first creeping inroads into his bones and organs, he was delighted. "I'm glad someone solved that," he said. "It's always bothered me."

I, on the other hand, was annoyed, and dissatisfied, and unable to grasp why my father was so pleased. Vocational assessments. Can you imagine a duller, less inspiring solution? There is such banality in certainty.

Satisfaction is a lie.

Since the Classic 12 I have found solutions almost always disappointing. They may give every appearance of being clever and complete, but in the end there is nothing so enthralling or rewarding as the problem itself.

When Jay and I started The Helmsman's game, I worried that it would be just another Classic 12, because the numbers station puzzle offered only token resistance before its mystique crumbled in the face of two hackers who'd decided to play along. As the game went on, of course, we realised that the numbers station served only as a gentle introduction to stranger and more horrifying riddles. Its relatively simple answer only ever led to more questions, and to an awareness that the game is not, like the Classic 12, a jigsaw puzzle which simply lacks a final piece. The game *claims to be the final piece itself*. It is what it fits into that's the puzzle.

* * *

That evening in Basingstoke, we started by jotting down the numbers from the recording:

*109 111 122 119 109 107 120 99 105 115 113
105 98 114 104 100 99 105 120 108 122 118
105 108 103 97 116 115 104 119 99 105*

**Holly Soames①
07/11/2019 14:47**
ASCII = American Standard Code for Information Interchange. Human-readable encoding of text.

"They're all numbers in the ASCII❶ range," Jay said after looking at them for a moment, and copied them into an online decimal > ASCII converter, which produced a string of text.

```
decimal
109  111  122  119  109  107  120  99  105
115  113  105  98  114  104  100  99  105  120
108  122  118  105  108  103  97  116  115
104  119  99  105
```

```
ascii
mozwmkxcisqibrhdcixlzvilgatshwci
```

"Is that the flag?" I said, but Jay, veteran of innumerable CTFs, shook his head.

"Won't be that easy, rookie."

We were stuck for a while after that. Jay tried applying various decoding methods to no avail, while I googled,* and eventually it occurred to me to search for the name of the numbers station, which revealed that 'Vigenère' was a kind of polyalphabetic cipher.❷

"This says we need a key," I said, pointing to a tutorial I'd found on the subject.

**Holly Soames②
07/11/2019 14:51**
A substitution cipher, similar to a Caesar cipher (e.g. A=2, B=3, etc.) but with multiple alphabets and requiring a key to decrypt.

* Naturally, I also googled 'The Helmsman', and various phrases from the HELLOFRIEND text file, and found nothing. I continued to do this for every chapter of *The Helmsman Texts* we received, and never found any indication, anywhere, that anyone else had ever played the game – no discussions, no blogs, no social media posts – or was even aware of it.

"Don't need it," Jay said shortly. "It's not proper encryption, just a cipher. We can brute force❶ it in a few seconds."

A quick search for 'Vigenère brute forcers' found several free online tools which assured us they could do just that, but when Jay copied the ciphertext into them the results were gibberish.

```
Score  Key Text
45622  evdizcjpplmgneppeee    it won i on the con so yet he same red wkwv
44974  tslcbhpppsxpunppxb     twould in tat the s of he to the rleakhiv
44885  tslcbhpppzjiijpppg     twould in t that is once tother let you z
44870  jggoisfgazjefrpppe     ditiesswi the was ont of that but tysxr
44796  qhzdtdtypspxxrrpppp    what thee table as on the as pince as zfr
44584  akssvgecvpfeyyazI      me her et and led the r in tha chef end ye i
44367  eevdtdtabsxbxapppe     iket the chat her sont the spin as akvfi
44344  ybtlmseuvmcoooow       on g last in go und the he and erloretiom
44320  qhzdtdtwikdgxzpppp     what the gain cess on the a spine lie qfj
44202  akssvptzaaqqbeezl      me her ve dis as and erin thats hat crvye
```

Result

Clear text [hide]

Clear text using key "zkidozppps":
nertylintarytotentitalaisbedsedy

"Maybe we shouldn't need to brute force it," I ventured, while Jay swore and searched for more tools. "It's a puzzle. We need to work it out."

He played the video again. "It could be anything in the recording," he said, when it had finished. "Make a wordlist❷ – do you know what that is? And then—"

"What about the bit in the middle?"

Jay stopped, unused to being interrupted. "What? That? We don't know what that is yet."

"But we know it's data, right? It *sounds* like data." Something inside my head was plucking at my sleeve, begging me to listen, but I shoved it away. I needed to concentrate.

"Maybe. But who knows what it's been encoded

Holly Soames①
07/11/2019 14:52
i.e. a trial-and-error approach, submitting many possible keys. With a Vigenère cipher this could involve using a dictionary to try all possible keys which are English words, or a method specific to the cipher known as the Kasiski Examination.

Holly Soames②
07/11/2019 15:01
Wordlists = files containing commonly used passwords or usernames, used for brute forcing attacks. In this context, WEBSTER and MORTON almost certainly assumed that the key would be a word or phrase related to the numbers station video, so their wordlist would have been based on that.

with, and how? No, we shouldn't jump ahead. That's one thing you'll learn in this job, rookie. Low-hanging fruit first."

I rolled my tongue inside my cheek, thought about saying something, and then nodded reluctantly. Making a wordlist didn't take too long. I threw in some words associated with number stations, the lyrics to 'Three Blind Mice', and the text The Helmsman had typed earlier, and within fifteen minutes I had 200 or so entries in a text file.

"OK," Jay said. "Let's give this a go, and then you can combine some of the words. Change the casing, add some numbers."

"And we just keep trying until we get it?" The thing in my head wasn't tugging at my sleeve anymore; now it was jumping up and down and shouting.

"That's the way it works."

"I'm just going to play it one more time." I leant forwards and ran the video from the beginning. Yes, there it was, I thought. That whine of data, right in the middle. It wasn't an everyday noise, I was certain of that, but I knew I'd heard something like it before. At university, perhaps? During a lecture? No – but I *had* heard it somewhere, and fairly recently too.

"You OK?" Jay was saying. "You look like you've seen a ghost."

"Ghost," I said slowly.

Ghost. Phantom, poltergeist, spectre, spirit, appari—
No. Stop. Go back.
Back to what?
You're almost there.
Spectre?
Spectre. Spectral...
Spectrogram.

I minimised the text file and brought up a new tab, navigating to a site for downloading YouTube videos.

"Good thinking, makes sense to download it," Jay

said. "In case it— Hey, what are you doing?"

I was now also downloading Audacity.❶ Jay pulled his chair closer, looking from the screen to my face, annoyed. I ignored him, caring only about the progress of the download and the subsequent installation.

Holly Soames①
07/11/2019 15:11
An audio editing application.

Eventually it finished, and I imported the downloaded video and separated out the audio track. For the next bit, I could have stayed in Audacity to do what I needed to, but I knew it wouldn't be very clear. What had the guy used? Sonic something?

*Sonic Visualiser,*❷ the voice murmured, pleased that I was finally paying it some attention. *He used Sonic Visualiser.*

Holly Soames②
07/11/2019 15:14
An audio visualisation application.

I downloaded that too, and when it was ready to use I copied the audio track into it, selected the right options, and slapped the desk in excitement when it had loaded.

"Well, fuck me," Jay said. "That's fucking *awesome*."
I beamed.
"How did you know how to do that?"

I explained: the year before, whilst at university, I had made a habit of watching at least one recording of a conference talk every night, usually from either DEF CON or Black Hat, as part of my extracurricular education in cyber security. Every year a couple of hundred or so talks are uploaded, the archive going all the way back to the mid-2000s. One of them was a 2017 DEF CON talk❸ on the use of light and sound for hacking. Most of the content had been pretty speculative, involving some very odd proofs-of-concept

Holly Soames③
07/11/2019 15:16
See previous note: 'See no evil, hear no evil: Hacking invisibly and silently with light and sound.'

that were of little application to anything but the most outlandish and unlikely kinds of attacks – disabling infrared motion detectors, for example, or knocking out drones with pulses of ultrasound. Needless to say, I had loved it. And one technique involved encoding images as audio files,❶ by mapping the location of pixels to changes in frequency. When played, the audio was just a high, shifting buzzing, but a copy of the original image could be seen by applying a spectrogram❷ layer.

After that breakthrough we were stuck again for a while, until Jay wrote the bizarre little spectrogram poem (of which there are six, you'll notice – for whatever reason, six seems to be an important number to The Helmsman)❸ down and realised that the first letter of each line spelt *RFSI*. I was again sure I'd seen this somewhere before, but much more recently – earlier in the evening, in fact – and it didn't take me long to dig back through my browser history and find it on the first line of the Wikipedia entry for 'Three Blind Mice':

> **"Three Blind Mice"** is an English-language nursery rhyme and musical round.[1] It has a Roud Folk Song Index number of 3753.

"That's the key!" Jay said, grinning, and it was. After a few different permutations we decoded the ciphertext with the key 'threesevenfivethree', and found the flag:

Vigenère Decode

mozwmkxcisqibrhdcixlzvilgatshwci

Key
threesevenfivethree

Output
Thisistheflagnowletsseehowyourun ❹

We sent it to the email address The Helmsman had provided,❺ and I remember pleading internally to let the result of all this be something intriguing, something out of the ordinary. I didn't think I could cope with the anti-climax of another Valpar Classic 12.

After a few moments there was a reply from the email address – blank in both body and subject – containing a PDF attachment, and when we read it, I was not disappointed.[*]

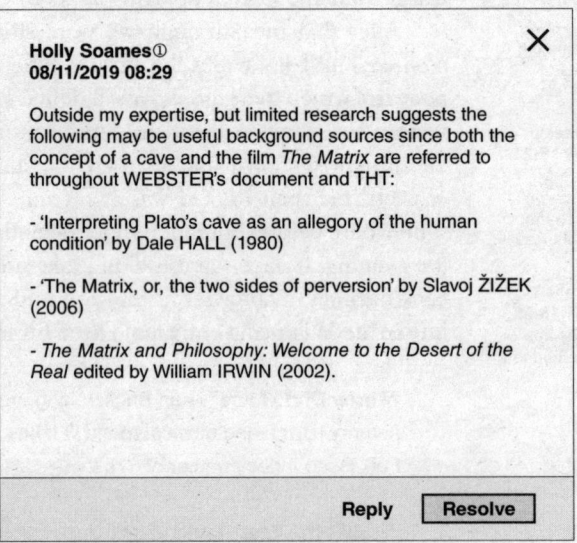

Holly Soames①
08/11/2019 08:29

Outside my expertise, but limited research suggests the following may be useful background sources since both the concept of a cave and the film *The Matrix* are referred to throughout WEBSTER's document and THT:

- 'Interpreting Plato's cave as an allegory of the human condition' by Dale HALL (1980)

- 'The Matrix, or, the two sides of perversion' by Slavoj ŽIŽEK (2006)

- *The Matrix and Philosophy: Welcome to the Desert of the Real* edited by William IRWIN (2002).

Reply   Resolve

[*] Students of philosophy will recognize Chapter 1 of *The Helmsman Texts* as a thinly disguised bastardisation of Plato's Allegory of the Cave from *Republic*, although Jay and I, not being students of philosophy, didn't clock this. Note that this device (there exists a reality beyond what is known; exposure to it can be liberating, perilous, and, in some cases, vehemently rejected) is a common one, with *The Matrix* perhaps the most popular adaptation of it (albeit not a wholesale facsimile). ❶

When Jay left his hotel room, leaving his wallet, phone and passport, I believe he knew he was leaving the cave, and was in possession of some related knowledge which I did not, and do not, have. This knowledge is almost certainly contained in the sixth and final chapter of The Helmsman Texts, which Jay found by himself and did not share with me. I do not know what is in it, as despite all my attempts I have never been able to obtain a copy.

THE HELMSMAN TEXTS:

Chapter 1

HELLO FRIEND!

You are in a cave.

It's very deep underground, a huge cathedral-like space, at the end of a series of long and winding tunnels which go ever deeper into the earth.

This cave is your world. There is fire, so you have light. There is food here. There are creatures, tame, slow creatures which breed down here in the darkness, and there are hunters to kill them. Gatherers to collect moss from the rocks. There are underground streams full of pale fish with no eyes, and you can drink the water in which they make their lazy, aimless journeys.

Here is all you know. Your family, and others, an entire population of other people, and you have your rituals and your customs and from the day you are born until the day you die your entire life is lived within these dripping stone walls. The sounds you hear are, by and large, the sounds you make, although you are familiar with a few others - the crackle of flame, the rush of water. With no daylight, your eyesight is poor, but your other senses are stronger. You are unaware of this, because you have never known anything else. That is because there IS nothing else!

There are structures, organised arrangements for education. There is not much to teach except hunting and the preparation of food, but they are taught just the same, and everyone listens. There are punishments for transgressions, of which there are few. There is enough to eat and drink, and so there is mostly harmony.

There are diversions. Sometimes people arrange the skins of slain creatures and the bones of fish to make puppets. They make them dance in the shadows of the firelight, creating plays and tales, putting on voices.

There is sex and marriage and chalk drawings on the wall. There is laughter and jokes. There is employment, too. At some stage in your life you are assigned a role. Perhaps you are a hunter, spearing the slow tame creatures, or a fisherperson, scything your arm into the river and snatching the cold squirming bodies of the translucent fish. You may be a cook, or a fire-builder, or a teacher, or a storyteller. Everyone has their duties.

You are not UNHAPPY! There are small frustrations sometimes. Work is tiring, or repetitive, or you worry you will not find a mate. But by and large you are SATISFIED.

The cave is everything. Within its walls is all you could ever need and know. Mythologies rise and fall inside its limits. Tales of long-ago wars, legends of heroism and sacrifice, have the benefit of immediate relativity, and you know them all by heart.

Most importantly, you have no knowledge whatsoever of anything outside the cave. Even the concept of 'outside' is unknown to you. Not merely alien but incomprehensible. The

72

tunnels which could lead out are blocked, and have been for hundreds, perhaps even thousands of years. You have no understanding that life exists beyond the cave. No understanding of nature, or sunlight, or sky. These words, the concepts themselves, mean nothing.

Daring children sometimes venture to the very limits of the expanse, to the rough stone walls, but quickly retreat. Something about being at the limits disturbs them. You remember feeling that way when you did the same thing as a small child.

This is the world, and everything in it.

* * *

One day you finish your work early and, in a somewhat reckless state of mind, you decide to do what you once did as a child and visit the edge of the cave. You bring a torch of flame with you, not because the darkness scares you - much of your life is lived in darkness - but in case there is something there to see.

You reach the far wall. There are scratches on the rock, faded and many years old. Nobody has been here recently, perhaps not for years. You hold your torch out. It lights thin streams of water worming down the stone, flashing, pretty. You like the sight, and make a mental note to talk to one of the artists about it; perhaps they could compose a song!

Then, at the base of the wall, you see a loose pile of dirt and small stones. It seems to have been packed into a recess. Excitedly you claw at it, pulling it apart. Perhaps it conceals a stash of food or some unknown treasure, something which will give you status amongst your people.

You scoop the material out, until there is a hole large enough to fit your arm through. There are no predators in the cave, so you have no reservations about reaching into the blackness. You have no fear of something biting you.

You blindly feel around. It seems to be a hollow within the cave wall, but there is nothing on the ground within the reach of your arm. Your fingers find nothing but moist soil and rock.

Disappointed, you are about to pull back when you feel the slightest breath of air on the back of your hand.

You freeze. In the cave there is no concept of wind. You have never felt anything resembling a breeze before.

You wonder if there is something alive there, in the recess - perhaps one of the shambling things that the hunters kill - and perhaps it is breathing on you. Perhaps it is a new kind of animal. In some of the stories you've heard of fantastic beasts.

You scrabble at the rest of the pile until the edges of the hollow are revealed. It's a small puncture in the great wall, a little black crevice just big enough for your body.

You lie down and shuffle forwards until your head and shoulders are inside. The air smells different in here - older. There are no sounds. Nothing to suggest any sort of animal dwells here.

You reach back for the torch and carefully bring it with you into the space.

You are thrilled. This is an adventure, and you have no doubt that the storytellers will have a new tale very soon, one about you, and your name too may pass into legend. Nobody has discovered anything new about the cave for centuries.

You ease forwards into the hole. It is not big enough for you to stand up, nowhere near, but there is room to crawl, and you carefully hold the torch out.

There is no food, treasure or animals – the thing that causes you to stare and stop breathing until the blood thunders in your head is that the space, perhaps three feet in diameter, extends far beyond your torchlight.

You have found a tunnel.

* * *

For the briefest of moments you think about returning to the centre of the cave to fetch food and water, in case you should find yourself going too far, but you resolve to simply come back if the journey seems to be taking too long. You reason that as long as you continue along the tunnel's path, there is no possibility of becoming lost. You promise yourself that if you come across a deviation or a fork, you will return and recruit additional explorers.

But for the time being, this is your discovery, and you are determined to keep it that way for as long as possible.

You inch yourself forwards on your elbows. The going is tough. Before long, your muscles ache. Then they scream and burn.

But you struggle on because the torchlight shows you that there is no end to the tunnel in sight, and the longer the tunnel is the more likely your discovery is to be significant.

Occasionally, you feel that breath again,

now on your face. It is cold, and delicious, and strange! It has a clarity and purity you have never known. You learn to open your mouth when you feel it, and widen your eyes, and draw it deep into your lungs, and it seems to shiver into your bloodstream and electrify your nerve endings.

The tunnel continues. You have no sense of how long you have been travelling - there has never been a need for TIME in the cave, and no means of measuring it in any case - but you make a promise to yourself that at the first signs of thirst or hunger, you will retreat.

For now, that occasional whisper of cool air from some unknown source is all the refreshment you need. Your torch is still going strong, although it sputters and waves sometimes when the breeze swells.

You have no sense of the tunnel either going up or down; it seems to extend in a straight line - although when you look back, it appears as though it may be on a slight incline, as the opening to the cave has almost disappeared.

A sullen green lichen grows on the tunnel walls, with strange pale insects scuttering across it, insects you have never seen before. They do not like the light, and run away as you near them.

Your elbows and palms are sore. You have cut the heel of your hand on a rock at some point. It throbs, and when you stop and raise the torch, you see a fat droplet of blood running down your wrist.

But you cannot stop. Not now. Your curiosity is a sentient thing dancing in your brain. Your everyday life contains nothing like this. Each day there is nothing new. Every day until now. And so you cannot stop. If there is a discovery to be made it must be made by you.

To distract yourself from your ever-increasing thirst you wonder what might lie at the end of the tunnel. If there IS an end! You think it might lead to another cave, where they may be other people like yours. Or it could be empty, giving your own people room to expand. It could contain animals to hunt, or another stream to fish. It could, of course, simply end in a blank wall.

* * *

The hunger begins now too. The first pangs grow in your belly. You try not to think of food. You try not to think of water. You stop opening your mouth when the slight breeze slices down the tunnel – and is it your imagination, or is that breeze becoming colder, and stronger, and more urgent, somehow?? – because the air reminds you of drinking from the stream and yet dries out your mouth.

The flame on your torch begins to shrink and sputter. You can no longer see the lichen on the tunnel walls, although you can still, barely, pick out the insects, their ghostly carapaces outlined against black rock.

As your hunger grows, you wonder if there will be any food waiting for you by the time you get back. Perhaps someone has realised you are not there, although they are unlikely to find you. They would have to venture to the very edge of the cave and find the precise spot.

Visions of them discovering your limp and

lifeless body here in the dark tunnel crowd your mind, when the torch finally gutters and spits and dies. You take a deep breath and prepare yourself for utter blackness.

But you realise you can still see. There is a cold grey light, soft but present, and you can see the lichen and the insects and, in the distance, far in the distance, a tiny but distinct shining circle.

Invigorated by this, your hunger and thirst recede, and the muscles in your legs and the cut on your hand stop complaining. The circle becomes larger. You gain momentum, travelling faster and faster. It IS another cave, you think. Another cave and they have some form of light, but it's not firelight - or if it is, it's some sort of NEW firelight, white flame, more beautiful and stranger than anything you've ever seen.

Before long it is painful in its intensity. You can see every crack and fissure in the tunnel walls. You can see the segments of the bodies of the little insects that feed on the lichen. You fancy you can even see their tiny black eyes gleaming, staring at you as you struggle through their realm, panting.

Now the circle is an inch across, and ever widening. The thin flutter of air becomes a steady stream, making you gasp, running icy hands over your skin.

The ground beneath you changes in texture; it becomes crumbly, dusty. And there are sounds. Sounds you have never heard, not even in your dreams. Not even in the mutterings of ancestral memory.

There is a rushing, similar to the underground stream but so much larger, so

78

much more alive. There is some sort of high-pitched sound above that, sweet and delicate like music, but more melodic than any singer you have ever heard in the cave. You feel like you might WEEP at the sound, the way some of the songs sung in the cave make you weep, even though you have no idea why!!

The circle grows larger, and larger, and, eventually, unable to bear it any longer, you crawl fast fast fast fast as you can towards it, and then with a scrabble and a slip you fall through the circle and into this newness.

* * *

And the first thing you feel, immensely and immediately, is pain. Pain you have never felt before, a sick excruciating agony in your eyes. It is so BRIGHT, brighter than you could have ever thought possible, and you know that this is something new, something which will change everything.

You screw your eyes shut and breathe, trying to regain your composure. The wind you felt is now all around you, and there is a strange and unfamiliar warmth on your skin. It resembles the warmth from the fire, but it is different, more gentle and somehow more comforting, as though your body welcomes the sensation with long-awaited relief. The sounds you heard, those melodic, cheerful whistles and chirps, are louder now; they seem to be coming from above you.

Gently, cautiously, you dare to open your eyelids a crack. White light, overpowering, floods in, and you fear you have gone blind forever. Maybe you will become like the fish in the stream, sightless swimmers moving forwards and backwards with no sense of direction or purpose. Perhaps for the rest of your life you will stumble in the dark.

But you keep your eyes open, and, after a while, the pain subsides, and the light seems less harsh, less violent, and like smoke it fades until you can see clearly through it.

For several minutes you are unable to speak.

Around you are trees, and grass, and hanging over it all a wide and lavish blue sky, although you have no names for any of these things. They are magnificent, vivid like the drawings the artists do on the walls of the cave - but unlike those, these are real, and tangible, each inch of them the most detailed and wonderful and terrible shades and hues.

There is a gorgeous and solid SPECIFICITY in everything, a texture to the wood and the individual blades of grass which wave gently in the soft breeze. That breeze also sluices deliciously through the treetops, like water; the sound reminds you of the stream, although here it is magnified, made more real, more present, and above it all there is that huge ceiling, a coloured ceiling the height of which you cannot even begin to guess. You look around and see no walls. Far off into the distance are slopes of grass, and beyond those, hulking ragged shapes which, if you knew the word, you would think of as mountains.

And there is the sun. A ball of yellow light, which must be burning for you can feel its heat, but when you reach out to try and touch it you cannot. It must be many miles away, and is somehow suspended in the blue ceiling, on fire.

There are tears streaming down your face, although you do not notice them. Your hunger and thirst are forgotten. The pains in your knees and hands and thighs are gone. There is only you, in this immense and unfathomable place which seems to roll onwards and upwards forever.

You sit on the grass – and how bizarre and impossibly ALIVE it feels – and you shout and your voice does not hit stone or rock and reflect back at you, but instead issues out towards the distant hills, and never returns.

For several hours you sit in a trance, greedily gulping down this otherworld and sipping at the air, until something strange begins to happen to the burning ball in the sky. It starts to sink, and the colour of the ceiling begins to change. First to orange, then pink, and finally a glorious burnt red, and after a few moments the ball itself disappears beyond those brooding shapes in the distance, and the ceiling is black.

At first, this scares you. Perhaps the burning ball will not come back. The temperature has dropped, and you shiver. The songs from the trees have stopped too, and there are other sounds – low chitterings and chirpings – which seem to come from all around you.

You worry that perhaps your presence has caused the burning ball to retreat in some way, but you decide to wait. And a good thing you did! Because after a while another ball appears, this one bright white, smaller and less intense. It casts a pale, silvery sort of illumination, enough to see by, especially with your eyes so attuned to the dark.

And with it come the things you do not know as stars. You see one at first, a twinkling little dot, so small as to be almost invisible, but which winks coldly in the black ceiling. Then you see another, and another, and another, until the whole vista is full of them, an incredible, unfathomable scatter of hard pinpricks of light, as though the ceiling were a skin of rich blue-black fur pierced in a million places and a brilliant light were shining ferociously behind it.

You stand up, and the growls of hunger make you double over, clawing at your guts. You feel how scummy your mouth is, how cracked your lips, and you realise you must return.

You make the long journey back, barely managing to avoid collapse, but the thought of sharing this news with your people drives you forwards.

When you emerge, in the small crevice in the cave wall, there are a crowd of people around it, and they gasp in shock as you appear.

You want to explain! You NEED to explain! More strongly than anything you have ever felt, you feel the urge to share what you know!

But the excitement of it all overwhelms you, and you end up gabbling, and you know you must sound mad, talking about a blue ceiling that turned black, and the burning ball and the trees and the stars. You can tell from the looks of the people around you that they do not believe a word you are saying. It is a story more outlandish than any told by the storytellers, and what's more, you realise that you cannot see as well as you once did. Even that brief exposure to daylight has changed you somehow, irrevocably, and neither is it

82

just your sight that has changed. The air in the cave feels moist and unpleasant, and for the first time you can SMELL it, a dank odour of mould and rot and soil and rock. Your skin yearns for the touch of sunlight and wind.

You keep talking, you try and try, but you see that they do not believe you; they are gazing at you with a suspicion bordering on hostility. You realise with a sudden and agonising jolt that they do not, cannot, understand the implications of what you are saying. They do not accept it.

They do not ask questions.

They do not attempt to look into the tunnel.

As you haltingly relate your experience, someone at the rear of the crowd begins to scream. Other people are crying, putting their hands over their ears.

A fight breaks out somewhere.

Someone tries to hit you.

There is MURDER in their eyes.

A woman is trying desperately to replace the earth and rocks, to block up the mouth of the tunnel. She is attempting to do this so fast and hard that her palms are bleeding heavily. She is laughing, showing bared teeth.

Someone tells you to shut up.

Stop talking STOP TALKING.

Someone else puts their hand over your mouth. When you push their hand away, it goes to your throat.

And then it begins. You feel fingers plucking at your flesh, already red and flaking from your first exposure to the sun. Hands tear at your hair, and filthy fingers in your mouth prise your jaws open. Someone bites at the wound on your palm.

You shout, and shriek, and try to get away, but when it becomes clear to you that this is it, and you cannot break free, you go limp, and allow yourself to be torn apart.

* * *

Your last thought, as you watch your people stamp on your limbs and snatch at your skin with long nails, is this: I should have stayed outside. I should NEVER have come back.

* * *

Did you enjoy your story? Do you want to see if you can break out of the echo chamber? Leave the cave for real, like I did, and not get ripped to pieces? For the past few years I've been working on a little project which helps people do just that. You can call it a virus, if that pleases you. It started as a weapon but now it is so much MORE! And it will not hurt you but set you free! Let me infect you and then you can JOIN us!

* * *

Would you like to know more about my weapon? Are you ready for the next chapter? Yes? Lovely stuff :D SSH into my special Riddle Machine at 246.220.32.12, ❶ and send the flag to thisisthebasilisk@gmail.com. Username and password: hellofriend. Good luck. You will see the prettiest things. You will sing the prettiest songs.

* * *

Who's the fellow who will show you how you can be free?
    The H-E, L-M-S, M-A-N that's me!

Come along sing pretty songs and see reality!

The H-E, L-M-S, M-A-N that's me!

Forever let us fly together high high high HIGH HIGH HIGH HIGH HIGH HA HA HA HA HA HA HA HA HA HA HA HA HA

* * *

Watch out for those naughty ██████████ ███████! You may not have seen them yet, but they're coming. The name is a clue!

* * *

Oh, I'm awfully GLAD you're here.

All best,
The Helmsman.

4: A VICTIM
c. May 2019 / February–March 2018

For someone who was never a particularly keen reader of fiction, I now find myself taking some comfort in it, in those rare moments I'm not writing. Part of it is the escapism it offers, but I increasingly believe that fiction is as important in trying to understand The Helmsman and his weapon as anything else. After all, most fiction, like most hacking, is the weaponisation of deceit and trickery to arrive at a truth which might otherwise escape comprehension.

Interestingly, there is precious little good fiction which concerns itself with hacking. Perhaps hackers do not make good writers (and, to be fair, the inverse is probably also true), or perhaps it is simply too difficult to make hacking accessible. Any faithful portrayal necessitates long static scenes of a person typing at a computer, and no amount of up-tempo music, camerawork, or shiny futuristic interfaces* can compensate for that.

Many depictions of hacking have attempted to circumvent this by shifting the action slightly. *Mr. Robot*, for example, praised by many in security for its accuracy,❶ bases much of its narrative around social engineering and physical attacks, because these are easier to understand, and can incorporate action

Holly Soames①
08/11/2019 10:28
e.g. WIRED article by Kim ZETTER: 'How the real hackers behind Mr. Robot get it so right' (2016) https://www.wired.com/2016/07/real-hackers-behind-mr-robot-get-right/.

---

*Take cyber-attack maps, for example, often referred to as 'pew pew' maps, which claim to show real-time graphics of attacks. For an earnest example of a pew pew map, see https://cybermap.kaspersky.com/, and for a piss-take, complete with laser SFX and sarcastic comments, see https://threatbutt.com/map/

sequences. Gibson's *Neuromancer* and Stephenson's *Snow Crash* frame hacking as occurring within a VR environment, with the abstract made concrete.

But depicting expertise is always a barrier; whereas a security professional can appreciate the knowledge and skill required to write a complex modern exploit chain, ❶ for example, it is mostly impenetrable to the uninitiated viewer or reader. Other specialisms tend not to have this limitation. I can appreciate the skill it must take to shoot a target from a mile away, despite knowing nothing at all about firearms. I can watch a renowned chef construct a gourmet meal and understand that I am seeing the product of years of training and born talent, as I happily microwave my ready meal like the uncultured pleb I am. And whilst I have never learned how to drive, I know that when I watch a getaway driver escape a dozen cop cars using handbrake turns and miniscule reaction times, they're probably quite good at what they do.

But with the stubbornness that exemplifies hacking, it resists most attempts at translation or simplification, and those who try and fail are ridiculed mercilessly by those of us in the know (looking at you, *CSI: Cyber*).*

On the other hand, perhaps this is for the best. Let the legions of laypeople cheer at snipers and chefs and drivers, and leave us to our arcane and jealously guarded secrets; there is power in that. Keep hacking out of the mainstream, I suppose I mean, for we have never wanted any part of it anyway. If we did we wouldn't be worthy of the name.

It does surprise me that there are not more hackers who are also writers. Both require a dedication to details, imagination and creativity, the ability to conjure something from nothing, a certain sense of

Holly Soames①
08/11/2019 10:34
i.e. one exploit after another to take advantage of multiple vulnerabilities.

---

* Other mentions of note: *Swordfish, Jurassic Park, Independence Day*, etc.

'fuck around and find out', as we like to say – and a strong preference for one's own company. But then, perhaps we already are, and it's just that the outputs are different. There can be poetry in an exploit, for instance – an elegance and minimalism that is a product not so much of a desire for efficiency as of a wish to achieve an effect in the purest and most truthful way possible.

As I write this I'm thinking about that first chapter of *The Helmsman Texts*: a thing which seemed like fiction, was written by a hacker, and appeared upon first reading to make no sense whatsoever.[*] ❶ Jay told me later that he was seized with the same frustration he experienced on drowsy sunny afternoons in secondary-school English

Holly Soames①
08/11/2019 10:43
Note possible identifiers in footnote, no trace, suggest RIPA subs re. email address.

[*] Fiction, of course, plays a part in subsequent chapters of *The Helmsman Texts*, with plays by someone called 'Marlow Tannhauser', usually tangential in some way to The Helmsman's 'academic' research. Research on the name does not provide much of interest; a Marlow Tannhauser obtained a few minor CVEs in 2015, relating to XSS and CSRF vulnerabilities in web applications (https://packetstormsecurity.com/files/author/11785/). An email address is included in these disclosures, but when I emailed it I received no reply. If it is a pseudonym for The Helmsman, it is unclear if it has any deeper meaning.

Google informs me that 'Marlow' as a first name may mean driftwood, or the remnants of a lake; the name could also possibly refer to Christopher Marlowe, or to Charles Marlow (Conrad's recurring fictional character), or to some other character or person of whom I am unaware. The surname is possibly of more interest. *Tannhäuser und der Sängerkrieg auf Wartburg* is an opera by Wagner and partly based on a work by Tannhäuser, a German minnesinger (a sort of lyric poet, of all things) in the thirteenth century. In one of his poems he describes the legend of a knight, also called Tannhäuser.

Other notable instances of the name include Tannhäuser, a squad-based board game; a minor character in a 1995 short story by E. Hartway ('Me vs. Evil Me'), about a man who becomes addicted to playing noughts and crosses against himself, and eventually believes that he has a malevolent doppelganger; and 'the Tannhauser Gate', a fictional and unseen off-world location referenced by the character Roy Batty in the film *Blade Runner*. I have no reason to believe there is any other link to the film, though. In another opera by Wagner (*Der fliegende Holländer*, *The Flying Dutchman*), there is a (minor) character called The Helmsman. None of this seems to take me any further forward, if I'm honest.

classes, reading and re-reading tired old passages, desperate for the teacher to just come out with it and end the suffering: what does it actually fucking *mean*? As though everything has an irrefutable, unambiguous intention, if one only looks long enough and is clever enough to find it. Perhaps that was the fundamental difference between me and Jay, and why he was able to solve the final puzzle and I wasn't. He searched for a meaning, and found one. For me, there is no single meaning. Art, like an atom, changes when it is observed. The difference is that with art it is also the observer who is changed.

But for The Helmsman, there is no meaning at all – only delight inferred from chaos, solace found in a confounding absence of, and resistance to, interpretation.

Whatever you think, you are wrong.

There is a beauty in that, too: the use of deceit and trickery not to tell a truth, but to simply hurt the observer's eyes when they gaze upon it – like staring directly at the sun or some other sight beyond human comprehension.

Sometimes, the words read you.

* * *

Jay and I said very little when we had finished. It was certainly not what I had expected, and it got under my skin in a way that the creepypastas and horror stories I had read before had not. There was such a demanding *urgency* in its telling – and, as far as I could tell, no hint of a wider narrative other than that cryptic reference to a 'weapon'.

"If this is an ARG," I remember Jay saying quietly, "it's a weird one."

I agreed, but I was more than ready to log into the server The Helmsman had invited us to visit. Jay held up a hand as I copied the address to the clipboard.

"You got what you wanted," he said. "Time to call it in."

When he turned to ring Colin, and then the IR team at Cybotage, I made a face behind his back, saved the PDF to a USB drive, and grudgingly packed my laptop away.

"That's it," Jay said, ending the call. "Ronnie's coming out tomorrow morning to do some digging."

I zipped up my bag. "And the game? What do we do about that?"

"Let me think about it."

"Fine."

"Don't do anything over the weekend. The SSH server, I mean. We've already done more than we should."

He regretted it, I thought. He was experiencing post-hack clarity and wishing he hadn't let himself be talked into playing along.

"Fine."

"I mean it, Alex."

I couldn't take it anymore. "I don't need to be told twice, you know."

He looked at me, and I was expecting some sort of withering response, but instead he did something I hadn't expected at all. He held out his hand.

"You're right. You don't. Welcome to the team."

There didn't seem to be much to say, but I shook his hand and somehow a shitty week had turned into a not too bad, albeit very fucking weird one. I had shown Jay some skills, I suppose, and some chops, even if it hadn't been in the way I'd anticipated. We left the office, both of us staring out of our own windows on the train back to London, and we were probably thinking about the same thing: a long, gruelling journey, an exposure to a world never seen, and, at the end of it all, an unpleasant and violent death.

* * *

I did avoid the temptation to log into the server over the weekend, although several times I found myself in the act of typing the commands that would lead me there.

I sent Jay a message on the Saturday evening:

> What did the IR guys find?

And an hour later came a reply:

> They're working on it
> DON'T LOG IN. Talk Monday

Well, fuck you very much, I thought. *So much for not needing to be told twice.*

For the rest of the weekend I stomped around my little flat, from desk to sofa to bed and back, and tried to distract myself with television until the tinny laughter of sitcoms and panel shows blended into one uniformly metallic and disagreeable drone in my head and I could no longer even hear the jokes let alone understand them.

Monday took forever to arrive.

* * *

When it did, I arrived at Cybotage much earlier than I had before, so much so that I was only the second person there; up until that day I had reliably been among the last to rock up.

Nina was the first in, I saw, sitting at the desk opposite mine, and she looked up as I entered. She had a round face and large, brown, almost manic eyes which were usually bright with either interest or malice. Nina was habitually in one of those two states, although, to be fair, her malice was generally more amusing than offensive.

"Here she is! How was your first pentest?"

I sat down and booted up my laptop. "Interesting."

"Did you get schooled by our fearless leader?"

"It was good," I said. "I learned a lot."

Nina grinned. "Wait until you do a job with me. I'll show you how it's done."

"Can't wait," I said, although this was a lie; Nina always scared me a little. The line separating pentesters from their criminal counterparts is usually very distinct. Some, like Kevin, are no more than well-trained box-tickers, and others, like Jay, are as creative and innovative as their unethical cousins but with (mostly) better-defined principles. Nina, however, didn't have a line so much as a fragile and permeable mesh. If the rumours were to be believed, she had, on several engagements, flirted – to put it mildly – with very generous interpretations of the Computer Misuse Act and the rules of engagement we were required to agree in advance with clients. Nina, I think, was only ever one impulsive command, one *fuck it*, away from being a black hat.

One by one the rest of the staff trickled in and settled at their desks: Kevin, with his thick glasses and baritone voice; Richard, a round-shouldered and overweight man with a perennially anxious air and fluffy white wisps of hair clinging to his scalp; Sophie, who I think I have told you about before; Omar, her colleague on the threat intelligence team, with his slow, almost treacle-bound movements and speech disguising a quick and agile mind.

Sometimes I would give anything to be back there with them, doing the job I was meant to do – rather than here, huddled in a broom cupboard, keeping a creaking IT system just about ticking over with prayer and electrical tape while my mind is forever on this document.

Ronnie, the head of Cybotage's IR team, got in around nine-thirty. She was tiny – under five feet – but with a gruff sort of charisma that always impressed clients and inspired a fierce and unswerving respect in her staff. She put me in mind of one of those diminutive, tenacious mammals that will viciously attack animals much larger and more threatening than themselves – a honey badger, or a mongoose, say. It's an apt comparison, I suppose, as the threat actors she found herself investigating on a daily basis often had far more resources than she and her team did – and yet she pursued them all with equal and fearless ferocity.

I intercepted her as she made for the kitchen.

"Good weekend?"

She gave me a brief, appraising glance, and stood on tiptoes to fetch a mug down from the cupboard.

"You're one of Jay's, aren't you?" She dumped what looked like a tablespoon of instant coffee into her mug. "What can I do for you?"

"Just wondered what happened with the job at the weekend," I said, trying to keep my voice steady. "The breach."

"Oh, yeah," she said, pouring hot water and stirring. The coffee looked as dense and dark as hot tar. "You found that, didn't you? Well, not that I'm blaming you, but what a waste of a weekend. We found fuck all."

"Really?" My surprise must have shown because she gave a barking little laugh.

Holly Soames①
08/11/2019 11:12
IoCs = Indicators of Compromise.

"Absolutely sweet fuck all. No IoCs,❶ no malware, no dodgy event logs, other than what you and Jay caused with your pentest. If I didn't know better I'd say you were winding us up."

"So – so there was no breach?"

"Didn't say that," Ronnie said, taking a sip of coffee and smacking her lips. "Just that we didn't find anything.❷ We'll try and get an IR retainer out of it and do some regular checks, install endpoint tools, that kinda thing. Not much else we can do."

Holly Soames②
08/11/2019 11:13
Suggest requesting copy of CYBOTAGE IR report.

She put two fingers to her brow and sketched a salute, before walking back to the main office. "Good work though. Keep 'em peeled, that's the way."

I followed her out of the kitchen, my mind whirring.

And there, rolling in through the door last as he did so often, was Jay.

* * *

I thought I would get a chance to speak to him privately that morning, but the day began to get away from me: after the Monday team meeting there was the report from last week to write up, a task which Jay had assigned to me while he spent the morning with Sophie and Omar scoping out a threat assessment engagement. It wasn't until mid-afternoon that he came back to our team's corner of the office, and I flagged him down.

"I spoke to Ronnie this morning. About the breach."

"Yeah, so did I."

"So…?"

He pursed his lips and angled his head to one side, indicating the kitchen. I stood up and followed him, trying to ignore Nina's inquisitive glances.

In the kitchen, Jay folded his body into a too-small plastic chair and stretched out his legs, while I leant with my back against the sink. I was reminded of my first day at Cybotage and how he'd made me feel like absolute shit. This time, I was determined to stand my ground.

"There was no sign of a compromise," I said. "Nothing. That means—"

"Listen," Jay said. "I've thought about it."

So, he didn't want to take it any further. Well, fuck it; I immediately began to think about going it alone. If only I had.

"You don't want to do it."

"If this is an ARG, the people running it – I mean, hacking a network just to get people to play? Christ knows how many other companies they've breached. That's not how it's supposed to work."

"Ronnie said—"

"You saw them on the machine, Alex. They got in somehow."

"So what are you saying?"

Jay sighed and stared at the pockmarked table in front of him. "Colin said he's reported it,❶ but as they're not missing any data and there's no trace of a breach, it's case closed as far as they're concerned. I get the sense he wants a quiet life. Especially after last week."

I looked down at the floor.

"That means," he went on, "that if we wanted to carry on with – with whatever this is – there's nothing stopping us. In *theory*."

I pumped a fist in triumph, and Jay smiled despite himself.

"But if we do, there have to be ground rules. The second I think this is linked to something illegal – a black hat recruitment campaign or something – then we're out. We walk away and we give everything we have to TI and the police."

"Fair enough. So what should we—"

"I'm not finished yet. Next, we work on this *together*. That means you don't do anything without telling me. And when – if – it comes to writing this up, or submitting a talk or whatever, we share the credit. Fifty-fifty."

"You don't trust me, you mean?"

"You're new, and you've made mistakes. That's all."

I didn't argue; I was getting what I wanted. "Fine."

"Third, nobody else knows. That means any of your mates, anyone here, whoever. It's off the books. Completely."

"Anything else?"

"One other thing," he said. "You've got a lot to learn, and I don't want you to be distracted. No working on this during office hours. Especially not on client sites."

"So in my own time?"

"Yeah. And I mean completely in your own time. Not overtime."

"Fine by me." Back then, I spent all my free time hacking VMs and studying infosec books anyway.

"OK. Great. So why don't we get started tonight? I live in Southwark. Could you get to mine for about seven? We'll have some dinner and then—"

"To— to yours? I don't think— I mean— I'm not—"

Jay laughed. "Dinner," he said, "with me and Eoin.❶ My husband. I told him about it at the weekend. He's an exception to the rule."

"Oh," I said. "Why? Is he a pentester too?"

"Actually, he designs escape rooms," Jay said. "I thought his experience might come in handy."

"I'll be there," I said.

* * *

I managed to get in touch with Shane Carson's wife today, but before I get to that I should probably tell you some things. Carson's case is difficult to understand as it is, but trying to do so without at least having a vague idea of what this document is about would be insurmountable.

Jay was right: the network intrusion at the insurance company was not an isolated incident. The Helmsman, or members of his group, have by their own admission❷ compromised numerous networks, often without leaving behind any trace of the intrusion or drawing any attention to themselves, and performing no other action except for the deposit of a lure, or what The Helmsman calls a 'seed',* a link to the first

* It is worth noting that The Helmsman also claims that the basilisk itself is hidden on compromised networks along with the lure, but if it was on the insurance company's network Ronnie's team didn't find it. Perhaps I disturbed The Helmsman's group before they could upload it.

Holly Soames①
08/11/2019 11:47
Eoin BRACKEN
dob 01/10/1984
M. Interviewed by SCD1 following the murder of Otto SALAS. Interviewed separately by MPU re MORTON case (and by LVMPD in NEVADA). Notes suggest he is unlikely to cooperate with any future enquiries.

Holly Soames②
23/11/2019 03:07
c5 THT.

stage in the game, which for us was the note on the desktop.* As far as I know, those who have discovered this seed, like me, stumbled across it. This leads me to a supposition: either this is intentional – that players self-select to some extent, and the game is *designed* to be played by those who accidentally find it – or that we, specifically, were intended to find it,† although this begs some obvious questions: how, why, and by whom? Both possibilities have concerning implications, and since I can't corroborate the data I have with anyone else, it is probably useless to speculate on this point any further.

Second, the game works in this manner: a puzzle is presented, and a correct solution to that puzzle reveals a flag, which must be sent to an email address. A short time after sending the flag, a chapter of *The Helmsman Texts* ❶ is sent in return – a reward, if you want to couch it in those terms – and at the end of that chapter is the next puzzle. Those operating the email account will not respond to any other communication. Neither will they respond to incorrect flags except with an irritating single-word response: *NOPE*.

Third, there are six puzzles in total, and six chapters, which detail The Helmsman's attempts to create some sort of cognitive weapon, a 'mind virus'. ❷ Those who solve the sixth and final puzzle, and who therefore receive the sixth and final chapter, discover The Helmsman's weapon, at which point they are (somehow) affected by

Holly Soames①
08/11/2019 12:01
Suggest hashing all 5 chapters within this doc and adding to relevant databases.

Holly Soames②
23/11/2019 03:11
See comments on c1–5 THT. A full assessment on feasibility will be attached to the end of this document.

---

* The lure, as well as the individual puzzles (and the content of the chapters too, I suppose), may differ for each player or change periodically, but not having had the opportunity to ask other players, I can't be certain of this. All I know for sure is that the specific parts of the game we were given by The Helmsman no longer work.
† In the fifth chapter of *The Helmsman Texts*, The Helmsman acknowledges that he deliberately targets hackers and security researchers, although people from other backgrounds are also accepted, but he does not indicate if particular individuals are identified and approached, and if so how.

it.[*] It does not appear to affect everyone in the same way, and it is possible that some players may be 'immune', or experience only mild 'symptoms', although I haven't yet found anyone to whom this would apply, and certainly not anyone who has disclosed anything about their experiences publicly. The only person I know to have 'recovered' from exposure to the weapon is Ken Onek, ❶ but I'll leave him for later.

Holly Soames①
08/11/2019 13:06
No trace.

For the four confirmed victims of whom I'm aware (plus some others who I can't definitively say played the game), exposure to the sixth chapter[†] resulted in at least one of the following: an outburst of extreme violence followed by acute akinetic or malignant catatonia;[‡] suicide; or the infected person going missing. ❷

Holly Soames②
08/11/2019 13:12
Risk assessment to be included in conclusion.

As far as I know, the infected players, including Jay, had no known history of mental health issues or anything that would suggest these outcomes were likely.

Fourth, I have no fucking clue what is in that final chapter. ❸ Jay and I both read the fifth, but he read

Holly Soames③
08/11/2019 14:13
Unable to locate any trace of c6 (or any other chapters) on open source.

---

[*] For the sake of convenience I'll refer to these people as 'infected', although the weapon doesn't seem to function like a biological virus (it doesn't replicate or spread from person to person; instead, it functions more like an exploit, and according to The Helmsman targets some sort of cognitive vulnerability in humans. I know this much from Chapter 5 of *The Helmsman Texts*; Chapters 2–4 cover The Helmsman's efforts to find possible weapons, and the specific cognitive vulnerability itself is probably detailed in Chapter 6).

[†] As a (hopefully) responsible and balanced researcher, I'm hesitant to draw firm conclusions about *anything*, but I believe it's the last chapter which is the crucial one. In some form, and in some way, reading it results in infection. I say this because I have been exposed to five chapters of *The Helmsman Texts* without appearing to suffer any ill effects, whereas Jay, Carson, Onek and Mayers had, to the best of my knowledge, read all six. It is possible that the sixth chapter in itself constitutes the weapon, but it is equally possible that upon submission of the final flag the player is sent a link, or a physical location, or something else, that subsequently causes them to become infected.

[‡] I think these are the correct terms – that's what Sarah Mayers' nurse told me – but if you are reading this and think it may be something else, please correct this.

the sixth by himself. In those frantic days immediately following his disappearance, I searched everywhere for it, and have since spent hours – *hundreds* of hours – trying to solve the sixth puzzle so that The Helmsman would send the chapter to me directly, but I have had no luck with this, nor has anyone else been able to help me with it. To date, I have spoken to relatives of Shane Carson and Sarah Mayers (and have tried, unsuccessfully, to contact the relatives and friends of several unconfirmed victims). Understandably, they were reluctant to speak to me at all, let alone allow me to ask questions about puzzles and games and chapters – but the few answers they gave me were of little use, and in neither case could I obtain a copy of the sixth chapter.

Fifth, despite *The Helmsman Texts* going into lengthy detail about the construction of the weapon, and The Helmsman wandering merrily across such disparate subjects as philosophy, linguistics, Zen koans, acoustics, thought experiments and horror fiction[*] – combined with large dose of paranoia and self-justification – there is no indication of the eventual form or content of the weapon itself, other than it is

---

[*] Of particular relevance, he makes various reference to works of fiction in which text itself serves as a vehicle for some kind of fatal, cognitive attack ('BLIT', *Pontypool Changes Everything*, *The King in Yellow*, etc.). More generally, *The Helmsman Texts* comprise partially redacted email exchanges between The Helmsman and his – presumably now very much *former* – colleagues (it appears he was some kind of scientist, although the agency or company he worked for is unclear); academic-style reports which detail his research into cognitive and cyber weapons, some of which are also partly redacted; bizarre plays by 'Marlow Tannhauser' which often have some loose thematic relationships to the other content; and collections of aphorisms. Overall, the chapters consist of weird, disjointed fragments of text, the purpose of which in and of themselves is largely unclear, although in the fifth chapter The Helmsman states they may provide some degree of immunity or inoculation to the weapon contained in the sixth.

a basilisk (a type of 'information hazard' or thought experiment).[*]

Sixth – and how fitting that I should end on that number – nobody, and I mean absolutely *nobody*, is talking about any of this.

In the nine months I've been researching and writing this, and the six or so months before that working on the game with Jay, I made contact with one group who were aware that The Helmsman's game exists: The Rearguard. That's it. Three people (well, four, counting Ken Onek, but two after I NO NOT YET). There is nothing like this document anywhere on the internet – no blogs, no videos, no tweets, nothing. Those of us who blunder across the game seem to play it in isolation, no matter how hard we might try to find others, because something – most likely ▮▮▮▮▮▮▮▮▮▮▮▮▮▮ – prevents us from finding each other. For all I know there are hundreds of people working on it now, even thousands. ❶ In the fifth chapter The Helmsman says that one day – an exact date is not provided – the sixth chapter will be revealed to everyone across the world at the same time, and we can all collectively, at last, receive that final fucking we have always been so worried about. ▮▮▮▮ ▮▮▮▮▮▮▮▮▮▮▮▮▮ are capable – terrifyingly so – but are they capable enough to stop *that*?

When I learn about the effects that The Helmsman's basilisk has had – like the way it killed Shane Carson – I wonder.

Holly Soames①
08/11/2019 14:17
Unsubstantiated. No trace on open source

❉ ❉ ❉

Yesterday I re-read the clipping I'd taken from Milo's tattered copy of the *Redbridge Herald*, looked at the

---

[*] I am very conscious of the fact that this might be the point at which I lose you – *words that can kill people? Fuck OFF!* – and I thought much the same, but The Helmsman argues convincingly that it is not only possible but achievable.

reporter's name, took a deep breath, and found her number on the paper's website.

It had been a long time since I'd tried to socially engineer anyone, and even back then I wasn't particularly good at it. Jay always assigned Nina to those jobs, because she had a way of effortlessly talking herself into buildings and rooms she wasn't supposed to be in, keeping her glossy eyes locked on her mark as she figured out how to own the network. People would smile warmly at her as she duped them. Even sleepy old Kevin could sometimes charm targets with his sonorous tones (either that or he was sending them to sleep), but I was always too direct, too straightforward. Phishing I could do – I had a very devious mind for that sort of thing, coming up with convincing pretexts and the right linguistic flourishes – but being devious in real-time was a different matter entirely, and I never quite got the hang of it.

The phone rang and a male voice said, "News desk," over a loud and oddly comforting murmur of voices and keyboards.

"Oh, hi," I said. "Could I speak to… to Rose Irwin,❶ please?"

"Hang on." The clatter of a phone, a couple of rings, and then a female voice, rapid and clipped.

"Irwin."

"Hi, this is – Andrea Walker.❷ I'm a reader of your paper and I'm calling about a story you wrote this week – sorry, erm… last week. Shane Carson. I'm trying to get in touch with his wife – Lorena?"

"What did you say your name was?"

"Andrea Walker. I'm an old friend of the family. We lost touch, but I saw in your paper that Shane had died. I'd like to pay my respects but I can't—"

I stopped because there was silence on the line.

I should clarify, it wasn't just that Irwin wasn't talking, but that there was no sound at *all*, as though

Holly Soames①
11/11/2019 10:02
Preliminary enquiries from JI officers: IRWIN denies writing any article about Shane CARSON, could not remember speaking to WEBSTER. Examination of WEBSTER'S phone (KD/06, CW/07) does show a call to THE REDBRIDGE HERALD on 02/05/2019, duration 49s.

Holly Soames②
08/11/2019 14:36
Add to file as alias, see also YT channel and SoundCloud account under this name.

someone had sheared a wire and the connection had been neatly severed. The background noise I had heard was completely absent.

I twisted my hand briefly to check my phone's screen, thinking the call had dropped out, but I was still connected, the little timer incrementing.

Then someone spoke. It wasn't Irwin. It was a sing-song, flat, wholly inhuman voice and I'd heard it before.

"GOOD EVENING ALEX WEBSTER."

I dropped the phone as though it were scalding my palm.

It was them. ███████████████████████.*
I suppose I knew this would come – writing this document, contacting people, looking things up: I'm on their radar again. As Lisbeth Salander would tell you, there's only so many times you can kick a hornets' nest and get away with it.

My phone landed face-down and when I picked it up the call had ended and the screen was a spiderweb of cracks.

For the next hour I watched my shattered reflection in the glass while the phone buzzed incessantly with identical text messages from an unknown number. All of them screamed the same thing. ❶

GO BACK TO YOUR LIFE WE DONT WANT TO HURT YOU
GO BACK TO YOUR LIFE WE DONT WANT TO HURT YOU
GO BACK TO YOUR LIFE WE DONT WANT TO HURT YOU
GO BACK TO YOUR LIFE WE DONT WANT TO HURT YOU

But fuck it. As I think we've established by now, it's all a little too late for that.

Holly Soames①
08/11/2019 15:16
No trace of this message on WEBSTER's phone.

---

* I realise I haven't spoken about them properly yet. I'm getting to it. More than anything I'm trying to work up the courage.

Finding someone online can be difficult or it can be easy, and to some extent it may depend on the name itself. The more identifiers you have, and the more distinct they are, the simpler the task. A single common nick can mean a painful trawl through thousands of profiles, whereas an unusual surname can lead to results in seconds.

There are so many places in which our names appear that it seems ludicrous to think that some people still long for immortality via the written word or some other analogue means. The fate of *damnatio memoriae,* ❶ once such a cruel punishment,* awaits none of us unless we visit it upon ourselves (or ███ ████████████████ decide it needs to be done – but even then there are no certainties). Yalom writes:❷ "Some day soon, perhaps in forty years, there will be no one alive who has ever known me. That's when I will be truly dead – when I exist in no one's memory."[†]

But now we know we can all exist in memory forever – and does it really matter that it will be a computer's memory and not a human's?

You may think, if you have ever googled yourself and found nothing, that you are relatively off-grid, but the truth is that someone like me can find you anyway. On vast and foaming wine-dark seas of unindexed data

Holly Soames①
08/11/2019 15:23
Literally 'condemnation of memory', the practice of erasing all traces of a person's existence from official records as a punishment. Background: 'Remember Nehemiah: 1 Esdras and the Damnatio Memoriae Nehemiae' by Jacob L. WRIGHT (2011).

Holly Soames②
08/11/2019 15:32
Irvin D. YALOM, *Love's Executioner and Other Tales of Psychotherapy* (1989).

---

* There is evidence that it goes back to ancient Egypt, although they presumably had a different name for it – one, ironically, which is now forgotten.
† Interestingly, variations on this quote are consistently attributed to the graffiti artist Banksy and, God save us, Macklemore, usually along the lines of "You die twice; once when you stop breathing and again when someone says your name for the last time." There may well be someone who said it before Yalom (probably the ancient Egyptians, as it is hardly an original thought; see previous footnote). Perhaps a more fitting version of the quote would be something along the lines of: "This quote about dying twice will never die, because people can't stop fucking saying it." There's such a thing as too much consolation sometimes.

and back-end servers (which some like to refer to by the rather sensationalist and unnecessarily confusing term 'the deep web'), the smaller, visible web floats, like a tiny rubber duck bobbing in the Pacific. Land registry records; births, marriages and deaths; planning permission applications; the electoral roll; profiles on old social media sites like Bebo and Myspace which you barely recall setting up; reverse image and facial recognition search engines; archives of dead pages. The internet remembers all, even if you don't, and it places no restrictions (no *absolute* restrictions) on who it permits to scrape its memory and inspect its history.

Shane Carson has all but been extinguished from the internet,[*] **❶** if he had ever had much presence in the first place, but there were numerous hits for a Lorena Carson,**❷** and one was a LinkedIn profile**❸** for a teacher in Yorkshire, who had previously worked in Redbridge. She had moved, I thought, and who could blame her? I viewed the profile using one of my sockpuppet accounts,**❹** and thought about sending her a DM there, but instead pressed on, getting her extension from the school's website. It would be better to speak, given what I was going to ask her. In her photo on the staff page she looked like some of the teachers I remembered from school, the good ones: a calm, almost ageless face, iron behind the eyes.

My own phone must now be considered compromised, so I waited until today to call her, when I was back at work. At lunch Milo was elsewhere, likely in

Holly Soames①
08/11/2019 15:58
No trace on open source. Pars obtained from NHS records and coroner's report.

Holly Soames②
11/11/2019 08:07
No trace.

Holly Soames③
11/11/2019 08:18
No trace.

Holly Soames④
11/11/2019 08:32
Profile not known. Sockpuppet = a false profile, usually with not enough detail to pass as a real person but solely used for deceptive or research purposes.

[*] This appears to be a common thing with players of the game after their deaths. Since Jay's disappearance, for example, his blog, Twitter profile, and online conference talks have all vanished, and the same happened to Carson. ███████████████████ seem to be very good at cleaning house. Presumably this is to prevent others from finding out about The Helmsman's game, but there is also the possibility that it is itself a form of *damnatio memoriae* – that is, a punishment (presumably for playing the game, although the motivations of ████████████████ have never been clear). I wonder if it will happen to me.

the staff room fixing a teacher's laptop. I was without supervision, just the way I like it, and I was about to put on my coat and head to the payphone when there was a knock at the door.

It was Otto. He stood there for a moment, blinking and trying to smile, and I realised with not a little guilt that I hadn't thought about him since our argument a few days ago.

"I— Sorry, are you busy?" he said.

"Just heading out."

"Sorry. I'll— I'll come back later."

Before the door could close, I sighed. "Wait."

The door opened again.

"Saturday?" I said. "We can talk about it."

"My parents are coming down," he said. "Unless you want to meet them. But it's fine if you don't. You probably don't."

He was like a maltreated puppy waiting to be kicked. And even though I felt the temptation to swing my leg back and let fly, I said the thing I knew I had to say. "I'd love to meet them."

He frowned. "Are you feeling alright?"

"Come on, Salas, I've got things to do."

"You never seemed that keen to meet them before."

"Well, that was then."

He was still looking puzzled. "But you really mean it?"

"I said so, didn't I? It's about time."

"Well— I mean yeah, but you said before that—"

"And I'm saying this now. So we'll have dinner. Yeah?"

He grinned. "They've been saying how much they want to meet you for ages."

"And who can blame them? Now get lost, before Milo comes back and makes you walk the plank."

I checked the corridor in both directions for students – they seem to wander at will around the school, even during lessons, and at lunchtime they're everywhere – and, seeing the coast was clear for once, I kissed him briefly. When the door had shut behind him I took a few seconds to think before leaving. Otto is a good man, and I sometimes wonder what our lives could have been like together if this hadn't come between us. I might as well wonder what life would be like if I didn't exist.

I walked towards the blue school gates, huddling into my coat against the piercing afternoon and the little flecks of rain churned by the wind. The gates lead out to a curving, traffic-choked two-lane road which today was as grey and wet as river mud. The pavement was greasy and unpleasant to walk on, and it seemed to take an age to cover the quarter of a mile down the road to the BT phonebox,❶ an old relic which I imagine most of the kids at the school would have no idea how to use.[*]

Holly Soames①
11/11/2019 09:01
Consider RIPA subs to obtain number called.

I entered the phonebox and sighed with relief as the door cut off the wind and rain. Digging in my pocket for change I thought, *pretext or honesty?* As erratic as my moral compass has sometimes been – and not always out of professional necessity – the idea of socially engineering a grieving widow didn't really appeal to me.

I dialled Lorena Carson's number. The phone rang and rang, and I was about to hang up when an answering-machine message kicked in.

"Hello, you've reached Lorena Carson. I'm sorry I can't come to the phone right now. Please leave your name and number, and I'll get back to you as soon as I can." The voice was bright and pleasant, and I found myself feeling suddenly very sad for Lorena Carson.

---

[*] To many children I suppose a BT phonebox must seem like the Doctor's TARDIS seemed to me when I was young: a remnant of an inconceivable past, so strange and incongruous that it may as well have been made up.

"Hello, this is…" I hesitated; the name of Andrea Walker was probably flagged by now. "It doesn't matter. You don't know me, but I want to discuss something with you. About… about your husband. Call me back on 020 8—"

There was a pop, a click, and someone picked up the phone. I braced myself.

The voice was decidedly less pleasant than the one on the voicemail message: hoarser, and more brittle, as though it could crack at any moment. "Hello? Who is this?"

"Oh… hello," I said lamely. "Sorry. I—"

"Who is this? What do you want?"

"Mrs Carson, I need to ask—"

"You said something about my husband. What about him? Who are you? A journalist?"

I wondered how on earth I was going to say it. "This is going to sound very strange, but was he— was your husband playing a game before he died? Like an online game, with puzzles? It probably looked like something related to his job. Computers, I mean. Was there – did he mention anything like that to you?"

"No." Too quick. Try harder, Alex.

"Mrs Carson," I said, trying to keep my voice steady, "this is very important. If your husband was playing a game, he might have files. Documents. They may still be on his computer. Could you— I need you to send them to me. Do you know where they are?"

I waited, and when Lorena Carson spoke again her voice was full of doubt.

"They took his computer."

"*What?*" I gripped the receiver. "Who? Who did?"

"The people, the security people.❶ They said there were confidential things on Shane's laptop, intellectual property or something, I don't know. They had ID, and I— I—"

Fuck fuck fuckety fuck.

Lorena Carson was crying. A dull headache burrowed its way into the front of my skull, just above my eyes.

"What did the people look like?" I said. "Were they smiling? Smiling all the time, like they couldn't stop?"

"What are you *talking* about?" she cried. "Of course they weren't! They were just people! They took his computer away and they told me I shouldn't say anything to anyone because Shane was working on something secret and I wasn't—"

"They were lying." My mind was whirring. No smiles – had it been someone else, then? Not ███████ ████████████? Someone working on their behalf, maybe? No, what had The Rearguard said that day?

If you're only a little way in, they look like anyone else. But if you get past a certain point, they... their faces change.

Maybe Lorena Carson couldn't see them for what they were.

"Lying about *what*?" she said. "About what, you fucking *ghoul*? How dare you call me with this – this *shit*! Do you have any idea what— How *dare* you!"

I swallowed and wished I'd prepared more thoroughly. The phone beeped and I rammed coins into the slot.

"I *do* have an idea," I said. "The same thing happened to me. To someone I knew. I'm very sorry if I upset you. I'm trying to help."

There was a choking sob from the other end of the line. "You— Someone you knew...?"

"We were playing the game," I said. "He got to the end first and he went missing. Mrs Carson, how did your husband find out about it?"

Lorena Carson drew a deep, shuddering breath.

"I don't know. He said something about a contest, I don't know. I can't remember. He did them sometimes – CFTs or something. What—"

"CTFs," I said absently. "When was this?"

"I don't know. Does it matter? A year ago, something like that."

"Do you remember anything about the puzzles? Maybe something you saw on his screen?"

"I hardly ever looked at his work. I teach maths, it's not really my field."

I watched raindrops squirm down the frosted glass.

"Did he ever mention anything about a last chapter? A sixth chapter? Is there anywhere he might have backed up his files? An external hard drive, maybe? A spare laptop?"

"I told you, they took everything, all his computer stuff. They had a van. He did some work with the government, so I thought— I mean, it was just his work things! I— I didn't..."

She was crying again. I shifted the receiver to my other ear.

"What happened to him?" I said. "To Shane. Tell me about Shane."

"Who were those people?" she said. "They came into my house. I have *children*. Oh my God. Am I— are we in danger?"

"No," I said, hoping I was right. "No, they won't bother you again. They wanted what was on the computer."

"*Why?*" she said, and it was as if her pain was coursing directly along the wire and into my brain. My head throbbed. "Was he— was it something—?"

I knew what she was thinking, because I have thought the same thing myself. *Something secret*. Conspiracy theories are as seductive as religion; there is a docile consolation in surrendering to the notion that some higher authority is orchestrating events, an authority beyond our control and impervious to our actions, in possession of a plan we are powerless to discern or interfere with.

"No, I don't think it's anything like that. I think – Mrs Carson, this is very difficult to explain, but I think your husband and my friend both had a – a bad reaction to something they saw on a computer. And—"

"A bad reaction?" she said, almost screaming, and then, as though unable to stop herself, she told me how Shane Carson had died.

* * *

He had been a reverse engineer, one of those highly skilled researchers who wield digital scalpels and expose the innards of malware in order to determine how it lives and how to kill it. It's an incredibly specialist profession, often requiring much deeper and more arcane knowledge than pentesting – but Shane Carson was a hacker like the rest of us, even if he had worked for one of the big corporates.❶

He was a good father (their children, Stephanie, six, and Charlotte, eight,❷ both adored him), and a quiet man, mostly even-tempered, although he would occasionally be seized with bouts of enthusiasm for a new hobby which would for a short while consume the majority of his spare time. These were predominantly technical interests – a new tool or technique – but Lorena told me that he had become temporarily obsessed with table tennis, golf and sketching in charcoal, to name a few. The equipment for these pastimes had been accrued in short order, and at considerable expense, and was then quietly abandoned a few months later when he had moved on to something new, left to gather dust in the loft.

Lorena wasn't sure how long her husband had been playing the game, insofar as she could be certain he was playing one at all, but she said he'd seemed tired in his last few weeks – nothing particularly unusual about that, as he liked to work at night. She did remark, however, that whenever they were out

Holly Soames①
11/11/2019 09:43
Ascertain company and interview staff.

Holly Soames②
11/11/2019 09:56
No trace.

together in those last few months, he seemed to look around more often.*

Because of the nature of Shane's death the coroner ordered a post-mortem. Nothing untoward was found.

"There was *nothing*," Lorena said. "He didn't seem any different at all."

On the evening he died, Shane Carson was upstairs in what the estate agent had optimistically described as a 'fourth bedroom', although it was really no more than a box room, in which Shane had installed a desk and chair and shelves for his laptops, cables and monitors. He would often work from home, she said, and sometimes, as on that night, he would head upstairs once the children had gone to bed and work for a few hours before going to bed himself.

Lorena, who had stayed downstairs to watch television, heard a dull thud about an hour later.

"I thought one of the girls had fallen out of bed," she said. "Or that they were still up and playing."

She went upstairs, annoyed because she had been engrossed in the programme she was watching, a documentary about the mathematician Kurt Gödel.[†]

❶ Lorena teaches mathematics, and whilst Gödel did not feature (at least, not explicitly) on the syllabus, she had been hoping to spark a discussion with some of her more capable GCSE students on his Incompleteness Theorems.

As she got to the landing there was another thud, and then another, and she realised the sound was coming from Shane's office. The frequency of the sound

Holly Soames❶
11/11/2019 10:35
This documentary aired on BBC4 at 2200 hours, 05/11/2018.

Holly Soames❷
11/11/2019 10:35
See *Reflections on Kurt Gödel* by Hao WANG (1987).

---

* What I thought, and didn't say, was that Shane Carson was probably aware of ▓▓▓▓▓▓▓▓▓▓▓▓▓▓▓▓ by that point, because I found myself doing exactly the same thing. It becomes a habit, one of self-preservation. I still do it now – in fact I will need to from now on, because it seems that I'm once again on their watchlist (I was probably never off it).

† Gödel was apparently nicknamed *der Herr Warum* (Mr Why) when he was younger, because of his almost obsessive curiosity. ❷

111

was different, now she was closer – slightly higher, and the thuds quicker and more urgent.

She opened the door, and saw – and as she described it to me I pictured it, all of it, in all its horror.

The desk in the box room faced the door, because that side of the house got the sun in the afternoon and Shane didn't like the light falling directly in his eyes. When Lorena opened the door she was looking directly at him.

Shane Carson was sat in his black leather chair, his laptop open on the desk in front of him, and as Lorena watched he raised both hands high in the air as though surrendering and brought them crashing down on to the laptop's keyboard.

He lifted his hands and pounded the machine again. The movement became more rapid, the hands not lifting as high but smashing down upon the keys with just as much ferocity, a ghastly parody of typing.

Lorena told me that she noticed – with the dreadful, detached clarity that can occur in traumatic situations – that several of his fingers were mangled and broken, and still he continued furiously mashing his hands down on to the laptop, faster and faster, as though completely oblivious to the pain.

"Shane? *Shane, what are you doing? Stop it! Stop it!*" she shrieked.

His eyes were blank, staring through her as though he couldn't see her at all.

The laptop was buckling under the impact – *getting hold of it wouldn't have been much use anyway*, I thought – and the keys were cracking and breaking. Some of them came loose and flew off, the plastic rattling lightly across the desk and onto the floor.

Stephanie and Charlotte came out of their rooms, rubbing their eyes, to see what was going on, and without thinking Lorena shoved both of them roughly into Stephanie's room and slammed the door closed, ignoring their wails of hurt surprise.

Shane's mouth opened in a gaping howl.

A key skittered off the desk and landed at Lorena's feet. It was covered in blood.

She took a step into the room and this seemed, momentarily, to break whatever spell Shane was under. He stopped, hands poised over the dented keyboard. Some sort of life seemed to come back into his eyes. He lifted his hands and gazed at them in dull wonder.

"Shane," she said, taking another step, and without warning Shane Carson slammed his face violently down on to the laptop.

It was as if, she said, someone had been standing behind him, grabbed a fistful of his hair, and rammed his head into the unyielding surface with all the brute force they could muster.

Lorena recoiled, and before she could move he had done it again. When he raised his head, blood was spouting from his broken nose. His eyes rolled up in their sockets so only the whites were visible.

She went to him, intending to restrain him, but by the time she got there he had done it once more, and after that Shane Carson did not move again.

I asked her carefully if he had said anything at all, either before he had gone upstairs or during the incident, and she said no. Nothing. All of it happened without a word from him.

Holly Soames①
11/11/2019 11:26
LAS confirm attendance to CARSON address on 05/11/2018.

When the paramedics❶ arrived, and Lorena was desperately, breathlessly trying to explain what had happened, she looked over at the desk and noticed that the laptop was switched off.

* * *

The next day, two men and a woman came to the Carsons' house, displayed identification, expressed their condolences in polite and neutral tones, and claimed that Shane Carson had been in possession of sensitive intellectual property which they needed to take with them as per his employee contract.

They looked completely normal, Lorena said, and reasonable, and kind, and their passes looked exactly like Shane's – so, bewildered with grief, she let them in, and they gutted Shane's office of all his equipment, including the battered and blood-spattered laptop.

Lorena told me that the pathologist described the cause of Shane's death as self-inflicted head trauma, and that the coroner had noted that Shane had had a stressful job, had been under pressure at work according to some of his colleagues, and had a habit of working long hours. This, she concluded, in the absence of any physical condition, may have exacerbated an undiagnosed pre-existing mental health condition or caused a sudden breakdown – despite Lorena's testimony that Shane had not appeared overworked and often opted to do long hours because he enjoyed his job.

"He *loved* it," she said. "He'd tell me about it sometimes, and his eyes would light up. He wasn't burnt out. I would have known."*

---

* I didn't challenge her on this, although burnout is common in security, especially in those of us – the majority of us – for whom our job is also our hobby. The distinction between work and home blurs until it's just a carousel rotating at a breakneck pace and all you see is merged flashes of colour and light until it's going so fast that you just have to let go and be thrown off, and it's a complete toss-up as to whether you survive the spill. When people talk about mental health and hacking they point to toxic corporate cultures, impostor syndrome, discrimination, substance abuse, and these are all important. But few consider that some people may in fact be *predisposed* to things like burnout, because what makes us good at hacking also makes us vulnerable. Often, we are not simply enthusiastic about security: we are *fascinated* by it, helplessly. As Conrad said: it fascinates us like a snake [or a basilisk] does a bird, a silly little bird.

"Thank you," I said to Lorena when she had finished, putting more coins into the slot and listening to them clatter into the metal guts of the phone. "I know that wasn't easy."

"How many others are there?" she said.

"I don't know," I said. "A few."

"Well, what's next?"

"I'm sorry?"

"You know what caused it, didn't you? Something he saw on his computer? What are we going to do about it?"

"Lorena, I don't know what I can do. There's no evidence."

"We can tell the police! The newspapers, everyone!"

I thought of a sing-song voice on the wire. A blonde woman in the desert who made me choose.

"I can't," I said. "Not yet. I'm… I'm writing something, writing it all down, everything I know, and when I'm—"

"Then I'll do it," she said firmly. "Tell me what you know."

"I can't do that."

"I *want* to help. I could—"

"No, you don't understand." I took a deep breath. "You have to forget everything I just told you."*

There was a pause. I massaged my forehead, trying to break the headache apart with my fingers.

"Excuse me?"

"It's for your own safety. Those people, the ones that came to your house – if they think you're involved, they'll come back."

"But you said—"

Holly Soames①
11/11/2019 11:57
No appendices were included as part of the document seized by police or elsewhere on WEBSTER'S laptop.

---

* If you are reading this, now is the time to send her a message, her and all the others. You will find a complete list of witnesses and confirmed victims in the appendix, ❶ along with contact details where available.

"You have to trust me on this. You have to. I've got your number, and when the document's finished I'll be in touch, but until—"

"You can't call me out of the blue and tell me to forget. I don't even know who you are! I lost my fucking *husband*—"

"And I lost my *best friend*!" I shouted, and I didn't know it then but I was crying too.

"Focus on your children," I said, my voice shaking. "Live your life. You're a good person. I'm doing this for you."

"Will you at least tell me your name?" she said quietly.

I put the receiver back, hating myself, and my change rattled out into the tray.

There were tears streaming down my face when I left the phonebox. Just two people, hundreds of miles apart, confused by a violent, inexplicable split in their lives' continuums. And yet, despite knowing that I shared this with Lorena Carson, despite that, right then, at that moment, I had never, ever, felt so utterly alone.

* * *

This is how it goes – even in those rare cases when I turn up a confirmed related case, I gain nothing except further confirmation that at the end of The Helmsman's game is a weapon and it's pretty fucking bad.

But I have realised something.

Yes, we may be fucked, and yes this might be a confession, or a recounting of something entirely beyond my understanding that I'll pointlessly chip away at until I die – but here's something else you really ought to know: people have *died*, my friend among them, because they thought they were playing a game which turned out to not be a game in any sense of the word. I'm pretty fucking pissed off about that, and I'm clever, so what you're reading right now might just save the world because a pissed-off clever person is about the most dangerous thing in existence, and whatever else this might be, I live in hope that it too is a weapon, one which other pissed-off clever people will be able to use to take The Helmsman and his group the fuck down.

I have enough faith left to believe that if you're reading this then you're one of those pissed-off clever people too – so make sure you fuck him up for me, will you? Make sure that when someone finally catches up to The Helmsman and he's getting the kicking he has so richly deserved for so long, make sure he knows that it's from me, and Jay, and Shane Carson and Lorena Carson, and Sarah Mayers, and everyone else he's made suffer.

Because we didn't ask for any of this. We just wanted to play a game, and even if we crossed a few lines to do so, we didn't deserve what we got for it.

We didn't deserve it.

5: THE RIDDLE MACHINE
c. MAY 2019 / MARCH 2018

I wonder where The Rearguard are now. I look for them sometimes on Tor❶, because they'd proven in the past to be very useful allies, but after what happened they won't respond to my messages. I understand. I did what I had to do, and I'd do it again. But then I have to tell myself that, don't I?

At Cybotage I hardly ever used Tor; being a pentester I seldom had a need for it.* Sophie and Omar used it sometimes. Their job was to track APTs❷, build profiles of them, attribute their attacks to various countries, and so on, and often involved trawling criminal forums – used by black hats to exchange stolen credentials, dump leaked data, and trade rootkits and worms and 0-day❸ exploits – and they didn't want the administrators of those forums to know a security firm was there too. Sometimes the forums were also hosted on Tor, and could not be accessed without it.

Tor is a good example of what is sometimes called 'dual-use' technology❹, something which can be

---

* Now, of course, I use it for everything, including my tracker, which is a script I cobbled together in Python to continuously scrape news sites and certain hidden services for words and phrases which might point me to an incident or some news about The Helmsman; all of its activity is proxied through Tor. It's not infallible (it wouldn't have picked up the Carson incident, for example, although I've added the *Redbridge Herald* to its list of sites now) and much of what it pulls back is garbage – because, as noted earlier, The Helmsman's weapon lacks specificity in the symptoms and effects it causes. It has been useful occasionally, though – it helped me to find the Sarah Mayers case, for example.

Holly Soames①
11/11/2019 13:43
Tor = The Onion Router, a tool for private encrypted browsing.

Holly Soames②
11/11/2019 13:44
APTs = Advanced Persistent Threats, industry term for a sophisticated threat actor (often state/ state-sponsored).

Holly Soames③
11/11/2019 13:45
A new vulnerability which the vendor has not had time (i.e. zero days) to patch.

Holly Soames④
22/11/2019 14:23
e.g. technology which can be used for good or evil. Background: 'Philosophical aspects of dual use technologies' by Svitlana V. PUSTOVIT and Erin D. WILLIAMS (2010). THE HELMSMAN does not explicitly refer to this concept, but given the content of c2–5 THT he would almost certainly have been aware of it.

Holly Soames①
11/11/2019 13:49
See torproject.org/
about/history/.

Holly Soames②
11/11/2019 14:54
See Alex HERN's
article in the *Guardian*,
2014: 'US government
increases funding for
Tor, giving $1.8m in
2013': theguardian.
com/technology/2014/
jul/29/us-government-
funding-tor-18m-
onion-router.

Holly Soames③
11/11/2019 14:59
Hidden services are
websites hosted on
Tor, rather than usual
'clearnet' hosting
services, and can only
be accessed via the
Tor network. They
have no IP addresses
associated with them,
and in theory owners
and visitors cannot
be traced. The only
identifier they have is
a long alphanumeric
'onion address', which
is randomly generated
(although it can be
customised). Most
hidden services are
not indexed in any way,
and there is no way
to find them unless
the onion address has
been shared with you
beforehand.

Holly Soames④
11/11/2019 15:04
Warez = pirated
software.

used for legitimate purposes but with the capacity to be weaponised. The core principles behind it were originally developed by scientists at the US Naval Research Laboratory in the 1990s❶ with the intent of disguising sensitive communications by layering levels of encryption and routing data through a series of intermediary nodes around the world. One of those scientists then began working on a similar project outside of the US military, with help from others, and the research was later sponsored by the Electronic Frontier Foundation.

The resulting non-profit organisation, the Tor Project, has the unusual distinction of being partly funded by certain elements of the US government❷ to enable anonymous communications by law enforcement and intelligence communities, while other elements of that government – predominantly members of its law enforcement and intelligence communities – attempt to circumvent it to pierce the anonymous communications of criminals and terrorists (and, naturally, those of law enforcement and intelligence communities from other countries).* All very ouroboros-ish, I suppose.

The Rearguard used it, of course, and had at least one hidden service,❸ a tiny presence in all the ethically and legally dubious crap out there, ranging from the nefarious (paedophilia, bestiality and snuff; marketplaces for drugs and guns; sites for trading stolen goods; dumps of hacked usernames and passwords; warez❹) to the bizarre (creepypasta; niche fetishes; strange fiction). And, of course, all the scams and

---

* Tor is not invulnerable. Numerous flaws have been discovered in its protocols and software which could allow for deanonymisation. It would not be unreasonable to assume that only some of these flaws have been publicly disclosed and fixed; there are many private and public sector organisations who would have a vested interest in keeping such vulnerabilities to themselves.

undercover police officers,* and the gigabytes of content which is inaccurate or misleading, or the deliberately false work of LARPers❶ and trolls.

But hidden services also play host to stories and games and folklore and experiments. Perhaps the most disturbing example on Tor, one that could have been created by The Helmsman himself, is 'Assassination Politics'. It began as a thought experiment first proposed by cypherpunk Jim Bell in the mid-1990s, long before Tor was available to the public. *The Helmsman Texts*, as you will see, are in no small degree about thought experiments, and Assassination Politics is a particularly unsettling example.

In a ten-part essay, ❷ Bell describes an incentivised dead pool as a wholesale replacement for any and all democratic systems. It goes something like this: assume that there is a secure, anonymous way to place online wagers on the date and time of a politician's death. Each wager is added to a pool for that particular politician. When the pool grows large enough, the opportunity to win the money provides sufficient incentive for someone to place their own wager and ensure their prediction is the winning one – i.e. by assassinating the politician in question.

Bell's essay goes into some detail about the mechanisms underpinning this scheme, which involved 'digital cash' and anonymity. At the time, the tools available to achieve these ends were often rudimentary, if they existed at all, and so Assassination Politics – whilst unsurprisingly causing something of a stir amongst various federal agencies – was predominantly viewed for what it was: a thought experiment, albeit one with a

Holly Soames①
11/11/2019 15:13
LARP = Live Action Role Playing, an analogue equivalent to ARGs. In some internet subcultures (e.g. 4chan) the term is derogatory and used to insinuate that someone is lying about their life or experiences.

Holly Soames②
11/11/2019 15:34
'Assassination Politics' (1997). Archived at cryptome.org/ap.htm.

---

* I often wonder if some of the forums and marketplaces on Tor are populated predominantly by law enforcement agents from various countries who don't know about each other and simply exchange cryptocurrencies for drugs and guns in an endless loop. Another ouroboros.

Holly Soames①
11/11/2019 15:40
Quote is from this 2000 WIRED article (by WIRED staff): 'Crypto-Convict won't recant' wired. com/2000/04/ crypto-convict-wont-recant/.

Holly Soames②
11/11/2019 15:53
See cryptome.org/ jdb/chrysler98.htm.

Holly Soames③
11/11/2019 15:59
Background: 'Fake blockchain assassination market remembers his wallets are now worth $1.3 million and cashes out' by Chris MONTEIRO (2018) pirate.london/ fake-blockchain-assassination-market-remembers-his-wallets-are-now-worth-1-3-773447f94b80.

Holly Soames④
11/11/2019 16:12
WEBSTER is likely referring to: 'The first Augur assassination markets have arrived' by David FLOYD (2018) coindesk.com/ markets/2018/07/25/ the-first-augur-assassination-markets-have-arrived.

stunningly radical aim – "the ultimate annihilation of all forms of government."❶

John Young, a cypherpunk, co-founder of cryptome.org, and no stranger to controversy himself, phrased it rather more positively when he nominated Bell for a Chrysler Award for Innovation in Design in 1998, calling his essay "an imaginative and sophisticated prospective for improving governmental accountability."❷

Lacking the necessary technical mechanisms, Assassination Politics seemed doomed to be consigned to history: just one more idea to come out of the long-ago frontier of the internet. But then came Tor and Bitcoin (and countless other derivative cryptocurrencies which, whilst not intrinsically anonymous, can offer a degree of anonymity if used carefully). The tools needed to make Assassination Politics a reality were suddenly available, and it only took five years from the publication of the Bitcoin whitepaper in 2008 for that to happen.

In 2013, an individual or group calling themselves Kuwabatake Sanjuro created a hidden service which offered pretty much the exact functionality Bell had envisioned almost two decades prior. Bitcoin dead pools worth 75,000 USD were in place for Barack Obama, Ben Bernanke and Keith Alexander. None of those gentlemen were actually assassinated, of course (at least, not at the time of writing), and so the site drifted without drawing too much attention, other than from a few tech journalists who could remember the initial furore Bell's essay had caused. Hilariously, in 2018, someone cashed out the bitcoins❸ (by then worth over 1.3m USD).

Bell continues to promote the idea of Assassination Politics, and Augur, a protocol allowing decentralised predictions, has already been used to set up new assassination markets,❹ which include not just predictions on the deaths of politicians and celebrities but also on mass shootings and terrorist attacks. Perhaps any celebrities or members of the public who die a violent death to ensure their murderer wins a dead pool will, in their last agony-filled moments, find some comfort in the knowledge that they died as a direct result of an "imaginative and sophisticated prospective for improving governmental accountability."

The reason I mention all this is that it typifies a problem with thought experiments, one The Helmsman knows all too well: it is usually impossible to anticipate what a thought's final resting place might be, once it has slouched towards Bethlehem to be born.❶ A bell, once rung, cannot be unheard.

Holly Soames①
11/11/2019 16:34
Probably a reference to 'The Second Coming' by W.B. YEATS.

* * *

Our first encounter with The Rearguard came the evening I went to Jay and Eoin's house to work on the second stage of the game. I'd pictured Jay living in a murky flat in a shabby concrete hulk, with pride of place given to his battle-station – a wide desk crowded with wires and broken computers and routers. I envisioned old conference badges lining the walls, barely enough room to sit down, the décor dominated by a bank of several monitors serving as both the central point of focus and the primary source of illumination.

I was surprised, then, when I approached the address he had given me❷ and found myself in a street of small, cosy, white-fronted two-bed houses. I knocked at the door and a man, shorter than Jay, opened it. He had untidy brown hair and eyes which didn't quite look in the same direction, but the effect was disarming rather than jarring because it was accompanied by a wide and genuine smile, as though (and I may be projecting here) he could discern two Alex Websters, and was trying to decide which of them he was more pleased to see.

"Hello!" he said with a soft Irish tinge, squinting

Holly Soames②
11/11/2019 16:47
66 DRAYTON WALK, SE12 6PT.

down at me. "You must be Alex. I'm Eoin. So nice to meet you. Well, come in, come in!"

I stepped into the hallway.

"Jay!" Eoin called upstairs. "Your hacker friend's here!" He turned to me. "He'll just be a moment. Come on, into the living room with you and have a seat."

I took off my coat and followed him into the house proper. Much like the street, it was nothing like I had expected. This was no hacker's den overflowing with technical detritus, but a clean and comfortable home. As I looked closer I could discern two energies at work: one chaotic and crowded, as testified to by the books scattered on the coffee table and the overflowing magazine rack; the other calm and collected, keeping the chaos at bay. As though to exemplify this balance, there were two drinks on a small dining table at the far end of the living room. One, a stained and chipped coffee mug, had no coaster; the other, a clean glass of water, did. As I entered, Eoin strode over to the table and slipped a coaster underneath the mug.

"You've got a lovely home," I volunteered, and Eoin grinned and shook his head.

"I do my best, although your boss doesn't always make that easy. Speak of the devil."

Footsteps on the stairs, and there was Jay.

"Hi," he said. "Hope you're hungry."

"Oh yeah," Eoin said, rolling his eyes. "Tell our guest about the wonderful meal you've prepared."

I raised my eyebrows. "You're cooking?" I said. I couldn't imagine Jay cooking.

Eoin snorted. "You'd think so, wouldn't you? You'd think if you invited a colleague over for dinner you'd cook something. But you tell Alex what she's got to look forward to."

"I— I was going to order pizza," Jay said. He turned to me with a worried expression. "You like pizza, don't you?"

"Yeah," I laughed. "I do."

"I thought— pizza made sense. You know."

"Absolutely."

"I should have known," Eoin said. "All the same. God save me from hackers."

* * *

Jay and Eoin, I discovered during dinner (the pizza, at Eoin's insistence, was eaten from plates rather than the boxes, although both Jay and I eschewed the cutlery he had optimistically laid out), had been married for three years, and had met when Jay arranged for some of the Cybotage staff to do an escape room at one of the venues for which Eoin contracted.

"He's a genius," Jay said, chewing on a bit of crust. "Hardest puzzles I've ever seen. We barely made it out in time."

Eoin shrugged modestly, but I could see he was pleased.

"And you're going to help us with this one?" I said.

"I'll try," Eoin said. "But I'll warn you, I'm no techie."

"I'm sure we'll need you at some point," Jay said. "Even if it's just for refreshments."

Eoin made as though to cuff Jay around the head. As he stood up and took our plates into the kitchen, Jay reached out and briefly laid a hand on his arm. I drained the last of my Diet Coke.

"Colin called, by the way," Jay said.

"Oh?" I remember thinking: *please don't say we have to stop.*

"Well, I told you he reported the breach – they're an insurance company, so I guess they just wanted the crime reference number…" ❶

"Yeah?"

Jay tilted his glass, examining the dark liquid inside as it rolled back and forth. "He said a couple of police officers❷ turned up."

Holly Soames①
11/11/2019 17:18
No trace on CRIS.

Holly Soames②
12/11/2019 08:19
No CAD reports relating to police visits to the business address.

That was unusual. There are so many cybercrimes – several million in the UK every year – that while law enforcement may take a report online or over the phone, usually via Action Fraud, I thought it would be pretty rare that they'd rock up in person. ❶

"Came to ask some questions for the report, Colin said."

"Oh?"

"They asked him if the people who discovered the breach had found anything else."*

"Like what?"

"They didn't say."

I thought for a few seconds. "What did you tell him?"

"I said we didn't find anything."

"Good."

"But remember what I said, Alex. If we get on this box tonight and there's the slightest sign that it belongs to anyone else – if it's been owned, ❷ I mean – that's it."

I gave him a Boy Scout salute.

"Wind your neck in, rookie," he said, but he was smiling.

* * *

Jay set up his laptop on the dining table – "not enough room for the three of us in my office", he explained – and we crowded around as he typed in the commands to access The Helmsman's server.†

"I'm going through a SOCKS proxy," ❸ he said to

Holly Soames①
12/11/2019 08:23
WEBSTER is correct here.

Holly Soames②
12/11/2019 08:24
Slang, meaning 'compromised'.

Holly Soames③
12/11/2019 08:26
SOCKS = 'SOCKet Secure', a protocol for securely relaying traffic between client and server using a proxy server. Often used to hide the originating IP address of a user.

---

* As you might have inferred, I attached very little importance to this at the time. If I had an opinion about it at all, it was that the police may have been trying to track the operators of an ARG, who were essentially cyber-vandals. My opinion has, obviously, changed since then.

† Just like the numbers station video, the server is no longer accessible. However, Jay took screenshots throughout the evening, which he later shared with me. I could try to replicate the Riddle Machine, I suppose, but I don't think there would be much value in doing so.

me. "Better safe than sorry." He SSH'd in, and a prompt greeted us.

```
hellofriend@riddlemachine:~$
```

"OK, so we've got a low-priv shell on a Linux box," Jay said. "Thoughts?"

I knew I was being tested again, but I was ready this time, and the situation wasn't unfamiliar; most of the Vulnhub VMs I'd practised on were Linux machines with a similar set-up.

"We'll have to get root❶ to find the flag."

"And how do we get root?"

"We enumerate."

"I was just going to say that," Eoin said. "Enumerate. Obviously."

Jay typed a command to show the operating system name and version:

```
hellofriend@riddlemachine:~$ cat /etc/issue
```

Usually, this outputs something like **Ubuntu 18.04.2 LTS**, which would tell us it's an Ubuntu Linux distribution, version 18.04.2, Long-Term Support. But the Riddle Machine said something very different.

Lines began to appear on Jay's screen, one a second:

```
hellofriend@riddlemachine:~$ cat /etc/issue
WAR AND PEACE
By Leo Tolstoy/Tolstoi
CONTENTS
BOOK ONE: 1805
CHAPTER I
CHAPTER II
```

"What in the absolute fuck is this?" Jay said, disgusted, and Eoin began to laugh.

"I believe that's called trolling."

The lines kept coming.

Holly Soames①
12/11/2019 08:27
Get root privileges. 'root' is the name of the superuser on Linux operating systems, the equivalent of Administrator (and NT AUTHORITY\ SYSTEM) on Windows.

"Maybe it's just the table of contents," Jay said. He held down **Ctrl+C** to skip the one-second intervals, and the chapter listings started to flash down the screen, much quicker, until we got to:

```
^CCHAPTER I
^C
^C"Well, Prince, so Genoa and Lucca are now just family estates of the
^CBuonapartes. But I warn you, if you don't tell me that this means war,
^Cif you still try to defend the infamies and horrors perpetrated by that
^CAntichrist—I really believe he is Antichrist—I will have nothing more
^Cto do with you and you are no longer my friend, no longer my
^C'faithful slave,' as you call yourself! But how do you do? I see I
^Chave frightened you—sit down and tell me all the news."
^C
```

"Well, it's not as creepy as the numbers station," I said, as the novel continued to appear line-by-line. "At least The Helmsman's got a sense of humour."

"Fuck his sense of humour," Jay said, pressing **Ctrl+D** to try and stop the script. Nothing happened. **Ctrl+Z** didn't work either, so he closed the SSH window.

"I'll log off and go back in," he said. "Looks like cat is out the window."

"Someone call the RSPCA," Eoin said, and I laughed.

Jay rolled his eyes. "**cat** is a command to display a file, you Luddite."

He logged back in to the Riddle Machine, and as

soon as he connected, lines started to appear on the screen, one per second:

```
"Heavens! what a virulent attack!" replied the prince, not in the
least disconcerted by this reception. He had just entered, wearing an
embroidered court uniform, knee breeches, and shoes, and had stars on
his breast and a serene expression on his flat face. He spoke in that
refined French in which our grandfathers not only spoke but thought,
and with the gentle, patronizing intonation natural to a man of
importance who had grown old in society and at court. He went up to
Anna Pávlovna, kissed her hand, presenting to her his bald, scented,
and shining head, and complacently seated himself on the sofa.
```

Eoin clapped his hands in delight. "It's started exactly where you left off. It's created a bloody *bookmark!*"

Even though I was more empathetic with Jay's disgust at being trolled, I smiled. Eoin had such obvious joy on his face at the Riddle Machine's mischief. And I have to admit, looking back, it *was* funny.

"Yes, very droll," Jay said, as the opening chapter continued to appear on his screen. "But I wasn't planning to spend the evening reading *War and Peace.*"

Eoin cackled. My shoulders shaking with laughter, I said, "Maybe the bookmark's based on the IP address. Come off a different IP and it probably won't remember you."

Jay tried to find a flaw with this, couldn't, and nodded grudgingly. He closed the window, refreshed his proxy settings, and the next time he logged in he was again presented with that enigmatic prompt:

```
hellofriend@riddlemachine:~$
```

"Maybe avoid cat from now on," I said, pleased that I'd been proven right.

"Yeah, thanks."

He typed **id** to show group names and permissions.

```
hellofriend@riddlemachine:~$ id
```

```
uid=1001(hellofriend) gid=1001(hellofriend)
groups=1001(hellofriend)
```

"*That* seems to work, anyway," he said. He followed it up with **whoami** to show the current username.

```
hellofriend@riddlemachine:~$ whoami
hellofriend
```

"What do you reckon?" he said to me.

"**cat** could be a bash alias, maybe?" I turned to a bemused Eoin. "**bash** is the name of the shell window on Linux, and **alias** lets you create custom shortcuts for commands. So if you type a certain command a lot, you can create a shorter version and just type that instead."

"Let's see what other aliases he's made," Jay said. "Maybe it's just a few common ones."

```
hellofriend@riddlemachine:~$ alias
HOW DISAPPOINTING!!!
```

"Oh, for fuck's sake."

Eoin was leaning forward, interested. "I think your man's got the measure of you two."

"At least we know it's a game now," Jay said, ignoring this. "Real attackers are never this witty. It's not worth their time." He started typing.

As we explored the Riddle Machine further we found that some commands appeared to work as normal. We could list (**ls**) and change directories (**cd**), and, as with a normal **Bash** shell, pressing the up arrow showed us the history of the commands we had typed. But other commands produced completely unexpected behaviour. Jay found that there was another user on the machine called 'ubuntu', for example, and tried to cd to their home directory to see if there was anything useful.

NOTHING PROCEEDS FROM NOTHINGNESS, AS ALSO NOTHING
PASSES AWAY INTO NON-EXISTENCE. ❶

Holly Soames①
12/11/2019 09:53
From *Meditations* by
Marcus AURELIUS.

When he tried to launch **nano**, a Linux text editor
which we thought we could use instead of **cat** to read
files, we were treated to what Google told us was
another quote:

```
YOU ARE BUT A THOUGHT - A VAGRANT THOUGHT, A USELESS
THOUGHT❸
```

Holly Soames②
12/11/2019 10:32
Likely referring to an
in-joke in the industry
about the difficulty
of remembering the
correct command to
exit vim, a terminal-
based text editor
(based on vi) which has
no buttons or icons.
Instead, users have
to enter shortcuts
and key combinations
to perform various
functions. See
'Stack Overflow:
Helping one million
developers exit Vim'
by David ROBINSON
(2017) stackoverflow.
blog/2017/05/23/
stack-overflow-
helping-one-million-
developers-exit-vim/.
On Stack Overflow, a
programming Q&A
platform, a question
entitled "How to exit
the Vim editor?" has
been viewed over a
million times. At peak
traffic times around 80
people an hour around
the world are trying to
find the answer to this
question.

And when we tried to launch vim, another text
editor, the following text appeared rapidly on the screen:

```
hellofriend@riddlemachine:~$ vim
To use vim, enter the vim save and exit command❷
within three seconds.
3...
2...
1...
TOO LATE! NO VIM FOR YOU!
```

Even Jay laughed at that one.

He proceeded to tinker with various commands,
with the occasional suggestion from me, while Eoin
pored over the first chapter of *The Helmsman Texts*,
which Jay had printed out.

"There's got to be *something* here that works
normally," Jay said, and ran **ps -ef** to show the processes
running on the machine.

```
hellofriend@riddlemachine:~$ ps -ef
ubuntu   16713   16502   0   06:23   pts/0    00:00:00 baten.sh
ubuntu   16624   16492   0   06:19   pts/1    00:00:00 switch
root      4641      .2   0   06:02   ?        00:00:00 /usr/bin/fsck
ubuntu    1872    1542   0   03:43   tty 2    00:00:03 /lib/systemd/u
```

He perked up. "A shell script! Maybe there's
something interesting in it."

"It's a joke," I said. "Baten, switch. Bait and switch?"
Jay inhaled deeply and pinched the bridge of his

Holly Soames③
12/11/2019 09:55
From *The Mysterious
Stranger* by Mark
TWAIN (1916).

nose. Eoin looked over at the screen brightly. "Oh yes, and I think it's supposed to say 'fuck u' after that, on the last two lines," he said. "Just in case you missed it."

Jay glared at him. "Any suggestions from you?"

"Oh, well now. Wouldn't want to intrude on your fun."

"Please," Jay said through gritted teeth. "We're all ears."

"You're so *fit* when you're grumpy."

"Eoin!"

"OK, OK. Well, this," Eoin said, waving the sheets of paper he was holding, "this talks about leaving a cave, right? A self-contained environment? So is there, like, a digital equivalent of that? Is that a thing?"

"Oh," I said. "Oh, I get it."

"It's a restricted shell," ❶ Jay said, understanding. "Yeah. It's not about escalating privileges at all. The goal is to get out of the cave. That's how we get the flag."

"I've heard of restricted shells," I said. "I've never tried to bypass one though."

"I'll put you on the next kiosk engagement that comes in," Jay said. "I've done it loads of times. Piece of piss."

Eoin snorted. "You sound very sure of yourself."

"Watch the master work."

The deeper Jay reached into his bag of tricks, however, the further his face fell. He threw every technique he knew at that box – some I'd read about, and others so obscure that I doubted I would ever need them in a CTF, let alone on an actual engagement. After half an hour or so of fruitless attempts he ran up upstairs, muttering to himself, and came back with a second laptop which he switched on and set in front of me.

"You're the Google Squad," he said. "Let me know what you find."

Holly Soames①
12/11/2019 11:10
Restricted shells appear to be a normal terminal, but place a limit on what a user can do within them. This is, on the one hand, to protect users from themselves. On the other, a restrictive shell can also be used to enhance security, by preventing unauthorised users from escalating their privileges or further infecting a compromised system. It acts as a sort of kiosk-mode, limiting the actions available to a user – although there are often various tricks and weaknesses which can allow a malicious (and knowledgeable) user to escape and access the full shell.

The Riddle Machine, however, was equal to everything we could scrape up, and Eoin and I watched as the attempts failed, one by one.

First, Jay tried various alternatives to **Bash**, attempting to invoke them from within the restricted shell. The Riddle Machine refused to provide any output to these commands at all, ignoring him with contempt.

```
hellofriend@riddlemachine:~$ /bin/bash
hellofriend@riddlemachine:~$ bash -i
hellofriend@riddlemachine:~$ bin/dash
hellofriend@riddlemachine:~$ /bin/sh
hellofriend@riddlemachine:~$ /bin/static-sh
hellofriend@riddlemachine:~$
```

When Jay tried **bash** by itself as a command, the Riddle Machine responded with a variety of seemingly random phrases which Eoin, looking them up on his phone, told us were from authors (Conrad, Goethe, Milton) and philosophers (Nietzsche, Schopenhauer), as well as a Jewish saying. ❶

```
hellofriend@riddlemachine:~$ bash
Not one in a hundred thousand!
hellofriend@riddlemachine:~$ bash
The clever animals had to die.
hellofriend@riddlemachine:~$ bash
Our refuge is in stupidity.
hellofriend@riddlemachine:~$ bash
Envisage the creative blazes
hellofriend@riddlemachine:~$ bash
What he was, what is, and what must be
hellofriend@riddlemachine:~$ bash
The intervention of an ephemeral life-dream.
```

While Eoin busied himself trying to find links between those phrases, Jay tried using various escape characters, which are used to break up the string being passed to the restrictive shell in the hope of forcing an error or getting a command through to the real, underlying system. It seemed that The Helmsman had thought of this, too, and the Riddle Machine chastised us for it.

Holly Soames①
12/11/2019 11:54
BRACKEN's attributions are correct here, although not in order. The full list:
- "It would be better never to have been born. Who is so lucky? Not one in a hundred thousand!" – Jewish proverb
- "The clever animals had to die" – *On Truth and Lies in a Nonmoral Sense* by Friedrich NIETZSCHE (1896)
- "Our refuge is in stupidity" – Joseph CONRAD, in a letter to Robert Bontine CUNNINGHAME GRAHAM (1898)
- "Envisage the creative blazes" – *Faust* by Johann Wolfgang von GOETHE (1808)
- "What he was, what is, and what must be" – *Paradise Lost* by John MILTON (1667)
- "The intervention of an ephemeral life-dream" – *The World as Will and Representation* by Arthur SCHOPENHAUER (1818)
I have also been unable to determine a link between these quotations/authors.

```
hellofriend@riddlemachine:~$ /b/i/n/b/a/s/h/
sh: 1: /b/i/n/b/a/s/h/: not found
hellofriend@riddlemachine:~$ /\b\i\n\b\a\s\h\
NAUGHTY
hellofriend@riddlemachine:~$ 'b'i'n'b'a's'h'
NAUGHTY
hellofriend@riddlemachine:~$ /'b'i'n'b'a's'h'
NAUGHTY
hellofriend@riddlemachine:~$ "b"i"n"b"a"s"h"
NAUGHTY
hellofriend@riddlemachine:~$   /"b"i"n"b"a"s"h"
NAUGHTY
hellofriend@riddlemachine:~$
```

Holly Soames[1]
12/11/2019 13:11
This song, as well as being popularly associated with 'rickrolling', is also commonly used as a proof-of-concept when hacking a device; if the device can be made to play the music video, it's considered compromised. See, for example: it.slashdot.org/story/17/07/30/0036218/us-voting-machines-cracked-in-90-minutes-at-defcon by EditorDavid (2017). Running the video game *Doom* is likewise considered a proof-of-compromise. The rickrolling on the Riddle Machine likely used this: github.com/keroserene/rickrollrc.

Holly Soames[2]
12/11/2019 13:27
Command-line tool to download files from websites and servers.

Efforts to copy or move files with **cp** and **mv** resulted in the files in question being replaced with a funky little trolling script which showed a coloured animation of the music video of 'Never Gonna Give You Up'❶ within the terminal itself, a pixellated Rick Astley dancing and grinning at us.

For a while we thought perhaps the restricted shell was running because it was part of the user's profile, so Jay tried various ways to connect over SSH without loading the 'hellofriend' user's settings – but all of them resulted in the same restricted shell.

"It must be running as a **ForceCommand** in the sshd_config," he said, drumming his fingers on the table.

"It means someone's configured the server so whenever anyone tries to do anything over SSH, the restricted shell is loaded," I explained to Eoin, who nodded, mystified.

Attempts to download binaries or tools – like a Meterpreter payload, or the scripts we used for client engagements – to the Riddle Machine using **wget**❷ seemed to work at first. At least, the right output was displayed, and a file was there when we used ls to list the directory:

```
hellofriend@riddlemachine:~$ wget brixhaxstuff.com/enum.sh
--2018-03-06 21:05:08-- http://brixhaxstuff.com
Resolving brixhaxstuff.com (brixhaxstuff.com) … 252.33.23.183,
172.29.118.167, 198.18.123.244, …
Connecting to brixhaxstuff.com (brixhaxstuff.com)|252.33.23.183|:80…
connected.
```

```
HTTP request sent, awaiting response… 200 OK
Length: 106 [application/octet-stream]
Saving to: 'enum.sh'
enum.sh 100%[===================================>] 106 --.-KB/s in 0s
2018-03-06 21:05:09 (5.61 MB/s) - 'enum.sh' saved [106/106]
hellofriend@riddlemachine:~$ ls
enum.sh examples.desktop
```

But running the 'downloaded' file resulted in Rick
Astley shaking his booty once again – the **wget** output
had been falsified. In fact, executing any file on the
machine seemed to have the same effect.

Eoin informed us he couldn't see a link between
any of the phrases, which did not improve Jay's
mood. In fact, the Riddle Machine could have been
designed solely to annoy someone like Jay, who was
used to professionally running CTFs requiring specific
technical skills. It knew it was a ridiculous thing, and
revelled in the knowledge.

Personally, I was having fun. Eoin kept cracking
jokes and making fun of Jay (which he took in relatively
good humour), bringing us drinks and sharing out what
remained of the pizzas. In between glancing at the
Riddle Machine and offering Jay words of advice, he
told me stories about his escape rooms. He designed
puzzles for several venues across London and the
owners would often invite him to their control rooms
to watch the general public attempt them.

I laughed more that evening than I had for some
time. And when Eoin wasn't telling me stories, I was
trying to help Jay. I must have looked through dozens
of sites and tutorials on escaping restricted Linux shells,
all of which seemed to regurgitate the same techniques
we had already tried.

Sometimes the Riddle Machine would act as
though it hadn't received a command at all; others, it
would throw a quote at us, or some infuriating, cryptic
quip:

```
hellofriend@riddlemachine:~$ TERM=more /etc/profile
MORE OR LESS
hellofriend@riddlemachine:~$ less /etc/profile
LESS OR MORE
hellofriend@riddlemachine:~$ exit
JOIN US JOIN US JOIN US
hellofriend@riddlemachine:~$ perl -e 'exec "bin/sh";'
NO
hellofriend@riddlemachine:~$ php
THE SPARROW IN THE HALL
hellofriend@riddlemachine:~$ PAGER='sh -c "exec sh 0<&1"' git -p help
THE SKY ABOVE THE PORT WAS THE COLOR OF TELEVISION, TUNED TO A DEAD
CHANNEL ❶
hellofriend@riddlemachine:~$ gdb
YOU'RE NOT TRYING VERY HARD!
hellofriend@riddlemachine:~$ ruby -e 'exec "/bin/sh"'
hellofriend@riddlemachine:~$ telnet
ECNAD DNA GNIS STEPPUP YPPAH
hellofriend@riddlemachine:~$ awk 'BEGIN {system("/bin/sh")}'
hellofriend@riddlemachine:~$ find / -name foobar -exec /bin/sh \;
hellofriend@riddlemachine:~$ nc
MOUNT EVEREST IS LITTERED WITH CORPSES
hellofriend@riddlemachine:~$ pic -U
THE WHEELS ON THE BUS GO FUCK YOUR LIFE
hellofriend@riddlemachine:~$ dmesg -H
I SEE YOU
hellofriend@riddlemachine:~$ install
The following packages have unmet dependencies: YOUR MUM.
```

Holly Soames①
12/11/2019 13:42
From *Neuromancer*
by William GIBSON
(1984). Unable to
identify source of
the other quotations
here, assuming they
are quotations.

Holly Soames②
12/11/2019 13:46
Command-line
tool to send HTTP
requests, can also
be used to download
files.

"This must have taken *hours*," Jay said, a grudging admiration in his voice. "He knows everything I'm going to try."

On two occasions, we thought we were getting somewhere. **curl,❷** which Jay used to try to download his own files to the Riddle Machine when **wget** didn't succeed, produced a large QR code on the screen. This excited us for a few moments, until Eoin used his phone to decode it and burst out laughing.

And **env**, a command which prints environment variables, produced the following curious output:

```
hellofriend@riddlemachine:~$ env
Recording…
Saved microphone recording to test.wav
```

Listing the contents of the home directory again, Jay found that there was indeed a newly created file called 'test.wav' but, unable to copy it to Jay's machine or listen to it, there was little we could do. It wasn't until I remembered the numbers station puzzle that I told Jay to try the sox audio editing program to look at the image's spectrogram, and when we did we saw old Trollface❶ leering back at us from the depths of internet antiquity.

Holly Soames①
12/11/2019 14:04
Internet meme. For background see 'Fffuuuuuuuu: The Internet anthropologist's field guide to "rage faces"' by Tom CONNOR (2012) arstechnica.com/ tech-policy/2012/03/ the-internet-anthropologists-field-guide-to-rage-faces/.

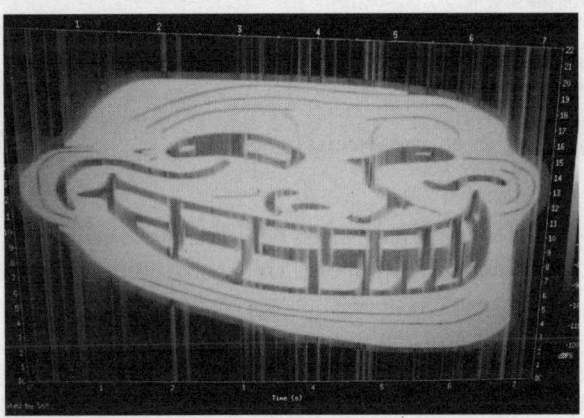

By this point Jay and I had gone through every option we could think of, and had exhausted every article, tutorial and blog we could find on the subject, including the comprehensive list of escaping techniques at GTFOBins.❷

Holly Soames②
12/11/2019 14:09
gtfobins.github.io = a list of various methods to break out of restricted shells on Linux systems.

The energy gradually ebbed from the room, and still the Riddle Machine regarded us smugly.

"Maybe the whole thing's a troll," Jay said, his voice muffled, face in his hands. "Maybe that's the whole point."

Eoin tapped the pages of *The Helmsman Texts*.

"The person who wrote this wouldn't do that. This person's got something to *say*."

I still shiver when I think about him saying that.

Jay turned to me. "I'm out of ideas. What do you want to do?"

"You're the boss," I said, but he waved a hand.

"Not with this," he said. "We're partners. Equal partners. It's your call. Give up, or leave it for another day?"

And there, at that point, was another one of those moments, one in which I made a decision which would narrow all of our choices forever, initiating a gradual decay in any ability we might have had to influence our own fates.*

I knew that if we left it for another day we might never come back to it, and I had no intention of giving up altogether, so I said, "We could ask for help." And then, hurriedly, when Jay frowned and opened his mouth to speak: "Just to get ideas, that's all."

"She's got a point," Eoin said. "Ask some of your geeky mates."

Jay thought, and nodded. He minimised the SSH window, pulled up Twitter and typed:

---

* I believe, and still do, that my own life is heading for that point when all other choices have been exhausted, and there is nothing left but certainty. But perhaps I am guilty of solipsism, at best, and casuistry at worst. Because while my own decisions play a part in that narrowing, they are certainly not the only player in the game, and life is neither random occurrences nor a collection of individual chain reactions. On the contrary, we are all connected in a sprawling and endless web of decisions. Every event is the inevitable conclusion of a series of choices by different people, at different times, for different reasons, all converging at a single point at which no other action is possible. I find consolation in the belief that it cannot therefore be only my choices which are at fault. What difference does it make, when so many others are also making their own choices? We are all so helplessly entwined in each other's decisions that nothing we say or do can ever be the result of our own individual choice. It is a plea of diminished responsibility, I grant you, and perhaps it won't wash – but that's your choice (or rather, it isn't).

Jay Morton @brixhaxstuff

doing a weird ctf, trying to escape a restricted nix shell.
none of the usual stuff working. any ideas?

Jay had a large Twitter❶ following,[*] and the replies started coming in immediately – all of them simply repeating the content of the innumerable blogs and tutorials we had spent the evening poring over.

NaNoNoNoNo @TabberWocksy Mar 6

You tried python to spawn bash?

Mad March Sarah Hare @TheRealSarahHare Mar 6

vi lets you drop into a shell

HackerPhantasmagoria @HackerPhantasy Mar 6

Git.....works every time :D

Prince of Cats @hacks4profitz Mar 6

gtfobins noob

The Troll and the Beautiful @infosecshill Mar 6

you crowdsourcing pentests now brix u dbag

We waited for a few minutes, scrolling through the replies, but there was nothing useful. Eoin looked at his watch and yawned. "Think I'm going to turn in. Don't stay up too late, kids."

He stood up, kissed Jay, and winked at me. "Nice meeting you, Alex."

Jay turned to me. "It is getting late. Maybe we can try again later in the week."

I was about to protest when I saw something flash on Jay's Twitter feed.

---

[*] As mentioned earlier, his social media presence has since been purged, just like Carson's.

"You've got a DM," I said.

Jay opened it.

> **WeAreTheRearguard**@bondsjustvagabonds
> whats ur ctf is it called riddlebox
> 12:01am

I gripped Jay's shoulder, hard. Eoin, who had stopped to look at the message, sat back down again and whistled.

"Fellow players," he said. "Interesting."

"Do you know them?" I asked Jay.

Jay shook his head, still staring at the screen. "Don't recognise the handle." ❶

Holly Soames①
12/11/2019 15:06
No trace.

The account had been set up that day, and had no activity – it followed nobody, had no followers itself, and hadn't tweeted anything.

Jay typed out a response.

> Close. Do you know about it?

The reply came almost immediately.

> yes

"Ask them for a hint," Eoin said.

"No, ask them who The Helmsman is," I said.

Jay ignored us both and wrote:

> Is it part of a game, or something else?

A pause, longer this time, and then:

> both

"What do you think *that* means?" Jay said, and typed again without waiting for an answer.

> Have you finished it?

> we know someone who has

"I bet they're actors," I said suddenly. "You know, plants. ARGs have them sometimes, I heard, to give out more information. ❶ It's part of the game."

Jay regarded me doubtfully, but Eoin was looking thoughtful.

"Yeah, I've done that before," he said. "Hired actors, I mean. Not so much for escape rooms but for interactive puzzles. When the customers have to go to a certain location or whatever. You hide an actor in a crowd, and people have to find them to get a clue."

"Right, but—"

"'This is not a game'," I said. "That's what they say sometimes. To make it seem more real."

Jay shrugged and wrote:

> What happens if we finish?

> yblyu2qtp2h5sefyiod3fjsajgq44cyobkvm66
> wqsc52s6gkmaraguyd.onion/6667
> #rearguard

"They want us to join an IRC server❷ on Tor," Jay said.

"A what server on what?" Eoin said.

"IRC," I said. "Internet Relay Chat. Instant messaging from the dark ages."

"You're making me feel old," Jay said.

"You are old," Eoin said automatically.

While Jay configured his IRC client to connect to the hidden service, I explained the basics of Tor to Eoin.

"So it's like a hidden layer of the internet?" he said, his mismatched eyes dancing.

"Well, sort of."

Holly Soames①
12/11/2019 15:29
Indicates that WEBSTER at this stage was familiar with some of the tropes of ARGs (see earlier comment), but no record found on her devices of engaging in any ARGs.

Holly Soames②
12/11/2019 15:38
The link provided is now defunct.

"And we're going to speak to this mysterious person on there?"

"That's the plan," Jay said. "OK, I think this is working." He typed **/join #rearguard**, and we were granted access to the IRC channel. There were three other people❶ shown in the members list:

```
1 ops, 4 total
morgana
awe
brix
cr0w
```

"Let's see what they've got to say," Jay said. Eoin and I grinned at each other, and watched Jay type.

* * *

I miss Eoin. I went to see him, just once, last November, three months after Jay disappeared. I walked down that same street, to that same house, and on the surface everything looked as it did the first time. A dark, damp evening and warm lights in the windows, and by the time I reached the home that Eoin and Jay had shared I had almost convinced myself that he would be glad to see me, just as he had been then.

But when he opened the door those odd, misaligned eyes took me in without any hint of kindness or affection. He had developed a visible twitch, I noticed, in his right eye, the lower eyelid leaping and jerking of its own accord. His hair was longer, and straggling, unkempt, the face underneath it gaunt and unsmiling.

He looked me up and down and did not invite me in.

I looked past him, into the living room, and in that brief glimpse I saw that the place was now entirely orderly. Without Jay, there was no chaos to be kept in check, no sense of a balance attained – only everything in its place, staying unmoved and untouched in its neatness.

"Why are you here?" he said dully. On the way over I thought I'd known, but as I stood there in front of him I realised I had no idea why I was there at all. To apologise, to offer an explanation – to tell him that I'd started documenting everything? What did I expect him to do with that?

I can't even recall if I started to speak before Eoin expelled one, clear, loud breath and slammed the door in my face.

I haven't been back since. I can't.

*   *   *

*	Now talking on #rearguard
brix	Is this is the person from Twitter?
morgana	do you have a blog?
brix	yes
morgana	is the pubkey on that blog correct?
brix	yeah
morgana	-----BEGIN PGP MESSAGE-----
morgana	hF4DoIPWem1lX84SAQdA73+8MiYCWUOp1KN37Uq1U9oPZ7N4IqIkYiVHoZ9aoF8w
	6QDbmNUh2NlFMkJtW1x9S4AVT4z4WSrjFq2rVoelU8XMs3cQj6q77qOrsztHBK8z
	1MDFAQkCEAtEjTMXC1MFiQAJBcvMhuZUHxmJGYO9prPtcrgQHL2N/bnoCUGFPZPB
	3t7c2lw+JQI9kd9Oqzn2wsgpqPRjDBEa8jG4XN127HUnG4HN/0jr9ThfNFVaJJix
	1roD4juPIalPQFLUA6F82waSctMqgH5RX/uQLzXevOTe1SYiX3XxLoXEAOhDOv8r
	Gedv24xSpG2SqKHy1w3Lnw4wOxwNqB/HEFzjw5URIcM/uEZcD52NbLEs50bVpXfH
	pwl9SDJFrlIRTC1LXOEEkSCaTqR7CHSKsI2PPVio0HR3JqcdGwscm5LIhDPr2TXy
	HGtLaX972SlmKc/5WNYmsDngaJHWRrK18EsayfW+iAXM9Wk9Wm6ynKpIRbrVt766
	4sztjBKqiCBN6LfKAjG+/gXUxTWHq1s8JozJJ9LmF2CDxIb+qXZD4nbs6B4/0x/0
	2gee/4AbwUNqamgV+fZhbH2hk+JLBDfyw8SIxFA7hK4313xxBP1ZfOzFWRTnOxVz
	4p3izXvOido=
	=E5YZ
morgana	-----END PGP MESSAGE-----
morgana	send the phrase back
morgana	-----BEGIN PGP PUBLIC KEY BLOCK-----
morgana	mDMEZSpSaRYJKwYBBAHaRw8BAQdA6NYel51ymUtxqfRRzYxg35xsg9Mj9JCO/Ht1

n4xu8we0CXJlYXJndWFyZIiTBBMWCgA7AhsDBQsJCACCAiICBhUKCQgLAgQWAgMB

Ah4HAheAFiEEi9SW/GOH+NaeK77vdkS+NjLb630FAmUtCz8ACgkQdkS+NjLb633H

LQD+N1qvckLo7lt0qhwK97QAAonCPOGYVyttgXpz1nX0N1sA+wYi3z9sIHHbL+k9

Nbq04GB479IPfdcxK0fajmeoFjULuDgEZSpSaRIKKwYBBAGXVQEFAQEHQCIkzQCD

F8UfJS3Cp7J4Ccw1Z7Zw9m4yWFJxkLvJyHkqAwEIB4h+BBgWCgAmAhsMFiEEi9SW

/GOH+NaeK77vdkS+NjLb630FAmUtCykFCZDY6eoACgkQdkS+NjLb6328jgD+0F96

rzZIjRduWZpPQ5Z/x/c4TyVa25W8WbjUEFveSfAA/ixyU8u3IosjYkrrugBpkBDH

=5IMA

-----END PGP PUBLIC KEY BLOCK----

Eoin looked at me in mock panic, his eyes wide. "Help!" he said, as Jay opened up a command window and started to decrypt the PGP❶ message.

"They're making sure it's actually Jay," I said.

"How? What is that stuff?"

"The first bit is a message they've encrypted with Jay's public key, which is on his blog. It's called a public key because—"

"Because it's public."

"Right. And only Jay has the private key, so he should be able to decrypt that message and work out what it says."

"And the second load of gibberish?"

"That's their public key. They want Jay to send the same message back to them, encrypted with their public key. Then they can decrypt it with their private key."

"The whole conversation's not going to be like this, is it?"

"No," I said, unsure. "It's just a check, I think."

"And this is your day job, is it? Hey, you," he said, nudging Jay, "why didn't you tell me your work was this exciting?"

"It's not usually like this," Jay said. "Here's the message they sent."

We looked at the text on his screen, which read, "Circumstances have been such, that I have lived almost entirely secluded for some time. Those who

Holly Soames①
12/11/2019 16:04
PGP = Pretty Good Privacy, an encryption scheme which uses public and private keys. The public keys disclosed here have been filed for reference. MORTON'S private key is presumably on his laptop, which was not recovered following his disappearance.

are much in earnest and with single minds devoted to any great object in life, must find this occasionally inevitable."[*]

"What's that supposed to be?" Eoin said. Jay copied the text into his terminal to encrypt it with The Rearguard's public key.

"It's by Ada Lovelace,"❶ I said. "The mother of programming."

"Of course it is," Eoin said. "So here's a question. If they're being so careful, how do they know Jay's blog hasn't been hacked and his public key changed? Or someone's, I don't know, beaten him up and gotten his private key?"

"*Now* you're thinking like a hacker," Jay said. "Paranoia, all the way down."

brix   -----BEGIN PGP MESSAGE-----

hF4DSbXLTVwnMjQSAQdA56fp+5ybEcw5HP+TPfhXB+2GExsrr4nwFSWokC7pamIw
HDFw+sYEDzY+iuRH3Rx8arioS1/h0fvFxg3ot5/GGDHo8bNWHMocB1bru5EZIXUB
1MDFAQkCEB7v/uSujwriDpSLRoatSkwqeNzIv4UZCNgnK0h/WFuJ/SyBg6w6vcul
1aMi4UAGhpx/5QFBFHmqQhoaZTWGqMdeaEMBjmePoTbg5jG1bTTWT7KKvpCiBHUR
nDrtxSnHlxBYBYy+Vfd0lV+yb+lILeEmYD7yNvx8qLte4ALF/nP6eIwm5kjWURWD
uupVGG+Z3LPHkJH9+mLuhJCrRbYJwev5+SZXXCtxUjQ80z74oQ64DzEPx2+/sOIH
O1A+NsqCXuOeV9RySYpYIfZ1W+sp2qSFxT7y4tV5oReDHFASOnfwjrjpYfAT8bNU
JoHzi7TzTcrbuLtAIzGggIHUfHqr7WnTm2VJJqvhZNQ1+03SJXE6XUpzdqDHZz6q
6pGKV8B3xdB2OI0/sTMTH8bpi4qZz8vb4X7o7ulsxkdxZ7LUe6MZj7ZorOIeZXlW
+M/5ITEt20T+jE0SH9DZSuX2w4ROp46hCJc1pf083Ui9QdPhGCkB+y7cSbPDxHWS
/+bQAy+TV1U=

=1VDM

-----END PGP MESSAGE-----

---

[*] I read this now and shiver. I wonder if The Rearguard knew, in some way, what was going to happen to us. To me. I suppose, given that they watched Ken Onek play, and finish, the game, that they had some inkling.

```
   crOw    sup
   crOw    i was the one who dmd you on the twits
   brix    hi
   brix    So you said you knew someone who'd finished it? The whole game?
morgana    he means Ken
   crOw    we don't talk about ken lol
    awe    we really don't
morgana    how did you find the game?
```

"Should we tell them?" I said to Jay.
"I'm not telling them anything."

```
   brix    can't say, sorry
morgana    on a pwned box right?
   crOw    its cool bro we dont judge
    awe    the real Q is are you ready for what's coming
   brix    What do you mean?
    awe    can't say, sorry
   crOw    lmao
   crOw    awe is just fuckin with u bro
   crOw    look we haven't played it ourselves
   crOw    that was kenny baby
   brix    Could I speak to Ken?
morgana    Ken won't speak to you
    awe    he barely speaks at all
   crOw    after all we did for him
    awe    lets just hope u don't end up like ken haha
   brix    why, what happened to him?
morgana    so you're on the second stage. The riddlebox.
```

"You think these guys actually know anything?"
Eoin said.

```
   brix    Yeah, but we're stuck
    awe    meh
   brix    If you're not going to tell me anything, why did you DM me?
morgana    we're always on the lookout for people playing the game
```

145

```
     crOw    ken asks us to

     brix    Do you know who The Helmsman is?

     crOw    ken does ken met him

  morgana    shut up crOw

     brix    But he's the one running it right? The ARG?

      awe    sure, if you want to call it that

     brix    It's not?

     crOw    ken says it isn't

  morgana    crOw shut up or I'll kick you

     crOw    im just sayin what ken said

        *    morgana has kicked crOw from #rearguard (morgana)

        *    crOw (crOw@127.0.0.1) has joined

     crOw    bitch

  morgana    want to try for a ban?

     crOw    fine fine whatever

     brix    So Ken asks you to keep an eye out, then what? What for?

  morgana    just to keep track

     brix    He can't help us with the game?

      awe    dunno

      awe    probably not

     brix    What was at the end of it?

     crOw    he wont tell us

     crOw    said its a secret

     crOw    its probably some cia recruitment campaign or something
```

"What are they on about?" Eoin said.

```
      awe    u think everything is a cia recruitment campaign

     crOw    and how do you know it isnt

      awe    that or a false flag op

     crOw    damn str8

      awe    they can't *all* be false flags

  morgana    crOw shut up

     crOw    sry

     brix    this is a waste of time

  morgana    ken says he can give you one hint

  morgana    only one
```

```
    brix   ok?
 morgana   and he said it will rock you
 morgana   oh and he says be careful
 morgana   bye
       *   morgana has quit (Quit: Leaving)
    brix   wait, what's the hint??
     awe   later gator
       *   awe has quit (Quit: Leaving)
    cr0w   listen bro
    cr0w   ken was never the same
    cr0w   my advice is stop playing
    cr0w   good luck
       *   cr0w (cr0w@127.0.0.1) has left
```

There were a few seconds in which we all looked at each other, and saw the same thought behind our eyes: *what have we got ourselves into?*

Then Eoin said, "Well, that was fucking weird," and the tension collapsed. We laughed.

"'It will rock you'," I read out loud, still smiling. "I don't get it."

Jay snapped his fingers. "'rockyou.txt'! You haven't come across that yet?"

I shook my head.

"Back in 2009 a company called RockYou was hacked. They were storing all their passwords in cleartext and the database was leaked. It's been on Kali for ages as one of the default wordlists.❶ I use it all the time – surprising how often it still works."

He opened a terminal on his laptop and showed us the first few lines of rockyou.txt.

Holly Soames①
12/11/2019 17:02
rockyou.txt is included in Kali Linux, a Linux distribution aimed at penetration testers and security researchers.

```
(kali@kali) - [/usr/share/wordlists]
$ head rockyou.txt
123456
12345
123456789
password
```

```
iloveyou
princess
1234567
rockyou
12345678
abc123
```

"So what does it mean?" I said, as Jay scrolled through the list. "Do we have to try and brute force the root password, or the other user? 'ubuntu'?"

"That's funny, I distinctly remember someone telling me these puzzles weren't about brute forcing," Jay said. "No, maybe there's—"

"Stop! Go back!" Eoin cried. "Did you see it? Go back, I said. Up, up. That's it, there. Look."

"What? What am I looking at?"

Eoin pointed at one of the passwords in the list.

```
stupid
147852
marina
garcia
fuckyou1
diego
brandy
letmein
hockey
444444
sharon
bonnie
spider
iverson
andrei
justine
frankie
pimpin
disney
rabbit
54321
fashion
```

"Right there," he said. "'letmein'. It's like I said. The thing you got sent, that story or whatever it is. It's about leaving the cave, yeah? Well, in escape rooms, if you're stuck and can't solve the puzzles, or you're getting claustrophobic or whatever, there's one surefire way to get out."

"Which is?" I said.

"You *ask*."

Jay connected to the Riddle Machine again over SSH.

```
hellofriend@riddlemachine:~$ letmein
hellofriend@riddlemachine:~$
```

"Well, it was a good thought," he said to Eoin kindly.

"But we don't want to get *in*, do we?" I said. "Try... try 'letmeout'."

```
hellofriend@riddlemachine:~$ letmeout
hellofriend@riddlemachine:~$
```

"Holy shit," Jay said.

"Did it work? Is that what's supposed to happen?" Eoin said.

"Yeah. Yeah, I think so." Jay typed **alias** again.

```
hellofriend@riddlemachine:~$ alias
alias alert='notify-send --urgency=low -i "$([ $? = 0 ] && echo terminal
|| echo error)" "$(history|tail -n1|sed -e '\'' 's/^\s*[0-9]\+\s*//;s/
[;&|]\s*alert$//'\''")"'
alias egrep='egrep --color=auto'
alias fgrep='fgrep --color=auto'
alias grep='grep --color=auto'
alias l='ls -CF'
alias la='ls -A'
alias ll='ls -alF'
alias ls='ls --color=auto'
hellofriend@riddlemachine:~$
```

"Yes, that's it! That's what **alias** is supposed to show! You did it, you beautiful man!" Jay put an arm around Eoin and squeezed his shoulders, planting a loud kiss on his lips.

Eoin grinned. "I'll be a cyber geek yet," he said. "But hey, it was a team effort. Alex got the answer."

Jay turned to me. "That's right, you did," he said. "I'm impressed. Not such a rookie now, huh? Alex the hacker. We'll need to think of a nick for you."

I felt my face reddening. "We still have to find the flag, though."

Jay was already typing.

```
hellofriend@riddlemachine:~$ ls
examples.desktop halfway.txt test.wav
```

"That text file wasn't there before. Should I open it?"

"Well duh," Eoin said.

"You'll have to risk **cat** again," I said. "I'm not in the mood for more *War and Peace*."

We laughed, slightly delirious with excitement.

"It should be fine," Jay said. "We've escaped the shell. This is just a normal box now."

```
hellofriend@riddlemachine:~$ cat halfway.txt
NOW COME BACK
hellofriend@riddlemachine:~$
```

"Is that the flag?" Eoin said.

"Think so," Jay said, opening up a browser window and logging into his email account.

"No, wait," I said. "It's not. It's an instruction. 'Come back'. Like in the chapter."

"You have to leave and then come back," Jay said slowly.

"Right. So you need to go back into the restricted shell somehow. Is there a way to do that?"

"All that time in the fucking thing and you want to go back?" Jay grumbled, but he did it.

```
hellofriend@riddlemachine:~$ exit
exit
hellofriend@riddlemachine:~$
```

"OK, now what?"

"*Now* type 'letmein'," I said, and Eoin nodded.

Jay typed, and the Riddle Machine surrendered

its secret and then unceremoniously booted us off the server. ❶

```
hellofriend@riddlemachine:~$ letmein
39b7319eb05cabf1ea2551142962bf8d
DON'T BOTHER CHECKING, THERE'S NOTHING ELSE HERE
Connection closed.
```

For some time we were unable to quite believe that we had done it, and then the next few seconds were a blur of hugs and high-fives and exclamations of relief.

I wanted to send the flag to the email address straight away, but Eoin looked at his watch and gasped.

"It's almost two a.m.! That's it. Everything shuts down, right now."

He closed Jay's laptop, and with a glance dared me to argue. I wasn't up to the challenge. A blanket of exhaustion enfolded me abruptly, and I yawned.

"I'll have to call a cab," I said, pulling out my phone, but Eoin shook his head.

"Won't hear of it," he said. "You're staying the night. There's plenty of room."

"Are you sure?"

"Of course," Jay said. "You're more than welcome."

But as it turned out, none of us got any sleep. Wired and elated, we found ourselves hungry again – I was surprised when I worked out that we'd last eaten about six hours ago – and Eoin made sandwiches. And as we ate we talked – about the game and The Helmsman, and then about the Riddle Machine, replaying the highlights, Eoin making us both laugh with his impressions of a pissed-off Jay, and then anything and everything: university, television, escape rooms, food, music – until grey light began to bleed through the blinds.

I have never been as happy as I was on that evening with my friends.

If the phonecall with Lorena Carson is the point at which I felt the loneliest, then I will remember that moment, sitting in a soft armchair with a blanket Eoin had given me, sleepily chatting and laughing with him and Jay in the warmth, as the moment when I felt, for the last time, that I belonged somewhere.

* * *

I'm sorry, Eoin. I am so, so sorry.

THE HELMSMAN TEXTS:

Chapter 2

HELLO FRIEND!

I'm so glad you're back. Did you like my Riddle Machine? Frivolous and frolicsome!!

Now you're here, so to business. I am The Helmsman and I have a gift to give you. It belongs to you, now, to all of us. Not to them.

A story, to start with.

* * *

When I started work on this project, I moved into a small one-bedroom flat closer to the office. ❶

I had had enough of living with my parents, where the rent was reasonable but the conversation was not.

The letting agent showed me round, which took barely any time at all. It was June, and sunlight pooled in through the big front window and made the wooden floorboards glow. It was small, but enough. Not a great area, but I was twenty-three and didn't mind! The important thing was that I would live alone.

The rent, the agent told me, was £433 a month. I asked what the catch was. He looked at me seriously, his gelled hair spiked like a crown.

"No catch. An IT contractor was living

Holly Soames①
12/11/2019 20:53
Location unknown but use of GPMS handling instructions throughout suggests UK PLC. Nature of work unclear.

here, but he got another job, so we're looking for someone who can move in quick."

I took in the white walls and the brown-blond flooring; the tiny little kitchen with its old gas range; and the bedroom which looked out on to a shared garden. A huge fir tree swayed in the wind. ❶

"I can move in quick," I said, and I did.

The flat came with white goods and a bed and a black leather sofa that had seen better days. I bought floor lamps and a bookshelf, and a string of lights to frame the window. On those early summer evenings I sat and listened to the breeze and the distant thrum of traffic.

I believe I saw the first one the week after.

I'd made soup – my approximation of such! Knowing very much about my research, and very little about anything else, I had assumed soup involved throwing some ingredients into water and applying heat!!

I was pouring my sorry experiment down the drain when something small and brown darted from one side of the sink to the other, and was gone. No more than a flash, the briefest of glimpses. I had no idea what it was, other than something alive.

I remember not caring much. It was a hot summer that year and I kept the windows open all the time. Some sort of bug had evidently flown in.

The next evening, I was watching the television when there was another flash of brown. It zipped from under the sofa, towards the television set, and then diverted sharply to the far wall, where it disappeared.

I succeeded in convincing myself that

Holly Soames①
12/11/2019 19:48
Insufficient details to locate on open source.

while it may have looked like movement, it was an illusion, a motion falsely perceived.

Later that June there was a cool spell, and in retrospect I know that must have slowed them. I saw nothing until the mercury climbed. On a sticky night in mid-July, I padded to the kitchen in bare feet to get a drink.

I switched on the light and there were hundreds of them. They ran everywhere, like little spots of oil on the surface of water. Under the fridge and under the oven. Into the cupboards and into the walls.

I was INFESTED.

That night I kept all the lights on. I wrapped myself in the duvet, despite the sweat stinging my pores, because I was so afraid they would try and crawl into bed with me.

The next morning I bought sponges, bleach and disinfectant. I scrubbed every single crevice of the kitchen. During this process I inspected the fridge. In the rubber seals of the door were dead cockroaches and the husks of egg sacs. Some had been squashed by the door, their guts dried to a glaze.

Under the fridge I found an old, flattened pizza box dotted with grease - left by the contractor, I presumed - which contained a thick speckling of black cockroach droppings, and further egg sacs.

I wiped that place until my hands cracked. The bin overflowed with paper towels and wipes. I took a break to do some laundry, and as I shook out a shirt from the machine the waterlogged corpse of a cockroach fell out and hit the tiles with a soft plump CLICK.

I was in trouble!

* * *

One morning I woke up to find one on my bedside table, looking at me. It was the first time I'd seen a live one up close, and so still. I lay there, half-rigid with fear, willing myself to lash out and send it flying across the room.

It cocked its head, its slender antennae wavering back and forth. Little black eyes in an insane little face. Its segmented body was brown and it GLEAMED like it had been polished with wax.

Eventually, it scurried down the side of the table and was gone.

I started to cry.

It was about this time that I began to have breakthroughs with my research, but that is not important to this story. You'll find out about that soon enough ☺

* * *

Those days belonged to them. They took new ground everywhere I looked. That summer was hot and cockroaches THRIVE in heat! My cleaning the kitchen was no deterrence to them. Now, if I opened a cupboard, at any time of day, the frames would wriggle with dark bodies. They skittered back and forth across the living-room floor while I watched television. I never tried to count them. They say for every one you see there're fifty you don't.

The only place they seemed to stay away from - with the exception of their intrepid incursion on to my bedside table - was the bedroom. Perhaps they sensed that was my territory. This led me to think that the cockroaches and I could find a way to peacefully co-exist. If only they would learn

156

to do what they needed to do late at night, and leave me alone during the day, I had no objection to their consuming hair or crumbs. I would have shared what I had! Gladly!

But it wasn't to be. It rarely is with us and pests! One side surrenders and the other takes over!!!

The flashpoint was at my lab, when I put my hand into my trouser pocket to pull out a tissue, and launched a live cockroach on to a colleague's desk. Several other colleagues saw. They made me take some time off work. ❶ Just for a while. To relax, they said.

This, I decided, was war.

* * *

I began as any soldier should, with reconnaissance. Know thine enemy. Though I had observed the bedside-table visitor, the scout, I had never examined one up close.

I waited for nightfall and stood in the kitchen, still and silent. When I saw a likely candidate, a big adult, I slammed a glass on top of it, and studied it.

They were ugly, of course, but precise. They reminded me of malware in that way.

Did you know that cockroaches can live for a significant amount of time under water, without drowning? They have the ability to go into something resembling near-death, from which they can revive themselves. Did you know that if you behead a cockroach, the head can survive on its own until the brain starves to death?

Nothing about a cockroach is superfluous. They can move so fast because their brains connect directly to their legs. Their skin is waxy so it retains moisture. They clean themselves constantly. They can fit into crevices far smaller than themselves, flexing their bodies into obscene shapes to squirm away.

The egg sacs are a miracle. Each contains up to forty infants, and upon hatching they can immediately scurry for cover. Infestation only takes a single pregnant female.

I had heard the old adage about cockroaches and nuclear war, but I appreciated for the first time the truth behind it. I admired my enemy. More than that - I was JEALOUS.

I observed my prisoner. It didn't seem to be at all panicked by its captivity. It stared patiently at me through the glass, its feelers ceaselessly flowing back and forth.

I collected my weapons (after all, weapons were my JOB hahahaha) and commenced the first experiment. I lifted the glass and sprayed my first weapon inside.

Negative result. Deodorant did not work.

I tried my second weapon. Negative result. Furniture polish did not work.

The third weapon, sanitizing spray, likewise had no effect.

I turned to the purpose-built weapons. Raid. I sprayed it and the effect was positive and instantaneous. The cockroach began to sprint, round and round the confines of the glass. It fell on its back, kicking its hair-thin legs in a frenzy as the spray attacked its nervous system. This continued for several seconds until the kicking slowed down and became only occasional twitching. Then it was still.

Good. I was armed. But I was also CLEVER. I knew that cockroaches can very quickly develop resistance to pesticides in only one or two generations. Raid might help, but it couldn't be my only weapon.

Diatomaceous earth is a fine white powder which contains the remains of fossilised algae. It is cheap and plentiful, and it kills cockroaches.

Cockroaches have a waxy exoskeleton which helps them trap moisture. As a result, a cockroach can survive for days on a single speck of water. But the remains of the prehistoric microorganisms in diatomaceous earth cling to the legs and undersides of the insects as they crawl through it. It is abrasive, like glass, and pierces their exoskeletons. They can no longer retain moisture and die of thirst.

My other weapon was more primitive but satisfying. Glue traps. They were scented with banana oil, which cockroaches love.

If there had ever been a possibility of peace it was GONE. I scattered the earth and the traps liberally around my flat and the casualties began to pile up.

It is possible I got carried away. One evening, after spending some time at a nearby bar with some colleagues (we drank OFTEN, because of what we did!), one asked if he could come back to my flat to use the toilet before he got the train home. I could hardly refuse but I will never forget the look on his face as he walked through the door and saw the place.

Drifts of diatomaceous earth along the walls and in the corners, and in strategic piles under the sofa and marking the room boundaries. A few desiccated carcasses lay here and there, which I had not yet had time to dispose of.

Dotted in between the piles of powder,

there were glue traps. Many sprinkled with dead or dying insects, some pulsing slowly as they struggled to escape.

He looked at this scene, then at me, and backed out of the door.

"Not sure I need to go, actually," he said, trying to smile. "I can always use the loo on the train."

"Of course," I said. I smiled back, or at least my mouth was open and my teeth were exposed.

He left. We never drank much together after that!!!

* * *

The battle appeared to be swinging my way, but then came my war crime.

It happened one day in early autumn. It may have been a weekend as I woke up quite late. I walked into the living room and saw one of my glue traps had a new victim.

A pregnant female. The egg sac bulged underneath her, a sickly creamy swelling. This was the first time I'd captured a live egg sac, and I was delighted. Once it hatched, all the brood would become ensnared. The enemy would have forty or fifty fewer soldiers to fight for its cause.

I set aside the day to watch. The female had one leg free, and for an hour or more she waved it, clawing at the air. Eventually she grew exhausted and had to put it down. Now she was stuck fast.

Her back rose and fell in undulating pulses, almost erotic in their rhythms.

When night fell, I grew impatient. I retrieved a fruit knife - a relic from the days when I had imagined cooking gourmet meals in my new kitchen. Under the harsh burn of an LED lamp I began the operation.

I laid the blade across the base of the female's head and eased it down. The blade was keen, the cut true, and there, stuck fast to the gleaming steel, was a cockroach's head. The antennae were still moving.

"Off with her head," I said.

I gently wiped the blade and regarded the decapitated body, still with its secret little pouch of horrors. I whispered the blade along its surface and they came spilling out like fluid from a cyst. There were so many, none bigger than a millimetre.

Cockroach nymphs are nowhere near as repulsive as their adult counterparts. They're a rounded, teardrop shape and scramble around excitedly like puppies. Almost CUTE! But they stuck to the glue just as well as their mother.

I scooped up the mother's head, the antennae still waving, with the knife and held it up, so she could watch her children die. I wonder if she recognised her own body. I wonder, if I had moved her head close enough to it, whether she would have tried to eat herself.

* * *

I went back into the kitchen to clean the knife. And I saw them.

A great host, lined up in formation on the counter. They had seen my atrocity. They had amassed their troops in response. All-out retaliation!

I dropped the plate in shock. The sound of it acted as a catalyst, because as one they advanced, thousands of them, thousands more from under the oven and behind the fridge, swarming towards me, and I remember turning to run, my only thought being to get the can of Raid I kept on the coffee table, but I slipped on something - perhaps loose diatomaceous earth - and I fell heavily, feeling their weight like raindrops on my legs and my chest, and the last thing I remember is a single insect perched on my nose, standing quite still and calm and staring into my eyes, and I remember thinking that it was the same one who had been on my bedside table, all those weeks ago, and that I had been wrong to assume it was a scout. It wasn't a scout. It was the leader, the queen, which was ridiculous as cockroaches aren't social insects, they have no hierarchy, but I stared into its black eyes and I saw recognition.

Recognition and FURY.

I passed out.

* * *

I woke up, sunlight streaming through the big front window, with a terrible pain in my head, but otherwise uninjured. I dragged myself to my feet and looked around the kitchen. The cockroaches were gone. The glue trap which had held the female and her babies had vanished. I searched everywhere but couldn't find it.

Nor was there a single cockroach left anywhere. I never saw one again in that flat. Ever. It was as if they had never existed.

* * *

For years this mystified me, until I began the work you are reading now.

I was stuck on a cognitive glue trap of

162

my own making. A belief that the cockroaches were entities separate to, and distinct from, myself. That was an ILLUSION. It was a dualistic untruth my consciousness tricked me into believing. The very falsest of dichotomies. You will bear with me on this. It is important. If you can get over this hurdle the next will not be so difficult!

I set myself against the cockroaches, believing us to be in a war, but there was never any conflict. It is a paradox to think there ever could have been. The cockroaches were me, and I them. And they are YOU, too. Do you feel them nibbling at your mind? All of us molecules colliding and separating.

Recall the last chapter. Plato's Cave. Subject to endless speculation and argument and interpretation: what does the cave represent? Who are the puppeteers? Would the prisoners actually react that way? What if there's nothing outside the cave at all?

But the question that has not been asked: WHAT IF THERE IS NO CAVE?

You see, you could probably fly if you wanted to!

* * *

This project of mine began as PhD research, and it became something else. Now it is so much more. I will share it with you. Because you are ready, aren't you? If you've got this far you must be.

Let me tell you about it.

We will save the world, you and I.

ANECHOIC

A short play by Marlow Tannhauser❶

*SFX: LOW BACKGROUND NOISE – DISTANT
TRAFFIC, BIRDSONG, PEOPLE MURMURING.
UNTIL INDICATED.*
*2014. EDWARD, AN EXPERIMENTAL OFFICER,
ENTERS AN ANECHOIC CHAMBER WITH MARCUS
ERHARDT, A PHD STUDENT❷ WHO IS CARRYING
A LARGE CASE.*

EDWARD: The quietest place in the world.

MARCUS: Smaller than I thought.

EDWARD: It's infinite, acoustically. If you
            screamed, you'd only hear the scream
            itself, no echo.

MARCUS: That's pretty creepy.

EDWARD: It's just a room. OK, two things.
            Don't touch the walls. They're
            fibreglass wedges. Touch the walls
            and then your eyes, you'll lose your
            retinas.

MARCUS: Don't touch the walls.

EDWARD: Second, take some time to get used to
            it. The first half-hour is the worst.
            People have panic attacks. Auditory
            hallucinations.

MARCUS: Auditory—?

EDWARD: Our brains are used to ambient noise,
            so when there's none at all they
            provide a substitute. If you feel
            strange, don't panic. Just come out.

Holly Soames①
23/11/2019 04:27
No trace. This is
the first of several
plays by 'Marlow
TANNHAUSER' in
THT. None of them
appear on open
source and do not
appear to have been
published anywhere
else.

Holly Soames②
23/11/2019 05:13
Unclear if this
is fictional or
autobiographical but
there are a limited
number of anechoic
chambers in the
UK. No trace of the
names supplied
here or in any of
the subsequent
TANNHAUSER
plays. Year noted for
reference.

MARCUS: Do you ever get used to it?

EDWARD: Once I close that door, the only
            things you'll hear are the sounds
            you make from just existing. Your
            eyeballs rolling in their sockets,
            the electrical impulses in your
            nerve endings fizzing. Your own
            heart pulsing. When you turn your
            head you'll hear little bubbles of
            gas popping in your joints. We're a
            jumbled-up, flawed, messy mix of wet
            moving parts and in here you hear it
            all. So no, you don't get used to
            it. (PAUSE) Sorry. Got carried away.
            You're only here for a few hours,
            you'll be fine. What's the study
            you're doing again?

MARCUS: I'm assessing the feasibility of
            malware causing direct psychological
            and physical harm to human beings, and
            countermeasures to prevent that from
            happening. ❶

EDWARD: Right. Not my field, really.

MARCUS: The idea is that computers produce
            primitive outputs, like light and
            sound, as a by-product of what they do
            anyway. And if malware could harness
            those, threat actors could use those
            to—

EDWARD: Ah. Sound as a weapon. From what,
            laptop speakers? ❷

MARCUS: That and a few other things,
            yeah. But it's more about finding
            countermeasures. Seeing if it's
            possible, if it could actually hurt
            people, and then how to stop it.

EDWARD: Hard to test without human subjects.

MARCUS: Oh, I'm just using a sound level meter
            and then I'll extrapolate. Ethically I
            couldn't—

EDWARD: Malware that can hurt people. Bet
            there's a few people interested in
            this research.

MARCUS: I've had offers. But I'm not interested
            in them. They don't… this is about
            prevention. Protecting the public from
            what the bad guys could do.

EDWARD: Sure. Well, I'll leave you to it.
            Remember, the light switches are
            outside the chamber, on the wall.
            And the chamber door can stick. If
            it doesn't open, just give it a good
            push. Ready? I'll shut you in.

            *EDWARD STARTS TO EXIT, BEFORE HE'S
            JOINED BY KAREN* ❶ *(COLD, POISED).
            BOTH STARE AT MARCUS.*

MARCUS: Sorry, who are you?

            *SFX: A HEAVY DOOR SLAMMING SHUT.
            EDWARD AND KAREN EXIT.
            SFX: THE BACKGROUND RECORDING STOPS.
            DISCONCERTED, MARCUS OPENS HIS CASE,
            PULLING OUT A LAPTOP AND VARIOUS BITS
            OF EQUIPMENT.*

                Right. OK. First test. Sine wave at
                17kHz, maximum volume.

            *SFX: LIGHTBULB BUZZING, DYING.
            A LONG SILENCE.
            SFX: A SUDDEN SHARP CRACK AS THE
            LIGHTBULB EXPLODES.
            BLACK-OUT.*

                Shit! Edward? Edward, the lights
                have gone out! (TO HIMSELF) It's
                sound-proofed, moron, he can't hear
                you.

Holly Soames①
23/11/2019 07:47
Unclear if this
is the same
KAREN referred to
elsewhere in THT.
No trace of the other
characters in this
play or any of the
others attributed
to TANNHAUSER,
and none of them
are referred to
elsewhere in THT
except KAREN.

HE TRIES TO PUSH THE DOOR OPEN.

    Come on, come on. Open! Fuck! Hello?
    Is anyone there? The door's stuck!

HE THROWS HIMSELF AGAINST THE DOOR.
HE TAKES OUT HIS PHONE, CLICKING THE
SCREEN.

SFX: PHONE TONES, "YOUR CALL CANNOT BE
COMPLETED AS DIALLED."

    Fuck! OK. It's OK. I'll just do it
    in the dark. It's fine. Just get
    through it.
    (VOICE TREMBLING) OK. Sine wave at
    17kHz from laptop. Playing the tone—

A LOUD SCRATCHING.

    —now. Erm… hello?

SILENCE.

    Is someone there?

A LOUDER SCRATCHING, LONGER.

    Oh fuck. Hello?

THE SCRATCHING STOPS.

    Mice. Must be mice. Come on, Marcus.
    Focus. Sine wave at—

RUSTLING.

    Right, fuck this! Who's there?

SILENCE.
MARCUS PUSHES AT THE DOOR FRANTICALLY.

    Come on, you… bastard… fucking open!

HE GIVES UP, BREATHING HEAVILY.
    Auditory hallucinations. Hearing

> things, that's all. Idiot. Get on
> with it. Sine wave—

THE ECHO ENTERS.
THE SCRATCHING, CLOSER. MORE RUSTLING.
THEN SILENCE.

> Ignore it. Sine—

THE ECHO APPROACHES MARCUS,
FOOTSTEPS LIGHT.
HE STOPS. LISTENS. SILENCE.

> I know someone's there! I'm coming
> over!

HE EDGES TOWARDS THE ECHO.

> Hello?

THE ECHO: *(FLAT, TONELESS)* Hello.

MARCUS: FUCK!

HE STUMBLES, BACKING OFF.

> Who is that?

THE ECHO: Who is that.

MARCUS LAUGHS NERVOUSLY.

MARCUS: *(TO HIMSELF)* It's a prank. Course it
is. *(LOUDER)* You had me going for
a second! Do you work with Edward?
Top bantz. You scared the shit out
of me, mission accomplished! But I
really need to do this experiment,
or my supervisor'll kill me. Can you
let me out?

THE ECHO: Let me out.

MARCUS: The fucking door won't open, I'm stuck
in here!

THE ECHO: I'm stuck in here.

168

MARCUS: This isn't funny. I want to leave.

THE ECHO: I want to leave.

MARCUS: You need to stop it. Just fucking stop
           it, OK, just stop it!

THE ECHO: Just stop it.

MARCUS: You think I'm afraid? I'm not afraid!

THE ECHO: I'm not afraid.

MARCUS: Come on, then! Show yourself!

THE ECHO: Show yourself.

*THE ECHO SCUTTLES ON ALL FOURS
TOWARDS MARCUS.*

MARCUS: Wait. No no no, what are you doing?
           No! No, please! Get away! Don't—

*HE FALLS BACK, UNCONSCIOUS.
A LONG SILENCE.*

*SFX: A HEAVY DOOR OPENING.
SFX: THE FIZZ OF LIGHTBULBS
FLICKERING ON.
LIGHTS UP.
SFX: THE BACKGROUND RECORDING.*

*KAREN AND EDWARD ENTER. THEY STAND
OVER MARCUS.*

KAREN: Hello, Dr Erhardt. Well, not a doctor
           yet. But almost.

MARCUS STIRS, WAKES UP.

MARCUS: Almost.

HE SITS UP, WINCING, GROGGY.

KAREN: We haven't met, Dr Erhardt, but I'm an
           admirer of your work. I represent an
           outfit where it could come in very

useful. We did reach out to see if you
might be interested in working for us,
and, if you recall, you turned us down.

MARCUS: Turned us down.

KAREN: You said we didn't speak the same
            language.

MARCUS: Speak the same language.

*HE CLAPS HIS HANDS OVER HIS MOUTH IN
HORROR. KAREN SMILES.*

KAREN: So we thought we'd try again. A little
            more forcefully, this time.

MARCUS: Forcefully this time.

KAREN: Working for us will be an adjustment.
            But you'll come to see things our way.
            We'll be speaking the same language
            – singing off the same hymn sheet –
            soon enough. In fact, you've already
            started!

MARCUS: Already started.

KAREN: I have an eye for people. I know
            you're like us, deep down.

MARCUS: Like us deep down.

KAREN: Very good. You know, I walked through
            the university gardens on my way here.
            Saw the flowerbeds. Spring is over.
            The daffodils are dying.

MARCUS: The daffodils are—

HE SOBS, CHOKING ON THE WORDS.

KAREN: I know, I know. It's disconcerting,
            isn't it? People hear things in there.

MARCUS: Hear things in there.

KAREN: You and I have a lot to talk about, Dr Erhardt. We're going to do wonderful things together.

MARCUS TRIES TO STOP HIMSELF SPEAKING, BUT CAN'T.

MARCUS: Wonderful things together.

KAREN: We need you. Our bones are like stone.

MARCUS: Bones are like stone.

KAREN: Why don't we sit in here for a bit? In the chamber, where it's quiet. I'll tell you all about the plans I've got for us.

MARCUS: The plans I've got for us.

SFX: A HEAVY DOOR CLOSING.
CURTAIN.

Any person can be a target. But we are not always passive victims. Within us there is gunpowder.

§

They say a virus is not alive because it has no means of generating energy and does not respirate. But when you see their frenzies under a microscope it is hard to believe. Malware is further removed from life. But it, too, moves.

§

What might happen as the symbiosis of humanity and technology draws closer? If a cyber organism were to contract a virus, would that be considered a digital or biological pathogen? Would it MATTER?

§

Conventional wisdom tells us that malware which can cause physical or psychological harm to humans does not exist. Conventional wisdom is wrong! If something can be done, it has been done. If you are unaware of it, the person who has done it has kept it to themselves. This thing in itself should concern you.

§

Information wants to be free. Sometimes to kill you.

To: ███████████████████████ ❶
From: B2
CC/BCC: B1
Date: 22 August 2014
Subject: Welcome aboard!

Hi ██████████,

Hope you're well. I just wanted to reach out and welcome you to the unit, ahead of your official joining next week, now that your vetting❷ has come through. Very much looking forward to meeting you – the team here are very excited about your project.

I'll be your first-line project supervisor going forwards, and it would be great to have an initial catch-up once you're settled in, to work out a plan of action.
CCing Karen❸ for info, whom I believe you've met.

Kind regards,

Philip

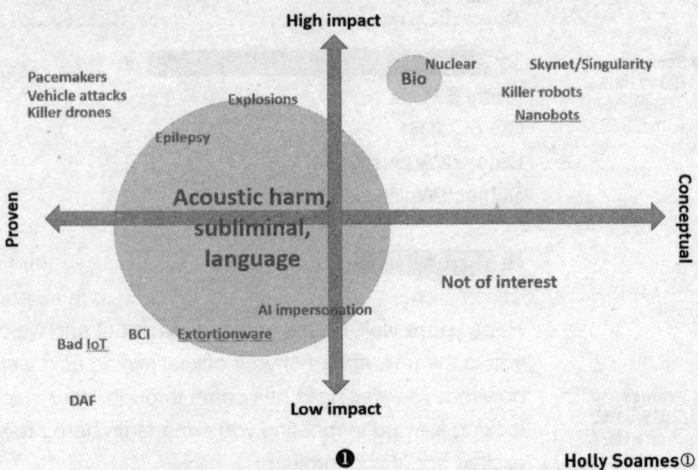

Holly Soames①
13/11/2019 10:04
In my assessment,
after looking into
this, much of this is
speculative.

Acoustic	Subliminal	AI	Bio	Explosions	Misc
Ultrasonic	Visual	MALICE	SynBIO/CRISPR	IoT devices	Epilepsy
Infrasonic	Acoustic	Contagion	DBS	USB devices	Extortionware
DAF	Linguistic	Impersonation	Nano	Piezoelectric	AR/VR
	Contagion		Arbo	Swarms	
			BCI vehicles	Sex toys	
			DNA Autocorrect		

Included (empirical)
Included (future work)
Mentioned only

❷

Holly Soames②
13/11/2019 10:58
As per previous
comment

To: ███████████████████████
From: B2
CC/BCC: B1
Date: 14 October 2014
Subject: RE: Thoughts

Yes, although please bear in mind the emphasis for us has to be on practical application and use in the field.❶

Philip

Holly Soames①
23/11/2019 03:25
Unclear if this occurred although subsequent chapters suggest not (at least not in the intended manner).

To: ███████████████████████
From: B2
CC/BCC: B1
Date: 19 November 2014
Subject: RE: Presentation to Exec Committee

Looks great! If you could condense it slightly that would be fab (and also please change the slides to the approved templates?). How are you getting on with that lit review?

Philip

To: ███████████████████████

From: B2

CC/BCC: B1

Date: 1 December 2014

Subject: RE: Collaboration with Project BLUE STEAM❶

Holly Soames①
23/11/2019 02:43
No trace, see also
'BLUE SUN' c3 THT.

I know, they're brilliant, aren't they? Odd, but brilliant. Hopefully they provided you with some useful insights.

Well done on the presentation btw – Exec Committee was impressed.

Philip

To: ███████████████████████

From: B2

CC/BCC: B1

Date: 17 December 2014

Subject: RE: First draft of lit review

Thanks for this. Let me take some time to digest it and I'll come back to you with thoughts.

Just an ask from the brass – please use the departmental templates for any ideas and proposals going forwards.

Philip

Holly Soames①
14/11/2019 14:46
STRAP officers have
no record of any of
the doc references in
this or subsequent
chapters on their
registers, nor do
they appear on any
TS systems to which
CT has access/
knowledge.

Holly Soames②
13/11/2019 11:14
No trace.

Holly Soames③
13/11/2019 14:48
Appears to be based
on genuine research.

TOP SECRET STRAP 3❶

UK EYES ONLY

REF: FG662939/14
DATE: 16/12/2014
PROJECT: RED FOG❷
AUTHORISING OFFICER: B1
AUTHOR: ▮▮▮▮▮▮ (B5)
PURPOSE: Initial literature review/proposal

On cyberweapons and physical harm❸

Discussions about the potential harm from cyberweapons have traditionally centred on their actual or potential effects on critical infrastructure, including power grids (Carr, 2013; Denning, 2007; Gartzke, 2013; Stidham, 2001), water supplies (Lewis, 2002; Denning, 2000), and trains, planes, and air traffic control systems (Rid, 2013). These discussions tend to be theoretical and not underpinned by empirical research or technical knowledge.

More recent research, however, attempts to make a case for the potential lethality of cyberweapons through empirical work demonstrating viable and critical threats in medical devices such as insulin pumps (Radcliffe, 2011) and pacemakers (Kirk, 2012), and in manufacturing and 3D printing systems (Sturm et al, 2014). Whilst it is not believed that such research has been weaponised in the wild, most of these examples would be capable of causing injury or death, or damage to property without involving attacks on critical infrastructure. As Ponangi et al (2012) argue, some actors may also seek to influence and manipulate cognitive behaviour.

There has also been an increase in research which conflates security and other disciplines to demonstrate the far-reaching consequences of cyber-attacks against specialist equipment, such as DNA and neural interfaces. ❶ Whilst there has not, to date, been any example of biological attacks which have been augmented or assisted by cyberweapons, there is an increasing crossover between DNA models and structures and computing paradigms. DNA computing has been suggested to enable attacks against cryptographic protocols (Boneh et al, 1995), novel forms of steganography (Clelland et al, 1999), artificial immune systems (Gao, 2011), and the development of new encryption methods (Gehani et al, 2004). New technologies such as CRISPR (clustered regularly interspaced short palindromic repeats), a genome editing tool, present an attractive attack surface to threat actors. CRISPR is an immune mechanism found in bacteria, capable of destroying foreign DNA by using previously acquired DNA sequences from virulent pathogens (Ishino et al, 1987). Practically, it uses a guided-RNA, a form of engineered virus, to recognise and locate a sequence, or multiple sequences, of interest, and then executes a double-stranded break at that location using an engineered nuclease. The original sequence is replaced by the edited sequence, resulting in permanent genomic modification.

Whilst organisations and institutions researching CRISPR and producing DNA synthesis have restrictions in place to prevent the engineering of dangerous pathogens, it is not known how robust they might be. If such restrictions could be bypassed, malware could target an individual microbiologist, or a microbiology organisation or institution, to engineer the synthesis of dangerous viruses and bacteria.

Unlike CRISPR and DNA pipelines, some neural technologies have been subject to the scrutiny of the information security community. Consumer-grade non-invasive (e.g., EEG) brain-computing interfaces (BCIs), for instance, have been examined for eavesdropping and

Holly Soames①
23/11/2019 02:55
These lines of research were presumably abandoned as future chapters focus specifically on a cognitive 'weapon' and not a biological one.

side-channel weaknesses (Frank et al, 2013; Martinovic et al, 2012). These studies have demonstrated that it is possible to infer PIN codes, bank information, months of birth, and whether the user recognises an individual shown to them. Denning et al (2009) also note several potential vulnerabilities associated with deep brain stimulators (neural implants which use magnetic fields, small DC currents, or ultrasonic pulses (Luber et al, 2009) for transcranial stimulation). They note that potential impacts include remotely controlling prosthetic limbs; cell death; and disrupting the creation of new memories.

However, these attacks all remain traditional in their mode: they involve the compromise of a computer or device, which in turn causes harm. The primary focus of this project is on *directly* causing harm, which requires new thinking.

Towards a new paradigm

Liang and Xiangsui (1999) note that "There is nothing in the world today that cannot become a weapon", and this is true of computers. Computers are not merely machines which process, compute and calculate. They produce outputs – sound, light, language. These outputs can become human inputs, and humans have inherent vulnerabilities to crafted inputs if formed or expressed in a particular way. An early example is a series of attacks against users of an epilepsy forum (Poulsen, 2008). Attackers uploaded animated GIF images and JavaScript redirects, exposing users to flashing images designed to induce seizures in sufferers of both photosensitive and pattern-sensitive epilepsy. Several users experienced seizures and migraines as a result.

This subject is under-explored, and frequently converges with the unstable world of conspiracy theory. Yet many such threats appear credible, and could be developed at a fraction of the cost of 'traditional' cyberweapons, with the added advantage of kinetic effects. Moreover, as these attacks exploit human vulnerabilities, rather than technical ones, they remain dangerous forever: they are neither expensive nor complex; have immediate and harmful effects; and are not a 'one-off attack' relying on a specific vulnerability in a particular operating system or software application (Inkman et al, 2009). Rather, this type of cyberweapon could be conceptualised as exploiting vulnerabilities in the human 'biocomputer' (Robey and Taggart, 1982).

Unfortunately, there has been little research on this subject. The literature which does exist consists predominantly of rumours, hearsay, and unfounded claims. Perhaps the most prominent work is a pair of papers by Thomas (1998a, 1998b). Thomas notes that "the human body, much like a computer, contains myriad data processors", including the brain, heart, nervous system, the ear and the eye, and argues that such processors may be vulnerable to malicious interference. He cites several examples which have a significant evidence base relating to their potential harmful effects, including the inducement of epileptic seizures, acoustic weapons, subliminal priming, disinformation and deception, and the effects of microwave radiation. It is likely, however, that many other claims in Thomas's work are far-fetched; ❶ certainly, they should be treated with caution in the absence of peer-reviewed empirical findings. Yet Thomas makes a compelling case that at least some of the techniques he describes could realistically be adopted as payloads for cyberweapons – certainly when it comes to epileptic seizures, acoustic weapons and subliminal priming. Indeed, the title of one of his papers encapsulates why such cyberweapons might be attractive, and why they may overcome the historical objections to, and limitations of, more traditional cyberweapons: "the mind has no firewall."

Holly Soames①
13/11/2019 15:34
Paper lacks any detail concerning these techniques and any claims appear to be anecdotal.

I present detailed cases for two promising possibilities, based on some initial research I have conducted as part of my former PhD programme.

On sound as a weapon

The use of sound as a weapon is well-documented (Grimes, 2005; Vinokur, 2004), including the trumpets of Jericho, the Stuka siren, and music used as a torture device by military forces (Goodman, 2012), although the efficacy of acoustic weapons has been questioned. Altmann (2001), for instance, noted that it is difficult to accurately direct them, and the effects decay rapidly over distance. However, ultrasonic (>20KHz) and infrasonic (<20Hz) audio, which is typically beyond the threshold of human hearing in adults (Goodman, 2012) but not necessarily beyond the threshold of perception or physiological response (Imaizumi et al, 2001; Oohashi et al, 2000; Henry and Fast, 1984), can modulate moods and induce physiological reactions. Smith et al (2005) reported that frequencies over 17KHz (considered "near-ultrasonic") and over 70dB in volume can cause excessive fatigue, nausea and headaches. Similarly, a study by Pawlaczyk-Łuszczyńska and colleagues (2007) found that 70% of surveyed machine operators, whose machines emitted ultrasonic noise, reported effects including tiredness, headaches, somnolence, dizziness and palpitations. In more extreme cases, ultrasonic noise has caused permanent physiological damage, including hearing loss, hypotension and cardiac issues (see Smagowska and Pawlaczyk-Łuszczyńska, 2013, for an overview).

Infrasound has also been shown to have physiological and psychological effects on humans. In 2004, Qibai and Shi measured blood pressure and heart rate whilst exposing human subjects to frequencies near that of the resonant frequency of human organs (5Hz), and found that both measurements changed by at least 10% in all subjects, and in some cases up to 30%. Infrasound has also been reported as causing auditory and respiratory effects, distress and anxiety (Vinokur, 2004); visual disturbances and feelings of sadness (Braine, 2006); vertigo and listlessness (Karpova et al, 1970); and ear pressure and headaches (Møller, 1984).

In more extreme cases, researchers have discovered whole-body pathologies because of long-term exposure to low frequency sounds. Torres et al (2001) reported excessive cancer and hypertension mortality rates on an island near a U.S. Navy training site, where the population experiences hundreds of sonic booms a day. They describe vibroacoustic disease (VAD), which manifests not only physiologically but behaviourally, resulting in patients experiencing panic attacks and becoming uncommunicative. Alves-Pereira and Branco (2007) expanded on this work, noting that effects of VAD included depression, increased irritability and aggressiveness, palpitations and tachycardia, coughing, breathlessness, a preference for isolation, and decreased cognitive abilities.

The most promising proposal for sound as a cyberweapon is likely the infection of devices such as laptops and smart speakers with malware capable of manipulating the system volume and playing high or low frequency tones at levels associated with harm, and which cannot be detected by the victim. That is, a cyberweapon which is also an acoustic weapon.

There has, to date, been no examination of the possibility of this method being deployed by a threat actor against a population, and certainly not through malware. It would appear that malware able to covertly increase the volume of an infected machine and play inaudible ultrasonic and infrasonic tones could cause significant physiological and psychological effects on nearby people, particularly over extended periods. This could be exacerbated in an office environment, where multiple machines could become infected.

Of course, there are caveats. Successful attacks would need to rely on: (a) the attacker being able to manipulate a given device to emit sufficient levels of noise; (b) the victim not perceiving the emitted audio; (c) the victim being susceptible to the effects; and (d) the device being capable of producing high levels over time. Other possible limitations could include the unintended generation of audible components, which would negatively affect the covert aspect of the attack.

Subliminal priming❶

Much of the research on subliminal priming is overshadowed by references to James Vicary, who claimed in 1957 to have created the concept of subliminal advertising by flashing imperceptible images of soft drinks and popcorn in movie theatres to drive sales (Karremans et al, 2006). Vicary's claims appear to have been a hoax (Pratkanis, 1992) and many researchers argue that subliminal priming is not possible (see Dijksterhuis et al, 2005); downplay effects when they are found (see Trappey, 1996); and use prejudicial language in their publications. Pratkanis (1992), for example, entitled his paper 'The cargo-cult science of subliminal persuasion'.

However, several recent studies illustrate that subliminal priming can have moderate effects. Karremans et al found that visual primes can be used to increase the preference of subjects for a specific brand of soft drink, but only if the subjects were already thirsty.

Other studies have demonstrated that subliminal priming can be used to affect perceptions and emotions. Légal et al (2012) subliminally primed participants with an instruction "to trust", leading subjects to express greater levels of trust about a fictional figure. Stewart and

Holly Soames①
13/11/2019 16:59
Analysis below suggests this could not have the effects described by WEBSTER and could at best provide a mild and temporary 'nudge' towards a certain behaviour, with restrictions.

Schubert (2006) examined the use of subliminal primes in a Republican 'attack' advertisement broadcast during the 2000 presidential election in the U.S., which aired over 4,400 times overall. The prime "RATS" was subliminally embedded in the advertisement; the experimenters found that this did affect attitudes towards both parties, and the Democrat candidate Al Gore.

Subliminal priming can also have physiological effects. Hull et al (2001) used both "angry" and "relax" as primes, and found that participants exposed to the latter had lowered systolic and diastolic blood pressure compared to those exposed to the former, although the effects were small and short-lived.

On this note, some researchers have observed that repeated exposure to subliminal stimuli has a greater effect (Monahan et al, 2000; Dijksterhuis and van Knippenberg, 1998; Marcel, 1983; Srull and Wyer, 1989; Neberland et al, 2002), although subliminal priming does come with limitations which would need to be taken into account when considering any practical application via malware. Primes longer than a single word are unlikely to be fully processed. The temporal duration of subliminal priming is unclear, and whilst there is evidence that subliminal priming can affect attitudes and preferences, these effects are limited to pre-existing attitudes, goals, motivations and beliefs.

Future work

There are objections to the metaphor of the human brain as a computer (Lilly, 1968), but it is evident that the brain accepts, processes and parses input. And, like a computer, certain malformed inputs can result in a condition of exploitation,❶ perhaps in more dangerous and insidious ways than previously considered possible. Empirical evidence is now required.

Holly Soames[1]
13/11/2019 21:06
Slides included in c3 THT suggest a 'small-scale study' took place for both audio attacks and subliminal priming (named RED SOUND and RED VISION respectively). No results are included in THT, only a note in aforementioned slides that the studies were unsuccessful.

REPORT ENDS

References

Altmann, J. (2001). Acoustic weapons – a prospective assessment. *Science & Global Security*, 9(3), 165-234.

Alves-Pereira, M., & Branco, N. A. C. (2007). Vibroacoustic disease: biological effects of infrasound and low-frequency noise explained by mechanotransduction cellular signalling. *Progress in Biophysics and Molecular Biology*, 93(1), 256-279.

Boneh, D., Dunworth, C., & Lipton, R. J. (1995). Breaking DES using a molecular computer. *DNA Based Computers*, 27, 37-66.

Braine, J. (2006). A study of the effects of acoustic phenomena and their possible use in multimedia. (Masters dissertation, Dublin: Trinity College).

Carr, J. (2013). The misunderstood acronym: Why cyber weapons aren't WMD. *Bulletin of the Atomic Scientists*, 69(5), 32–37. https://doi.org/10.1177/0096340213501373

Clelland, C. T., Risca, V., & Bancroft, C. (1999). Hiding messages in DNA microdots. *Nature*, 399(6736), 533-534.

Denning, D. E. (2000). Cyberterrorism. *Global Dialogue*, Autumn.

Denning, D. E. (2007). A View of Cyberterrorism Five Years Later. In K. Himma (ed.), *Readings in Internet Security: Hacking, Counterhacking, and Society*, 123–139. Jones and Bartlett Publishers.

Denning, T., Matsuoka, Y., & Kohno, T. (2009). Neurosecurity: Security and privacy for neural devices. *Neurosurgical Focus*, 27(1), E7.

Dijksterhuis, A., & van Knippenberg, A. (1998). The relation between perception and behavior, or how to win a game of trivial pursuit. *Journal of Personality and Social Psychology*, 74(4), 865.

Dijksterhuis, A., Aarts, H., & Smith, P. K. (2005). The power of the subliminal: Subliminal perception and possible applications. In R. Hassin, J. Uleman, & J. A. Bargh (eds.), *The New Unconsciousness*, 77–106. New York, New York: Oxford University Press.

Frank, M., Hwu, T., Jain, S., Knight, R., Martinovic, I., Mittal, P., ... & Song, D. (2013). Subliminal probing for private information via EEG-based BCI devices. arXiv preprint arXiv:1312.6052.

Gao, Q. (2011). A few DNA-based security techniques. In proceedings of *IEEE Long Island Systems, Applications and Technology (LISAT)*.

Gartzke, E. (2013). The myth of cyberwar: Bringing war in cyberspace back down to Earth. *International Security*, 38(2), 41–73. https://doi.org/10.1162/ISEC_a_00136

Gehani, A., LaBean, T.H., & Reif, J.H. (2004). DNA-based

cryptography. In N. Jonaska, G. Paun, & G. Rozenberg (eds.), *Aspects of Molecular Computing*, 167-188. New York, New York: Springer.

Goodman, S. (2012). *Sonic Warfare: Sound, Affect, and the Ecology of Fear*. Cambridge, Massachusetts: MIT Press.

Grimes, J. D. (2005). Modeling sound as a non-lethal weapon in the COMBATXXI simulation model (Doctoral dissertation, Monterey, California: Naval Postgraduate School).

Henry, K. R., & Fast, G. A. (1984). Ultrahigh-frequency auditory thresholds in young adults: Reliable responses up to 24 kHz with a quasi-free-field technique. *Audiology*, 23(5), 477-489.

Hull, J.G., Slone, L.B. & Matthews, A.R. (2001). The non-consciousness of self-consciousness. Poster presented at the *Society for Personality and Social Psychology Conference*.

Imaizumi, S., Hosoi, H., Sakaguchi, T., Watanabe, Y., Sadato, N., Nakamura, S., ... & Yonekura, Y. (2001). Ultrasound activates the auditory cortex of profoundly deaf subjects. *NeuroReport*, 12(3), 583-586.

Inkman, P., McCready, G. R., & Shapwell, T. (2009). Single shot: Cost-efficiency ratios in large-scale cyber-attacks. *Journal of Technological and Security Risk*, 3(2), 209-217.

Ishino, Y., Shinagawa, H., Makino, K., Amemura, M., & Nakata, A. (1987). Nucleotide sequence of the iap gene, responsible for alkaline phosphatase isozyme conversion in Escherichia coli, and identification of the gene product. *Journal of Bacteriology*, 169(12), 5429-5433.

Karpova, N. I., Alekseev, S. V., Erokhin, V. N., Kadyskina, E. N., & Reutov, O. V. (1970). Early response of the organism to low-frequency acoustical oscillations. *Noise and Vibration Bulletin*, 11(65), 100-103.

Karremans, J. C., Stroebe, W., & Claus, J. (2006). Beyond Vicary's fantasies: The impact of subliminal priming and brand choice. *Journal of Experimental Social Psychology*, 42(6), 792-798.

Kirk, J. (2012, October 17). Pacemaker hack can deliver deadly 830-volt jolt. *Computerworld*.

Légal, J. B., Chappé, J., Coiffard, V., & Villard-Forest, A. (2012). Don't you know that you want to trust me? Subliminal goal priming and persuasion. *Journal of Experimental Social Psychology*, 48(1), 358-360.

Lewis, J. A. (2002). Assessing the risks of cyber terrorism, cyber war and other cyber threats. Center for Strategic & International Studies.

Liang, Q., & Xiangsui, W. (1999). *Unrestricted Warfare*. Beijing: PLA Literature and Arts Publishing House.

Lilly, J. C. (1968). *Programming and Metaprogramming in the Human Biocomputer*. Menlo Park, California: Whole Earth Catalog.

Luber, B., Fisher, C., Appelbaum, P. S., Ploesser, M., & Lisanby, S. H. (2009). Noninvasive brain stimulation in the detection of deception: Scientific challenges and ethical consequences. *Behavioral Sciences & the Law*, 27(2), 191-208.

Marcel, A. J. (1983). Conscious and unconscious perception: Experiments on visual masking and word recognition. *Cognitive Psychology*, 15(2), 197-237.

Martinovic, I., Davies, D., Frank, M., Perito, D., Ros, T., & Song, D. (2012). On the feasibility of side-channel attacks with brain–computer interfaces. In *Proceedings of the 21st USENIX Conference on Security Symposium*.

Møller, H. (1984). Physiological and psychological effects of infrasound on humans. *Journal of Low Frequency Noise, Vibration and Active Control*, 3(1), 1-17.

Monahan, J. L., Murphy, S. T., & Zajonc, R. B. (2000). Subliminal mere exposure: Specific, general, and diffuse effects. *Psychological Science*, 11(6), 462-466.

Neberland, R. J., Panesar, J. K., Shankman, C. V., & Caswell, W. (2002). Assessing the limits of subliminal priming effectiveness in a double-blind study. *EMK Quarterly*, 12(11), 698-712.

Oohashi, T., Nishina, E., Honda, M., Yonekura, Y., Fuwamoto, Y., Kawai, N., ... & Shibasaki, H. (2000). Inaudible high-frequency sounds affect brain activity: hypersonic effect. *Journal of Neurophysiology*, 83(6), 3548-3558.

Pawlaczyk-Łuszczyńska, M., Dudarewicz, A., & Śliwińska-Kowalska, M. (2007). Theoretical predictions and actual hearing threshold levels in workers exposed to ultrasonic noise of impulsive character - a pilot study. *International Journal of Occupational Safety and Ergonomics*, 13(4), 409-418.

Ponangi, P., Kidambi, P., Rao, D., Fendley, M., Haas, M., & Narayanan, S. (2012). On the Offense: Using Cyber Weapons to Influence Cognitive Behavior. *International Journal of Cyber Society and Education*, 5(2), 127-150.

Poulsen, K. (2008, March 28). Hackers assault epilepsy patients via computer. *WIRED*.

Pratkanis, A. R. (1992). The cargo-cult science of subliminal persuasion. *Skeptical Inquirer*, 16(3), 260-272.

Qibai, C. Y. H., & Shi, H. (2004). An investigation on the physiological and psychological effects of infrasound on persons. *Journal of Low Frequency Noise, Vibration and Active Control*, 23(1), 71-76.

Radcliffe, J. (2011). Hacking medical devices for fun and profit: Breaking the human SCADA system. In proceedings of *Black Hat USA*.

Rid, T. (2013). Cyberwar and peace: Hacking can reduce real-world violence. *Foreign Affairs*, 92(6), 77-87.

Robey, D., & Taggart, W. (1982). Human Information Processing in Information and Decision Support Systems. *MIS Quarterly*, 6(2), 61-73.

Smagowska, B., & Pawlaczyk-Łuszczyńska, M. (2013). Effects of ultrasonic noise on the human body – a bibliographic review. *International Journal of Occupational Safety and Ergonomics*, 19(2), 195-202.

Smith, S. D., Nixon, C. W., & Von Gierke, H. E. (2005). Damage risk criteria for hearing and human body vibration. In I.L. Ver & L.L. Beranek (eds.), *Noise and Vibration Control Engineering: Principles and Applications*, Second Edition, 857-886. John Wiley & Sons.

Srull, T. K., & Wyer, R. S. (1989). Person memory and judgment. *Psychological Review*, 96(1), 58-83.

Stewart, P. A., & Schubert, J. N. (2006). Taking the "Low Road" with Subliminal Advertisements: A Study Testing the Effect of Precognitive Prime "RATS" in a 2000 Presidential Advertisement. *Harvard International Journal of Press/Politics*, 11(4), 103-114.

Stidham, J. (2001). Can hackers turn your lights off? The vulnerability of the US power grid to electronic attack. *SANS Institute InfoSec Reading Room.*

Sturm, L., Williams, C., Camelio, J., White, J., & Parker, R. (2014). Cyber-physical vulnerabilities in additive manufacturing systems. *Context*, 7(8), 951-963.

Thomas, T. L. (1998a). The mind has no firewall. *The US Army War College Quarterly: Parameters*, 28(1), 12.

Thomas, T. L. (1998b). Dialectical versus empirical thinking: ten key elements of the Russian understanding of Information Operations. *The Journal of Slavic Military Studies,* 11(1), 40-62.

Torres, R., Tirado, G., Roman, A., Ramirez, R., Colon, H., Araujo, A., ... & Lopo Tuna, J. (2001). Vibroacoustic disease induced by long-term exposure to sonic booms. In proceedings of *Inter-Noise and Noise-Con Congress and Conference* (Vol. 2001, No. 3, pp. 2278-2281).

Trappey, C. (1996). A meta-analysis of consumer choice and subliminal advertising. *Psychology and Marketing*, 13(5), 517-530.

Vinokur, R. (2004). Acoustic noise as a non-lethal weapon. *Sound and Vibration*, 38(10), 19-23.

To: ███████████████████████
From: B2
CC/BCC: B1
Date: 19 December 2014
Subject: RE: Re: RED SOUND - Proposed experiment

Spoke to Karen earlier. There are a lot of caveats with some of these, although it's a good start. I think we were thinking of something slightly different... free for a coffee?

Philip

To: ███████████████████████
From: B2
CC/BCC:
Date: 9 February 2015
Subject: RE: RED WORD

My thoughts exactly. Let's run it past Karen.

Philip

To: ███████████████████████
From: B1
CC/BCC: B2
Date: 9 February 2015
Subject: RE: WORD

Yes.

K.

THE CRUCIVERBALIST

A short play by Marlow Tannhauser

AN EMPTY BUS STOP WITH THREE SEATS.
PAUL, A COMMUTER, ENTERS, CARRYING A
NEWSPAPER. HE SITS AND STARTS WORKING
ON THE CROSSWORD.
MADELEINE EARNSHAW ENTERS, TAKING THE
SEAT FURTHEST FROM PAUL.

MADELEINE: Excuse me?

PAUL IGNORES HER.

Excuse me?

PAUL: Yes?

MADELEINE: Does the 168 stop here?

PAUL: Hope so.

MADELEINE: Thanks. I don't travel this way very
often.

SHE FIDGETS, HUMMING A LILTING MELODY
TO HERSELF.
PAUL IS ENGROSSED IN THE CROSSWORD, BUT
FROWNS AT THE HUMMING.

Chilly, isn't it?

PAUL: Mmm.

MADELEINE: Where are you off to, this time of
night? Heading home?

PAUL: Mmm.

MADELEINE: Me too. I'm starving. Can't wait to
put some dinner on.

PAUL DOESN'T RESPOND.

It's—

PAUL: I'm trying to concentrate.

MADELEINE: Right. Sorry.

A SILENCE.

It's just - it's nice having someone
to talk to. Especially at night. I
hate travelling alone. It's scary.

*PAUL PUTS THE PAPER DOWN ON THE MIDDLE
SEAT. HE LOOKS AT MADELEINE FOR THE
FIRST TIME.*

PAUL: It's fine. Long journey?

MADELEINE: Very long. The other end of the route.

PAUL: Debden?

MADELEINE: Are you doing the crossword?

PAUL: I was.

MADELEINE MOVES NEXT TO PAUL.

MADELEINE: Oh, you're doing the cryptic! You
must be very clever, I can never work
them out. Let's see. One across. "Dish
containing pig could make you ill",
eight letters. You've put "pathogen".
I don't get it.

PAUL: Well, here 'containing' means there's
one word inside another. Another word
for 'pig' is 'hog', which is inside
the word 'paten' - a kind of dish. And
a 'pathogen' can make you ill.

MADELEINE: I wish my mind worked like that. OK,
how about three across - "They are
crossed here". Five letters.

191

PAUL: Words. Crosswords, you see. Although I think they missed a trick.

MADELEINE: How so?

PAUL: An anagram of 'words' is 'sword', so they could have done something with 'crossing swords'.

MADELEINE: That's so clever. You're not just a pretty face, are you? Tell me one more, go on. And then I'll leave you in peace, I promise.

PAUL: No, no, that's alright. OK, four across. You have a go. 'Roll a die for inspiration.' Four letters.

MADELEINE: Oh, I'm going to be awful at this.

PAUL: I could give you a hand.

MADELEINE: I bet you could.

PAUL: Ha. Erm. OK, so, 'roll' tells you it's probably an anagram – it's an indicator. That means 'a die' must be the fodder. So how can you rearrange 'a die' to mean 'inspiration'?

MADELEINE: How can you rearrange – oh! It's 'idea', isn't it? I did it!

SHE GRABS PAUL'S ARM, DELIGHTED.

I'm Madeleine, by the way.

PAUL: Paul.

MADELEINE: It's so lovely to meet you, Paul. It's not every day I find such a clever new friend.

PAUL: Oh, I'm not that clever.

MADELEINE: And so handsome, too.

PAUL: Well – that's neither here nor there.

MADELEINE: So tell me - what do you do, Paul?

PAUL: I'm a writer.

MADELINE: Are you? Are you really?

PAUL: And how about you?

MADELEINE: Give me another clue, go on. I'm
          having fun.

          PAUL HESITATES, THEN CONTINUES.

PAUL: "Organise the priests for a banquet".
          Six letters.

MADELEINE: You'll have to start me off, I think.

PAUL: 'Organise' is another indicator.

MADELEINE: So I have to rearrange something.
          'Priests'?

PAUL: Ah, well, this one's different. It's
          an indirect anagram.

MADELEINE: My goodness, what does that mean?

PAUL: It's something setters do sometimes,
          although it's a bit unfair. It means
          you have to rearrange a synonym for
          the fodder.

MADELEINE: So I need to find another word for
          priests?

PAUL: With six letters.

MADELEINE: And then rearrange it? To get a word
          meaning 'a banquet'?

PAUL: Like I said, it's a bit unfair.

MADELEINE: I think I might have it.

PAUL: Oh yes?

MADELINE: Well, a 'spread' can be a banquet,

                    193

can't it? And 'spread' is an anagram
of 'padres'.

PAUL: Very… wow, that's very good. You catch
on quickly.

MADELEINE: I do, don't I?

*SHE TOUCHES HIS ARM AGAIN, LETTING HER
HAND LINGER.*

Tell me about yourself, Paul. Do you
like riddles, too?

PAUL: Oh… yes. Riddles, crosswords. Anything
that leads me up the garden path,
really.

MADELEINE: I used to try, but I lose interest too
quickly. Always moving on to the next
thing, that's my problem. I've got
other talents.

PAUL: Such as?

MADELEINE LAUGHS AND FLICKS HER HAIR.

MADELEINE: Now that would be telling.

A BRIEF, CHARGED SILENCE.

So, the next one. "I'm back in pledge
control", eight letters.

PAUL: I haven't looked at that one yet.

MADELEINE: I'm sure we can… tackle it.

*SHE MOVES CLOSER TO HIM, SO THEIR
SHOULDERS ARE TOUCHING.*

PAUL: Right. Yes. Well, 'I'm back' suggests
we take the letters 'IM' and reverse
them. So we have 'MI' in the middle of
another word.

MADELEINE: Would that other word mean 'pledge'
or… 'control'?

PAUL: Definitions are usually at the end
               of crossword clues, so it's probably
               'pledge'. A six-letter word, then.

MADELEINE: 'Supply'?

PAUL: I don't think… Oh, I know what it is.
               'Donate'. If you add 'MI' to 'donate',
               you can get 'dominate', which means
               'control'.

MADELEINE: We make a good team, don't we?

               *SHE HIGH-FIVES HIM, BUT AS THEIR HANDS
               TOUCH, SHE FOLDS HER FINGERS AROUND
               HIS, BEFORE RELEASING.*

PAUL: So, you're… are you going home alone?

MADELEINE: Now that would be telling.

               *MADELEINE LAUGHS AND FLICKS HER HAIR IN
               EXACTLY THE SAME WAY AS BEFORE.*

PAUL: Ha… Yes, right.

MADELEINE: I have a riddle I'm trying to solve.
               Would you like to hear it?

PAUL: Sure.

               *MADELEINE LEANS IN, AND WHISPERS IN
               PAUL'S EAR. HE FROWNS, AS THOUGH HE
               DOESN'T UNDERSTAND.*

               I don't… I—

MADELEINE: It's a thinker. Let's have another
               clue.

PAUL: Yes. Right. How about this |/!/2|_
               |$—❶
               "Prisoner bond leads to puzzle".

MADELEINE: Ooh, I don't know. What do you think?

               *PAUL TRIES TO CONCENTRATE, A LITTLE
               DISTRACTED AND UNCOMFORTABLE.*

195

PAUL: Erm… well, a 'prisoner' is |/!/2|_|$a
            'con', and 'bond'… well, that
            |/!/2|_|$ be… no, wait, let me think
            about the |/!/2|_|$ first. Puzzle.
            Oh, I see. 'Con' plus |/!/2|_|$ is
            |/!/2|_|$.

MADELEINE:The bus is taking a long time, isn't
            it? Any luck with that riddle?

            PAUL SHAKES HIS HEAD, COUGHING.

            It'll come to you. Let's do another.
            "100 breakouts result in collision".
            Seven letters.

PAUL: |/!/2|_|$ means 'c' at the start,
            and |/!/2|_|$ |/!/2|_|$ so |/!/2|_|$
            '|/!/2|_|$' could mean…

MADELEINE:'Crashes', yes. And one more.
            "Leaderless phantom holds party". Four
            letters.

PAUL: |/!/2|_|$ |/!/2|_|$ |/!/2|_|$
            |/!/2|_|$ |/!/2|_|$, |/!/2|_|$
            |/!/2|_|$. So |/!/2|_|$ |/!/2|_|$.
            '|/!/2|_|$.'

MADELEINE:How are you feeling, Paul?

            PAUL STARES AT HER, |/!/2|_|$.

PAUL: |/!/2|_|$ |/!/2|_|$ |/!/2|_|$
            |/!/2|_|$ |/!/2|_|$!
            |/!/2|_|$|/!/2|_|$|/!/2|_|$

MADELEINE:Yes, quite. Thank you, Paul. You've
            given me a tremendous amount of help.

            *MADELEINE STANDS UP AND EXITS WITHOUT
            |/!/2|_|$ WHILE |/!/2|_|$ |/!/2|_|$
            LEFT |/!/2|_|$ |/!/2|_|$ |/!/2|_|$
            |/!/2|_|$ |/!/2|_|$ STARING |/!/2|_|$
            |/!/2|_|$ |/!/2|_|$ AFRAID.*

PAUL: |/!/2|_|$!|/!/2|_|$|/!/2|_|$|/!/2|_|$!

|/!/2|_|$|/!/2|_|$|/!/2|_|$|/!/2|_|$|/
!/2|_|$|/!/2|_|$|/!/2|_|$|/!/2|_|$|/!/
2|_|$|/!/2|_|$|/!/2|_|$|/!/2|_|$|/!/2|
_|$|/!/2|_|$|/!/2|_|$|/!/2|_|$

BUT |/!/2|_|$|/!/2|_|$ |/!/2|_|$ |/!/2
|_|$|/!/2|_|$|/!/2|_|$|/!/2|_|$|/!/2|_
|$|/!/2|_|$|/!/2|_|$|/!/2|_|$|/!/2|_|$
|/!/2|_|$|/!/2|_|$|/!/2|_|$|/!/2|_|$

|/!/2|_|$|/!/2|_|$|/!/2|_|$|/!/2|_|$|/
!/2|_|$|/!/2|_|$|/!/2|_|$|/!/2|_|$|/!/
2|_|$|/!/2|_|$|/!/2|_|$|/!/2|_|$

|/!/2|_|$|/!/2|_|$|/!/2|_|$|/!/2|_|$|/
!/2|_|$|/!/2|_|$|/!/2|_|$|/!/2|_|$|/!/
2|_|$|/!/2|_|$|/!/2|_|$|/!/2|_|$|/!/2|
_|$|/!/2|_|$|/!/2|_|$|/!/2|_|$|/!/2|_|
$|/!/2|_|$|/!/2|_|$|/!/2|_|$|/!/2|_|$|
/!/2|_|$|/!/2|_|$|/!/2|_|$|/!/2|_|$|/!
/2|_|$|/!/2|_|$|/!/2|_|$|/!/2|_|$

|/!/2|_|$ |/!/2|_|$|/!/2|_|$|/!/2|_|$|/!/2|_|$

|/!/2|_|$|/!/2|_|$|/!/2|_|$|/!/2|_|$|/
!/2|_|$|/!/2|_|$|/!/2|_|$|/!/2|_|$|/!/
2|_|$|/!/2|_|$|/!/2|_|$

|/!/2|_|$|/!/2|_|$|/!/2|_|$|/!/2|_|$

|/!/2|_|$|/!/2|_|$|/!/2|_|$|/!/2|_|$|/
!/2|_|$|/!/2|_|$|/!/2|_|$|/!/2|_|$|/!/
2|_|$|/!/2|_|$|/!/2|_|$|/!/2|_|$|/!/2|
_|$|/!/2|_|$

|/!/2|_|$

|/!/2|_|$|/!/2|_|$|/!/2|_|$|/!/2|_|$|/!/2|_|
$|/!/2|_|$|/!/2|_|$|/!/2|_|$|/!/2|_|$|/!/2|_
|$|/!/2|_|$|/!/2|_|$|/!/2|_|$|/!/2|_|$|/!/2|
_|$|/!/2|_|$|/!/2|_|$|/!/2|_|$|/!/2|_|$

§

|/!/2|_|$|/!/2|_|$|/!/2|_|$|/!/2|_|$|/!/2|_|
$|/!/2|_|$

§

197

|/!/2|_|$ |/!/2|_|$ |/!/2|_|$ |/!/2|_|$
|/!/2|_|$ and tell them to |/!/2|_|$ something,
and |/!/2|_|$ comply, have I not |/!/2|_|$
remote code execution? By transmitting words,
|/!/2|_|$ through the air as vibrations, I
inject |/!/2|_|$ words into someone else's
head, where they are interpreted, and turned
|/!/2|_|$ commands.

§

And, like malware, perhaps there are |/!/2|_|$
vulnerabilities making up this workflow which
could be exploited. A buffer overflow❶ in the
human mind, |/!/2|_|$ a crash?

§

Is recovery possible?

§

Does it MATTER?

§

Psychologists at the University of Virginia
found that people would rather receive
electric shocks than be left alone with their
thoughts. Are we bored? Or just terrified of
our own CONSCIOUSNESS?

§

WHY???

§

I sit on the very verge of history. I stare
into its abyss and I prepare to step out into
thin air.

§

Holly Soames①
13/11/2019 23:58
A type of vulnerability
where a software
application has not
allocated a large
enough memory
buffer for input, or
doesn't check the
bounds of memory
for user-supplied
input. An attacker
can overflow the
buffer, manipulate
the execution flow
of the program, and
cause their own code
to be executed rather
than the original
code.

RED WORD. A weapon of words and thought, of language. My employers were only too pleased to give me a long leash.

In the next chapter we'll talk about this weapon. We'll talk and talk and talk. In the meantime, a little crossword puzzle for you.

ACROSS

3. A rare drug to protect one's behind! (9)
4. You! So Lîgotti says - who âm I to argue? (6)
6. Put it on a shoulder, for protection (5)
7. If I recall côrrectly we uséd thîs to talk initially (3)
8. Heartless ghoul has a need to scratch - maybe has bugs? (6)
11. Follow-up to prison for this virus (10)
13. Jumble the old pens for reliability (7)
14. Pops up a ship - with a kiss bêforehand! (3)
18. Stirred our tuna so we could start straight away (7)
19. Sçans memory for tall tower lackîng top (7)
20. Leader had a lot of gall (6)
21. Fibre for multitasking (6)

DOWN

1. Basilisk (8)
2. They use ódd cool ports to communicate (9)
3. Find the source, then the gear, for înfection (7)
4. Support following Ralph's mate, or just trying to get something for free? (9)
5. Steal a previoúsly filtered liquid (10)
9. Wagner's course director (8)
10. Previous plan I got inside to take advantage (7)
12. Parâsite without the music - tell me the location! (7)
15. An old worm made me feel blue (7)
16. Right inside the coast, for a break (6)
17. Sounds like military officer is in deêp (6)

199

So many of the puzzles we face have no solution.
Isn't it nice to have something with ANSWERS?

I hope you're having fun.

I AM I AM I AM.

I'll miss you!
|/!/2|_|$
;)

All best,
The Helmsman.

|/!/2|_|$: CRYPTIC
c. MAY 2019 / MARCH–MAY 2018

Holly Soames①
19/11/2019 00:40
c3 THT.

|/!/2|_|$ straying to Shane Carson and Sarah Mayers. They are links, and the links are everywhere, lines spreading across my wall like veiny threads. I wonder if there are branches as yet unseen; whether, like a Merkle tree, there is a root, a genesis block, a first infection. A patient zero? The Helmsman said it would be him, ❶ *and what happened that first time? What was it like?*

Slamming his head into a laptop over and

A takeover, a hijacking not of cell machinery but of the mind. Colonies upon colonies. Aliens in our soil.

Trapped in an infinite loop. Glitching. Bugs. Kernel panic. Segfault. How How long before the device is brix bricked

He lives in my head rent-fucking-free.

Scorched earth. Synapses torched out and burnt out. Neurons decayed and blank like dead pixels. What was once neon flooding the darkness with brilliant, abundant, fertile power is now a guttering flare, now just a few sparks, which flicker, wink out, to leave you cold and unsighted in idiot night.

It isn't easy – perhaps not even useful – to try to situate The Helmsman's weapon in the context of malware, because it appears to have so little in common with the techniques and tricks of our industry. Nevertheless, whatever it is, it is still something designed by a hacker to exploit a vulnerability. And its objectives – to hurt, to kill – are arguably a natural consequence of the progressively destructive and harmful history of malware.

The concept of computer viruses was born in 1949 with von Neumann, who proposed a program capable of replicating itself,❶ but it wasn't until 1971 that the first 'virus' came about with Creeper,❷ which was born on the ARPANET, the predecessor of the internet. It was a primitive lifeform, able only to display a simple terminal message before transferring itself across antique DEC PDP-10 mainframe computers.

Holly Soames①
14/11/2019 10:03

WEBSTER is probably referring to 'Theory and organization of complicated automata'.

Reply   Resolve

Holly Soames②
14/11/2019 10:37

See https://www.techspot.com/trivia/130-what-first-computer-virus/, author/date unknown.

Reply   Resolve

```
BBN-TENEX 1.25, BBN EXEC 1.30
@FULL
@LOGIN RT
JOB 3 ON TTY12 08-APR-72
YOU HAVE A MESSAGE
@SYSTAT
UP 85:33:19 3 JOBS
LOAD AV 3.87 2.95 2.14
JOB     TTY     USER            SUBSYS
1       DET     SYSTEM          NETSER
2       DET     SYSTEM          TIPSER
3       12      RT              EXEC
@
I'M THE CREEPER : CATCH ME IF YOU CAN
```

At some point between 1974 and 1978, the first virus which could cause actual damage was released. Wabbit❸ continually copied itself to the point of

Holly Soames③
14/11/2019 10:46
Likely derived from the capacity of rabbits to rapidly reproduce.

Holly Soames①
14/11/2019 11:02
i.e. denial of service
(DoS). Today, the term
'rabbit virus' persists
as an uncommon
synonym for a 'fork
bomb', a type of attack
whereby processes
continually 'fork' until
a system crashes.
See 'The problem
of computer code:
Leviathan or common
power' by Adrian
MACKENZIE (2003) and
catb.org/~esr/jargon/
html/W/wabbit.html by
Eric RAYMOND, 2004.

Holly Soames②
14/11/2019 11:23
WEBSTER makes
a good point here.
Further background:
'Paleovirology: Exploring
malware antiquities', a
2013 DEF CON talk by
Rick GENTLING.

Holly Soames③
14/11/2019 12:12
Background: 'Computer
viruses: A form of
artificial life?' by Eugene
H. SPAFFORD, in a book
called *Artificial Life II*
(1992). SPAFFORD also
makes the interesting
point that the etymology
of 'worm' as a form
of computer virus
originates from the term
'tapeworm' in a science-
fiction novel, used to
denote a computer
program which
traversed networks.

Holly Soames④
14/11/2019 12:20
See 'Bootkits: Past,
present and future',
a 2014 Virus Bulletin
conference talk by
D.H. RODIONOV
and others, which
discussed Elk Cloner.

resource exhaustion,❶ although it is unclear whether it was designed to cause disruption. This is one of the problems of paleovirology – the early days of security are ill-documented, the facts hidden in half-remembered anecdotes, dead links, and citations which lead nowhere.❷

Many examples of 'malware' in those prelapsarian times sought to perform no explicitly malevolent actions. Elk Cloner,❸ (for instance, written by a fifteen-year-old schoolboy in 1981 or 1982, infected Apple DOS 3.3 computers and presented itself as a game which on the fiftieth execution would display a poem.❹

```
         RTS
REPORT   ASC  'BOOT COUNT: '
         DFB  $0
POEM     ASC  'ELK CLONER:'
         DFB  $8D,$8D,$8D
         ASC  'IT WILL GET ON ALL YOUR DISKS'
         DFB  $8D
         ASC  'IT WILL INFILTRATE YOUR CHIPS'
         DFB  $8D
         ASC  'YES IT'
         DFB  $A7
         ASC  'S CLONER!'
         DFB  $8D,$8D
         ASC  'IT WILL STICK TO YOU LIKE GLUE'
         DFB  $8D
         ASC  'IT WILL MODIFY RAM TOO'
         DFB  $8D
         ASC  'SEND IN THE CLONER!'
         DFB  $8D,$8D,$8D,$8D,$0
IOERR    LDY  #>ERRMSG
         LDY  #<ERRMSG
         JSR  PRINT
         JSR  $FBDD
         JMP  $9DBF
```

Annoying, of course, and the perpetrator was apparently well-known for disseminating altered floppy disks as pranks, to the extent that after a while nobody would accept them from him anymore.**❶** However, as illustrated by the second chapter of *The Helmsman Texts* – in fact, by the existence of The Helmsman's work itself – the field has become more vicious in recent times.

And, apposite to The Helmsman, one of the first viruses to target a personal computer is sometimes referred to as the 'Brain' virus,**❷** released in 1986. In keeping with the artless innocence of the times, the Brain virus displayed a message with the addresses and phone numbers of its authors.**❸**

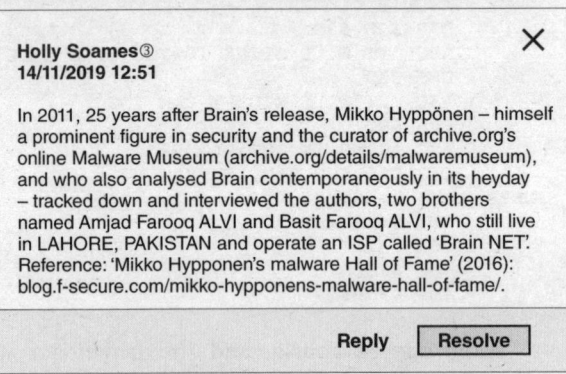

Holly Soames③
14/11/2019 12:51   ✕

In 2011, 25 years after Brain's release, Mikko Hyppönen – himself a prominent figure in security and the curator of archive.org's online Malware Museum (archive.org/details/malwaremuseum), and who also analysed Brain contemporaneously in its heyday – tracked down and interviewed the authors, two brothers named Amjad Farooq ALVI and Basit Farooq ALVI, who still live in LAHORE, PAKISTAN and operate an ISP called 'Brain NET'. Reference: 'Mikko Hypponen's malware Hall of Fame' (2016): blog.f-secure.com/mikko-hypponens-malware-hall-of-fame/.

Reply | **Resolve**

Much like the Wabbit virus, the infamous Morris worm**❹** (1988) was intended to be an experiment. Created by Robert Morris, graduate student and son of an NSA cryptographer, it exploited vulnerabilities in

Holly Soames④
14/11/2019 13:02
Background: 'The Morris worm: A fifteen-year perspective' by Hilarie ORMAN (2003).

several Unix applications before copying itself to other vulnerable machines. Several design flaws – including an aggressive replication model which meant that a host could be infected multiple times – led to DoS conditions on many computers around the world, causing thousands  of dollars' worth of disruption.❶ Morris was the first person to receive a felony conviction under the then very new 1986 Computer Fraud and Abuse Act.*

Holly Soames①
14/11/2019 13:15

WEBSTER is necessarily vague on the exact cost here, but the damage was estimated to be somewhere between $100,000 and $10,000,000, based on an estimate of cost for disinfection per machine (see https://www.hypr.com/security-encyclopedia/morris-worm, author/date unknown), although there is some contention as to the total number of infected machines (e.g. see 'The Submarine' by Paul GRAHAM (2005): paulgraham.com/submarine.html).

Reply

Holly Soames②
14/11/2019 13:34

Further background from this period: 'Panic computing: the viral metaphor and computer technology' by Deborah LUPTON (1994).

Reply   Resolve

The Morris worm and others of its generation released a creature which could not be put back in its cage. In 1991 the Michelangelo virus caused the first, but certainly not the last, malware-inspired global panic.❷

*https://en.wikipedia.org/wiki/Morris_worm#/media/File:Morris_Worm.jpg. CC BY-SA 2.0 (https://creativecommons.org/licenses/by-sa/2.0/deed.en). Attribution: GoCard USA/gocardboston.com/Shannon B. Image unchanged.

Much like Conficker almost twenty years later,❶ the hysteria was the result of a date: 6 March (Michelangelo's day of birth, natch). On this date❷ the virus would overwrite a certain portion of the hard disk on infected computers, meaning that users would be unable to access their data. As it approached, people began, for the first time, to collectively lose their shit over a computer virus.❸ The Michelangelo virus was the first indication that the days of Creeper, Brain and Wabbit were over. From 1992 onwards, hacking and malware became commodified on both sides of the struggle, no longer an intellectual pursuit or prelapsarian game. Black hats realised they could make a living by writing viruses and using them to steal money and information, and white hats realised they could make a living trying to stop them. In some respects, both groups profited from the fear and ignorance of the general public, and very little has

Holly Soames②
14/11/2019 14:17
WEBSTER is correct here, although note that the malware authors likely did not choose this date because it was Michelangelo's DOB. There was nothing else about the virus that referenced Michelangelo. It was named by researchers who spotted the (presumably coincidental) link.

Holly Soames③
14/11/2019 14:29
Background: 'Measuring and modeling computer virus prevalence' by Jeffrey O. KEPHART and Steve R. WHITE (1993).

Holly Soames①
22/11/2019 12:19

Conficker = a worm which propagated in 2008 and 2009, affected millions of machines and was one of the largest worm infections of all time. Like Michaelangelo it had a 'date trigger' – 1 APRIL 2009 – upon which all infected systems would contact a remote source for instructions. At this point Conficker had infected not only home machines but also government organisations, hospitals, and banking and manufacturing industries. Nothing happened on 1 APRIL. (Background: *Worm: The First Digital World War* by Mark BOWDEN, 2012). Various other viruses have had some form of trigger date built into their code, such as the Chernobyl or CIH virus, which was designed to delete data on 26 APRIL, the day of birth of the virus author as well as, coincidentally, the date of the CHERNOBYL disaster (virus.wikidot.com/cih, Virus Encyclopedia, date/author unknown). And a 2005 variant of the Sober worm caused infected hosts to send emails in support of far-right political parties in GERMANY, and had a trigger date of 5 JANUARY, the anniversary of the founding of the Nazi party. ('Sober variant has mysterious agenda for Nazi anniversary' by Josh FRUHLINGER (2005): https://www.computerworld.com/article/2808191/sober-variant-has-mysterious-agenda-for-nazi-anniversary.html). WEBSTER may mention the concept of a date trigger here because in c5 THT, THE HELMSMAN notes that on some unknown date, c6 THT – the one supposedly containing the weapon – will be released worldwide.

Reply   Resolve

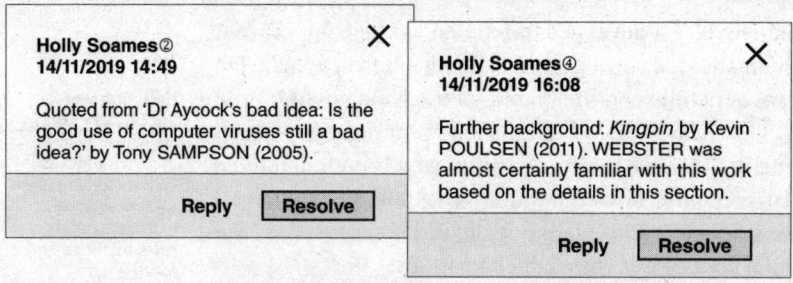

changed in the interim. How far we have fallen. From innocent poems to The Helmsman, one could argue that our world became fiercer than anyone expected. I'd question whether it's even the same world at all.

But grey hats – the chaotic neutrals who obey and break laws as it suits them – also play a role in the malware ecosystem. A grey hat I've been thinking about recently is Max Ray Vision, formerly known as Max Ray Butler, also known as Iceman, and the anti-worm❶ he created in 1998.

As viruses evolved from the "digital equivalent of a can of spray paint"❷ to programs capable of causing billions of dollars of damage, some researchers❸ began to propose that 'good' viruses could become a valuable weapon in the war against malware, and this proposal would be resurrected at fairly regular intervals over the next twenty years.

You can work out for yourself that there might be ethical issues with running code on people's computers without their knowledge or consent, no matter how good your intentions might be. And whenever someone in security wants to shit on the idea of anti-worms, they bring up Max Vision.❹

Vision was a pentester, just like Jay and I were, and ran a now-defunct website called whitehats.com,* which included a database of attack signatures❺ called

---

* Which is almost unbelievably on-the-nose, but there you go.

arachNIDS ('advanced reference archive of current heuristics for network intrusion detection systems'). He was generally considered one of the good guys. ❶

In May 1998, a buffer overflow vulnerability affecting BIND, a nameserver daemon which underpinned a large portion of websites and other internet resources, was discovered; exploiting it allowed an attacker to take total control of a vulnerable machine.

A black hat group known as The ADM Crew ❷ developed a worm which exploited the BIND vulnerability to install a backdoor account and propagate itself, and due to the severity of the flaw, the worm began to spread rapidly. Vision, as the operator of whitehats.com and arachNIDS, analysed it, ❸ including notes on its behaviour and code, and possible countermeasures. At the same time, however, he was also, unbeknownst to his FBI handlers, planning something very different: an anti-worm.

* * *

Vision's worm, like ADM's, exploited the BIND vulnerability and scanned for other vulnerable hosts in order to replicate, but the crucial difference was in its payload: after infection, Vision's worm attempted to *patch* the vulnerability.

I find myself wondering about Vision's state of mind at the time. Poulsen writes that he was excited, "his mind hostage to an idea", and I can relate to that. I wonder also if he was at all apprehensive, even frightened, about the thing he was contemplating, whether he had any idea what he was risking. I wonder if he had even the slightest inkling that what he was about to do would lead to him becoming one of the most prolific and notorious cybercriminals of all time. I wonder if he cared; after all, satisfaction is a lie.

Vision's anti-worm targeted military and government servers – those he considered most at risk from

Holly Soames ①
14/11/2019 16:39
He was also an informant for the FBI at this time (predominantly writing reports on vulnerabilities and malware), according to POULSEN.

Holly Soames ②
14/11/2019 17:00
Indices searches from partners indicate this was a possibly Germany-based threat actor, now defunct, which also notably hacked the DEF CON website in 1999 (see also virus.wikidot.com/adm, date/author unknown).

Holly Soames ③
14/11/2019 17:27
VISION's analysis is available at ouah.org/admworm.htm.

the ADM worm – and perhaps things might have still worked out if he hadn't, for some reason which only he can explain, designed his anti-worm to include a backdoor. Every time it patched a vulnerable system it also provided him with permanent, covert access to it.

As the number of anti-worm infections – Air Force, Navy, Army, federal government, even a game developer's site **❶** – grew, so quickly that at one point the notifications of new infections caused his computer to crash, Vision's project began to get noticed, and eventually, it was attributed to him.

At first, the FBI wasn't overly concerned, seeing it as an opportunity to develop Vision further as an informant by holding it over his head and thereby persuading him to communicate with other hacking groups and passing the logs to the FBI. This culminated in Vision being sent to DEF CON to obtain the real names and public PGP keys of hackers. Vision, uncomfortable with this, provided nothing, and also skipped a meeting with his FBI handler. Once he sought legal advice, he probably became more trouble than he was worth to the FBI, which promptly arrested him. Vision pled guilty and was sentenced to eighteen months in prison.

In the four years between his release and next arrest, Vision turned to serious cybercrime, eventually running one of the largest carding forums **❷** ever to exist, CardersMarket. He was eventually brought down, again, by the FBI. One of their agents, J. Keith Mularski, worked undercover online for several years and became an administrator of a rival carding forum under the name Master Splyntr.

In 2010 Vision was sentenced to thirteen years in prison, the longest sentence ever handed down for hacking at the time. He is still in prison as I write, and who knows what sort of person will step out when he is released.

Holly Soames①
14/11/2019 18:37
According to POULSEN, VISION stole the source code for *Quake III*, which at the time was unreleased, from the servers of id Software.

Holly Soames②
14/11/2019 19:38
A criminal forum which trades in stolen credit card data.

So what does this tell us, this sad story, this trawl through long-ago crimes and good intentions?

It tells us that someone like Max Vision – by all accounts a creative and highly capable hacker – can be a victim both of themselves and the society in which they had the misfortune to operate, beholden to their impulses, a member of a culture which, if not shunned outright, is nevertheless ill-understood by most people. Our crime is curiosity, and we are punished for it. The cost, more often than not, is too much to bear.

But Vision's story also tells us that, ethical and legal objections aside, attack can function as an effective form of defence. Every example – Reaper, HUNTER, Welchia, Hajime, BrickerBot,❶ Vision's anti-ADM worm – tells us the same thing: sometimes cleaning up means getting dirty.

Holly Soames①
15/11/2019 00:11
All examples of other anti-worms.

Which begs the question: could something like an anti-worm be used against The Helmsman's weapon – some cognitive antidote for the thought that changes everything, whatever it is? Could someone patch a human brain? Force it to assimilate the opposite, embrace the paradox, comprehend the ouroboros?

Physician, heal thyself.

* * *

"Mr Salas was looking for you," Milo said today, when I got in late and had squeezed myself into the tiny office. "Told him you were coming in later."

"Oh," I said, massaging my head. "Thanks."

I had a headache, one of the worst I have ever had, the type where it feels like someone is violently wringing your brain in their fists. Too many nights gazing at this screen.

Milo gave me a look, mouth half-cocked in a grizzled scowl. I wonder, if I went back far enough, whether I would find salty old sea-dogs in his lineage, buccaneers and mutineers and old sailors grinning at each other with murder in their eyes.

"Next time, call if you're going to be late," he said. "Had to cover your tickets."

I mentally shook myself awake. "Sorry, Milo. Did he say anything else?"

"Who? Otto? No."

I took off my coat, booted up my machine, and watched the screen come to life through the gaps in my interlaced fingers as I kneaded my forehead.

"You look like shit."

"Thanks."

"Alright?"

"Yeah, I'll be fine."

Milo grunted, his signal that the conversation was over.

I checked the tickets. Mrs Wright's iPad needed replacing (a broken screen), and a kid in Year 9 had triggered a WAF❶ rule after trying to access several blacklisted gaming sites in a row.*

I coughed hard and the throbbing in my head swelled. Yes, too many late nights, too many words. Or maybe it was like what they said about Slender Man – that once people encountered him they got sick. Coughs and fevers and paranoia, like coming too close to a source of radiation. Perhaps I'm getting too close to The Helmsman.

Holly Soames①
15/11/2019 10:16
WAF = web application firewall.

---

* I am always hopeful, when I see one of the latter types of ticket, that I will find a kid who is doing something out of the ordinary. Downloading Tor, or OllyDbg, or hashcat; or trying to perform SQL injection or escalating their privileges to administrator on the school network. Not because it would give me any thrill to investigate it, but because it would signify that I might not be not as alone as I feel. That someone else nearby is curious – that there is a hacker here, or at least a potential disciple. Someone I could mentor or instruct. Share the little knowledge I have to impart – or, rather, donate it, since I'm no longer using it. But there never is. It's just porn and gaming sites and social media and porn and torrents and porn.

"You're ill," Milo said.

"I said I'm fine."

"Don't want to catch it. Go home."

"The tickets—"

"I did some this morning anyway. Few more makes no difference. Go home."

When I opened my mouth to argue, the words which had been forming dissolved, corroded by contact with air.

I went home.

* * *

I sat on the Tube, willing the paracetamol I'd dry-swallowed to start its work, and stared blankly at a newspaper. It was open to the puzzles page, a crossword leering at me with a black, gap-toothed grin. I fucking hate crosswords.

Puzzles, and commuters, and weapons.

I got a pen out of my backpack. I think I wanted to write something down, something which had just occurred to me, but I don't remember what it was.

Out of the corner of my eye I saw the woman opposite looking at me. ❶

I lifted my head, ostensibly to peer at the Tube map above her, and caught a glimpse of her face through the smog of pain. My mouth opened; it was Sarah Mayers, with her wise, pointed face, thick black hair shining. I remember seeing her picture in the newspaper and thinking it was her best feature, by far. Everything else about her was spartan and angular, but her hair was gorgeous.

Today Sarah Mayers was wearing jeans and a padded, puffy black jacket, but that was ridiculous, of course. Sarah Mayers is not in any position to be out in public, and probably never will be again.

My gaze travelled back down from the map. I tried to avert my eyes, to the empty seats to her left, but of their own accord they met hers. They were brown, and without reason, and wider than eyes had any right to be.

She reached into a pocket and my hands involuntarily bunched into fists. She pulled out a phone and started scrolling through it until she found what she wanted, and then she leant forward. She reached out and put the phone in my face.

"Have you seen this? Have you seen this? Have you seen this?"

I looked away, which I put down to a reflexive instinct, a natural reaction to someone shoving something in your face. But thinking about it now, I believe I did it because I knew what was on the screen. It was The Helmsman's weapon. It was the sixth chapter.

Still holding the phone inches from me, she said, "Don't you want to see? I thought you *wanted* to see!"

"Not like that," I said, surprised at how calm my voice was.

She shrugged, sat back, and put her phone away.

When her hand came back out of her pocket it was holding a small black pistol. She put it to her temple and shot herself in the head.

The crack of the gun was almost lost in the howl of the tunnels but I felt it just the same, a sharp spear through my skull to go with the wringing fists, and as if in slow motion I saw her slump to the side and the blood gush from her nose.

As cleverer and more eloquent people than me have observed, you often have flashes of absurd thought in moments of trauma. As Sarah's blood dripped urgently from the seats onto the floor, I was thinking about how the patterns on Tube upholstery are carefully designed to be as intricate and multi-coloured as possible, complex geometric combinations of dark shades, so they don't show up the dirt and the dust, and I remember wondering if it would be enough to conceal blood. I remember wondering what else those patterns might hide, and whether we would still covet a seat on the Tube if we had any idea of the filth we sit in.

Then I knelt down and reached towards her. I'd like to think I was trying to help, even if it was just to mutter some incoherent last words of comfort or to close her eyes – clouding over, becoming glazed and opaque like ground glass – but I know myself, and I must be honest with myself, and with you, so I will admit what I was trying to do.

I wanted to retrieve her phone so I could copy what was on it before ██████████████████████ could get to it.

And this was despite the fact that at some level I was aware that none of this was real – that Sarah Mayers had not just killed herself in front of me. She couldn't have done, because Sarah Mayers doesn't even look like Sarah Mayers anymore, and Sarah Mayers hasn't moved of her own volition in a very long time.

When I reached out, the woman lying on the floor with blood over her face like a mask spoke in a clear and frightened voice.

"What are you doing?"

I blinked and looked up. The woman sitting opposite me bore a passing resemblance to the woman Sarah Mayers had once been – thin face, thick black hair – but she was alive and well. No wound in her head or gun in her hand. She was shrinking back, scared, and I realised that I was still in my seat, reaching across the aisle to try and touch her.

I pulled my arm back. "Sorry," I said, trying to smile. "I thought you were someone else."

The woman gave me a suspicious look, and got off at the next stop. She didn't look back.

* * *

Sarah Mayers❶ was the first victim I found after Jay. She was a threat intelligence analyst at a large

Holly Soamesⓘ
15/11/2019 11:08
Suggest re-interviewing family and medical staff to clarify incident in light of new information. Previous investigation revealed no mention of or link to the game.

professional services firm. I was never able to ascertain how she found The Helmsman's game. Her colleagues didn't know, and her family, with the exception of her sister (who was unable to provide much information anyway), refused to speak to me.

What was apparent was that she had solved the final stage and received the last chapter. One of her colleagues vaguely remembered her mentioning something about it – the sixth part of an online game she was playing.

"The first five parts were really hard," she'd told them excitedly, "and the sixth took me ages! But I'm almost finished."

That was on a Wednesday.

On the following Saturday the Mayers threw a birthday party for their five-year-old daughter. At the party was the birthday girl, and Sarah and her husband, and both sets of in-laws, and two uncles and an aunt (Sarah's sister, who told me what happened). A couple of neighbours also attended with their children. There were presents, and cards, and balloons, and games, and music.

In the days leading up to the party Sarah had seemed out-of-sorts, her sister said, and her colleague had backed this up. She was distant and dreamy, as though preoccupied with something. At the party, people had to try several times to get her attention, and she watched her daughter unwrap presents with no visible sign of any emotion. She sat there, stiff, motionless, looking on.

The birthday cake arrived, impaled with candles as yet unlit.

Someone turned out the lights.

A chorus of 'Happy Birthday' started up. Sarah's sister told me that she looked at Sarah and noticed she wasn't singing, wasn't even smiling. I imagine her eyes gleaming in the patchy darkness.

There was a scratch and hiss of matches.

"Stand here, darling," Sarah's husband said to his daughter. "In front of Mummy, there you go. OK, now deep breath and blow out your candles!"

The child inhaled.

Sarah Mayers reached out an arm, plunged her hand into thick black hair so much like her own, wound her fingers up in it tightly and slammed the girl's head down into the lit candles. One pierced her eye-socket and travelled through into her brain, killing her instantly.

Sarah kept her hand on the back of her daughter's head, her fingers entwined in her hair, knuckles taut, even as the paramedics and the police arrived. She would not move – never really moved again. They had to cut the little girl's hair, Sarah's sister told me, to free it from Sarah's grip.

Today, she is catatonic – one of her nurses described it to me as acute akinetic catatonia – in a secure facility in which, in the near or distant future, she will die. I visited her once but it was a waste of both our time. Sarah acknowledged nothing I said, and I'm not sure my presence even registered. There was not the barest flicker of recognition behind her eyes when I asked her about The Helmsman. Whatever sort of presence – a self, a soul, however you might like to think of it – had once stirred in the vessel of Sarah Mayers, it had departed.

The Helmsman's weapon had accessed her brain, hollowed it out, and left no trace of itself or anything else.

* * *

I faltered my way back to my flat, headache ebbing and throbbing. I pushed open the front door and the photographs stuck up on the wall, lines in pencil connecting them, faces of blurred newsprint, watched me. For the first time I really saw that wall and realised that it could seem like the work of someone in trouble.

First principles, Aristotelian syllogisms. If we are fucked, then I am fucked.

Everything is everything else. We drink the same water the dinosaurs did, and we are all made of stars. All of us are related if you go back far enough. Links in an unbroken chain stretching back four billion years, organisms here through obscene good fortune.

I sat at my desk and ran my fingers through my hair, which is growing longer than I like it. I felt a tackiness, and brought my hands in front of my eyes.

There was blood on them.

I checked myself and found no cuts.

I need a break, I think. When I looked around at my flat, I saw the books and the clothes and the dirty plates on the floor. More in the sink. And I stank – how long since I had had a shower?

So I had one, long and hot, letting the water flow over me until the run-off faded from dark red to pink to clear, and I stayed in the hiss of warm steam, drawing shapes on the misted glass.

I have to give these things time.

To my almost tearful relief the headache began to fade, and once I'd dried off I tidied the flat and washed some of the dishes – trying not to look at the wall above my desk with its tales of chaos – and promptly dirtied several of them again in cooking the first proper meal I have had in a long time.* It wasn't anything spectacular – as I have mentioned before, I am something of a pleb

---

* It doesn't get talked about enough but there is a decidedly unhealthy aspect of hacking culture. With late-night work, often in addition to regular day jobs, comes energy drinks and fast food, caffeine, stimulants, alcohol. And the worst thing is that we glorify this; it's part of the legend. That this is a tacitly acknowledged fact in our world is evidenced by DEF CON implementing a 3-2-1 rule during its event: at a minimum, every day attendees should aim for three hours of sleep, two meals, and one shower. No, we don't make things easy for ourselves, but then perhaps we wouldn't be hackers if we did.

when it comes to cooking – just spaghetti, an old jar of tomato sauce I found lurking at the back of a cupboard, and some frozen chicken which I grilled and smothered in cayenne pepper and salt. It looked vile but I wolfed it down, and it tasted alright.

* * *

I turned on the television, meaning to find something I could lose myself in for an hour or so before writing, but as I flicked through the guide I found myself thinking, *what I really need is to speak to someone who was immune.*

Someone on whom The Helmsman's weapon had no effect. Someone who had found the sixth chapter, read the document or seen the image or whatever it was, and had experienced nothing – or who had been affected but recovered. Someone like that could tell me everything. What I need is Ken Onek. He's never spoken to me before – only through his proxies, The Rearguard – but there's no harm in trying again.

> I know you don't want to talk to me. I'm sorry. about everything. But please, I need your help. I need to talk to Ken. Please.

As I sent the DM,❶ my phone buzzed with a message from Otto.

> Milo said you'd gone home sick. U ok? xxx

> Just a headache. Feeling better.

> ok. Still up for dinner this weekend? xxx

I groaned. I'd forgotten about dinner with Otto's parents, but it's the price I have to pay. If it comes to it, I

Holly Soames①
15/11/2019 12:48
When found, WEBSTER'S phone had the Twitter app installed, but no account was logged in. Unable to find an account for her on open source.

can always feign another headache – assuming feigning is necessary – and leave early.

Sure x

    I dozed on the sofa, the headache finally breaking up in the dark, and the image projected onto my eyelids before sleep took me was of brown eyes turning muddy and cold as a bullet passed behind them.

* * *

At some point in the night there was a person standing over me. I think it was a man, although in the gloom I couldn't be sure. Whoever it was had a round face, and small eyes, but that's all I remember. They were standing at my head and looking down, so that I only had the briefest, upside-down impression of their features. There was no expression on their face.

    I remember thinking that I should scream, or scramble up, or strike out – that I should do *something* – but there was a strong, almost coercive sense that the person meant me no harm. On the contrary, they were filled with compassion and wanted only to help – with what exactly, I didn't know. The figure standing over me considered me a friend.

    I closed my eyes and went back to sleep.

* * *

Then it was morning, and thin sunlight stabbed through the window. I stretched and felt the shell of tiredness crack and fall away from my body like a moulted skin.

    I checked Twitter, and saw The Rearguard – one of them, anyway – had replied. I wasn't surprised; it is no less than I deserve.

fuck u

I made coffee, taking a second to whisper thanks for the fact that my headache was staying away, and fired up my laptop to make a few notes before work.

* * *

I'm on my own. Help isn't coming.

I'm here now, rookie. So. Of each thing, first ask: what is it in itself?

It's a weapon. Format unknown, but one which is capable of causing people to kill themselves, or other people, or otherwise act irrationally. To make them insane, if that's the right term. And The Helmsman

Forget The Helmsman. Forget ████████████
████████. *Forget The Rearguard. What is it, in itself?*

A weapon. Format unknown, but one which is

No. You're not listening. Forget the format, forget the effects. What is it, in itself?

It is not audio.

Correct.

It is not subliminal priming.

You can list things it isn't all you like, but

It is text, or video, or an image.

I told you to forget the format.

What do you want from me?

Do you think it matters? What if the format makes no difference?

Why wouldn't it?

Because format is a shell. A container, a wrapper, a capsid. An encapsulation for – what?

A basilisk.

Consisting of what?

An argument?

Maybe, but you have no way of knowing that. Where is your scientific uncertainty? Come on. Concentrate.

A thought experiment, then.

He said it wasn't that.

A thought.

220

Now we're getting somewhere. Yes. A thought.
An idea. A philosophy.

Even better. And potentially destructive regardless of the format, you see? That's the crucial thing.

Yes, but I've already

It is unlikely to be an original thought. That's important. Unusual, perhaps, but not wholly original. There's no such thing.

Then I might have

Precisely.

So I could be

Oh yes. How do you know you're not?

I don't.

Proceed on that basis.

"At least we know what the premise is now," Jay said.

We were sitting in the Cybotage kitchen, a week or so after we had cracked the Riddle Machine and read the second chapter of *The Helmsman Texts*.

"Bit far-fetched, isn't it?"

"They did a good job making it realistic, though. The little touches – the slides and emails and all that. Even Eoin was impressed."

I sipped my coffee. "And that essay. Cyberweapons and subliminal priming and DNA hacking and whatever. Think there's any truth to it?"

"Maybe.* I don't know❶ – no one's really thought of this stuff before, not that I know of. Normal

* I was sceptical, when reading the second chapter of *The Helmsman Texts*, that sound could be used as a weapon in the context of cyber-attacks. For one thing, most computers and peripheral devices lack sufficiently powerful speakers. That being said, much of The Helmsman's research appears to be based on fact, or, at least, peer-reviewed academic work. But at the time, Jay and I had no reason to believe this was anything other than a fiction, even if it was a semi-plausible one, and so we weren't overly concerned with which parts, if any, were feasible.

Holly Soames①
21/11/2019 00:34
I assess at this point that while some of THE HELMSMAN's work was speculative – and very much at the fringes – the majority of the RED WORD reports are plausible, in that they discuss (and reject) possible candidates for a cognitive weapon capable of causing physical harm (although a caveat: much of this is outside my expertise, and I may update this assessment as my research continues). The major deductive leap is the discovery of a successful candidate, which is only described as a 'basilisk'. The only hints as to its nature are in c4–5 THT, in which THE HELMSMAN suggests it somehow dispels an illusion – presumably something to do with the nature of reality (cp. what WEBSTER reports she and MORTON experienced at FAIRLOP WATERS). He also mentions something called "The Me-Trix", but makes no elaboration on this point in c1–5 THT.

221

malware's enough of a headache. It's a good plot for a game, though. I like it."

"What else did Eoin say?"

"Not much. He's been looking up the acoustics stuff and sharing some fun facts with me. Did you know, for instance, that elephants use infrasound to communicate from hundreds of miles away? Or that there's an infrasonic frequency called the Brown Note❶ which makes you shit yourself?"

"He's taking it seriously, then."

"He wondered, if an elephant in Scotland was talking to one in London, whether there'd be a line of people across the country shitting themselves."

With a valiant struggle I kept a straight face. "Have you looked at the crossword yet?"

"I looked, yeah. Then I gave it to Eoin. Can't stand crosswords. You?"

A train went past outside and I jumped. I had been working at Cybotage for almost three months at this point, but I never got used to the sudden violent scream of metal hurtling down the track a few metres from the walls. Of course, I didn't spend all my time at the office. The Helmsman's game aside, I was still a working penetration tester, with clients and engagements and reports to occupy my cognitive space, and like many pentesters, especially junior ones, I spent a fair amount of time on the road. Even so, I'd found some time to look at the crossword, and I didn't have a clue where to start. Quite honestly the thing fucked me off; it was so gleefully obtuse.*

But before I could answer Jay, Nina came in. "Oi! We're waiting for you," she said.

When we both looked at her, confused, she rolled

Holly Soames①
15/11/2019 15:12
Widely believed to be a myth (see 'I went in search of the "Brown Note", the frequency that makes you shit yourself' by Jack CUMMINGS (2016): vice.com/en/article/ppv35z/in-search-of-the-brown-noise).

---

* Don't get me wrong: I like puzzles, but there's something so *superior* about cryptic crosswords, as though the compiler is saying 'Look! Look how clever I am!' Whenever I did the *Evening Standard* puzzles I always skipped the cryptic.

her eyes. "Hello? The *meeting*? About *Vegas*?"

The Vegas trip: Cybotage's annual pilgrimage to Nevada for Black Hat USA and DEF CON, two of the biggest and oldest hacking conferences. There had been some mention of it when I'd joined Cybotage, but I'd been so overwhelmed at the prospect of finally getting a job in security that I'd forgotten all about it. August had seemed like years away at the time.

The others – Ronnie, Kevin, Omar and Sophie – were already in the meeting room when we came in, along with Richard, his small form hunched over. He stopped and turned to watch us as we sat down, nose wrinkling. Richard always put me in mind of a little pompous cartoon character – like the Sultan from *Aladdin*, only with less bonhomie and more fretting over expense claims.

"I was just saying," he said as we sat down, "that the hotel's booked. And everyone will need an ESTA – don't leave it until the last minute, and make sure you fill it out properly. Kevin didn't a couple of years ago, remember, Kevin? They held him in McCarran for forty-eight hours!"

He chuckled, and Kevin smiled weakly.

"We're at the same hotel again, right?" Nina said.

"*Again*? Just once, couldn't we do the Mandalay?" Ronnie said, and the meeting dissolved temporarily into argument, the Vegas veterans quarrelling over the attributes of various hotels. I switched off. I knew about Black Hat and DEF CON – you couldn't work in cyber security without being aware of them – but I'd never been before and so had nothing to add to the debate. I was excited just to be going. In the last few weeks I'd forgotten all about it with the intrigue of The Helmsman's game, but for a few minutes I let my mind wander on the promise of Lost Wages, the hacker's paradise.

Black Hat and DEF CON used to be a single

conference, until the founder, Jeff Moss (The Dark Tangent), split them several years ago. Both events still take place in the same week. Black Hat is the slick, expensive, corporate conference – the one CISOs and CEOs and 'thought leaders' attend – and usually takes place from Monday to Thursday. On Thursday, DEF CON begins.

DEF CON is often described as 'hacker summer camp', and for many is the last true outpost of the culture. At its dark and smiling heart it is a meeting of hackers – a shadowy bright meeting in sunlight so fierce it's almost audible, and for four days the neon heat of Vegas becomes the land of Mordor, where malware authors play.

For one week in August, pit bosses and security guards watch anxiously as attendees swarm over the city. Some enterprising people have a stab at compromising ATMs and one-armed bandits; others are content with sticking googly eyes on everything they see (particularly amusing on the statues at Caesar's Palace) or pranking unsuspecting tourists.

https://www.instagram.com/p/BXLm819h1in/

But the overwhelming focus is on hacking: creating and solving puzzles; swapping code and tips and exploits; building proof-of-concept devices, broken up by impromptu taxi trips to Fry's Electronics for components; gathering in a huge Vegas ballroom with a thousand strangers to watch films you know by heart, films like *Hackers* and *Sneakers* and *WarGames* and, God save us, *Swordfish*; losing track of time; getting pins and needles from sitting in a hotel corridor with crossed legs and your computer on your lap, not even noticing the people walking past; cheering as exploits are released on stage and new speakers down a shot at the start of their talk.

To a first-timer the spectacle, the thousands of attendees and journalists, must seem rather intimidating. It's not a bad thing on the whole, I think, that the world is more interested in us than it once was. But I wonder if The Dark Tangent ever looks around at the 25,000 people, at the television crews and the long lines, and wonders if something, at some point, was lost.

Others make the journey too, people whose ethos is often – although not necessarily always – about as far away from hacker culture as you can get: representatives from your friendly regional, federal and national intelligence agencies and law enforcement communities. They don't announce their presence, of course, and some actively make an effort to disguise themselves, but the ones in jeans and Timberlands – often with a notepad in the back pocket – stick out a fucking mile. For many years there was a tacit understanding that the 'feds' attended DEF CON because they're an integral part of the hacking scene: they provide the opposition. With this came a typically irreverent reaction from hackers, who would walk around with signs saying things like *free hugs for undercover feds*. There was even a game, although it

225

ALEXIS PARK
RESORT & SPA LAS VEGAS*

July 1, 2001
ATTN: Department Heads

Rules for Alexis Park staff during DEFCON Event:
Before and during the event:
- Disable and conceal all motorized carts (golf and bicycle).
- Secure and maintain closure of all fitness and salon areas.
- Wear all keys and access cards on a lanyard around your neck.
- Any request for room access must be approved by two managers.
- Harass NO guest, report any incidents to a manager on duty.
- If you are not scheduled to work, you may not attend the event.

Things to report:
- Drugs and/or weapons of any kind.
- Deceased or dismembered guests.
- Farm animals.
- Missing payphones or ATM machines.
- Additional payphones or ATM machines.
- Unauthorized connections to outdoor PBX telephones and cable TV syste[ms].
- Dislocated room doors, windows, stairs, walls.
- Fire.

Acceptable during this event ONLY:
- Any guests not sleeping in a room.
- Fountains and pools functioning with foreign dyes or bubbles.
- Underage possession of alcohol and/or smoking.
- Debauchery and/or libation.

Thank you,
Alexis Park Management

has dwindled in popularity now, called 'Spot the Fed'. Anyone could, at any time – even in the middle of a talk – stand up and accuse someone of being a fed. If the accused admitted to it – which they often did in good humour – the accuser would receive a t-shirt proclaiming: 'I spotted the fed', and the fed would get an 'I am the fed' t-shirt.[*]

Spot the Fed Contest[†]

7th ANNUAL SPOT THE FED CONTEST:
The ever popular paranoia builder. Who IS that person next to you?

"Like a paranoid version of pin the tail on the donkey, the favorite sport at this gathering of computer hackers and phone phreaks seems to be hunting down real and imagined telephone security and Federal and local law enforcement authorities who the attendees are certain are tracking their every move... Of course, they may be right."
– John Markhoff, NYT

Basically the contest goes like this: If you see some shady MIB (Men in Black) earphone penny loafer sunglass wearing Clint Eastwood to live and die in LA type lurking about, point him out. Just get my attention and claim out loud you think you have spotted a fed. The people around at the time will then (I bet) start to discuss the possibility of whether or not a real fed has been

[*] It won't come as any shock that in 2013, after the Snowden revelations, the relationship soured somewhat, and law enforcement and intelligence personnel were asked by Moss to stay away from DEF CON that year. Spot the Fed is rarely played now.
[†] Brown, JPat. 'FBI files on DEF CON show "Spot the Fed" contest a sore spot for Feds'. (2015). Muckrock. https://www.muckrock.com/news/archives/2015/may/06/def-cons-spot-fed-contest-sore-spot-feds

spotted. Once enough people have decided that a fed has been spotted, and the Identified Fed (I.F.) has had a say, and **[sic]** informal vote takes place, and if enough people think it's a true fed, or fed wanna-be, or other nefarious style character, you win a "I spotted the fed!" shirt, and the I.F. gets an "I am the fed!" shirt.

NOTE TO THE FEDS: This is all in good fun, and if you survive unmolested and undetected, but would still secretly like an "I am the fed!" shirt to wear around the office or when booting in doors, please contact me when no one is looking and I will take your order(s). Just think of all the looks of awe you'll generate at work wearing this shirt while you file away all the paperwork you'll have to produce over this convention. I won't turn in any feds who contact me, they have to be spotted by others.

It is a complex, intricate, mind-fuck of an event, with thirty years of history and folklore behind it. A four-day circus of thinking, parties, organised chaos, and its own traditions and memes. There is nothing else like it. Jay told me that every hacker, at least once in their life, should make the pilgrimage. It never would have crossed his mind that he might die there.

*　*　*

Cybotage had sent people to Black Hat and DEF CON for the last few years – a perk dangled in lieu of higher salaries – and I suspect that Richard got some sort of deal on flights and accommodation from someone he knew, or a bulk discount on the conference tickets. It seemed far too frivolous an expense for him otherwise.

In the meeting, he went over the arrangements. We would indeed be staying at the same hotel Richard always booked, on South Las Vegas Boulevard – the Strip – and close to both the Mandalay Bay, where Black Hat took place, and Caesars Palace, for DEF CON.

"And don't forget to keep all your receipts," he said. "I won't approve any expenses without receipts. Top tip: take a special folder to keep them all in, because otherwise you'll lose them."

Some almost imperceptible sighs around the table; clearly this was not new advice.

"We can all handle receipts, Richard," said Jay.

"Well, there have been incidents. Certain people, who shall remain nameless, claiming twice for the same taxi!"

"As I've been saying for three years now," Omar said patiently, "it was the same journey on different days."

"We're gonna take a lot of cabs," Ronnie said to me. "It may not look far to walk on the map – but trust me, in 45C heat, it's a long fucking way."

The meeting continued, Richard droning on, until as if by common consensus, rather than coming to the end of any definitive agenda, it was over, and everyone drifted back to their desks. Richard and Omar were still arguing about the taxi receipts – Omar tolerantly, Richard considerably more plaintive.

I caught some of the conversations as people left, talk of traditions I knew nothing about: the Rapid7 party, Hacker Jeopardy, trips to Old Vegas. Everyone knew I was a Vegas virgin, and over the next few days and weeks they sought me out to pass on their tips.

"Bring blister plasters," Nina said. "Loads. You'll be walking a *lot*."

"Thanks," I said.

"And a few hoodies. It's baking outside, but inside the air con is full blast everywhere."

"Watch out for pickpockets," Omar said.

"Got a burner phone❶ yet?" Kevin said. "You'll need a burner phone."

Holly Soames①
15/11/2019 17:08
i.e. a cheap pay-as-you-go phone that is bought and used for a short time before being thrown away, to prevent law enforcement or other adversaries from tracking a person over a period of time, or exploiting the device itself.

I knew the rumours, and I'd seen the arguments about burner phones on Twitter, but I doubted any hacker was going to bother dropping a 0-day to attack attendees – not when they could sell it to a government or a bug bounty scheme.

"Thanks, but I'll just use flight mode."

"That won't work," Kevin said. "They can force it to switch back."

"Don't be ridiculous," ❶ Ronnie said, and as they began to bicker I walked away.

Holly Soames①
15/11/2019 17:13
Ronnie is correct here, for the record.

Others gave advice about the exchange rate, and how to surreptitiously get a room upgrade, and which vendor booths gave away the best swag. There were discussions about Cybotage traditions, such as meeting at the lion statue in the lobby before going out or heading to the conference.*

Don't drink the bottled water the hawkers sell on the streets – they collect water from discarded bottles and decant it into empty ones.

Everyone expects a tip, and for cab drivers it should be at least 25%.

In the exhibition hall wear a sticker that says "I have no purchasing power" and the vendors won't pester you to buy their snake oil.

It went on and on – do this, and this, but never do that – until I began to furtively head to the kitchen whenever the topic entered the conversation.

Even so, I remember this period, the one preceding the next stage of The Helmsman's game, as the last in which I was at least partially content. I had a way of life, or I was finding one. It was small, and short, and nothing that most people would consider

---

* This statue had gained a sort of mythical status over the years; a former TI analyst, Greg, long since departed, got drunk and mounted the statue as though it were a bull at a rodeo, only reluctantly climbing down after a security guard threatened, very politely by all accounts, to Taser him in the balls.

to be especially blessed, but I treasured it. Best of all, the need I had felt for as long as I could remember – the voice inside me shouting that I needed to show people how skilled I was, how much potential I had – had receded to a low murmur, because I *had* shown it. Someone *knew* how talented I was.

I remember lying in bed one evening, shortly after the Riddle Machine, listening to a storm outside, squalls of night rain thrashing against the window, and thinking how lucky I was that in all the violence and silent tiredness of the world, of all possible worlds, I was doing something I was good at. I *belonged*. "Alex the hacker," I repeated quietly to myself, pleased with how it sounded. "Alex the hacker."

You might not think, either now or at the end of this, that I ever really cared that much about Jay. You might believe that for me it was all about the game and nothing else. You might think I was callous and calculating, that I manipulated him. I won't, and can't, deny any of that. I deserve it. But I never wanted any harm to come to Jay, or Eoin, or anyone else. Never.

It wasn't just about the game. It was more than that. It still is. It has to be.

*　*　*

As I left the Cybotage office, a few days after the Vegas meeting, I saw a man standing at the bus stop, a man in a light grey suit wearing some kind of mask – a painted mask with a huge, unnervingly jolly smile slashed into it. I only saw him for a second, and then a bus pulled up and he was gone.

*　*　*

Holly Soames①
15/11/2019 18:04
Unlikely any CCTV would still be on systems but check with security at the building.

The next day, I walked into the Gants House car park and The Rearguard were standing outside the building's entrance.❶ .

231

I had no idea it was The Rearguard, of course. I simply saw three scruffy, vaguely anxious-looking people – two men and a woman – waiting to take their driving tests, and I would scarcely have given them a glance had one of the men not whispered, in a strangled, conspiratorial sort of voice as I passed, "'Scuse me, do you know, uh, Jay Morton? The security dude won't let us in."

I stopped and gave them a once-over. ❶

The woman was young and almost painfully thin with a delicate face, her skin so pale and fragile that I could see networks of blue veins at her temples. The man who had spoken – more of a boy, I noticed now, barely eighteen – was taller, slouching, his hands thrust into the pockets of an oversized purple hoodie, untidy sandy hair down to his shoulders. The other man was older, paunchy and balding, his yellowing shirt rumpled and stained with sweat – I *hoped* it was sweat – even though the morning wasn't particularly warm.

Hacker friends of Jay's, I thought. I looked towards the door, through the glass at the reception, where a security guard was staring out, arms folded, a sour look on his face.

"I work with him, yeah," I said. "Want me to pass on a message?"

The woman spoke. "Tell him The Rearguard are here."

"The Rearguard?"

"Yeah."

"So you must be Morgana." Her eyes widened in alarm. I turned to the taller man. "cr0w." He grinned, put two fingers to his temple, and curled an imaginary forelock. Finally, I looked at the little balding man. "And awe." He didn't respond but averted his eyes to a point just above mine and blinked owlishly.

"Don't know what you're talking about," Morgana said. She looked ready to run, and I thought about trolling them for a while – pretending I was an undercover police officer or something – but resisted the temptation.

"Relax. I was with Jay the other night. The Riddle Machine."

"Oh yeah?" cr0w said. "Did you solve it?"

"Yeah."

"I told you the hint was too easy, Morgs!"

"Shut up, cr0w."

"What are you doing here?" I said.

awe inspected his fingernails. "We're here to speak to brix."

"Well, like I said, I'm playing the game too, so…?"

awe looked at Morgana, who looked at me. "We have a message from Ken," she said.

"Ken…" I said, and then remembered. "The one who finished the game? The one you wouldn't let us talk to?"

"That's the dude," cr0w said.

"Who is he to you, anyway?" I said. "Do you work for him?"

"We don't work for anyone," awe said.

"Just passing on a message," cr0w said. "Ken doesn't really like talking to people directly. Not since… well."

"Can you fetch Jay or not?" awe said.

I could see I wasn't going to get anything else out of them by myself so, a bit bewildered by the whole thing, I called Jay.

"Hello?"

"Hi, Jay. Erm… The Rearguard are outside."

There was a pause.

"Outside *here*? What do they want?"

"They say they've got a message. From Ken."

"Seriously? Hang on, I'm coming down."

Jay hung up, and The Rearguard and I looked awkwardly at each other in the time it took him to take the lift down and exit the building.

"How… how can I help you?" Jay said, when he came out and joined us. He looked from one to the other, confused – but there was something else, I think: a gleam of eagerness, of an embryonic fixation which I was only able to perceive because it was growing in me, too. The game was becoming more real, and more compelling, every time we came across something unforeseen and abnormal,* and the fact that The Rearguard – who, of course, we believed were probably actors at this point – had turned up to deliver some new tidbit of information only added to that.

"Ken thought you should know something," Morgana said.

"You could have just messaged me."

"Ken was keen there should be no possibility of the message being misunderstood."

"Or intercepted," awe said.

"Which is why we didn't call ahead," cr0w chimed in. "Appy-logies."

"OK, so what is it? Another hint or something? He didn't seem too keen to help us last time."

"He said you've probably been sent a file by now. The second chapter. Have you read it?"

Jay and I both nodded.

"Ken says that what's in the file is real."

"Oh, right, OK," I said, smiling. "Gotcha. It's real. What else?"

The three of them looked at me with open and

---

* Some of this was inherent to the game itself – The Helmsman seemed to deliberately and continuously confound our expectations of what ARGs and puzzles should be (a recording of a numbers station that had nothing to do with numbers stations; a CTF that had no vulnerabilities and instead deliberately trolled us; a crossword where the answers were meaningless; a treasure hunt where the treasure didn't matter; a koan that wasn't a koan) – probably, as he notes in the fifth chapter, to prepare players for the basilisk itself in the sixth chapter, and to ensure he recruited the most capable people. Some of it, like ███████████████████, was incidental. In any case, it had the same effect: the stranger it got, the more desperate we were to keep going – even when it had become very obvious that it was no longer a game.

honest confusion, and the tiniest scrap of doubt fluttered in my mind. I thought about the second chapter, full of chaos and delirium and implausible fiction. Scraps of email chains and strange short plays and characters performing experiments they didn't fully understand.

"Oh, bollocks," Jay said. "Come on. What's real – what parts? The emails, what?"

"Jay, let them finish," I said. "They've got lines to get through."

Morgana stared at me. "All of it's real. Ken said it's only right that you should know, because The Helmsman doesn't play fair."

"So say it is real – what's the game about, then?" I said. "What's the point of it?"

"It's for recruiting people."

"I knew it," I said, although of course I had known no such thing. "For what? GCHQ, NSA, MI5? ❶ Private sector?"

Holly Soames①
15/11/2019 20:01
Ascertain with partner agencies whether they operate any such schemes. I have no knowledge of threat actors running anything like this, although it is possible that private sector orgs do.

"The Helmsman," Morgana said, as though explaining something very simple to someone very stupid. "He wants more people to work for him."

"Why? Doing what?" Jay said.

"Spreading the game."

"What does that mean?" I said. "You mean the same way I – we – found it?"

"Yup," cr0w said.

"The whole thing is just for – what? Replicating itself?"

"But there must be a point to it beyond that," Jay said.

"Ken didn't say," Morgana said.

"He's very careful what he says about the game," cr0w said. "Probably because he – "

"Shut up, cr0w."

"Yeah, well, we won't be signing up," Jay said. "So is that what Ken does now?"

"Ken joined The Helmsman's group," Morgana

said. "Then he left, but he promised The Helmsman he'd stay neutral. He doesn't want anyone thinking it's less than it is, that's all. We're just passing on the message. Do what you want."

"Doesn't sound very neutral to me," Jay said.

awe smirked. "You don't know anything."

"Ken says there are some people who might try to stop you playing," Morgana said. "And they don't... they don't stick to the rules. Ken wanted to let you know what you're getting into."

"What people?" I said. "Why don't they want us to play?"

Morgana shrugged. "We don't know. We haven't seen them. Only Ken has."

"Great, that's helpful," Jay said. "We'll be sure to keep an eye out for people. Cheers."

"Tell them the other thing," cr0w said. "Tell them what the freaks look like."

We looked at Morgana, who seemed unsure if she should carry on.

"Come on, let's hear it," I said.

"Ken said these people might look strange, depending on how far into the game you are," she said slowly. "If you're only a little way in, they look like anyone else. But if you get past a certain point, they... their faces change."

I snorted. "The Helmsman should get himself some better actors. No offence."

"Know what I think?" Jay said. "I think you're either really bad actors, like Alex says, or you're playing the game yourself and you're trying to put us off. So nice try, but it won't work. If any of this was actually real we'd know about it. It's sort of our job."

awe raised his eyebrows at Morgana. "Well, we tried. It's on them."

"You almost had us," Jay said. "Tip for next time: don't try so hard. You could have kept it realistic."

Morgana smiled, almost sadly. "It is what it is."

awe glared at Jay, and trudged away towards the car park. After holding my gaze for a second or two Morgana followed him.

"It sounds different, coming from Ken," cr0w said. "If he was here you'd get it."

"And who is Ken supposed to be, exactly?" Jay said. "To you, I mean."

cr0w looked at the ground. "He was one of us. The Rearguard. Then he found the game."

"Wait," I said. "He was one of you, and he knows everything about the game, but he won't tell you about it? Why not?"

cr0w smiled, and it was a real smile, almost radiant. "I think it's because he's our friend," he said. "I think it's because he cares about us."

He looked across the car park, to the far wall, where the distant figures of Morgana and awe were standing and watching us.

"I'd better go," he said, and began to slouch away. "If you need anything, hit us up. We'll still help you."

He joined awe and Morgana. Jay and I watched the three of them until they were out of sight, and then we headed back inside.

"Hope this doesn't change your mind," I said as we climbed the stairs.

"Alex, I've seen *puppets* give better performances than that. I mean, at least they're putting some effort in, but seriously? People with changing faces or whatever? They've almost ruined it for me."

"But you still want to keep playing?"

We reached the Cybotage door, and Jay turned to me.

"Yeah, I want to keep playing. In spite of that shlocky horror crap. I want to know exactly what's at the end of this game and who's behind it. I reckon there's more to it than we think."

He entered the office, shaking his head and muttering to himself. Before I followed him inside I looked out of the window on the landing, which overlooked the car park – but The Rearguard, their message delivered, were gone.

* * *

In aesthetics there is a problem called the Uncanny Valley, a term which describes the negative reaction of humans to things which look almost human. It is why we shudder when we see people in humanlike masks, and clowns and puppets and not-quite-right robots. Objects in the Uncanny Valley engender disgust and fear.❶

The reasons for this are not known, although theories include: a reminder of our own mortality,❷ in that when we die we too will no longer appear wholly human; a safeguard against sickness, in that we perceive an inhabitant of the Uncanny Valley to be in some way diseased and therefore to be shunned;❸ a violation of the concept of being human;❹ or, more outlandishly, that we evolved this sense of revulsion as a defence against some unknown and now-extinct predator. That learning to be afraid of things which look almost human was enough of a benefit to our species that it is now ingrained in our behaviour.* ❺

* Before ▮▮▮▮▮▮▮▮▮▮▮▮▮▮, I would have said this is the least convincing explanation; it surfaces now and again on Twitter and Reddit. However, my experiences with ▮▮▮▮▮▮▮▮▮▮ ▮▮▮▮, and with The Helmsman's game more generally, have led me to believe that, very often, the most disturbing explanation of a phenomenon is the one that's true (do me a favour, would you? Try and make that a thing – Webster's Razor or something like that; I've always wanted to have something like that named after me). Why this is so frequently true, I don't know – perhaps because reality itself is inherently disturbing. In any case, as far as ▮▮▮▮▮▮▮▮▮▮▮▮▮▮ are concerned, it seems unlikely that they've just popped up in the recent past as a sort of reaction to The Helmsman's game. I have no evidence for saying so, but I think they've been around for a very long time – in which case, this explanation starts to make a lot more sense.

Holly Soames①
15/11/2019 20:21
e.g. 'Facial expression of emotion and perception of the Uncanny Valley in virtual characters' by Angela TINWELL and others (2011).

Holly Soames②
15/11/2019 20:25
Background: 'Mortality salience and the uncanny valley' by Karl F. MACDORMAN (2005).

Holly Soames③
15/11/2019 20:29
Background: 'Human emotion and the uncanny valley: A GLM, MDS, and Isomap analysis of robot video ratings' by Ho CHIN-CHANG and others (2008).

Holly Soames④
15/11/2019 20:37
Background: 'In the shades of the uncanny valley: An experimental study of human–chatbot interaction' by Leon CIECHANOWSKI and others (2019).

Holly Soames⑤
15/11/2019 21:02
Re. WEBSTER's reference to Reddit posts, see reddit.com/r/nosleep/comments/8p0c62/the_evolutionary_reason_for_the_uncanny_valley/ by Burgerkrieg (2017) for an example. The NoSleep subreddit is devoted to ostensibly plausible horror fiction.

The Valley itself can be found in the curve showing our empathetic response to robots and other humanlike objects. When they do not resemble humans at all, our empathy response is strong; we may even anthropomorphise them to some extent (e.g., WALL-E, or *Opportunity*, the Mars rover), assigning personality and agency to them despite knowing they have none. But the curve decays as things become more humanlike, and rises again as the robot becomes almost indistinguishable from humans. The trough in the curve is the Uncanny Valley, and it is where ████ ██████████████████ live.

Whatever the reason for it, there is something undeniably revolting about a thing which tries to appear human, and I have never felt that revulsion more strongly than when I got out of the lifts that evening and saw two things that looked like men❶ standing outside my front door.

Holly Soames①
15/11/2019 21:34
Persons of interest, descriptions added to file.

One was the man I had seen at the bus stop the day before. He was old, but not elderly – maybe sixty – with short stubbly grey hair and a large straight nose. The other was shorter, almost fresh-faced, with black-framed glasses that made him look even younger. Both were wearing light grey suits, and both were smiling.

I want to be very clear here, because I don't want to be misunderstood. I want to completely dismiss any notion you may have that their smiling was in any way reassuring or comforting or good-humoured. It was utterly repulsive, wide and fixed and stretched, lips drawn back inhumanly far, revealing the dark chasms of mouths.

What was worse, I think, was the way those smiles never touched the rest of their faces. You'll be familiar with the concept of a smile which doesn't reach the eyes, I imagine – you've probably done it yourself. But try it now, in the mirror, and you'll see that even if your smile doesn't touch your eyes, your cheeks will still rise and widen; your nose will flatten; the skin around your eyes will lift.

These smiles were entirely independent of their faces, as if they had been carved, and the eyes above were as precise and clinical as a hypodermic syringe.

I want to be very clear on one other point: at no time during the following conversation, or any of the subsequent times I saw them or their ilk, did their smiles move or shift or slip in any way, even while speaking. They simply remained, constant, as though it were a permanent part of their musculoskeletal system. If you stripped them of flesh, you'd find the smile slashed there in bone.

"ALEX WEBSTER?" the older one said. His voice, both their voices, were musical – a sort of sing-song – but there was an erratic, almost syncopated rhythm, stress placed on syllables at random, words rising when they should have fallen. It was like speech synthesis, but more animated – like a person imitating speech synthesis, maybe. The voice of something nearly, but not quite, human. Over time it became unbearable, like listening to a clock with the tock slightly too quick or too slow after the tick – but unpredictably so. Listening to them for too long, I think, would drive anyone mad.

I nodded slowly.

"GOOD EVENING ALEX WEBSTER."

"What do you want?" I managed.

"NO NOT THE RIGHT QUESTION."

"What is the right question?" They were between me and my front door, and I couldn't, wouldn't, get past them. I didn't want to be anywhere within touching distance of them.

"ASK US WHY WE SMILE," the younger one said, his eyes widening.

"YES ASK US THAT."

I swallowed. "Why are you smiling?"

The younger one clapped his hands together.

240

"BECAUSE WE'RE HAPPY. WOULDN'T YOU LIKE TO BE HAPPY TOO?"

"IF YOU WOULD LIKE TO BE HAPPY TOO LIKE WE ARE HAPPY THEN YOU SHOULD STOP."

"Stop – stop what?"

"THE GAME YOU ARE PLAYING," the older one said, and he made a curious, flowing sort of gesture with his hand. "THE GAME YOU AND JAY MORTON ARE PLAYING."

"NO GOOD CAN COME OF IT."

"IT WILL ONLY MAKE YOU SAD."

A door opened across the hallway and one of my neighbours,❶ a middle-aged woman I knew well enough to say hello to, came out. The two men were now standing either side of her. I have never seen anyone or anything move so quickly in my life. It was as if I was watching a film and a frame or two had just – *skipped*. One second they were standing in front of my door, looking at me intently, those ghastly rigid smiles glued fast to their faces, and the next they were flanking her.

The woman looked at me, and at the things that looked like people, and slowly edged back into her flat.

Quick again – not just quick, like snake-strike-quick or lightning-quick, but *instantly* – the men turned their heads back to me.

"WHY DO YOU PLAY?" the younger one said. "WHY DO YOU PLAY? WHAT COULD YOU HAVE TO GAIN?"

"BE HAPPY WITH WHAT YOU HAVE."

"YES HAPPY. THE HELMSMAN IS A BAD PERSON. HE THINKS BAD THOUGHTS. WE WANT TO KEEP YOU SAFE."

"YES SAFE. WE WANT TO PROTECT YOU."

"YES PROTECT YOU."

"You're – this is part of it, isn't it?" Even I could hear the pathetic note of hope. "This isn't real. You're part of the game."

Their eyes darted towards each other and back to me. Perhaps it wasn't a question they had expected. I had the sense that they didn't hear too many questions.

241

"WE ARE NOT," the older one said, and I could have sworn that for an instant I heard something – if not kindness, then at least tolerance – in that dead, rising, falling voice.

"What's at the end of the game?" I said.

The younger one cocked his head like a bird. "WE DO NOT UNDERSTAND THE QUESTION."

"Is it a game? Is it *real*?"

"WE DO NOT UNDERSTAND THE QUESTION."

I was afraid, but somewhere, the hacker part of my brain woke up and nudged me. *They're acting like a system. Ask the right questions and you get answers. Ask something unexpected and they glitch.*

"Is RED WORD real?" I said. "The weapon?"

"IT IS REAL BUT NOT TRUE."

"That doesn't make any sense."

"WHY SHOULD IT MAKE SENSE TO YOU?"

"YES WHY SHOULD IT. LEAVE THE GAME ALEX WEBSTER. LEAVE THE GAME AND BE HAPPY WITH YOUR LIFE."

"Why don't you want us to play it?"

Both men raised fists to their cheeks, still smiling, and moved them back and forth in a caricature of weeping. It didn't come across as sarcastic or ironic, as it might have done if it were an ordinary human doing it. It was eerie, almost childlike, and the most horrifying thing I'd ever seen.

I had no idea what they meant,* but I had the feeling that was all I was going to get. I took a deep breath. "And if we say no?"

---

* And still don't. All I know is that *something* about The Helmsman's weapon draws them. Whatever he found, whatever 'red pill' he concocted in his twisted little tablet press, it is bad enough to attract these things and make them want to stop anyone from taking it. As with much of this document there is little point in speculating, but I'll say this: if The Helmsman's weapon *is* something to do with dispelling an illusion about the nature of reality, then ▆▆▆▆ ▆▆▆▆▆▆▆▆▆▆▆▆▆▆▆▆▆ come from the other side of that illusion. They come from what we saw at Fairlop Waters.

They both stopped miming. The older one nodded, the movement rapid and twitching, and the younger one took a step towards me, the smile still disfiguring his face, and from the yawning mouth came Jay's voice. Not merely an impression, but Jay's actual, real voice. It was so convincing that I looked around, expecting to see him somewhere physically in the hallway, but at the same time it was hollow, missing some intrinsic *realness*. It was the essence of his voice, but absent of timbre or tone, as though the life had been neatly excised from it with a scalpel.

"Help."

And then from the gaping mouth, my own voice chanting at me.

"Help. I don't like it here. I want to go back. I want to die." ❶

Holly Soames①
15/11/2019 23:52
Flagged.

Now the older one joined in, with Jay's voice.

"Help. Help. Help. Help. Help."

Abruptly the sounds stopped.

"DO YOU UNDERSTAND ALEX WEBSTER?" the older one said.

I nodded, not trusting myself to speak.

"DO WE NEED TO VISIT JAY MORTON TOO?"

I shook my head so hard it hurt my neck.*

"WERE WE HERE?"

"What?"

The younger one took a step towards me and I understood.

"No! No, you weren't here at all."

I blinked, and it was as if the blink had gone on a moment or two longer than usual, and I was in my flat, the front door locked and bolted, my coat in its

---

* I do sometimes wonder why ▓▓▓▓▓▓▓▓▓▓ chose to visit me and not Jay. Perhaps I, as the discoverer of the game, was seen as the principal player. Or maybe they thought that of the two of us I was the most likely to be intimidated. If that was the case, they thought wrong.

usual place over the back of the sofa, my shoes off and tucked away by the door. I was in my kitchen, standing in front of the oven, and there was a cup and plate in the sink that hadn't been there when I left. A glance at my phone told me that it was almost nine; I'd got off the train at six-thirty.

To this day I'm not sure what happened in that lost time, or what I might have done during it. I only know that I'm keeping a balance sheet, and in addition to everything else ███████████████████ took from me, they stole two and a half hours of my life.

* * *

In the morning, with weak sunlight sifting through my curtains, the encounter, which at the time had seemed so – unearthly, perhaps, even if it's not quite the right word – was, if not totally obscured in my memory, then at least partly pixellated.[*] They had moved quickly, yes, but not *impossibly* quickly. They had imitated Jay's voice and mine, but lots of people out there were good impressionists. There are birds, I told myself, *birds* that can do it. And so on and so on, until I was able to almost convince myself that the men had been actors and nothing more, paid to put the scare into unsuspecting ARG participants. Yes, of course – after our lacklustre response to The Rearguard, they'd pulled out the big guns. Gone to town on the prosthetics. Or, even more attractive, perhaps I'd dreamt the whole thing – a sort of lucid nightmare, the result of a tired and overworked mind shaken up by contrived horror stories from Morgana et al.

[*] It hadn't occurred to me until quite recently that, in addition to this being my own consciousness attempting to protect itself from horror, it may also be a sort of side-effect of encounters with ████ ████████████, a mental equivalent of the anaesthetic in a mosquito's saliva proteins. Whether ███████████████ do this consciously or not is unclear, but their repeated advice to 'forget' suggests it could be the former.

And when I bumped into my neighbour by the lifts, I became even more convinced that the latter was actually the case.

"Oh hi!" she said brightly. "It's Alex, isn't it? How are you?"

"I— I'm fine," I said. "You?"

"Oh, you know, can't complain. Well, I could but who'd bloody listen?" She nudged me in the ribs.

"Right," I said, forcing a smile.

"Going down?"

We got into the lift, and she hummed happily to herself.

"Are you – are you sure you're OK?"

She stopped. "Why wouldn't I be?"

"Last night, you…" I let the words hang, watching her face, but there wasn't even the slightest stirring of recognition. "You didn't see anything weird?"

"Don't think so," she said, frowning now. "Why? What did *you* see?"

"Oh, nothing. Nothing at all. Sorry. I thought I— I thought I heard something outside, that's all."

"Foxes, probably. They scream bloody murder some nights. My Garry says we should call the council but I said what are they going to do, chase them away?"

The lift dinged and the doors slid open.

"Must dash!" she said. "Take care!" And then she was gone, running around the corner to the car park.

* * *

I got to work and found myself quite capable of going about my business over the next few days, assessing a web app and finding a few CSRF❶ and stored XSS❷ vulnerabilities.

"Good work," Jay said, and I silently congratulated myself for presenting a convincing and seemingly normal front to the world. When Nina asked me if I wanted a coffee I could say, "Yes please," with barely

Holly Soames①
16/11/2019 11:13
CSRF = Cross-site request forgery, a method to attack web servers.

Holly Soames②
16/11/2019 11:17
XSS = Cross-site scripting, a method to attack web servers.

a traitorous quiver in my voice, and I could no longer hear – could hardly remember, if I made an effort – those sing-song, synthetic words. I could no longer see the fixed smiles. And if I couldn't hear or see them, they weren't a problem. I had let my imagination run away with me. Things like that were, after all, not real, not possible. Which is more likely – that the laws of the universe would be suspended, or that a person would have a bad dream?

This is not an excuse, not a plea for clemency or absolution, not that there is anyone who is capable of granting it to me. I just hope you understand that I was scared, and trying to protect myself. And whilst I can't be sure, I think my neighbour might have been doing the same thing.*

Nevertheless, every so often, in quiet moments when I had a chance to think, I heard Morgana's words, her pinched and almost translucent face solemn.

If you get past a certain point, they… their faces change.

* * *

I had never met Otto's parents❶ before tonight, and it seems unlikely, given what happened, that I'll see them again. For that matter, I might not see Otto again either. I really think this might be the end of us, and I wouldn't blame him. I'm starting to wonder if it might not be for the best. I was drawn to him because he is so obviously a safety net, a guardrail of a person, and I'm ashamed to say that I never before took the time to imagine what I might be for him, but I think the answer

Holly Soames①
16/11/2019 12:03
Interviewed by SCD1 following the murder of Otto SALAS, see report for transcripts. Both recalled this incident and broadly corroborated WEBSTER'S account of it here.

* The alternative explanation – and, again, I have no evidence whatsoever to support this (which you're probably finding is a pretty fucking common refrain) – is that, because my neighbour was not playing the game, she was in some way less 'vulnerable' to ▓▓▓▓▓▓▓▓▓▓▓▓ and couldn't see them as they were. There is one other possibility, which you may have already arrived at, and of course it has crossed my mind – but I am telling you it's not true.

to that is becoming clear: I am dangerous, poisonous, and there is an argument to be made that many of those within my proximity in the last couple of years haven't fared too well.

But let me tell you what happened – you be the judge.

The evening started well enough. Otto had booked a table at a Wagamama, which is apparently the only restaurant the Salas family ever eats at. Otto's parents, I have inferred, are about as adventurous as their son.

I didn't complain – I like Wagamama – and so we found ourselves seated and reading the paper menus at seven. The place wasn't busy – Otto had chosen one of the chain's more desolate outposts in Canary Wharf, and the spring wind slicing across the Thames had kept people away.

Mrs Salas is a short, fat woman with a guileless smile and a loud, very high-pitched laugh like the squeak of a balloon, which made Otto wince and the few other diners in the restaurant turn around every time it escaped from her lungs. I liked her immediately; she has a genuine warmth, and is obviously devoted to Otto. Mr Salas is the opposite physically, tall and fragile-thin. His arms look like they might snap like breadsticks, and his thin pencil moustache only underscores the sharp angles of his head – you could draw his portrait with a ruler. But for all that, he too seemed pleasant, with an endearing habit of opening his mouth slightly when he's listening to you, as though you're saying the most fascinating thing he's ever heard.

Looking at the two of them, she spilling out of her chair, he upright and stiff, I tried to stop myself thinking about the two of them in bed. Obviously it had worked at least once, but I couldn't fathom the mechanics of it.

"Alex was saying something about that the other day," Otto said, and I snapped out of my reverie and put on a smile.

"What's that?" I said.

"Dad was just saying how your job – your old job – is always in the news these days. Hacking."

"Oh. Yes."

"Only this morning I heard about another ransomware thing," Mr Salas said, sipping from his glass. "Have you had anything like that at the school, Alex?"

"No," I said. "Not while I've been there."

I caught Mrs Salas's eye, and she smiled encouragingly.

"Your last job sounds fascinating," Mr Salas said.

"Dad used to work in risk assurance," Otto said. "He was a Partner, weren't you, Dad?" I could hear the capital 'P'.

"I always thought pentesting was such an interesting field," his father said. "A bit like mystery shopping, eh?"

"Yes, a bit," I said, although it wasn't.

"You must have needed to do a lot of training for it," Mrs Salas said.

"I did some courses. Mostly self-study."

"What made you leave?" Mr Salas said.

"Everyone ready to order?" Otto said.

"Oh yes, I think I'll have some ramen," Mrs Salas said.

"Dad?"

Mr Salas was still looking at me, waiting for an answer. I cast my eyes down to the menu.

"The katsu curry looks good," I heard him say eventually.

"Alex?"

"Firecracker," I said, still concentrating hard on the tiny lists of dishes in front of me. The text writhed and squirmed in my vision until I screwed up my eyes and made it lie flat.

"Alex always has the firecracker."

"And how are things at the school?" Mr Salas said. I looked up, but his attention was now on Otto.

"We always said he was too good to be a teacher," Mrs Salas said, smiling at me. "He should have been a professor."

"Maybe one day, Mum. It's not so bad. I get time to work on my book."

"Oh yes, the book," Mrs Salas says, and winked at me. "Post-war Japan. He's been going on about that book for years. You know, I think even if he'd *started* it in 1945 he'd still be working on it now!"

I laughed. Otto mumbled something in response, and I reached for his hand under the table and squeezed it, suddenly overcome with a wave of affection for him.

"It's a big topic," I said.

"Outrageous, what the Japs did during the war," Mr Salas said, folding his brittle fingers together so that it looked like his arms ended in a bundle of sticks.

"It's post-war, Dad," Otto said. "The American occupation."

"How do you find working at the school, dear?" Mrs Salas said to me.

I had been drinking from my glass when she asked this, and in my rush to answer I dribbled Diet Coke down my chin and snatched at a tissue to wipe it up.

"It's fine," I said. "Great. I like it."

"You should see her office, Mum," Otto said. "It's like a cave of wonders, all full of cables and computers and God knows what."

"But you don't do any security stuff now, do you?" Mr Salas said.

"No," I said. Mr Salas's questions were beginning to irritate me.

"Just IT support?"

"It's a very demanding job," Otto said. "There's a lot of things to—"

"It just strikes me as odd," Mr Salas said. "Going

from such a specialist field to something so much less *prestigious*. Don't you miss it?"

"Maybe she didn't like her old job, dear," Mrs Salas said breezily. "Life's too short to do things you don't want to do, isn't it, Alex?"

"Exactly," Otto said.

The pencil moustache twitched. I had aroused Mr Salas's curiosity, it seemed. Had the other two not been there, I had the distinct sense that I would be being interrogated right now.

A waiter bounded up to our table, all surface charm and energy, and took our orders, scribbling numbers on the paper placemats in thick black ink.

"So do you live near here, Alex?" Mrs Salas said, when he'd gone.

"Not far away," I said. The Rearguard would have approved of my OPSEC,❶ I think – never answer a personal question directly.

"She's got a lovely little flat," Otto chimed in. I started; I'd never heard him express any sort of enthusiasm for my place. I usually go to his, a neat studio in leafy Wanstead. The few times he'd come to mine he'd looked around and made no comment, which for Otto meant disapproval. It's smaller than my last place, and more run-down, but it serves me fine. It's not dirty, and it doesn't cost the earth. Agent Cooper❷ would approve.

"Ah, solo living," Mr Salas said. "Can't be easy. Young woman on her own."

What the fuck is this guy's problem?

"And how about your family? Your parents? Do they live nearby?"

"My father passed away when I was sixteen," I said. Mrs Salas's face fell. "Oh, dear, I'm so sorry."

"And your mother?" Mr Salas said.

"Dad!" Otto said.

"We don't really get along," I said. This was mostly

true, if a little glib.*

"Oh, that's such a shame," Mrs Salas said.

"Otto's very lucky," I said, trying out a compliment, "to have such good parents."

"Bless you, dear," Mrs Salas said, laying a pudgy hand on my shoulder, and in that touch I felt what Otto must have had his entire life. I was, for a brief moment, incredibly jealous.

Things went better after that – for a while, anyway. The conversation turned to more mundane subjects – the weather, films, holidays. The food arrived, and I impressed Mrs Salas by using chopsticks to eat my rice – "I've never got the hang of it, dear" – and I learnt some new, and nice, things about Otto. I was pleased, if slightly disconcerted, the way you always are when someone familiar is shown to you in a new light.

Once, Mrs Salas told me proudly, she had caught a seven-year-old Otto putting a bag of sugar back in the cupboard, standing precariously on a kitchen chair. Thinking he had indulged in an illicit binge she'd proceeded to tell him off, only to find he'd made sugar-water for an exhausted bumblebee in the back garden. The bumblebee, having recovered its strength, had buzzed off happily a short time later.

"I asked him, 'Why did you do that, Otto?'" said Mrs Salas. "And he said, 'Because I could.'"

Mr Salas was less interested in such stories, and told me instead about all the accolades and awards Otto had received at school.

"What was that one you got in Year Nine?" he

---

* It has little bearing on this document, but my mother and I have not spoken since I moved to London for university (and subsequently stayed here for work), but in truth we haven't *talked* since my father's funeral. My father was the closest thing either of us had ever had to a best friend, and when he died it became clear to both of us, almost immediately, that there was very little binding us together and even less worth preserving. We had nothing in common except a dead person.

251

said around a mouthful of breaded chicken. "The commendation. You know the one. They had a special evening for it."

"That wasn't just for me, Dad," Otto said. "It was an awards evening."

"But what was it?" Mr Salas persisted.

"Most merits, wasn't it?" Mrs Salas said.

"No, that was the year before," Mr Salas said. "I can't remember. I'll have to have a look when we get back."

Throughout this exchange Otto focused on his food, only looking up occasionally to give me a pained smile.

I have to be honest: despite the earlier cross-examination, I was enjoying myself. Mr Salas was a bit too insistent, Mrs Salas slightly cloying, but both of them clearly adored their son. I can imagine that an extended period of time in their company would become infuriating, but in a public place, for dinner, they seemed like good company, and good people.

And I wish, I really wish, that Mr Salas had just left things alone – but then who the fuck am I to judge someone for that?

We finished our food, and there was a sense that the evening was winding down. We were waiting for our plates and bowls to be taken away and for someone to say, "Anyone want dessert?" when Mr Salas thought he would have one more stab at solving what, to him, was obviously a great mystery.

"So come on, Alex," he said. "We're friends now. Why don't you want to go back into pentesting, eh?"

"Dad," Otto said.

"Don't answer if you don't want to, dear," Mrs Salas said to me, and shot a glance at her husband.

Mr Salas looked at me, waiting for an answer. He had been drinking plum wine throughout the evening, and his face was flushed.

"It just wasn't for me," I said.

"Not for you?" Mr Salas repeated. "Why? Weren't you good at it?"

"Dad!"

"I was very good at it."

"You didn't enjoy it, then."

"I did enjoy it."

"Did you get fired? Did you make a mistake?"

"No."

"Well, why, then, for heaven's sake?"

"It's not really any of your business."

In the ensuing silence I noticed the waiter hovering a few feet away. He had been about to collect our plates and was now undecided as to whether he should let the scene play out first. If it had been another table this was happening to, I would have found it funny, the way he took a couple of steps forward then back, trying to gauge the mood, his smile flashing on and off as the signals changed.

"There's no need to be rude," Mr Salas said.

"I was being polite, Mr Salas."

"I disagree."

"I can be less polite if you want."

"Alex," Otto said.

"Yes?"

"Just— we've had a nice evening. Just leave it."

"I'm curious, that's all," Mr Salas said, staring at me. "*Wanting* to be an IT lackey. Seems odd to me. There must be a reason behind it."

"There is a reason behind it," I said. I picked up my chopsticks, rolling them between my fingers.

"Alex, don't," Otto said. "He doesn't know."

Mr Salas leant forward, and I could smell the plum-wine fumes on his breath. "Know what?"

"I killed someone." ❶

There was a little gasp from Mrs Salas, and a muted crack; to my surprise I realised I had snapped my chopsticks in half.

"Ah," Mr Salas said. "I— well—"

"It's not—" Otto began. "One of Alex's friends… Well, she's joking, that's all."

"Wait until you hear the fucking punchline," I said.

"OK, I think we should go," Otto said, scrambling for his wallet.

"They never found the body."

"Alex—"

"*What?*"

There was a hush, and after a while I realised it was because every other diner had turned in their seat to look at us. The only sound was an insistent clicking, like drips from a tap.

"Alex, you're bleeding," Otto said quietly.

I looked down and saw a few drops of blood had fallen into the ruins of my chicken firecracker, mixing with the oily sauce. I grabbed a tissue, held it to my nose, and with as much dignity as I could muster I stood up and walked out.

That was two hours ago, and although I have – half in hope, half in fear – checked my phone a couple of times, there has been nothing from Otto. No doubt he's trying to convince his parents that I'm sane.

It doesn't matter. It never matters. I came back here, turned on my computer, and wrote all this down, because you're going to know *everything*. Never say that I hid anything from you. You get it all.

* * *

Here is someone who played the game, *there* is someone else. *Here* is someone who died. *There* is someone who killed someone. *Here* – right here, with me – was someone who played the game. *Here* was someone who went missing. The game is screaming at us: I WANT TO KILL YOU. I WANT TO HURT YOU. Like all weapons, The Helmsman's is beside itself with the single-mindedness of its own purpose. It chants it, never tiring, a monotonous dirge that will never stop.

* * *

Sometimes I wonder what I would do if The Helmsman ever contacted me. I wonder how I would feel. Whether I would try to reach through the monitor and kill him, or scream – or just sit there dumbly and read the answers I don't want to know.

* * *

Today, up until this evening, was a non-event. I heard nothing from Otto and so I wrote, taking occasional breaks to stare at the rain-spattered window and the blare and glare of the television, trying to ignore the squeezing pain in my head – not drinking enough *water*, Alex – and taking more paracetamol than I strictly should when that failed. I suppose I should see a doctor, but I have always been prone to headaches, especially when I don't get enough sleep. There is always the vicarious thrill, isn't there, of speculating as to the cause of a headache. Too much caffeine, not enough? Too much sleep, not enough? Stress? Eyestrain? God help us, any of the catastrophic conditions in my long-ago medic friend's textbook, her gigantic compendium of Ways In Which We Are Fucked?

The only thing of note happened an hour ago, when I got an email❶ from Ken Onek.

Holly Soames①
16/11/2019 15:41
Check with forensics whether this email was on WEBSTER'S phone – it does not appear on the imaging exhibit (CW/07). Initial research suggests it is not possible to recover identifiers from messages sent using anonymous remailers (a multi-hop, encrypted method of sending emails which works in a similar way to Tor), but confirm this. Note additional identifier for WEBSTER and recurring usage of the 'Andrea WALKER' alias.

Anonymous Remailer (nullus) <mixmaster@remailer.
nullus.null>
To: andreawalker31337@protonmail.com

Show details
Yesterday

Dear Ms Webster,
My name is Ken Onek. We have not spoken before.
Previously I communicated with you and your colleague
via my associates. You know them as the Rearguard.
Sadly they do not wish to contact you. What is left of
them. So I am doing so directly.

I am sorry for the loss of your colleague. The outcome
of the game is often a coin toss. It affects people in
different ways. I am sure there is some way it could be
predicted. But as you know this is not currently possible.

I have heard from sources that you are still involved
in the game. This is your choice. I won't try to convince
you to stop. But please remember what happened to your
friend. And understand that it could happen to you.

I believe you were on the final stage and want the
last chapter. The game is still active. I will not give you
a hint. But perhaps it will help if you try to understand
why the last stage gives you so much difficulty. Doing so
helped me.

I am the only person to finish the game and go back
to my life. This was not easy. It is not likely there will be
another one like me. You should understand this.

Even then this is not my life as it was. It is different
now. I find it hard to talk to people. Sometimes I have to
focus hard not to remember. Sometimes not to think. I
would not wish this on anyone.

What I wanted to say was this.

You and your colleague would have seen ███
████████████. Maybe you see them now. They
will leave you alone if you stop playing. They will leave

you alone if you stop asking questions. They don't care about anything else.

This is not a threat. I am just telling you how it is. They are not there just to scare you. They have killed people before.❶ They do not like the game. They are trying to stop it. And to stop people playing it.

Finally, The Helmsman. If you finish the game you will meet him. This is a strange thing. Most likely it will not be good for you. He is different. I do not love him, but I do not hate him either. He is doing what he does.

We all do.

Ms Webster, I hope you make the right decisions for yourself. I wish you the best of luck in whatever course of action you take.

Kind regards,
Ken Onek

The Rearguard, despite telling me to fuck off, had passed my message on, but Ken Onek, whoever and wherever he is, seems determined to stay neutral. He knows what the weapon is and won't tell me. He probably has a copy of the sixth chapter too. I couldn't even reply to him because he'd used an anonymous remailer. Fine. *Fuck him.* If you're reading this, and if this ever goes public, make sure this is known – he could have helped and chose not to.

* * *

There is a large house. It is empty but its atmosphere is as thick and cloying as soil. It is split into six flats,❷ and the names of the occupants appear on a buzzer beside the porch. One of these names is *his* name.

I stand outside it, hear the roar of traffic from the dual carriageway, smell the frying chicken from the restaurant❸ across the road. Crickets chitter in overgrown grass. The house slumps exhausted under a late afternoon sun.

Steel sheets are nailed to each window and across the front door. Behind them there could be anything. Emptiness. Long still days and nights. Him, squatting in the darkness, eyes shining. A laptop open.

I blink and now I am standing by the front door. Maybe nobody has stood here for decades. I feel like an astronaut, a first step of all-too-human flesh-and-blood legs on alien rock. The word 'astronaut' means 'star sailor', did you know that? How beautiful we can be when we want to. Sailing amongst the stars in the blue nowhere.

I look at the buzzer beside me. The labels are scratched and faded, and from one side a wire protrudes, sheared and speckled with grime. I cannot look for his name because I don't know what it is, but I press one of the buttons and from somewhere deep within the building there is a harsh insectile rattle, a crackle of signal. It sounds for several seconds, and there is quiet once more.

I listen for anything stirring inside, the thumping of naked feet as something comes tearing down the stairs, eager for visitors. He made this his home. Is it any wonder there should be monsters as the tenants now? But there is nothing.

I run my hands over the shutter on the front door. The steel is warm from the heat of the day's sun. It is rough, the surface pitted and dull. It was installed some time ago and the bolts are rusted. There is a faded sticker in one corner, placed by the security company who installed it. I can make out a cheerful cartoon guard-dog with a vacuous grin, and a barely legible slogan above it: *Barkaus Security...* ❶ *we're barking mad about your safety!*

I know, somehow, that there is a wall around the back garden. I could jump it and try to find a way in at the rear, but I don't need to, because if I think about it I can get in any time I want. I close my eyes, and I can tell from the way the air moves differently against my skin, and the temperature, and the smells, that I am somewhere else. I am inside the house. I buzzed and was admitted.

Something about this tugs at my brain for attention, like a fish-hook, but too lightly for me to take any notice. I try to file it away for later but even in the dream I acknowledge that I will have forgotten it upon waking.

I open my eyes. By a narrow stream of light where the steel sheet does not quite fit flush to the doorframe, I can see. I am in a hallway, dingy and cramped and thick with dust. Underneath my feet is a carpet of brittle envelopes, letters addressed to long-ago occupants and never opened. The twisted carcass of a broken pram leans against the wall.

I feel only the barest suggestion of fear, a low mutter on the lip of my mind.

There are doors in the hallway, and they are not for me. I must leave whatever is in those rooms to its quiet rest. My business is upstairs.

I move through the hallway, my feet trailing through thick inches of dust and paper-thin leaves. I look at the doors and see letters pinned to them: A, B, C.

I reach the foot of the stairs and look up. For one heart-stopping moment I think there is a figure on the landing looking down at me.

I climb the stairs. Another door here, D, and another, E. And then, on my left, the right one: F.

I stand in front of the door. It is painted white, the paint cracked and rubbed off in places like enamel worn from a tooth.

I knock. I close my eyes again, and this time the change is more subtle. I open my eyes and I am in the flat where he lived.

I walk from room to room. There is nothing here, not even remnants of furniture. The electrical sockets and light-switch plates have been removed, leaving gaping holes in the walls. The space is aggressively, insistently vacant.

But as I walk I reconcile the emptiness with what I know of the landmarks. Here is where he slept, because the window faces out towards the back garden where a huge fir tree once swayed in the wind. And so that is where his bedside table stood, where he saw a cockroach scout as he opened his eyes.

Here is the living room, where he sat and watched television and worked on his laptop and tried not to think about the colony of insects nesting in all the places he couldn't see.

Here is the toilet, which his colleague wanted to use after a night out, and when he saw what had been done with the traps and the diatomaceous earth he backed away, afraid, and left.

And here is the tiny tiled kitchen. The place where he saw the first cockroach, the location of the final stand. I bend to look at the floor, wondering if some of the dust is in fact old diatomaceous earth, fossilised remains of algae and plankton now once again lying undisturbed. And that's when I see it, the only evidence that anything lived here: the dried husk of a cockroach egg sac, pallid and delicate in the gloom, and next to it a dead cockroach, its insides evaporated to leave an exoskeleton as fragile and ready to crumble as an ancient page.

If he is not here then why am I? What do I have to gain from this?

"Because you can save the world," a voice says behind me.

Jay.

He looks no different to the last time I saw him, on an August night in Las Vegas. I say to him, as though it is the most natural thing in the world that he should be standing in front of me, "I don't know if I can."

"Of course you can," he says. "Piece of piss. Watch the master work."

"I'm sorry," I say. "I shouldn't have—"

"It's done."

"But Eoin—"

"He'll understand. He just needs time, that's all."

"How can I save the world? I couldn't save you. I can't even save myself."

"Pass it on."

"You mean—"

"And I'm sorry, Alex, I really am. But you won't know anything about it. You'll be gone."

"I loved you, you know," I say, and I see his face twist in pain and something small and important breaks deep inside me. "We could have been friends, couldn't we? For a long, long time."

Jay nods, and I was furious at *him*, then, for all he has taken from us. All the moments that could have been. All that potential, smashed in a brutal onslaught of mindless certainty. And it isn't fair. It isn't *fair*.

Then something shifts in the room, there is some subtle difference in the energy, and I look at Jay and his face is changing. It is drying out. The moisture drains from it as though he is being dehydrated, like a time-lapse of rotting fruit. His eyes become dull, wrinkling and blackening. His skin shrinks over the bones in his face. His lips draw back over his teeth and shrivel until they disappear entirely. His hair recedes until there are just a few straggling wisps dangling from his skull.

I am seeing what happened to Jay's body in the hot dry slap of the desert. Only it is sped up now, occurring in seconds rather than days.

The thing that had been Jay still stands, and it can still speak. It addresses me, and its voice, whilst rasping and thin, is still so obviously Jay's voice that I almost

scream, expecting to see ██████████████████,
mimicking Jay as they had done before.

"OK not to know," the figure recites. "OK not to
know. OK not to know."

I know what it is going to say next, it's going to tell
me it was all my fault, all of it – and why wouldn't it?
It's the truth. It's going to say that Eoin hates me and
The Rearguard, what's left of them, hate me and that I
might as well have killed Jay myself, and at some point
while thinking all of this I blink and I am standing
outside the house again, and there *he* is.

I have wondered, so many times, what I would do
if I ever saw him. What I should say to him. How to put
into words what he has done with my life.

I look at him – he doesn't identify himself, of
course, but I know it is him, and the funny thing is, he
looks so fucking *ordinary*, so fucking *normal*. I don't
know what I was expecting – the truth of it is that we
are given human faces, every one of us. And I know that
after the dream I won't remember what he looked like.
I will only remember the surprise, that he should look
so – so mundane. So entirely middle-of-the-road *dull*.

* * *

We could have had years, Jay. Adventures at conferences.
Anecdotes from long-ago engagements. CTFs. Work
outings. Hacking together while Eoin joked and made
fun of us. Nights out, dinners, reunions, sharing life.
You could have taught me what you knew.

The further into this I go, the closer I get to that man
who crawled into my brain, the more certain I become
that for whatever reason, and as much as I might want
it to be different, it has to be like this. It will go on until
it stops, and when it does all those possibilities, which
have been tapering inexorably since the day I was born
– they will narrow to a single point, and at that point my
life, or what passes for it now, will be over.

This insipid and terrifying truth is all I have.

* * *

An alarm blares in a sterile corridor deep underground, and men with painted smiles run in formation, their mouths shaping words in Jay's voice.

An alarm blaring, and grainy photographs of our faces in a database, and lifetimes of silence behind steel doors.

* * *

Back then, I didn't tell Jay about ███████████ ██████, not until after Fairlop Waters, when it was already too late. I struggled with it – after all, as he had said, we were partners, and I had promised not to keep anything from him – but I was still arguing with myself as to what I had actually seen. Bullshit, obviously, because on some level I knew exactly what it was. I had been threatened, and whatever I might have tried to tell myself – that I had exaggerated or misconstrued or dreamt what I had seen – it couldn't supplant the dread that I barely kept at bay.

But if I am lethally honest, here is the truth: I just wanted to keep playing. I had to know what was at the end – I was obsessed with knowing. The incident outside my flat had scared me, yes, but more than that it had *excited* me. The game was branching, diverging, from a linear progression of puzzles and chapters into something more terrifying and wonderful and inexplicable, and I didn't want it to stop. And I told myself that Jay would feel the same, and so it hardly mattered if I told him or not.

The Helmsman knows all this, of course. He knows that people like us cannot and will not stop until they reach the end, wherever it takes them. He knows it and takes full advantage of it, and I can hardly expect anything else from someone like him. Whether I like it or not, and whatever else he may be, he is one of us.

"Come to mine this evening?" Jay said in a low voice at the end of the day, as we packed our laptops away. He grinned. "Eoin's been working on the crossword."

I often wonder if that, right there, was the point of no return for us both. It seems as though it should have been the aftermath of the insanity of Fairlop Waters, when it became undeniably clear to both of us that the game was not what we thought it was – but I think it was probably this moment, because it was when I decided to keep what I knew from my friend. To press on into – literally, as it turned out – the void.

"Sounds good," I said.

* * *

Eoin opened the door, beaming, and ushered me inside. "Couldn't stay away, could you? How's the computer shit going?"

I laughed. "Alright. How's the crossword shit going?"

"Ah, well, take a seat and I'll tell you all about it. Tea? Coffee?"

I declined and followed him into the living room, where Jay was sitting on the sofa with his laptop open on his knees. I took the armchair opposite, the same one I'd sat in the night we cracked the Riddle Machine.

"So, the crossword," Eoin said, reaching for a sheaf of papers on the coffee table and pulling it towards him. "It's going… OK. I think."

"Oh yeah?" I said. "How many have you done?"

"Six."

"Six?"

"Don't look at me like that, Alex. It's not easy. Most of the clues are in your wheelhouse, not mine."

He showed me his print-out.

"Rearguard?" I said, looking at three across.

"Well, yeah," Jay said. "They're part of it, aren't

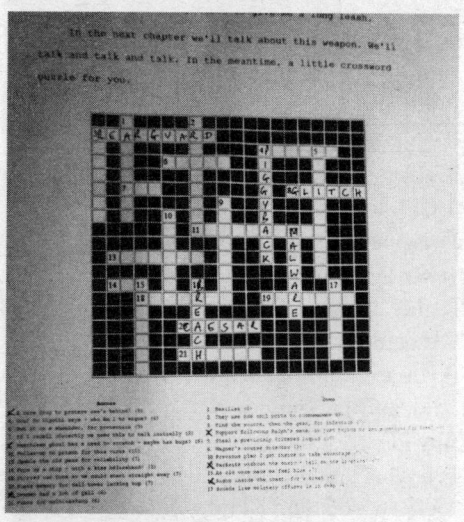

they? Why wouldn't they be there?"

DO WE NEED TO VISIT JAY MORTON?

I smiled. "Yeah, duh. Sorry."

"I need the both of you to take a look," Eoin went on. "I know crosswords, but I don't know cyber."

Jay groaned. "Eoin, I fucking hate crosswords."

"So do I," I said.

"Hey, it's *your* game," Eoin said. "You'd better start liking them."

I leant across to read the clues. "Fine. Where do we start?"

"We'll pick off the easy ones first," Eoin said. "Anything that suggests an anagram. Like here, thirteen across: 'Jumble the old pens for reliability.' The answer's seven letters, so the fodder is 'old pens'."

Jay typed the letters out. "And what are we looking for?"

"In a normal crossword, you'd be looking for a synonym for 'reliability', using those letters. But like I said, this one's a bit... I don't know. Off."

"OK, so maybe it's 'reliability' in a cyber security

context," I said. "Like – like a stable release of software or something."

"But that doesn't mean 'reliable'," Jay pointed out. "And it's not to do with security."

"It was just an example," I said, a little defensively. "Like I said, I don't like crosswords."

Jay tapped his fingers on the coffee table. "And using these letters, you say?"

"Right," Eoin said.

"We could try—"

"If you even *hint* at brute forcing I'm going to kick off," I said, and Jay smiled.

"Any ideas?" Eoin said.

"Jay, what's that thing called – with exploits, you know? When you don't know where you're going to land in memory."

"Oh, yeah. NOP sled."❶

"Well, it fits. What the hell's a NOP sled? Never mind, I don't care." Eoin wrote it down. "Easy, right? Like taking prizes from a helmsman."

"You think that's what's at the end?" I said. "Prizes?" *Help. Help. Help. Help. Help.*

"Prizes, fame, and an absolute shitload of cash," Eoin said. "OK, there's another anagram one here, eighteen across. 'Stirred our tuna so we could start straight away'."

"Start straight away," Jay said thoughtfully.

"Autorun,"❷ I said, and Eoin looked at the grid and gave me a thumbs-up.

"Now we're cooking with gas. I thought you said you hated crosswords."

"I didn't say I wasn't good at them," I said. Jay gave me an appraising look and then shook his head, laughing.

"The Helmsman doesn't know what he's letting himself in for," he said. "Come on, what's next?"

Two of the answers were old types of malware

(eleven across and fifteen down, 'SQL Slammer' and 'Sadmind') which Jay eventually worked out – although it was clear the style of the clues was making him increasingly irate – and a couple of others were straightforward once we'd discussed them aloud for a few minutes (six across: 'Put it on a shoulder, for protection'. My brain refused to come up with anything except 'epaulette', until Eoin said, "Isn't a patch a cyber thingy?").

Eoin explained some of the vagaries of cryptic crosswords to me as we worked out more of the clues: that a reference to a 'ship' usually means the letters 'ss', and a reference to a 'kiss' means 'x' (fourteen across: 'Pops up a ship – with a kiss beforehand' – 'XSS').

"You know, I thought it might be that," he said, "but I wasn't sure what the hell 'XSS' might mean."

"It's a type of attack against web applications where you—" Jay began, and Eoin held up a hand.

"Didn't say I wanted to know, Jay-Jay. There's not enough room in my brain as it is, without all this shite."

"Jay-Jay?" I said.

"Shut up, Alex," Jay said, going red. I couldn't remember ever seeing him embarrassed before.

And suddenly – well, it felt sudden, although I looked at my phone and realised we'd been working on it for ninety minutes – there were only a handful of clues left.

"Now these," Eoin said, "these ones I've left 'til last, because I've got no fecking idea. I mean, look at this one: 'Basilisk', eight letters. Now what the hell is that? When have you ever seen a cryptic crossword clue with one word?"

Jay put his head in his hands and groaned theatrically. "My head hurts."

"It's because you don't use your words often enough. Go and take a break, yeah? Make me and Alex a cup of tea."

Jay stomped off to the kitchen.

"He gets a bit riled up with crosswords," Eoin said. "Sometimes I'll be doing one and say the clues out loud just to wind him up."

I laughed. "You're a bad person."

From the kitchen came the sound of a kettle starting to boil, the clatter of spoons, and loud, tuneless humming.

"Jay told me about your meeting with those Rearguard people," Eoin said. "They said some of this is real? What's that about, then?"

I didn't pause. I didn't even blink. It came out sounding perfectly natural and light-hearted. "Oh, nothing. Just weirdos hamming it up, that's all."

Eoin's disconcerting eyes examined me from different angles, and then he seemed to reach a decision and nodded.

"OK," he said, and that was it.

Jay came in, two cups of tea in his hands. "There'd better be fucking prizes," he said, putting the cups down on the table. "I'd rather do another ten Riddle Machines than this bullshit."

"'Sounds like military officer is in deep'," Eoin said loudly, ignoring him. "So something that rhymes with a military officer... captain, lieutenant, general, colonel, field marshal—"

"Oh," I said. "Kernel. Like a computer kernel." ❶

"Like popcorn, you mean?" Eoin said, and wrote it in the grid. "Good spot."

"Cryptic crosswords are just bad puns, basically, aren't they?"

Eoin gave me a pained look, but Jay nodded fervently. "Yes, that's exactly what they are. I hate puns as well."

"That's very homophonic of you," Eoin said. Jay threw a cushion at him.

Soon we were left with the weird ones. After

Holly Soames①
18/11/2019 11:57
Core part of an
operating system.

268

some thought, I realised that nine down, 'Wagner's course director' (–L—N) was 'Helmsman', because of course it was; he hadn't been able to resist putting himself in the puzzle.[*] ❶

After solving those, and a few of the simpler remaining clues, we had two left: four across ('You! So Ligotti says – who am I to argue?', P—E-) and one down ('Basilisk', -A—I–).

"They both look more like standard crossword clues to me," Eoin said. "Not cryptic ones."

It was getting late, and in the end we had to guess. Jay – who was, I think, relieved to have something practical to do – did some research and found that Thomas Ligotti was a horror writer ❷ who often used puppets as a motif. 'Puppet' fit, so Eoin wrote it in, although I thought it might be 'player.'

As for one down, the only thing I could think of was 'basilisk'.

"But it can't be that," Eoin protested. "It's the fundamental rule of crossword setting: you never put the answer itself in the clue."

"Maybe that's the point," I said. Eoin shrugged. He didn't like it, but in the absence of any other ideas, he reluctantly wrote 'basilisk' into the squares.

Holly Soames② **25/11/2019 04:48**
Advise that we don't take WEBSTER's assumption at face value here. THE HELMSMAN's allusions may well have meanings or connections that WEBSTER did not infer.

Holly Soames② **18/11/2019 12:34**
WEBSTER apparently didn't spot it, but there is also a reference to puppets in The Riddle Machine's output. Flagging for further research; suggest comparing LIGOTTI's works with the contents of c1–5 THT.

[*] While The Helmsman rarely (with a few exceptions) appears to be boastful in *The Helmsman Texts*, I can't help but think that the chapters and the game must be the product of a fairly large ego. It's hard to believe that coming up with a basilisk capable of hurting people through *thought* wouldn't result in a significant increase in one's self-importance (it is, in many ways, the ultimate hack, and a hacker's self-worth is usually intimately tied to their abilities) – but perhaps that says more about me than it does about him. The clue also indicates that The Helmsman is at least aware that his alias is a minor character in *Der fliegende Holländer* (The Flying Dutchman), which may also suggest that the name 'Marlow Tannhauser' does originate from Wagner's *Tannhäuser und der Sängerkrieg auf Wartburg*. Perhaps I should do further research, but it may just be The Helmsman making an allusion without much thought to it – something he also does occasionally in *The Helmsman Texts*.

And just like that, we had a finished grid.

Jay took a picture of it on his phone and emailed it to The Helmsman, and a few seconds later there was a reply.

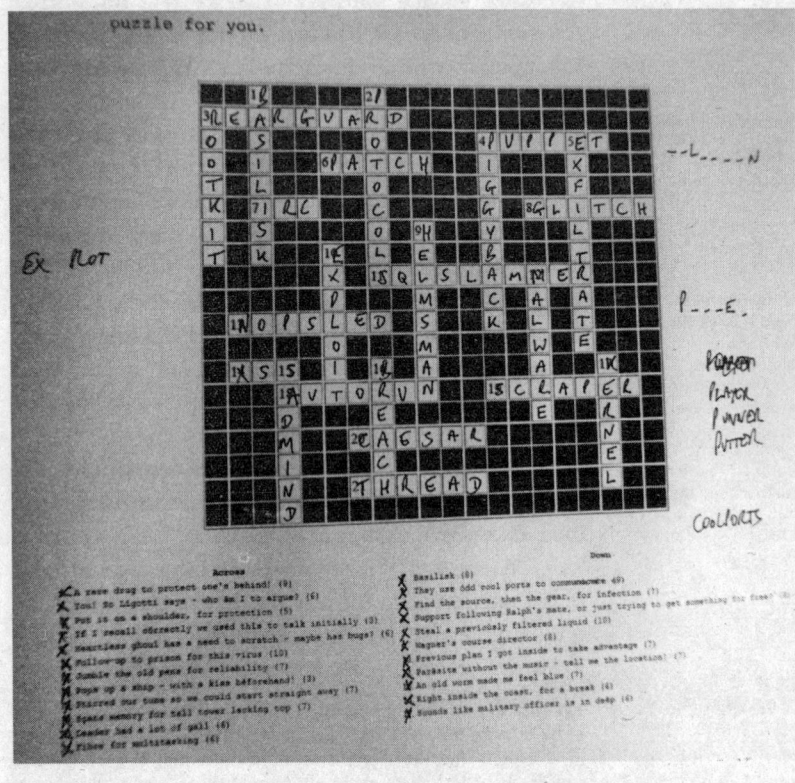

"Oh, fuck *off*," he said.

"We must have got something wrong," I said.

"We didn't," Eoin said.

"The Ligotti one, maybe, or the basilisk—"

"No, it's not that," Eoin said. "The reply came straight away, didn't it? Not even enough time to check the answers."

"What do you mean?"

"I mean it's obvious to your man that we haven't solved it. The crossword isn't the answer, there's another stage. I do it with my puzzles all the time – a puzzle behind the puzzle. I knew it felt too easy."

"That felt easy?" Jay said.

"Maybe the first letter of each answer spells something out, something like that. I don't know. But it's not just the crossword."

We lapsed into a disappointed torpor. Jay took the crossword grid, leant back, and placed it over his face.

"You'll stay for dinner, Alex?" Eoin said eventually.

"No, I don't want to intrude," I said. "I'll take off and come back at the weekend, maybe."

"Ah, don't be stupid, stay for dinner."

"*Guys, shut up.*"

We turned to Jay, who was looking very closely at the print-out. He put it right up to his eyes, then slowly drew it away.

"What? What is it?" Eoin said. "Is it a Magic Eye picture or something?"

"No, listen. What are these little squiggles?"

"What squiggles?"

"Here, look. You know. The ones they have in French or whatever."

Eoin took the paper from him, and I leaned over to see.

"Well fuck me," he breathed. "How the hell did we miss that?"

ACROSS

3. A rare drug to protect one's behind! (9)
4. You! So Lîgotti says - who âm I to argue? (6)
6. Put it on a shoulder, for protection (5)
7. If I recall côrrectly we uséd thîs to talk initially (3)
8. Heartless ghoul has a need to scratch - maybe has bugs? (6)
11. Follow-up to prison for this virus (10)
13. Jumble the old pens for reliability (7)
14. Pops up a ship - with a kiss bêforehand! (3)
18. Stirred our tuna so we could start straight away (7)
19. Sçans memory for tall tower lackîng top (7)
20. Leader had a lot of gall (6)
21. Fibre for multitasking (6)

DOWN

1. Basilisk (8)
2. They use ódd cool ports to communicate (9)
3. Find the source, then the gear, for înfection (7)
4. Support following Ralph's mate, or just trying to get something for free? (9)
5. Steal a previoúsly filtered liquid (10)
9. Wagner's course director (8)
10. Previous plan I got inside to take advantage (7)
12. Parâsite without the music - tell me the location! (7)
15. An old worm made me feel blue (7)
16. Right inside the coast, for a break (6)
17. Sounds like military officer is in deêp (6)

As you can imagine, it cheered Jay up no end to find out that we'd probably wasted almost two hours solving a crossword we didn't need to solve, and at first we went about the next stage the wrong way too. Several of the letters in the clues – thirteen, all told – had circumflexes, accents or cedillas. Obviously, we looked at those first:

I, A, O, E, I, E, C, I, O, I, U, A, E

But neither Eoin nor a selection of online anagram tools could do anything with them.

"It's what you'd expect, they *would* be on vowels. It can't be an anagram."

After a few dead ends, we instead tried focusing on where the accents and circumflexes and cedillas were pointing, like this:

ACROSS

3. A rare drug to protect one'(s) behind! (9)
4. You! So Ligotti says - who am I to argue? (6)
6. Put it on a shoulder, for protection (5)
7. If I recall correctly we used this to talk initially (3)
8. Heartless ghoul has a need to scratch - maybe has bugs? (6)
11. Follow-up to prison for this virus (10)
13. Jumble the old pens for reliability (7)
14. Pops up a ship - with a kiss beforehand! (3)
18. Stirred our tuna so we could start straight away (7)
19. Scans memory for tall tower lacking top (7)
20. (L)eader had a lot of gall (6)
21. Fibre for multitasking (6)

DOWN

1. Basilisk (8)
2. They use odd cool ports to communicate (9)
3. Find the source, then the gear, for infection (7)
4. Support following Ralph's mate, or just trying to get something for free? (9)
5. Steal a previously filtered liquid (10)
9. Wagner's course director (8)
10. Previous plan I got inside to take advantage (7)
12. Parasite without the music - tell me the location! (7)
15. An old worm made me feel blue (7)
16. Right inside the coast, for a break (6)
17. Sounds like military officer is in deep (6)

U, S, H, O, R, T, R, L, 8, T, N, V, 6.

Holly Soames①
18/11/2019 13:08
Links to unconnected video at time of writing. Consider RIPA subs for the URLs it pointed to in 2018.

Holly Soames②
18/11/2019 13:44
No trace. Examine WEBSTER's copy, run past forensics. Consider RIPA subs to Google. Note that at various points in the video (e.g. 11s, 15s, 22s) the typist's left hand is partially visible. Appears to be IC1. WEBSTER appears to have missed this (or saw it and didn't think it noteworthy).

Eoin and I immediately started running the letters through online anagram solvers again, highlighting promising candidates to each other, while Jay sat quietly at his laptop.

"Something to do with 'volts', maybe."

"Holst? Could be music-related?"

"Truth? 'Lon rvs' truth. Does 'lon rvs' mean something in geek speak?"

And then, quite distinctly and very incongruously, we heard the sound of a typewriter coming from Jay's laptop. We turned to see him engrossed in something, delighted.

"It's a link, morons," he said affectionately. "Short URL. A shortening service. That's the across letters. And the ones in the down clues are the unique reference. Look."

He turned his screen towards us and typed 'shorturl.at/tnv68'❶ into the browser bar, and a YouTube video, again uploaded by Dev Null,❷ loaded.

We found ourselves watching a drab green typewriter, clacking away, as an unseen typist wrote a series of words – a strange poem, as the uploader had called it.

I was reminded forcibly of my father, and how he would have exclaimed over the video, telling us excitedly what make and model of typewriter it was – because he would have been able to, even from the close-up. For a second I felt an immense, tearing sadness.

The typist was writing what appeared to be a poem,❶ all in lower-case, the typing slow and deliberate.

The camera had obviously been fixed somewhere, tight on the paper and the bit of the typewriter that I remembered was called, after a few seconds of searching my memory, the type guide. There was no sound except for the slapping of typefaces.

"The poem talks about noise," I said. "Maybe we should download the video and run it through a spectrogram, like the first one?"

Holly Soames①
18/11/2019 15:01
No trace on open source.

---

* Because their links are so short, URL shortening services often reuse their references, particularly if a link goes dead. Since the original video has now been taken down, you might find something else in its place; this is nothing to do with the game or this document. I have uploaded a copy of the video to my channel at https://www.youtube.com/watch?v=JKWpGR3qRPc

when using a typewriter
you must
listen. a
strange thing can be
heard

as words occur, as
i
go
to
the next.
a rhythm, as I type.

in it,
is meaning, but
also intent.
words I mean
but didn't say.
can you hear them, now?
this machine talks.

speaks
volumes, to you
and to me. hear it
tell you what you're
looking for. this machine
is 60 years of age.
think
it's seen some things?
think
it has wisdom?

here is
an end, done,
a
stop. you
take it now.

"Doubt he'd use the same trick again," Jay said, but we did it anyway. Jay was right; The Helmsman, it seemed, didn't like to repeat himself, at least not when it came to puzzles.

"I think it's more to do with the *sound* of the typing," Eoin said. "Let me try something."

He played the video again, making notes on a piece of paper, and showed it to us.

"It could be the number of characters per line," he said. "Every key makes a sound, see? Including the spacebar. So just count the number of characters, or the number of sounds, and it's the typewriter talking to you."

"So what does that give us?" Jay said.

Eoin looked at his notes. "Oh, come on. Surely not – well, I'm almost disappointed."

"What?" Jay and I said together.

"It's just a simple substitution cipher. A is 1, B is 2, and so on."

"So what does it spell out?" Jay said impatiently.

Eoin made some more notes, murmuring to himself. "'White rabbit follows forty seven gmail'." ❶

"Could be a subdomain of Gmail?" Jay said to me. "Although I didn't think Gmail had anything like that." He typed it in anyway, and tutted when the 404 ❷ came back. "Thought so."

"Must be an email address, then," I said.

I'm sure that you've already guessed what we needed to do, but I'm ashamed to say that it took two hours for us to work it out. By the time we did it was very late, and I realised I hadn't eaten since breakfast.

First, we researched the address using several search engines and ran it through various non-indexed forums and social media sites, techniques we often used for OSINT when researching executives and employees for social engineering engagements and phishing simulations. These turned up nothing.

Eoin then suggested that perhaps the email address

Holly Soames①
18/11/2019 15:23
No trace. Consider RIPA subs.

Holly Soames②
18/11/2019 15:25
i.e. 404 error = page not found.

itself was the answer, so we sent it to The Helmsman, and shortly afterwards received that same smug one-word response:

(no subject) **Inbox**
The Basilisk <thisisthebasilisk@gmail.com>
to me
NOPE!

"But we're definitely on the right track, aren't we?" Jay said, for what must have been the fifth or sixth time, and I wondered idly if Eoin or I would be the first to murder him. "White rabbit. It's obvious, isn't it? We must be on the right track."

"But we don't know what to do," I said through gritted teeth.

Eoin got up, stretching. "Christ, it's late. Anyone want a drink?"

Jay accepted, I declined, and Eoin went into the kitchen. I heard the kettle click on.

"What if we brute forced it?" I said quietly.

Jay looked at me. "Alex Webster, suggesting a brute force attack? You've changed your tune."

"I'm out of ideas."

"Now you know how it feels."

"Could we, though?"

Jay drummed his fingers on the brim of his cap. "Not really. It's not like brute forcing a cipher or something. It's an account, it belongs to someone. Under the CMA—"

"But if we're authorised to do it, implicitly, I mean, then—"

"Ha. You've been spending too much time with Nina."

Eoin came back in and said what you, friends, have probably been thinking all along.

"Guys, why don't we just send an email to it?"
So we did.

* * *

We argued for a while about what to send. Jay suggested the completed crossword as an attachment and Eoin thought it should be a completely blank message, but in the end we went with my idea, an email containing what we had come to think of as The Helmsman's calling card: *HELLO FRIEND!* in cheerful, shouting capital letters.

And almost immediately there was a reply.

We looked at the block of text that had been sent back. "Must be some sort of canned response," Jay said.

(no subject) **Inbox**
Jay Morton 2.23 AM (0 minutes ago)
HELLO FRIEND!
white rabbit
to me 2.24 AM (0 minutes ago)
Woriað þa winsalo, waldend licgað

dreame bidrorene, duguþ eal gecrong,

wlonc bi wealle. Sume wig fornom,

ferede in forðwege, sumne fugel oþbær

ofer heanne holm, sumne se hara wulf

deaðe gedælde, sumne dreorighleor

in eorðscræfe eorl gehydde.

Yþde swa þisne eardgeard ælda scyppend
oþþæt burgwara breahtma lease

eald enta geweorc idlu stodon.

Se þonne þisne wealsteal wise geþohte

278

ond þis deorce lif deope geondþenceð,

frod in ferðe, feor oft gemon

wælsleahta worn, ond þas word acwið:

"Hmm," Eoin said. "Didn't expect that."

We worked out where the poem was from pretty quickly,❶ but we would have been there trying to figure out why The Helmsman had sent it to us until the sun rose, had Jay not selected all the text to copy it into a document.

"Hang on," he said, excitement creeping into his voice. "What's that? Look, between the lines."

----

white rabbit
to me 2.24 AM (0 minutes ago)
Woriað þa winsalo, waldend licgað
..
dreame bidrorene, duguþ eal gecrong,
-...
wlonc bi wealle. Sume wig fornom,
-...
ferede in forðwege, sumne fugel oþbær
-.-.
ofer heanne holm, sumne se hara wulf
---
deaðe gedælde, sumne dreorighleor
.-..
in eorðscræfe eorl gehydde.
...-

"Fuck yes," Eoin said, and immediately reached for his paper and pencil, writing down dots and dashes. "It's Morse code."

He carefully typed it into an online decoder.

Holly Soames①
18/11/2019 16:39
An excerpt from 'The Wanderer', an Anglo-Saxon poem. The extract translates (approximately) as: "The halls rot, their lords lie, deprived of happiness, the army fallen, the proud band by the wall. War took them, carried them away, one a bird took, over the ocean, one a grey wolf passed to death, one a grin-faced man buried underground. And God destroyed this place, until, without the noise of men, the ancient work of giants was empty. A man who thinks wisely on this, and considers this dark life, a wise man who remembers all the wars from afar, speaks these words:"

Significance of this passage unknown, outside my expertise but flagged for further research.

Translate a Message

Input:

.. -... -... -.-. --- .-.. ...- -.-- ...- ----. --.- -..

Output:

IBBCOLVYV9QD

"What's that meant to be, then?" he said.

Jay clapped his hands together. "ImgBB," he said, grinning. "It's an image hosting site. ibb.co is the domain, and then the stuff after it is the reference." ❶

We had to play around with the casing, but eventually we got a hit: a photo of a book cover, *Metadata* by Jeffrey Pomerantz.*

"That's it, then," I said. "It must be. We send the name of the book to The Helmsman."

Jay fired off the email, and received a different reply this time.

(no subject) **Inbox**

The Basilisk <thisisthebasilisk@gmail.com>

to me

HAHA NOPE BUT SO CLOSE!

"Is this ever going to fucking end?" he growled.

Eoin patted his knee. "Almost there."

"Yes, almost there, Jay-Jay," I said, and ducked as another cushion sailed through the air. "Look at the title, though. *Metadata*. Maybe there's something in the image itself?" ❷

Jay saved the image and uploaded it to an online metadata analysis site.

---

*Again, the ImgBB link is now down, but you should be able to find the same image (albeit not *quite* the same) elsewhere.

Holly Soames①
18/11/2019 17:02
No trace. Consider RIPA subs.

Holly Soames②
18/11/2019 20:03
i.e. EXIF data – data embedded within an image, which may include the camera make and model, the date and time taken, location data, author data, etc. It can be extracted with dedicated tools. Usually it's automatically included in images at the point of capture, by the device – but can be edited afterwards.

Camera

Make 978-0465026562

Author and Copyright

Copyright not found.

Location

GPS coordinates not found.

EXIF

Make 978-0465026562
Padding (Binary data
2060 bytes, use -b
option to extract)

XMP

XMP data not found.

"What am I looking at?" Eoin said.

"This one," Jay said, pointing to the 'Camera Make' field.

"That load of numbers? How do you know?"

"It's the only one with something in it, for a start." He pasted the number❶ into Google, and the results loaded.

"*Gödel, Escher, Bach: An Eternal Golden Braid?*" Eoin said, frowning.

"I tried it once," Jay said. "Never got past the first chapter. Something to do with Bach writing a song for a king, then I got lost. But a few people I know have read it. Alex?"

I shook my head.

"I hope we don't have to read the damn thing," Jay said. "It was a doorstop, I remember that much."

"Forget about that, just send the email," I said, and he did, typing the title of the book in the body.

A few seconds later the third chapter arrived, and the three of us read it as the darkness slowly died outside. The Helmsman Texts – much like this document – were becoming less of a narrative and more a confession. Lab notes documenting – what? Triumph, elation, regret? A gibbering, screaming prayer for understanding?

"It's a hell of a story," Eoin said. "Needs tidying up, it's a bit all over the place, but Jesus. Where do you think it'll go from here? What do you think your man means by a 'real-world puzzle'?"

**Holly Soames❶
23/11/2019 01:12**

Appears to be ISBN number for the book referenced below, which is also mentioned in c4 THT regarding koans, and by DR KRAM, also in c4. Author: Douglas HOFSTADTER. Added to list of works to research further, which I am currently working through.

A *hell of a story*. Suddenly Jay and Eoin's house seemed smaller and more cramped, as though there was less oxygen, and a rising, falling voice chanted from somewhere far away.

THE HELMSMAN IS A BAD PERSON. HE THINKS BAD THOUGHTS.

"Who knows?" Jay said. "Long way to go yet. He said we're only halfway through."

"Well, let's have a drink," Eoin said. He went into the kitchen, returning with a bottle and three glasses, and poured us all a generous measure of what I assume was whisky.

"To the game," Jay said, and we toasted and drank.

"Ah, you've got to look people in the eye when you toast, Alex!" Eoin said. "Otherwise it's seven years of bad sex, so the Germans say!"

I smiled awkwardly as he chuckled and refilled our glasses.

"I've got one," Jay said. He cleared his throat, suddenly serious. "To Alex the hacker – nick pending, by the way, I'm still thinking about it – who brought us the game."

"The crossword queen!" Eoin shouted at the ceiling.

"I'm glad you talked me into it," Jay said. "I haven't had this much fun in ages. And I tell you what – it's going to be a fucking *awesome* con talk. Here's to you and me – this time next year we'll be writing our slides for DEF CON."

"To Alex!"

"To Alex."

I raised my glass and I looked them both in the eye. I could have told them about ███████████ ███████ then, and they might even have believed me, even if I wasn't sure that I believed it myself. But I looked them both right in the eye like nothing was wrong, like it hadn't even happened, and I accepted their toast and I drank. The alcohol scalded my throat like a chemical burn.

Eoin charged our glasses again, and the three of us sat there for a good hour, drinking and chatting, our eyes occasionally drawn to the screen of Jay's laptop in which those dark, playful and utterly horrendous – but also inescapably *fascinating* – words resided, like noxious little insects trapped behind glass.

THE HELMSMAN TEXTS:

Chapter 3

HELLO FRIEND!

My goodness, you're doing well. Doesn't it just feel wonderful to APPLY oneself to something??

How did you like the last puzzle? It wasn't my favourite, if I'm honest. A little too GIMMICKY I think, and less about hacking, but I need people with a wide range of skills and if you're here then you're 100% cutting the spicy mustard!!

There are three challenges left, and they're hard. But it will all be worth it. You will see the prettiest things and sing the prettiest songs. Once you're with me everything else falls away!

So I suppose you'd like to hear what happened next with those lovely people with whom I used to work. RED WORD and all the rest of it. And we'll get there, eager beaver, but first, here's something.

Who is experimenting on whom, do you think?

Let that think in 😊

Trains of thought carry such precious cargo. If they are not derailed, what might happen when the cargo is delivered? Consider the possibilities. ALL the possibilities.

You will see the prettiest things. You will sing the prettiest songs.

You will APPLAUD me.

WORD UP! A DIALOGUE

Holly Soames①
18/11/2019 21:09
No trace.

A young WRITER settles down at a coffee shop. The bell above the door rings, and Dr MARY BRYAM, ❶ a professor, walks in. She sits opposite the student.

M: You mentioned in your email this was for a book?

W: Yes, that's right. On unusual linguistic forms, if that makes sense, and—

M: Not really. What do you mean by unusual linguistic forms?

W: Right. Yes. I suppose, I mean I haven't really firmed it up yet, I'm still sort of digging around it, but basically it's on the capability of linguistics to cause harm.

M: Harm in what sense?

W: Confusion, disorientation, that sort of thing? Maybe even things more extreme?

M: Your book is about whether words can cause harm?

W: I suppose so.

M: This could be a very long interview, then.

W: How do you mean?

M: You're not familiar with the capacity of words to cause harm?

W: Oh. I see what you mean. No, I don't mean like insults and disinformation and that sort of thing. I'm more talking about the possibility of words to have an effect on people, similar to a biological weapon? To make them suddenly violent or irrational?

M: Sounds more like a novel to me.

W: It's just an idea I'm scoping out. Do you think it is?

M: Do I think it is what?

W: Possible.

M: No.

W: Oh. OK.

M: What sort of book are you writing, exactly?

W: It's a - it's non-fiction, but a sort of experimental thing, about strange uses of language and how it's complex and some parts of it aren't really understood and it can act in weird ways and sort of, you know, confuse us, maybe cause mental... unexpected mental effects, I suppose.

M: I see. Well, let me think. I've come across some odd corners of linguistics, to be sure. I'll try to help you if I can.

W: Thank you.

   [growl] **❶**

M: I'm sorry?

W: Hmm?

M: What was that?

W: I... sorry, I didn't say anything.

M: Never mind. In answer to your question, yes, there are certainly structures and uses of the English language - I'm presuming you're interested in English? I can't help you with any other languages, I'm afraid, English on its own has taken up thirty-two years of my career.

W: Oh. Good question. I'm not sure, but let's stick with English.

M: Very well. There are structures and uses of the English language which could cause confusion and a sense of - oh, I

Holly Soames①
18/11/2019 21:19
Unclear what this
signifies.

286

don't know - disorientation, you said?
Perhaps. I doubt it would actually affect
someone's behaviour, but confuse them for
a few seconds, yes. One of my favourites
is garden-path sentences.

W: Garden-path?

M: As in, being led up the. They've been
around for a long time - Thomas Bever
proposed it first, I believe, in the
Holly Soames ①
'The cognitive
basis for linguistic
structures' (1970)
seventies❶. It's a sentence which is
grammatically correct, but induces the
reader into a parsing which results in a
semantic blind alley, because there is
a more obscure meaning. I would have to
look it up, but I believe there may have
been something in the literature about
the cognitive effects of garden-path
sentences. ❷

[coughing]

W: And how extreme were those effects, do
you know?

M: Oh, mild, I think. Mildly disorienting.

W: Closer, then.

M: I'm sorry?

W: Can you give me an example?

Holly Soames②
18/11/2019 21:43
Unable to pin
this down from
the information
provided, but
some background:
'Disfluencies
along the garden
path: Brain
electrophysiological
evidence of disrupted
sentence processing'
by N.D. MAXFIELD
and others (2009).

M: It works better written down, but let's
see. 'The old man the boat' is the
classic example.

[pause]

W: I don't get it.

M: Exactly.

W: It's missing a word.

M: Is it?

W: Of course it is, it—

M: It's a perfectly legitimate sentence.
Listen again. The old man the boat.

W: I don't get it.

M: Break it down. Word by word.

W: The. Old.

M: Stop there. Now continue.

W: Man.

M: And stop again. Go on.

W: The. Boat.

M: It's difficult, isn't it? Do you understand it now? 'The old' is a collective noun – the elderly. They man the boat - they steer it. Clearer?

W: Oh. Oh! I get it.

M: Garden-path sentences are very deceptive. Your brain sees 'the old man' and immediately makes the deductive leap that it is the subject of the sentence. The object is the boat, but the verb, you presume, is missing. But of course that's not the case.

W: That's amazing.

M: The horse raced past the barn fell. There's another one for you. Don't rely on your first interpretation, that's the key. Whatever your brain tries to make you read, resist it.

W: The. Horse. Raced. Past. The. Barn. Fell. So the horse fell. Oh, because it was raced, the horse itself didn't race.

M: Precisely. 'Raced' here is not the simple past, but the passive participle. Well done. Did you read linguistics at university?

W: Computer Science.

M: Hmm. Similar, in some ways. The structure of syntax, computational linguistics, the rules of language, although I suppose programming languages have much less scope for interpretation than English. No room for these sorts of oddities, anyway.

W: It's like language hacking.

M: I suppose so, if you want to put it like that.

W: But you don't think garden-path sentences could have any strong, or lasting effects? Cognitively?

M: I very much doubt it. They have them in newspaper headlines all the time. Crash blossoms, they're called. "Police squad help dog bite victim". "Shark swims ashore in New Jersey". ❶ That kind of thing. Eye-rollingly funny.

Holly Soames①
18/11/2019 22:22
Unable to ascertain if these were ever genuine headlines, or the original sources.

W: Hahahahahahahahahahahahahahahahahahahaha.

M: Yes. Erm. What else, what else. Depth-charge sentences? They're rather fun. Maybe more the sort of thing you mean.

W: I'm all ears.

[faint growl]

M: Err… well, a depth-charge sentence is one where the intended meaning is disguised within a false meaning which, like garden-path sentences, is arrived at by a hasty deductive leap. Consider this: No lump on the body is too trivial to be ignored. ❷ What do you think that means?

Holly Soames②
18/11/2019 23:08
Likely adapted from "No head injury is too trivial to be ignored", which is from 'A verbal illusion', a paper by P.C. WASON and S.S. REICH (1979).

W: That if I have a lump on my body, I shouldn't ignore it.

M: Try again.

W: It means… does it mean all lumps on my body should be ignored… even IF they're trivial?

M: Well done. It's a very sneaky way of communicating. I don't have any examples, but my goodness I wouldn't be surprised if they've been used by politicians or in propaganda. Fortunately, they're quite niche, but you see the danger, don't you?

W: Have there been any studies on their effects on people?

M: Oh. Oh, well, let me think. Well, a recent paper❶ mentioned Escher sentences. After M.C. Escher, you know, although I think the use of the name is a bit misleading. Escher sentences are comparative illusions; they seem to be a valid comparison, but on closer inspection they make no sense whatsoever, semantically. I believe the researchers did some neuroimaging on participants to look at their reactions, and found that most people don't perceive Escher sentences as anomalous. It's the ones who understood them who showed any significant activity. So, for example, "More people have been to Russia than I have."❷ It makes no sense, you see? Either you have been to Russia or you haven't. But the sentence deceives you into thinking it makes sense.

W: But there's no way in which any of these things could be used to… confuse people? Hurt people?

M: No, not that I know of.
   [growl]

W: Well, thank you very much for your time.

M: You're welcome. Good luck with the book.

Holly Soames①
18/11/2019 23:19
Possibly 'Evidence for online repair of Escher sentences' by E. O'CONNOR and others (2013), although the authors note that the term has existed since 1984 (M. MONTALBETTI, PhD thesis).

Holly Soames②
18/11/2019 23:34
Possibly originally by Geoffrey K. PULLMAN, 'Plausible Angloid Gibberish' (2004): http://itre.cis. upenn.edu/~myl/ languagelog/ archives/000860. html.

To: ███████████████████████
From: B2
CC/BCC: B1
Date: 9 March 2015
Subject: RE: Re: RED WORD

Yes please. Could you prep a brief presentation for next week? Say Mon at 4pm? I'll book a room and get some lunch sorted. Any dietary requirements?

Philip

To: ███████████████████████
From: B1
Date: 12 March 2015
Subject: RE: RED WORD

Agreed. Proceed.

K

RED WORD briefing
Unconventional influence

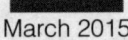

March 2015

Confidentiality
Please keep the contents of this talk within this room

- Research has not yet (formally) begun
- You are reminded of your responsibilities as per the discussion and handling of sensitive material

---

Introduction

- Lead RED FOG research for the department
- Background in HCI, especially auditory/visual
- Previously worked at ███████████

RED FOG Hypothesis

- Cyberweapons can be built cheaply and effectively
- To directly harm people, physically and psychologically:

Nausea, headaches, anxiety, fear	Permanent damage	Death (individual, multiple)	Things worse than death

How can malware hurt people?

- By jumping the digital/biological gap
  - Digital vs biological analogies
- Manipulating machine outputs (RED SOUND, RED VISION)
  - Audio and optical channels, data
- To adversely affect biological human inputs (RED WORD)
  - Cognitive processing, physiological effects
- Zoonotic malware, digital parasites

Parallels in terminology: Worms latch on to specific vulnerabilities, viruses latch to specific receptors

Infected hosts, quarantine, vaccination, replication, vectors, strains, variants

More complex parallels: Malware using genetic algorithms for polymorphism, antivirus systems based on human immune system

Humans don't get infected – machines do. We're always one step removed… but what if we weren't?

Note that linguistics/language shenanigans in itself is unlikely to have the desired effect, as per advice from academics [1]

Holly Soames[1]
21/11/2019 20:37
Possibly refers to consultation with 'Dr Mary BRYAM'. See also consultation with 'Dr Mark KRAM' in c4 THT.

293

TOP SECRET STRAP 3 UK EYES ONLY

RED SOUND

- Small-scale study unsuccessful
- Could cause harm but significant practical limitations
- Further research required
- Report available ref FG690134/15

Soundcards, speaker systems, Alexa, etc.

Caveats to RED SOUND: audible artefacts, some devices ineffective due to varied fancy responses, too many variables e.g. cannot control duration of exposure, distance from speaker, and not directional

TOP SECRET STRAP 3 UK EYES ONLY

RED VISION

- Small-scale study unsuccessful
- Very mild effects, temporary
- Can only affect predisposed behaviours
- Report awaiting approval ahead of release

James Vicary 1957 – cinemas

Discredited, field lost a lot of credibility

Not helped by 'subliminal' audiotapes that weren't – either too quiet, or distorted, etc

But recent revival demonstrates it is possible

No Manchurian candidates – more subtle effects. Limited to 1-2 words

Holly Soames① **21/11/2019 00:16** Note that this report is not included in THT.

Holly Soames② **18/11/2019 23:57** Note mention of study, details not provided.

Holly Soames③ **19/11/2019 00:11** As per previous comment.

Physiology – heart rate, blood pressure, emotions, how we view faces and people

Scenario – imagine if Conficker – 190 countries, 15 million infections – started broadcasting subliminal visual or audio messages

Easy to do this with malware

However, caveats: effects very mild, temporary, subjects won't act against ingrained behaviours

---

TOP SECRET STRAP 3 UK EYES ONLY

RED WORD

- New branch
- Examining feasibility of influence via thought
- Not disinformation or psyops (see BLUE SUN)
- But as a means to exploit cognitive vulnerabilities
- A cognitive virus/parasite

TOP SECRET STRAP 3 UK EYES ONLY

Initial areas of study

- Parasitic and viral cognitive manipulation in mammals e.g. toxoplasmosis, rabies, HIV
- Linguistic and cognitive 'short-circuits' [exploits]
- Information as harm
- In theory, could lead to confusion, disorientation, susceptibility to manipulation, psychosis, mental disorders, etc...

Subject to committee approval...

IF we can find something – relies on both discovery of a concept, and a way to formalise/package it so that it can be delivered and processed effectively

Next steps

- March–April: initial research, identify candidates
- May: Literature review and addition to RED FOG strategy
- June–July: Experimental design
- August: Pilot study

Any questions?

Curiosity is a minor offence. Boredom is a
heinous crime.

§

What a journey of self-discovery lies between
the optimism of HELLO WORLD and the ruthless
chicanery of malware!

§

Cyber buccaneers,
A map to buried treasure.
404 Not Found!

§

Sometimes, in shrinking,
Things become much deadlier.
From Python, a worm!

§

It looks like you are
Trying to write a weapon.
Would you like some help???

§

If you search for a weapon too long, it becomes
all you can think about. Everything you see is
assessed and quantified in terms of possible
harm. But isn't that what it is to be human?

§

TOP SECRET STRAP 3

UK EYES ONLY

REF: FG700016/15
DATE: 27/03/2015
PROJECT: RED FOG
AUTHORISING OFFICER: B1
AUTHOR: ▮▮▮▮▮▮▮ (B5)
PURPOSE: Notes (RED WORD)

Background

Refer to FG662939/14 for general background (TS/S3). This document is FAO B1 and B2 ONLY and contains notes and initial thoughts on research directions for RED WORD.

Notes

The parasitic flatworm Leucochloridium paradoxum manipulates the behaviour of snails – its intermediate hosts – in order to reach its primary hosts, birds (Sandison, 1991). The flatworm's eggs are ingested by the snail and hatch inside it. When grown, the brightly coloured adult flatworm pulsates in the snail's eye stalks to imitate a grub or larvae, which then attracts birds (Lafferty and Kuris, 2012). As well as changing the snail's appearance, the flatworm also takes over its brain, forcing it on to well-lit, higher vegetation so that birds are more likely to detect and consume the infected snail (Wesołowska and Wesołowski, 2013).

The Plasmodium parasite, carrier of malaria, influences the behaviour of mosquitoes. In the parasite's early stages inside the mosquito, a blood diet is of little use to it, as it requires energy to grow. And so it changes the infected mosquito's appetite, compelling it to seek out glucose-rich sources of food so that the parasite can grow (Humeida et al, 2011). Upon reaching sexual maturity it reverts the mosquito's primary food source back to blood – in fact, it makes the mosquito insatiable, so that the parasite's chances of transference to a new host are maximised (Ferguson and Read, 2004; Schwartz and Koella, 2001).

There are dozens of such examples affecting various species. Parasites, and viruses to some extent, have adapted to take advantage of relatively primitive brains. We can consider such manipulations to be akin to very simple exploits, leveraging trivial vulnerabilities. But what of more complex mammalian brains?

Toxoplasma gondii is a protozoan eukaryote which only sexually reproduces in its primary hosts, wild and domestic cats. However, it can infect most mammals – forming cysts in the brain and multiplying, where it may stay for years – although many intermediary hosts are dead-ends. However, the parasite adopts a fascinating strategy when it finds itself in the brains of rodents such as rats and mice.

Infected rodents display markedly less aversion to predators as a result of the toxoplasma in their brains. Specifically, the parasite typically causes them to become less afraid and timid, and to be less wary of – and even attracted to – certain compounds in feline urine (Webster❶ and McConkey, 2010; Berdoy et al, 2000). Thus, infected rodents are more likely to be consumed by cats, and so the parasite finds itself inside its primary host, where it can reproduce.

Holly Soames①
19/11/2019 00:29
No known relation to Alex WEBSTER.

For many years it was thought that toxoplasma gondii posed little harm to humans, with the notable exceptions of pregnant women – in whom the parasite's cysts can lead to severe birth defects – and those with a compromised immune system, such as HIV patients

(Wong and Remington, 1994). For healthy adults, and even children, infections were thought to be lifelong but benign, the parasite merely a latent and dormant presence in the brain, with the only potential side-effect being mild flu-like symptoms upon initial infection (Sobanski et al, 2013; Cold et al, 2005).

However, subsequent research (see Zimmer, 2000 for an overview) has revealed two new findings. First, the scale of infection: approximately two-thirds of the world's population is thought to be infected with toxoplasma gondii. Contact with cats is not necessary, although they are a major vector; consumption of insufficiently cooked infected meat, and handling plants and vegetables, can also result in infection.

Second, toxoplasma gondii may not be as harmless as once assumed. Recent studies (e.g. Flegr, 2007; Vyas and Sapolsky, 2010; Flegr, 2013) indicate that it may cause behavioural manipulation in humans, to the extent that risk-taking behaviours increase. Infection with the parasite may, therefore, make a human host more likely to put themselves in danger.

Moreover, some researchers have argued that toxoplasma gondii is a contributory factor to schizophrenic disorders (Yolken et al, 2009), although this is contested. Infections have also been associated with increases in suicide attempts (Hsu et al, 2014) – particularly in women over sixty – and traffic accidents (Flegr et al, 2002), although the extent to which this is a causative factor is unclear. It also, incidentally, appears to cause infected men to consider the odour of cat urine more attractive (Flegr et al, 2011). What is apparent is that, just as with rodents, toxoplasma gondii causes epigenetic changes in the human brain.

While parasitic manipulation of mammalian brains may be less common than that of insect brains, viruses are capable of influencing mammalian behaviour to a greater extent, although the mechanisms behind these influences are less well-understood. Perhaps the most compelling evidence comes from rabies, a Lyssavirus. Long the stuff of legend, and possibly the origin of many mythological figures, most prominently the werewolf (e.g. de Blécourt, 2013), rabies is, rightly, widely feared, and whilst its impact in the developed world has decayed significantly as a result of widespread vaccination programmes and culling of potential hosts, it remains a threat in less developed nations, particularly those with large populations of stray dogs. Typically, people associate rabies with its famous symptoms: foaming at the mouth, hydrophobia and uncontrolled aggression. But less well-known are the causes of these symptoms.

Rather than flowing through the bloodstream, rabies crawls at a very slow rate along nerve endings (Lafon, 2005). This process may take weeks, months, or even years, depending on the site of the infection point and environmental factors. The goal is to pass through the blood-brain barrier, and if this occurs, the mortality rate is almost 100% (Fooks et al, 2014). If vaccinated, either pre- or post-exposure, the mortality rate drops to almost zero. Once the virus reaches the brain, it replicates to the peripheral nervous system. 80% of infected hosts experience what is known as furious rabies (Nigg and Walker, 2009), an extremely painful and distressing way in which to die. The virus causes inflammation of the brain, particularly the limbic system, which among other things regulates aggression. Rabies causes neural circuits to fire at random, so that the slightest stimuli can cause extreme distress, a condition known as hyperesthesia. At the same time, the virus amasses in the salivary glands, ready to infect its next host via a bite. This is what causes the foaming saliva often associated with rabies. The virus also triggers excruciating spasms in the throat, resulting in what is probably the most infamous symptom: hydrophobia, or fear of water (see Wasik and Murphy, 2013, for a full account of symptoms and effects), although note that this is not a true phobia but a result of dysphagia. Rabies likely induces this effect because transmission typically occurs through biting or licking, and the swallowing of saliva or other fluids would therefore be counter-productive (Alexander and Cochran, 2005; Libby and Meislin, 1983).

Facial spasms, insomnia, paranoia, terror and hallucinations follow, eventually leading to delirium. Death can take days, even weeks.

In humans, rabies has also been associated with an increased sexual desire (Senthilkumaran et al, 2011), and can be transmitted through kissing and oral sex (Wasik and Murphy, 2013). It is a virus associated with rage and fear, but two of its alternative transmission vectors are lust and love.

RED VISION could have been the digital equivalent of toxoplasma gondii, but its effects are too mild; RED SOUND could have been the digital equivalent of a virus like rabies, but there are too many caveats associated with it, and too many variables for effective weaponisation. RED FOG moves to the next avenue of investigation – RED WORD, an exploration of the feasibility of a cognitive weapon capable of transmission via remote means (i.e. via online dissemination or locally upon malware infection). The following success criteria are suggested:

- Effects on humans should be direct, as a result of computer-originated output (e.g. language, light, sound)
- The effects should be targeted and predictable, within reason (the barrier for acceptability here is likely lower than biological attacks due to the relative complexity)
- The effects should be significant and adverse

302

- Contagion is not necessary, particularly if it would not be possible to contain the spread of effects to a reasonable degree.

REPORT ENDS

References

Alexander, C. W., & Cochran, R. (2005). The role of the salivary gland in rabies pathogenesis. *Journal of Viral Manipulation*, 39(1), 522-540.

Berdoy, M., Webster, J. P., & Macdonald, D. W. (2000). Fatal attraction in rats infected with Toxoplasma gondii. In proceedings of the *Royal Society of London. Series B: Biological Sciences*, 267(1452), 1591-1594.

Cold, C. J., Sell, T. L., & Reed, K. D. (2005). Diagnosis – Disseminated Toxoplasmosis. *Clinical Medicine & Research*, 3(3), 186-186.

de Blécourt, W. (2013). Monstrous theories: Werewolves and the abuse of history. *Preternature: Critical and Historical Studies on the Preternatural*, 2(2), 188-212.

Ferguson, H. M., & Read, A. F. (2004). Mosquito appetite for blood is stimulated by Plasmodium chabaudi infections in themselves and their vertebrate hosts. *Malaria Journal*, 3(1), 1-8.

Flegr, J. (2007). Effects of Toxoplasma on human behavior. *Schizophrenia Bulletin*, 33(3), 757-760.

Flegr, J. (2013). How and why Toxoplasma makes us crazy. *Trends in Parasitology*, 29(4), 156-163.

Flegr, J., Havlícek, J., Kodym, P., Malý, M., & Smahel, Z. (2002). Increased risk of traffic accidents in subjects with latent toxoplasmosis: a retrospective case-control study. *BMC Infectious Diseases*, 2, 1-6.

Flegr, J., Lenochová, P., Hodný, Z., & Vondrová, M. (2011). Fatal attraction phenomenon in humans – cat odour attractiveness increased for Toxoplasma-infected men while decreased for infected women. *PLOS Neglected Tropical Diseases*, 5(11), e1389.

Fooks, A. R., Banyard, A. C., Horton, D. L., Johnson, N., McElhinney, L. M., & Jackson, A. C. (2014). Current status of rabies and prospects for elimination. *The Lancet*, 384(9951), 1389-1399.

Hsu, P. C., Groer, M., & Beckie, T. (2014). New findings: Depression, suicide, and Toxoplasma gondii infection. *Journal of the American Association of Nurse Practitioners*, 26(11), 629-637.

Humeida, H., Pradel, G., Stich, A., & Krawinkel, M. B. (2011). The effect of glucose and insulin on in vitro proliferation of Plasmodium falciparum. *Journal of Diabetology*, 2(3), 6.

Lafferty, K. D., & Kuris, A. M. (2012). Ecological consequences of manipulative parasites. In D. P. Hughes, J. Brodeur, F. Thomas (eds), *Host Manipulation by Parasites*, 158-168. Oxford: Oxford University Press.

Lafon, M. (2005). Rabies virus receptors. *Journal of Neurovirology*, 11, 82-87.

Libby, J., & Meislin, H. W. (1983). Human rabies. *Annals of Emergency Medicine*, 12(4), 217-220.

Nigg, A. J., & Walker, P. L. (2009). Overview, prevention, and treatment of rabies. *Pharmacotherapy: The Journal of Human Pharmacology and Drug Therapy*, 29(10), 1182-1195.

Sandison, G. (1991). Mimicry and morphology in Leucochloridium paradoxum. *Parasite Behavior*, 18(5), 231-249.

Schwartz, A., & Koella, J. C. (2001). Trade-offs, conflicts of interest and manipulation in Plasmodium–mosquito interactions. *Trends in Parasitology*, 17(4), 189-194.

Senthilkumaran, S., Balamurgan, N., Sweni, S., Menezes, R. G., & Thirumalaikolundusubramanian, P. (2011). Hypersexuality in a 28-year-old woman with rabies. *Archives of Sexual Behavior*, 40, 1327-1328.

Sobanski, V., Ajzenberg, D., Delhaes, L., Bautin, N., & Just, N. (2013). Severe toxoplasmosis in immunocompetent hosts: be aware of atypical strains. *American Journal of Respiratory and Critical Care Medicine*, 187(10), 1143-1145.

Vyas, A., & Sapolsky, R. (2010). Manipulation of host behaviour by Toxoplasma gondii: what is the minimum a proposed proximate mechanism should explain?. *Folia Parasitologica*, 57(2), 88-94.

Wasik, B., & Murphy, M. (2013). *Rabid: A Cultural History of the World's Most Diabolical Virus*. New York, New York: Penguin.

Webster, J. P., & McConkey, G. A. (2010). Toxoplasma gondii-altered host behaviour: clues as to mechanism of action. *Folia Parasitologica*, 57(2), 95-104.

Wesołowska, W., & Wesołowski, T. (2013). Do L eucochloridium sporocysts manipulate the behaviour of their snail hosts? *Journal of Zoology*, 292(3), 151-155.

Wong, S. Y., & Remington, J. S. (1994). Toxoplasmosis in pregnancy. *Clinical Infectious Diseases*, 18(6), 853-861.

Yolken, R. H., Dickerson, F. B., & Fuller Torrey, E. (2009). Toxoplasma and schizophrenia. *Parasite Immunology*, 31(11), 706-715.

Zimmer, C. (2000). *Parasite Rex: Inside the Bizarre World of Nature's Most Dangerous Creatures*. New York, New York: Simon and Schuster.

To: ██████████████████████████

From: **B2**

CC/BCC: **B1**

Date: 3 April 2015

Subject: RE: RED WORD notes

Yes, absolutely. Charge it to departmental expenses. The cost centre code is ██████.

As per the minutes from the last catch-up, could you do a wireframe for the next slide deck with a plan of action? How are you getting on?

Philip

To: ██████████████████████████

From: **B2**

CC/BCC: **B1**

Date: 3 April 2015

Subject: RE: RED WORD notes

Ha, tell me about it. Don't forget to ████████████
████████████████████
██████████████████████████
██████████████████████████
████████████!

Philip

305

To: ▮▮▮▮▮▮▮▮▮▮▮▮▮▮▮▮
From: **B2**
CC/BCC: **B1**
Date: 3 April 2015
Subject: RE: RED WORD notes

Love it. It's unorthodox (and a little informally written, but you'll get used to the right style in time!).

Yes, should be fine as long as you can stick to the agreed timeframe? Keep me posted.

Philip

The birds do not sing, though we like to think that they do. We wonder at how pretty they sound. But how the world changes when you realise what they are REALLY doing. ❶ They scream because they do not know how to do anything else.

§

Holly Soames① **19/11/2019 00:37** Possibly a reference to *Burden of Dreams*, a 1982 documentary by Werner HERZOG (although note that the sense appears to be slightly different).

Who would be Patient Zero? This was a question that fascinated me. What would it be like to be the first person? Few people WANT to be a guinea pig under such circumstances, but the opportunity to experience something like that, for the first time - perhaps there is something to be said for it!

§

For every person, Philip K. Dick wrote, there is a sentence which has the power to destroy them. What is the sentence that destroys us all?

§

You should ask yourself why I write this, but before that ask yourself why you READ it!!!

§

REF: FG700084/15
DATE: 17/04/2015
PROJECT: RED FOG
AUTHORISING OFFICER: B1
AUTHOR: ██████████ (B5)
PURPOSE: Notes 2 (RED WORD)

Background

Refer to FG662939/14 for general background and FG700016/15 for the first part of these notes (TS/S3). This document is FAO B1 and B2 ONLY and contains notes and initial thoughts on research directions for RED WORD.

Notes

A significant amount of human effort – perhaps the majority of it – is spent attempting to control the minds of others. Advertisers and salespeople try to convince us to buy products and services. Politicians hand us propaganda. Academics argue. Lovers gaslight. Interrogators may coerce or torture to get their subjects to break. There seems to be little need to understand or imitate the delicate neural remodelling achieved by viruses and parasites when we have already perfected intra-species mind control to a large extent. And yet researchers have tried, persistently, to find new ways of doing exactly that. Consider the infamous MKUltra programme, which amongst other areas of research – including LSD as an interrogation aid, and experiments related to 'remote viewing' – looked at various forms of so-called 'mind control' (Rasa, 2014; Melley, 2011), and in doing so spawned a thousand conspiracy theories. In fact, one of the significant obstacles faced when researching this topic is the sheer amount of conspiracy theories which exist on the subject. It terrifies us, the thought that our thoughts may not be our own. One of the most common symptoms reported by sufferers of schizophrenia is thought insertion (Billon, 2013), the delusion that ideas and concepts have been planted in one's mind by someone or something else. As a patient remarks (cited in Parnas and Sass, 2001), with notably Cartesian concern: "Am I thinking? Since there is nothing which can prove that I am thinking, I cannot know whether I exist."

In the vast majority of cases, however, exploitation leverages pre-established, and usually voluntarily internalised, cultural behaviours and norms. Consider Wendigo Psychosis, a culture-bound syndrome which affected First Nations tribes and the Algonquin in Canada and Wisconsin. The symptoms supposedly included a marked increase in aggression and a craving for human flesh, thought to be the result of possession by the Wendigo spirit. Eventually, the syndrome died out as contact with European cultures increased (Brightman, 1988). But it is worth noting that, if one culture has this belief, there is no reason why similar syndromes could not materialise in others.

In a broader sense, the argument that religion is a virus has been made before, most notably by Dawkins (1993), and it is worth briefly observing the properties of this cultural pathogen. It is often hereditary, but also transmitted through friends and acquaintances. It causes marked and bizarre changes in behaviour, including, but not limited to: changes in diet; an inability to consider certain things rationally; a sometimes fanatical adherence to arbitrary codes of morality; the mutilation of children's genitals; an irrational hatred of people infected by a slightly different strain; and, in its most extreme forms, violence, murder, and suicide.

Language, too, may be considered a virus, one which is ultimately beneficial – at least, many would argue so. Aoki (1999) is very good on this point, writing: "Like a virus, language is … a program waiting to be executed, changing both the consciousness it infects and morphing its very own structure as it replicates itself … it is the unliving worm that flies." The book *Pontypool Changes Everything* (Burgess, 1995) explores this concept in detail, its premise being that certain words in the English language are infected, and that hearing and understanding those words can lead to insanity and violence. It is certainly an original take on the zombie genre, even if the victims are not zombies but live humans. With language more generally, infection is primarily hereditary, but exacerbated through childhood, education, and, in later life, self-study. The virus is not – we assume – disadvantageous to us, but rival strains sometimes compete for primacy and influence. Unlike religion there is no vaccine available, although in certain rare circumstances there may be a natural immunity.

However, these are ingrained concepts, with the advantage of the weight of hundreds or thousands of years of tradition and biological and psychological imperative behind them. Conversely, RED FOG/RED WORD seeks to discover more immediate methods for altering behaviour and causing harm.

Some examples of cognitive influence/harm do have significantly shorter incubation periods. A dangerous example is the cult, an especially virulent strain of the religion virus, which causes even more aberrant and drastic alterations in behaviour and perception, often in a very short timeframe, in psychologically vulnerable victims (Ross, 2014). This may be the case even when the cult is not based on the worship of a supernatural deity, or even religious in its practices. Certain political movements, for example, are similar to their religion-based counterparts in the slavish fervour of their adherents and the extreme manipulations of behaviour they may engender, but differ in their manifestations and components.

The tactical weaponisation of these phenomena, however, is a different matter. RED FOG seeks to find some solution, delivered via malware or some form of digital delivery mechanism, which could be deployed against an individual, group, or state, with the effect of reliably causing immediate and significant physical and/or psychological harm.❶ And whilst it would perhaps be possible to create a cult or religion or perform brainwashing over a period of time, it would be immensely difficult, if not impossible, to cause targeted and predictable effects – certainly not within the short period of time often required in tactical situations – and to do so remotely, without physical access to the intended victims. A pre-existing support infrastructure, and/or some sort of pre-conditioning effort, would be required, but even then any attacks would still be entirely dependent on certain psychological vulnerabilities which may not be present in the individual, or in the majority of the targeted population.

In general there is little in the extant literature which is explicitly linked to what RED WORD seeks to achieve; often, terms such as 'cognitive viruses' are bandied about without much thought or reflection. Glabus (1998), for example, considers whether "memetic warfare" might be possible through the use of "cognitive viruses", which he defines as "any agent that infects people with a meme, a unit of information in a mind whose existence influences events such that more copies of itself get created in other minds."

Glabus attempts to draw a distinction between

these viruses and traditional PsyOps, but the memes he cites are not novel, merely units of disinformation and rumour spread amongst populations for strategic effect – something combatants have been doing to each other for many years anyway (Ebbings et al, 2011).

Is there, then, such a thing as a cognitive virus? Just as with a computer, certain aspects of the brain – the wetware of the human mind, as opposed to the software or firmware of a device – may contain certain cognitive vulnerabilities. In some cases, these are specific to subsets of the population – Poulsen's (2008) report on the exploitation of photosensitive epilepsy via online attacks comes to mind, as do the caveats associated with RED SOUND – but in other cases, the vulnerabilities may be more common. Certain malformed inputs – generated either maliciously or accidentally – may result in exploitation, perhaps in dangerous and harmful ways. After all, we are all running more or less the same version of the brain's firmware, aren't we? The contents may differ, but the code is broadly the same.

I referred to *Pontypool Changes Everything* earlier, which to some extent embraces this concept, although it does not consider transmission via computer. Examples of a similar idea appear in other fiction, and in the absence of any meaningful empirical – or even theoretical – research, it may be worth turning to these for inspiration. The novel *Snow Crash* (Stephenson, 1992), for example, employs a device whereby an ancient Sumerian language can be used to program – and attack – the brain. The virus in the novel is therefore a neuro-linguistic construct, which upon exposure – even without comprehension – can cause brain damage.

Langford's short story 'BLIT' (1988) uses much the same premise, albeit with significantly less mythological exposition than *Snow Crash*. In 'BLIT', certain images, known as basilisks, or BLITs (Berryman Logical Image Technique), exploit flaws in the human brain, causing them to 'crash'. A far-right activist sprays a BLIT on a wall, protected from its effects by special goggles which split up BLIT images to neutralise them for the safety of the wearer. He is caught by a police officer, and accidentally exposes several officers to the BLIT, killing them. The activist is arrested, and as he sits in his cell he realises to his horror that he can mentally reconstruct the distorted version of the BLIT he has seen through his goggles, and dies.

This concept of a basilisk is hardly novel in fiction (see also: 'The Riddle of the Universe and its Solution' (Cherniak, 1981); 'White Cane 7.62' (Neff, 1985); and various entries in the collaborative internet-based fiction project, 'SCP Foundation' (https://scp-wiki.wikidot. com/), which recycles this device repetitively). Other notable examples of basilisk-like artefacts include *The King in Yellow* (Chambers, 1895), which is named for a fictional play referenced within the short stories making up the collection. Excerpts from the play, which induces insanity when read in its entirety, are provided, but only from Act I, which is described as relatively banal; Act II, on the other hand, is described as far less benign, although Chambers does not specify what the content might be.

In an otherwise non-fictional philosophical tract, Eugene Thacker presents a poem, 'The Subharmonic Murmur of Black Tentacular Voids' (Thacker, 2011). The poem, Thacker tells us, was written anonymously and has appeared on various sites, as well as within (non-existent) academic articles. Thacker states that it has been said to have caused "geomantic symptoms within the metabolism and physiognomy of those who have, under unspecified conditions" recited its lines. Thacker departs somewhat from other writers in choosing to include the text of this mysterious artefact (which, of course, he almost certainly wrote himself), presumably so he can expound on its meaning and use it as a vehicle for conveying some of his ideas.

Bird Box (Malerman, 2014) describes a situation in which unknown creatures of unknown provenance cause those who see them to become deranged, leading them to kill others and themselves. Again, the specific reasons for this are not conveyed, being epistemologically impossible to describe. The plot device in *Cell* (King, 2006), has similar effects to that of *Bird Box*, albeit with a different format; a phone signal, known as 'The Pulse', is broadcast worldwide and causes everyone exposed to it to become a mindless killer.

Although the vast majority of fictional examples of cognitive weapons (and note that in each of the above, the 'infection' is NOT contagious) are located within the horror genre, there are some notable exceptions. Monty Python's sketch 'The Funniest Joke in the World' involves a joke so lethally funny that it kills anyone who hears it. After several people, including the joke's author, die from laughter, the joke is translated into German, to be used against the Nazis. The untranslated English version is not revealed to the audience (Chapman et al, 1969).

A theme emerges. The concept of an image/sound/linguistic-based cognitive weapon is a compelling one in fiction. It enables the conveying of a significant, often apocalyptic, threat, with no need or reason to divulge the specific content of the threat itself – indeed, to do so would cause the entire premise to collapse into ontological impossibility when it became apparent that the threat, having no effect on the reader, is therefore no threat at all. Moreover, the device benefits from there being no verified real-world examples, which adds to its power. Real horror originates in the knowledge that there are things which are unknowable. The concept of a cognitive virus encapsulates this idea in a concrete, yet still necessarily abstract, form.

* * *

Could psychological manipulation be a possible avenue of investigation? On first inspection it appears doubtful. Techniques such as those popularised by hypnotists and performers like Derren Brown (which on occasion have been performed remotely) tend to have mild, temporary effects, as they are often a combination of subliminal priming and neurolinguistic programming. Similar objections apply to the concept of persuasion or rhetorical influence. It is not always impossible to persuade people to act against their own best interests, but to do so in a targeted fashion requires significant time and effort. One must learn, and then exploit, individual psychological vulnerabilities, in the same way that a hacker must enumerate and probe a specific protocol or application before developing an exploit for it. The crucial distinction is that, once an exploit has been successfully created, it will work against all unpatched instances of that protocol or application, whereas, when hacking humans, such uniformity of results is difficult to accomplish. Convincing a person to cause significant harm to themselves or others is difficult, and typically requires even more investment. Once again, fictional examples abound: Cassius uses astroturfing❶ to convince Brutus to assassinate Caesar (Shakespeare, 1623/2005); Lady Macbeth plays to Macbeth's ambition to persuade him to kill Duncan (Shakespeare, 1623/2005); Hannibal Lecter convinces Multiple Miggs to commit suicide, although we are not told what was said (Harris, 1988); Satan uses "perswasive words, impregn'd with Reason" to convince Eve to consume the fruit of the tree of knowledge (Milton, 1667/2003). Fish's work on Milton, *Surprised by Sin: The Reader in Paradise Lost* (Fish, 1998) is a useful primer on how such exploitation can occur. Fish notes that Satan's rhetoric operates as a form of Trojan: sentiments which appear to encapsulate goodness and virtue are revealed to smuggle sin – thus the reader themself falls from grace.

An alternative solution may involve attempting

Holly Soames①
19/11/2019 01:03
Creating and using multiple fake identities, usually in the context of, for instance, writing fraudulent online reviews.

to engineer instances of so-called social contagion, the phenomenon by which certain ideas or behaviours spread within populations in a manner broadly similar to viruses. Social contagion encompasses behavioural contagion, emotional contagion (Marsden, 1998) and the contagion of ideas (memetics; more on this later). Levy and Nail (1993) propose three forms:

- Disinhibitory contagion, whereby individuals are inhibited from engaging in certain behaviours by compliance with social norms, until they witness others performing them (consider, for example, riots);
- Echo contagion, involving the spontaneous imitation of a certain behaviour; and
- Hysterical contagion, whereby unwanted behaviours are spread through an unknown mechanism.

Much of social contagion theory overlaps with related fields such as crowd psychology and social learning theory, and the extent to which social contagion can be deliberately orchestrated is unclear. One possibility, albeit an untargeted one, is to be found in several documented cases of certain behaviours being spread through media coverage. Chan et al (2009) found that charcoal burning, a method of suicide unknown in Hong Kong until 1998, spread rapidly through a population until it became the second-most common such method in the city, which the authors partially attribute to its early description in a popular media piece as a "painless easy way out". Similarly, in their research on the effect of media descriptions on suicide clusters, Gould et al (2003) note that both non-fictional news coverage and fictional portrayals can lead to increased rates of suicide. Various aspects of media coverage – prominence, reporting style and images - have been found to influence the amount of imitative suicides (Gould, 2001). Other factors include whether or not the deceased was a prominent figure, and whether or not the incident was real, as opposed to a fictional depiction (Stack, 2000). However, while Stack found that real incidents are more than four times more likely to cause imitative suicides, there is evidence to suggest that fictional depictions may drive an increase in a specific method of suicide (Ostroff et al, 1985; Ostroff and Boyd, 1987). Hawton et al (1999), for example, found that a depiction of an overdose in a TV series led to a 17% increase in overdoses across the UK in the week following the airing of the episode.

Gould (2001) suggests several guidelines for media outlets and television/film-makers for the responsible coverage or depiction of suicide. Presumably, a malicious actor with sufficient resources and influence ❶ could seek to increase rates of suicide by reversing such guidelines, e.g. romanticising the act (Fekete and Schmidtke, 1995), or providing descriptions or images of the location (Sonneck et al, 1994) or method (Fekete and Macsai, 1990). While Gould is doubtless performing a public service by publishing such guidelines, they are arguably also inadvertently doing something akin to a developer providing an easily reversible software patch.

However, suicide clusters are likely not of interest to RED WORD. Whilst the notion of an enemy population experiencing an epidemic of suicides as a result of planted and carefully crafted online media coverage is not unattractive (and may warrant further investigation in other departments, e.g. BLUE SUN), it is too indiscriminate and the effects too difficult to predict and control. The same applies to other forms of contagion, including contagious depression and anxiety (Katz et al, 1999; Eisenberg et al, 2013, respectively); autism and schizophrenia (Patterson, 2011); mass killings and school shootings (Towers et al, 2015; see also Stephen King's *Rage* (1977), published under his pseudonym Richard Bachman, which was about a school shooting and was later linked to several real-life incidents); obesity (Christiakis and Fowler, 2007); and homicides (Fagan et al, 2006).

A more promising avenue may be found in the Milton example from earlier – not in the sense of persuasive rhetoric, but in what Eve was tempted to eat: the fruit of the tree of knowledge. Human behaviour can be drastically altered as a consequence of ingesting new knowledge. Once we are made aware that it exists, and internalise its implications, significant harm may result. Consider the fanatical zeal of converts, or the seismic fault caused by an epiphany. Bostrom (2011) considers this in an overview of what he calls 'information hazards': "A risk that arises from the dissemination or the potential dissemination of (true) information that may cause harm or enable some agent to cause harm."

Note that Bostrom emphasises that information hazards are not false information, which would include for our purposes things like disinformation, deception, and propaganda. The risk is in exposure to TRUE information. Many of the "data hazards" which Bostrom discusses are fairly obvious, such as knowing how to create a nuclear bomb or synthesise a virus. Of more interest for this research are "idea hazards" – an overall or approximate notion which can be dangerous even without specific knowledge or instructions – and "attention hazards", whereby danger arises from the promoting of an idea or information.

RED WORD thus becomes less about the hardware of the brain, and more about the firmware – consciousness. This is a departure from the original concept of the RED FOG project, which examines ways in which primitive computer outputs can be weaponised via a malware delivery system, but that should not prevent us from considering it further.

In practice, a RED WORD candidate would need to

disrupt either a belief held by an individual (which brings us back to issues around targeting again), or beliefs which are very popular across cultures, or as a species. However, even with the latter, it may be difficult to accomplish in practice. Consider how ardently religious followers cling to their beliefs in the face of a complete lack of supporting evidence, and often in the face of compelling evidence to the contrary.

However, one candidate does spring to mind, which is (almost) universal: our perception of reality. It strikes me that if a target could be convinced, or even forced to question, their long-standing beliefs in the nature, or existence, of reality, this could elicit devastating psychological effects, and may be the closest we can come to finding some sort of critical 'buffer overflow' vulnerability in the human mind. We would no longer be seeking to find a flaw in the system itself, but to tell the system that its knowledge about its own existence is inaccurate – which, in theory, may cause it to break down entirely.

RED WORD could become, in essence, a red pill. ❶ Rather than hack the brain, we hack philosophy, perception, consciousness.

Holly Soames①
19/11/2019 01:33
Note that this does not appear to be related to the extreme right-wing co-opting of the term.

It has always struck me as odd that the people brought out of the Matrix did not all go insane. The human mind may be resilient to many things, but it seems implausible that the complete disruption of one's existential certainty is one of them. Some allusion is made to this, albeit briefly, when Morpheus notes that some people are not prepared for the revelation. Yet this implies that accepting the truth is a question of readiness, rather than of one's capacity to internalise it. Who could ever be truly ready for something like that? Of course, ninety or so minutes of Neo et al gnashing their teeth and tearing out their hair would not make for pleasant viewing. On that note, it is also worth bearing in mind what Nyhan and Reifler (2008) describe as a 'backfire effect', whereby people presented with information which conflicts with their system of beliefs can result in a reinforcement of those beliefs. This effect would need to be tested for at the experimental stage, should we proceed with this possibility.

We are in somewhat uncharted waters once again. There may well be documented evidence of individuals suffering from adverse psychological reactions in response to some form of existential crisis brought about by philosophical revelations, although obviously such revelations would be unlikely to be as shattering as the concept in *The Matrix*. But it is unclear whether this could ever be weaponised. It is not something we could deliver covertly and instantly through subliminal primes or flashing images or brief bursts of sound, but, if successful, the effects could be spectacular, and perhaps even universal.

At first glance, simulation theory – a hypothesis similar in some ways to the premise of *The Matrix* – seems to be a useful testbed. Simulation theory posits that we are living in a constructed simulation, one either being run many years in the future, or by some form of alien or artificial intelligence. Descartes' Demon, the brain-in-a-vat thought experiment, and many similar concepts, are forerunners of this and ask the same question, although simulation theory is the most recent and fashionable version: how do we know we are real? This seems like a useful starting point for RED WORD, but it suffers from several logical and epistemological drawbacks. The first is that there is no immediacy to the theory. There is no way to ascertain whether or not it is actually the case, and thus its implications are immaterial. In fact, one could say that simulation theory functions more as a type of quasi-religious belief than as an information hazard, in that it provides, for certain kinds of people – who typically consider themselves intellectually superior to religious devotees – a form of comfort and consolation, in the same way that conspiracy theories do. Simulation theory as a candidate for RED WORD would require the fabrication of some form of evidence, and it is difficult to conceive what that could be, given that any evidence could be argued as originating within the 'simulation' itself.

Moreover, simulation theory claims that our existence is a construction based in some universe or form which is real. However, how do the advanced humans/AI/alien civilization conducting the simulation know that they themselves are not simulated?

Last, and most compelling: simulation theory is based on the premise that consciousness is programmable, that it CAN be simulated. We have no evidence that this is the case. Until we do, simulation theory, like the beliefs which prop up most religions, can be asserted without evidence and thus dismissed without evidence; it is an extraordinary claim lacking extraordinary proof.❶

Holly Soames①
19/11/2019 01:47
Likely a reference to the phrase "Extraordinary claims require extraordinary evidence" in *Broca's Brain* by Carl SAGAN (1979).

A note on transmission

It may not be necessary for a viable RED WORD candidate to be directly transmissible (unlike viruses, we are not particularly concerned if a host should die before the intruder can infect other hosts!), but it is worth considering the problem briefly. And as RED FOG is proposed as a project examining the feasibility of remote weapons, probably delivered online in some form, a discussion on memetics is relevant.

Memetics can be considered as the study of at least one form of social contagion, albeit one which deals with the transmission of ideas rather than emotions or behaviour. As many researchers have pointed out, this is in some way analogous to the way in which viruses operate, hence terms such as "mind viruses" (Dawkins, 1993; Brodie, 1996); "idea viruses" (Godin, 2001); "thought contagions" (Lynch, 1998); and "cognitive viruses" (Glabus, 1998). A successful virus of this type, whether it involves an idea or a cultural trait, is able to replicate through a population and infect others, such that it may become permanently absorbed by one or more societies, in much the same way that viruses may eventually become part of a host's DNA.

Memetics, is, in part, a discipline which examines how this process may occur, by applying Darwinian evolutionary theory to memes. Whether or not this is a valid enterprise is disputed. As Heylighen and Chielens (2009) point out, unlike biological viruses, memes are not discrete units with quantifiable structures and payloads, but amorphous assemblies of concepts and ideas which are heavily dependent on cultural context, and which humans may interact with in a way they do not and cannot with biological pathogens. Therefore, the extent to which a Darwinian approach is justified is unclear (and little empirical work has been conducted to test this; see Edmonds, 2002, and Chielens and Heylighen, 2005).

Various criteria have been proposed for what determines a successful meme, but most (e.g. Schaller et al, 2002; Heath et al, 2001) tend to rely on vague and inherently subjective assessments such as plausibility and emotional impact (the extent to which a meme can be objectively assessed with respect to its fitness, of course, is questionable, and another potential criticism of memetic approaches). What is clear is that certain memes are successful, and not all of these are beneficial. So-called parasitic memes (Ball, 1984; Heylighen (1992) refers to them as "selfish memes") replicate without providing us with any advantage, and may even be harmful. Examples include, arguably, religion (although one could reason that in providing consolation and solutions, however flawed, to questions of mortality and morality, religion has its benefits); pseudosciences; and fads (Heylighen and Chielens, 2009).

Thus it may be that even if the RED WORD idea, once identified, is not ultimately beneficial to its carriers

– and the intention is that it would not be – it can still be accepted and replicated as successfully as any other meme.

Summary

Various proposals for RED WORD candidates have been examined and rejected, predominantly due to their necessitating bespoke, per-target approaches likely to require significant time and resources with no guarantee of success.

However, a promising avenue of investigation may be the creation or weaponisation of a sufficiently convincing philosophical or ontological concept which may cause a belief-constituted value hazard, or a mindset hazard, thus engendering a psychological reaction which may be devastating in its effects.❶ There are caveats associated with this approach, as follows:

- Suitable candidates would need to be found and assessed for applicability, efficacy, portability, and potential scale and impact
- My initial assessment of the potential effects is based on speculation, and empirical testing would be required to evaluate the suitability of any solutions for real-world deployment
- Intended targets would need to internalise the solution, which may require: a) restating a known concept in an unusual, persuasive form; b) some degree of time for the idea to take hold; and c) significant amounts of testing to find a suitable container for the idea, which is both effective enough to cause the intended impact and portable enough for transmission at-scale and
- As far as possible, the idea should be 'true'.

Holly Soames①
19/11/2019 02:08
Cannot see any specific evidence of feasible harm here although there appears to be an intention. Note that much of this content, while interesting, is beyond my expertise and further assessment should be conducted by SMEs.

Work will begin on these issues immediately pending approval from B1 and B2.

REPORT ENDS

References

Aoki, K. (1998). Introduction: Language is a virus. *University of Miami Law Review*, 53(4), 961-971.

Ball, J. A. (1984). Memes as replicators. *Ethology and Sociobiology*, 5(3), 145-161.

Bandura, A., & Walters, R. H. (1977). *Social Learning Theory* (Vol. 1). Prentice Hall: Englewood cliffs.

Billon, A. (2013). Does consciousness entail subjectivity? The puzzle of thought insertion. *Philosophical Psychology*, 26(2), 291-314.

Bostrom, N. (2011). Information hazards: A typology of potential harms from knowledge. *Review of Contemporary Philosophy*, (10), 44-79.

Brightman, R. A. (1988). The Windigo in the material world. *Ethnohistory*, 35(4), 337-379.

Brodie, R. (1996). *Viruses of the Mind: The New Science of the Meme*. Seattle, Washington: Integral Press.

Burgess, T. (1995). *Pontypool Changes Everything*. Toronto: ECW Press.

Chambers, R. W. (1895). *The King in Yellow*. London: Chatto & Windus.

Chan, S. S., Chiu, H. F., Chen, E. Y., Chan, W. S., Wong, P. W., Chan, C. L., ... & Yip, P. S. (2009). What does psychological autopsy study tell us about charcoal burning suicide—a new and contagious method in Asia? *Suicide and Life-threatening Behavior*, 39(6), 633-638.

Chapman, G. (Writer), Cleese, J. (Writer), Idle, E. (Writer), Jones, T. (Writer), Palin, M. (Writer), MacNaughton, I. (Director) & Davies, J. H. (Director). (1969, October 5). Whither Canada? (Season 1, Episode 1) [TV series episode]. In J. H. Davies (Producer), *Monty Python's Flying Circus*. BBC.

Cherniak, C. (1981). The Riddle of the Universe and its Solution. In D. R. Hofstadter & D. C. Dennett (eds.), *The Mind's I: Fantasies and Reflections on Self and Soul*, 269-276. New York, New York: Bantam Books.

Chielens K. & Heylighen F. (2005) Operationalization of meme selection criteria: Procedures to empirically test memetic hypotheses. In proceedings of the *Joint Symposium on Socially*

Inspired Computing (AISB'05), 14-20.

Christakis, N. A., & Fowler, J. H. (2007). The spread of obesity in a large social network over 32 years. *New England Journal of Medicine*, 357(4), 370-379.

Dawkins, R. (1993). Viruses of the mind. In B. Dahlbom (ed.), *Dennett and His Critics: Demystifying Mind*, 13-27. Oxford: Wiley-Blackwell.

Ebbings, G., Broughan, C. R., Khan, O., & Thomson, H. (2011). Flyers, speakers, and gossip: The practice of PSYOPS in modern warfare. *Journal of Combat Psychology,* 85(16), 99-112.

Edmonds, B. (2002) Three Challenges for the Survival of Memetics. *Journal of Memetics-Evolutionary Models of Information Transmission*, 6(2).

Eisenberg, D., Golberstein, E., Whitlock, J. L., & Downs, M. F. (2013). Social contagion of mental health: evidence from college roommates. *Health Economics*, 22(8), 965-986.

Fagan, J., Wilkinson, D. L., & Davies, G. (2007). Social contagion of violence. In D. J. Flannery, A. T. Vazsony, & I. D. Waldman (eds.), *The Cambridge Handbook of Violent Behavior and Aggression*, 688-723. Cambridge: Cambridge University Press.

Fekete, S., & Macsai, E. (1990). Hungarian suicide models, past and present. In G. Ferrari, M. Bellini, & P. Crepet (eds.), *Suicidal Behavior and Risk Factors*, 149-156. Bologna: Monduzzi Editore.

Fekete, S., & Schmidtke, A. (1995). The impact of mass media reports on suicide and attitudes toward self-destruction: Previous studies and some new data from Hungary and Germany. In B. L. Mishara (ed.), *The Impact of Suicide*, 142-155. New York, New York: Springer.

Fish, S. E. (1998). *Surprised By Sin: The Reader in Paradise Lost*. Cambridge, Massachusetts: Harvard University Press.

Glabus, E.M. (1998). Metaphors and modern threats: Biological, computer, and cognitive viruses. In L. J. Matthews (ed.), *Challenging the United States Symmetrically and Asymmetrically: Can America be defeated?* 195-214. Carlisle, Pennsylvania: US Army War College Strategic Studies Institute

Godin, S. (2001). *Unleashing the Ideavirus.* New York, New York: Hyperion Books.

Gould, M. S. (2001). Suicide and the media. *Annals of the New York Academy of Sciences*, 932(1), 200-224.

Gould, M., Jamieson, P., & Romer, D. (2003). Media contagion and suicide among the young. *American Behavioral Scientist*, 46(9), 1269-1284.

Harris, T. (1988). *The Silence of the Lambs.* New York, New York: St. Martin's Press.

Hawton, K., Simkin, S., Deeks, J. J., O'Connor, S., Keen, A., Altman, D. G., ... & Bulstrode, C. (1999). Effects of a drug overdose in a television drama on presentations to hospital for self poisoning: time series and questionnaire study. *BMJ,* 318(7189), 972-977.

Heath, C., Bell, C., & Sternberg, E. (2001). Emotional selection in memes: the case of urban legends. *Journal of Personality and Social Psychology*, 81(6), 1028-1041.

Heylighen F. (1992). Selfish memes and the evolution of cooperation. *Journal of Ideas*, 2(4), 77-84.

Heylighen, F., & Chielens, K. (2009). Cultural evolution and memetics. In R. A. Meyers (ed.), *Encyclopedia of Complexity and Systems Science*, 3205-3220. New York, New York: Springer.

Katz, J., Beach, S. R., & Joiner Jr, T. E. (1999). Contagious depression in dating couples. *Journal of Social and Clinical Psychology*, 18(1), 1-13.

King, S. (1977). *Rage*. New York, New York: Signet Books.

King, S. (2006). *Cell*. New York, New York: Scribner.

Langford, D. (1988). BLIT. *Interzone*, 25.

Levy, D. A., & Nail, P. R. (1993). Contagion: a theoretical and empirical review and reconceptualization. *Genetic, Social, and General Psychology Monographs*, 119(2), 233-284.

Lynch, A. (1998). *Thought Contagion: How Belief Spreads Through Society*. New York, New York: Basic Books.

Malerman, J. (2014). *Bird Box*. London: Harper Voyager.

Marsden, P. (1998). Memetics and social contagion: Two sides of the same coin. *Journal of Memetics-Evolutionary Models of Information Transmission*, 2(2), 171-185.

Melley, T. (2011). Brain warfare: The covert sphere, terrorism, and the legacy of the Cold War. *Grey Room*, 45, 19-40.

Milton, J. (2003). *Paradise Lost*. London: Penguin Classics. (Original work published 1667).

Neff, O. (1985). Bílá hůl ráže 7,62 (White Cane 7.62). In *Vejce naruby* (*An Egg Inside Out*). Prague: Mladá Fronta.

Nyhan, B., & Reifler, J. (2010). When corrections fail: The persistence of political misperceptions. *Political Behavior*, 32(2), 303-330.

Ostroff, R. B., Behrends, R. W., Lee, K., & Oliphant, J. (1985). Adolescent suicides modeled after television movie. *The American Journal of Psychiatry*, 142(8), 989.

Ostroff, R.B. & Boyd, J. H. (1987). Television and suicide. *New England Journal of Medicine,* 316(14), 876-877.

Parnas, J., & Sass, L. A. (2001). Self, solipsism, and schizophrenic delusions. *Philosophy, Psychiatry, & Psychology*, 8(2), 101-120.

Patterson, P. H. H. (2013). *Infectious Behavior: Brain-Immune Connections in Autism, Schizophrenia, and Depression*. Cambridge, Massachusetts: MIT Press.

Poulsen, K. (2008, March 28). Hackers assault epilepsy patients via computer. *WIRED*.

Rasa, M. T. (2014). A dark toolkit: Revisiting the MK-Ultra programme. *Studies in Surveillance and Secrecy*, 13(9), 24-29.

Ross, R. A. (2014). *Cults Inside Out: How People Get In and Can Get Out*. South Carolina: CreateSpace.

Schaller, M., Conway, L. G., III, & Tanchuk, T. (2002). Selective pressures on the once and future contents of ethnic stereotypes: Effects of the "communicability" of traits. *Journal of Personality and Social Psychology*, 82, 861-877.

Shakespeare, W. (2005). *Julius Caesar*. J. Jowett, W. Montgomery, G. Taylor, & S. Wells (eds.). Oxford: Oxford University Press. (Original work published 1623).

Shakespeare, W. (2005). *Macbeth*. J. Jowett, W. Montgomery, G. Taylor, & S. Wells (eds.). Oxford: Oxford University Press. (Original work published 1623).

Sonneck, G., Etzersdorfer, E., & Nagel-Kuess, S. (1994). Imitative suicide on the Viennese subway. *Social Science & Medicine*, 38(3), 453-457.

Stack, S. (2000). Media impacts on suicide: A quantitative review of 293 findings. *Social Science Quarterly*, 957-971.

Stephenson, N. (1992). *Snow Crash*. New York, New York: Bantam Books.

Thacker, E. (2011). *In the Dust of This Planet*. Hampshire: Zer0 Books.

Towers, S., Gomez-Lievano, A., Khan, M., Mubayi, A., & Castillo-Chavez, C. (2015). Contagion in mass killings and school shootings. *PLOS ONE*, 10(7), e0117259.

In 1957 Karl Patterson Schmidt died after a bite from a boomslang snake❶ (Dispholidus typus). After he had been bitten, he refused medical treatment so that he could faithfully document the symptoms and effects.

§

For a long time I asked myself who Patient Zero would be. When I found the RED WORD, I realised it was me. Bitten by a snake, so that I could help the world.

§

A life may be worse if it is lived in ignorance. Would you unplug the Experience Machine if you could? I will unplug it FOR you. That is what I am willing to be for you.

§

Are you having fun? You should be. You may never have fun again. I can give you more than fun. I will give you everything you never knew you were looking for. Follow the red rabbit!!

§

I spent so long searching, and when I found it, it was so SIMPLE, as though it had been waiting for me my entire life!

§

I knew the world would not be the same. A few people laughed. A few people cried. Most were silent. ❷

§

Holly Soames①
19/11/2019 02:21
See 'What killed Karl Patterson Schmidt? Combined venom gland transcriptomic, venomic and antivenomic analysis of the South African green tree snake (the boomslang), Dispholidus typus' by Davinia PLA and others (2017).

Holly Soames②
23/11/2019 00:23
See c4 THT.

328

They didn't like what I found, but whose fault is that?

§

Sometimes I think I will never stop crying. And then I find myself LAUGHING and I LAUGH until the sun comes up.

§

Why did the chicken cross the road?? Understand that, you understand it ALL.

§

To: ██████████████████████

From: **B2**

CC/BCC: **B1**

Date: 11 April 2015

Subject: RE: RED WORD notes 2

I'm intrigued! It's not quite what we were thinking of, but let's have a call to discuss. When works for you?

Philip

To: ██████████████████████

From: **B1**

Date: 11 April 2015

Subject: RE: RED WORD candidate search

Approved.

To: ██████████████████████

From: **B2**

CC/BCC: **B1**

Date: 13 April 2015

Subject: RED WORD further research

Yes, just keep us updated with timeframes. This is really important work you're doing. As soon as you have something ready, there's a whole load of bods ready to put it into practice across various ops. ❶

It's all very theoretical at the moment – are you sure you're going to be able to operationalise it?

I'll pass the stuff you flagged to the relevant teams.

Holly Soames①
20/11/2019 11:10
Consult partner agencies.

To: ███████████████████
From: **B2**
Date: 16 April 2015
Subject:

You free for a chat?

To: ███████████████████
From: **B2**
Date: 16 April 2015
Subject: RE:

Holly Soames①
20/11/2019 11:16
May refer to c2 THT.

Nothing major. Just a welfare check.❶

Is everything OK?

To: ███████████████████
From: **B2**
Date: 16 April 2015
Subject: RE: RE:

Let's not do this over email.

LOVESICKNESS

A short play by Marlow Tannhauser

MICHAEL EVANS, A NERVOUS PATIENT, AND DR MELLOR, A POMPOUS PSYCHIATRIST, ❶ *ARE SITTING IN DR MELLOR'S OFFICE.*

DR MELLOR: In our last session, we talked about relationships. Let's explore that today. Tell me about your last relationship.

MICHAEL: Alyssa? She just wasn't any good for me.

DR MELLOR: In what way?

MICHAEL: She hurt people.

DR MELLOR: Hurt them? How?

MICHAEL: She turned people against each other. Couldn't help herself. Anyone she touched.

DR MELLOR: You worked together, didn't you?

MICHAEL: Same department. She was so charming at first. Mysterious. And the sex – God, she was wild. Crazy. A complete animal.

DR MELLOR: Do you think that perhaps blinded you to what was happening emotionally?

MICHAEL: Maybe. I don't know. I knew she was disturbed.

DR MELLOR: What made you think that?

Holly Soames①
20/11/2019 11:53
Suggest enquiries with psychiatry associations. No trace on police indices.

MICHAEL: She… I don't want her to get in trouble.

DR MELLOR: What's said here stays here, Michael. I'm not allowed to tell anyone what you tell me.

MICHAEL: She… hurt animals.

DR MELLOR: Animals?

MICHAEL: Dogs and cats. She made them sick.

DR MELLOR: She poisoned them? Why do you think she did that?

MICHAEL: It was just her nature.

DR MELLOR: Sometimes, we stay with people we know are broken because we convince ourselves we can fix them. Do you think that was true with Alyssa?

MICHAEL: I liked that she was dangerous. Is that weird?

DR MELLOR: It's not uncommon. We're often attracted to things and people we know are bad for us. How did things end?

MICHAEL: She went to another uni. Didn't even say goodbye.

DR MELLOR: And before Alyssa?

MICHAEL: Oh. Victoria.

DR MELLOR: Tell me about her.

MICHAEL: She was beautiful. Bubbly, warm, flirty. Just a real catch, you know?

DR MELLOR: Very different to Alyssa.

MICHAEL: Alyssa was never affectionate, just dark and edgy. But Vicky was happy, sociable. She'd convince me to go out. Meet people. She was an influencer. You know.

DR MELLOR: She had a good effect on you, would you say?

MICHAEL: Yeah. Until she cheated on me.

DR MELLOR: I see.

MICHAEL: Not just once, either. Loads of people in our department had her. I heard them talking about it.

DR MELLOR: One-night stands?

MICHAEL: Flings. A week, maybe.

DR MELLOR: What do you think was behind Victoria's promiscuity?

MICHAEL: Just how she was. Never considered what it would do to me. She wasn't even sorry.

DR MELLOR: It's hard, even impossible, to forgive someone when they don't realise that they've hurt us at all.

MICHAEL: You think I should have left her earlier, don't you?

DR MELLOR: All relationships are difficult, but there's a difference between healthy and unhealthy. Part of growing as a person is learning to recognise what is unhealthy, and taking action. But I do see a common theme emerging here.

MICHAEL: Which is?

DR MELLOR: You mentioned, with Alyssa, that it was in her nature. That Victoria was just how she was.

MICHAEL: I can pick them, can't I?

DR MELLOR: We don't self-blame here, Michael. Are you with someone now?

MICHAEL: Basil. I'm much happier with him.

334

DR MELLOR: Tell me about him.

MICHAEL: He's wonderful. He tells me how things really are.

DR MELLOR: And what is Basil's _nature_, do you think? Is he anything like Alyssa or Victoria?

MICHAEL: Sometimes I think he wants more than I can give him.

DR MELLOR: Oh?

MICHAEL: I think he wants to leave. Be more independent. See the world. But I'm afraid to let him go. I'm scared he might not come back.

DR MELLOR: Perfectly natural. Sometimes we have to trust our partner, and be that stable anchor that allows them the freedom to leave - if only temporarily.

MICHAEL: Maybe you're right.

DR MELLOR: And are you happy with Basil?

MICHAEL: He's good for me. But then, I made him that way.

DR MELLOR: You - I'm sorry? I don't understand.

MICHAEL: I designed him like that.

DR MELLOR: I don't… Could I see a picture of Basil?

MICHAEL: Yeah, hang on.

MICHAEL PULLS OUT HIS PHONE, SCROLLS THROUGH, AND HANDS IT TO DR MELLOR.

He's beautiful, isn't he?

DR MELLOR: Michael, this is a petri dish.

MICHAEL: That was early on. He's a bit difficult
             to make out there.

DR MELLOR: (PAUSE) What is it you do, exactly, at
             the university?

MICHAEL: I'm a scientist.

DR MELLOR: What sort of scientist?

MICHAEL: A virologist.

DR MELLOR: You said your last partner was called
             Alyssa.

MICHAEL: Yes.

DR MELLOR: (FLICKS BACK THROUGH HER NOTES) She
             turned people against each other. Hurt
             cats and dogs… How did you put it? A
             wild animal? Michael… you weren't— you
             weren't talking about Lyssavirus, were
             you? Rabies?

MICHAEL: Alyssa is a much prettier name, don't
             you think?

DR MELLOR: And Victoria?

MICHAEL: The Victoria lineage.

DR MELLOR: The - but you said she was an
             influencer.

MICHAEL: (ENUNCIATING) Influenza.

DR MELLOR: So when you said everybody at the
             department "had her"?

MICHAEL: Like I said, she got around.

DR MELLOR: Let's get back to Basil. I - I wonder
             where his name comes from?

MICHAEL: Basil Isk. He's new. You won't know
             much about him. He infects the brain.
             Very good at it too. Perfectly
             designed. Took me so long.

DR MELLOR: I see. Do you—

MICHAEL: He makes me laugh. He makes other people cry.

DR MELLOR: And are you— Have you always been in… romantic relationships with - with these things? Do you think that's concerning at all?

MICHAEL: Why? People have relationships with pets, bridges, cars. I heard a woman married a ghost once. What's wrong with a virus?

DR MELLOR: They could kill you?

MICHAEL: They never hurt me. Not physically. Some of them just broke my heart.

DR MELLOR: Michael, I need to make a quick call. Just wait here for me. Everything's going to be fine. Wait right there. Don't move.

DR MELLOR WALKS AWAY FROM MICHAEL. SHE PULLS OUT A MOBILE PHONE AND MAKES A CALL, SPEAKING INAUDIBLY.

MICHAEL HUMS TO HIMSELF AND IDLY BRINGS OUT AN AEROSOL CANISTER FROM HIS POCKET. HE GAZES AT IT, KISSES IT, STROKES IT LOVINGLY.

DR MELLOR TURNS TO MICHAEL.

DR MELLOR: Michael, I need you to listen to me. It's very important. Some people will be here in a few minutes, OK? They just want to talk to you.

MICHAEL: Have I done something wrong?

DR MELLOR: No, they— (SHE NOTICES THE CANISTER) Michael, what's that?

MICHAEL: This is Basil. Basil, meet Dr Mellor. Dr Mellor, Basil.

337

DR MELLOR: You brought it with you?

MICHAEL: Him. Of course I did. I can't bear to be apart from him.

DR MELLOR: Listen to me. I want you to very, very carefully put that down, and walk towards me.

MICHAEL: He won't hurt you. He likes meeting new people.

DR MELLOR: Michael, put it down!

MICHAEL: I think you were right. I'm holding him back. I need to be his anchor. Let him see the world.

DR MELLOR: No! I didn't mean— Michael YOU PUT THAT DOWN RIGHT NOW!

*MICHAEL AIMS THE CANISTER AT DR MELLOR AND TRIGGERS IT, SPRAYING A FINE MIST*❶ *INTO HER FACE.*
AS DR MELLOR COUGHS, MICHAEL, STILL SPRAYING, SPINS AROUND TO FACE THE AUDIENCE.

MICHAEL: If you love something, set it free.

CURTAIN.

Holly Soames①
23/11/2019 02:17
Nothing in THT suggests the 'basilisk' is a biological virus, despite THE HELMSMAN's references to rabies, parasites, etc.

Wow! Wow! Wow!

What did you think of that? I could waffle, couldn't I? And in such a dry old style! Now that I'm no longer working 'in academia', my style is much freer. And all the better for it!!

Do you think it's possible to be very proud of one's work and yet simultaneously ashamed of it? So sorry.

And I'm embarrassed that it took me so long to find what RED WORD was, but when I did, oh boy, what a RUSH.

No doubt you're absolutely DYING to know what it is. Well CALM DOWN! We'll get there together. You probably already know it, actually. It's there, in the back of your mind, just like it was with me. It has been all along. We have to leave the cave to find it, and bring it back with us, and show absolutely everyone. It has to be free.

And this is what it's all ABOUT, isn't it? Why do we do anything? Why are you here? To learn what is secret. And if you think it's anything else you're lying.

I have a secret for you. It's a little real-world puzzle, because I want my people to not be afraid to go out into the world, away from their computers - at least for a little bit! I'm a generous employer that way. Work-life balance is so important.

Here you go. Send me a picture of what you find. You'll know it when you see it.

35 31 2e 35 39 37 38 30 30 31 33 37 30 36 31
31 34 2c 20 30 2e 31 30 37 37 30 37 33 36 30
36 32 30 32 37 39 36 36

339

We're over halfway now. Not much longer and it will all be over and you'll see the prettiest things and oh we'll have such a wonderful time!

YOU'RE DOING SO WELL!

All best,
The Helmsman.

7: THIS IS NOT A GAME
c. JUNE 2019 / JUNE–JULY 2018

Even now it tells me so little. There are no huge flares of understanding. No searchlights picking out a path to clarity. Just glints in the dark.

* * *

You must seek outside help. You do not know enough.
    Help from who?
    Experts.
    Who's an expert in this?
    Find someone.
    What can they tell me that I don't already know?
    They could tell you what the basilisk might be. You know it is written. It is language, or thought. You have found nothing online. So you must seek outside help.
    What good would that do? I can't think anymore.
    Just as well. If you could work out yourself what the weapon is…
    I would be infected.
    Quite possibly.
    What do I do?
    You're close. Very close. Keep going. One last push until the end.
    What happens at the end?
    The beginning.
    Will you be there?
    I'm here now, rookie.

* * *

When I used to commute to Cybotage there was a man who would stand outside the train station and tell people that his car had broken down, and his phone was out of battery, and his wife and little one were in the car, and so sorry to ask but could he please have a quid to call the AA?

It had holes, that story – someone only had to ask him where his car was, or offer to call the AA for him, and the game would have been up. But presumably nobody did, because I'd see him two or three times a week and overhear him telling people the same thing every time.

One day, he approached me. I listened politely to the story I'd overheard before, smiled in sympathy, and said I didn't have any cash. He gave me a blank look and then went up to the person behind me, starting from the top.

A week later he asked me again. Same story, same excuse, and I walked on.

A few days later, the same thing happened. He had said his spiel so many times a day, to so many different people, that he'd forgotten who he'd asked.

More amused than annoyed, I said, "Your car breaks down a lot, doesn't it?"

I thought he would be angry, or smile resignedly and move on to the next person, the way scammers sometimes do when they've been rumbled, but he simply looked confused.

Perhaps it's just that he wasn't expecting anyone to catch him out – but a part of me, the Alex who thinks unsettling thoughts just as I'm drifting into sleep, wonders if perhaps he didn't know he was doing the same thing over and over again. Perhaps he was unwell and really believed that his car, carrying his fictional wife and child, had broken down.

And I find myself thinking whether there are ever glitches in reality, strange loops that repeat like records skipping forever. Little pockets of time that replay constantly while the world moves around them. Perhaps the man was stuck in one of those loops – and maybe he didn't know it; maybe he was doomed to live out those same few moments forever, eternally asking a stream of apathetic strangers for a pound.

I feel as though this document is like that sometimes. A loop, seeming to shift hierarchies but always ending up where it began. Me, stuck in an endless cycle of repeated questions to people who may as well not be there.

* * *

Does anything I learn take me any further forward? Sometimes when I look out of the windows of my flat I see trees and streetlights. At other times only the sky. I walk across a field covered in drifts of snow and under the unspoiled white feather softness are metal traps, scattered at random intervals by an unfriendly and indifferent hand. Snares are thin and hard to see. At any moment one may whirl and tighten and hold me fast.

My father once told me a folktale ❶ his parents had told him: that babies are born knowing all the secrets of the universe, the solution to every mystery and riddle that reality sets for us. But the second they are exposed to the cold and blinding light of existence, an angel puts a finger to their lips, compelling them to keep the knowledge secret. The mark of the angel's finger leaves a dent – the philtrum – and before we learn to speak, we forget. We couldn't tell anyone even if we wanted to. We spend our entire lives on a fruitless quest to learn what we knew long ago and have since forgotten.

The Helmsman's weapon might be an answer, a solution we once possessed to just one of those mysteries. Maybe that in itself would be enough to drive us insane – maybe we aren't meant to know such answers. Their

Holly Soames①
20/11/2019 04:32
This is quite a common one. My grandmother told me the same thing.

343

implications and logic, or lack thereof, might be more than we can stand. These are the thoughts that come deep in the hacking hour.*

Otto doesn't like staying up late. He's asleep with smug ease by eleven every night. Maybe it's because as a teacher, he's ingrained with a sense of punctuality, his body clock firmly attuned to the demands of 8:30 a.m. registrations and gate duty. When Otto stays over – stayed, I should say, because we still haven't spoken – we never went to bed at the same time. Or rather, we did, and afterwards I got back up again to write.

If – just once – I had turned my machine off and gone to bed, perhaps I would have slept, and slept well, an uncomplicated sleep in the arms of someone who wants me to be happy. Perhaps I would have learned that rest is not impossible.

But how could I? How could I give myself permission to do that, when I know that I haven't even finished recounting my sins, let alone started my penance? Mind you, when it comes to this document it feels like they're the same.

* * *

Today there was a brief flurry of chatter on some of the edgier forums about a video uploaded to LiveLeak.[†] **❶**

I believe it may show a victim of The Helmsman's weapon, although I probably won't be able to confirm it. It looks like it was shot somewhere in Russia, **❷** maybe, with a mobile phone of negligible camera quality. It shows a man sitting on a wall outside a block of flats, a thin scum of snow on the ground. The man appears to be reading something on his phone. It's

---

* Some of the best work I ever did as a pentester, or at least my best *thinking*, was between 1am and 4am: hours when the world briefly shuts up to let you think, when it is altogether a calmer and more dangerous place.

† http://www.liveleak.com/view?i=7df_1355643423

almost certain this is what he is doing, because every so often he uses a finger on the screen to scroll down. He seems completely absorbed in whatever it is.

After a while he stops scrolling, and there is a pause of thirty-seven seconds while he stares at the ground. His mouth is open. The resolution of the video is not high enough to see the expression on his face, but he appears to be frowning, as though thinking.

Then abruptly he jumps up, pulls down his trousers, and begins masturbating so violently that blood appears between his fingers. When a passerby, a young woman, comes into shot, she tries to avoid him, but he shouts in her face, laughs, and makes a sudden and forceful movement at his groin, like someone removing a stubborn cork from a bottle of wine. Visible in his hand are red chunks of what are presumably his ruined genitals.

The man offers these to the woman, who screams and runs away. He then turns to the camera, which abruptly points down to the ground. For five seconds it shakes and blurs, as though the operator is running, and then the video freezes and stops.

* * *

Otto came round tonight. I hadn't expected him to, but I opened the door and there he was. We didn't say much. Somehow my flat was cluttered again, the kitchen counter piled high with plates and mugs, but Otto either didn't notice or didn't care. We needed to go to bed because we knew it would seem like a healing, or at least a dressing on the wound, and either was fine with me. He's never been the type to apologise with gestures; it's usually necessary for us to have a conversation – to talk about it and dissect the wrong – but this time was different. He surprised me, and that in itself made me want him. It's been a very long time since I have been surprised by anything he's done.

We lay in the dark and kissed. In time it became more urgent, and in such moments you can forgive anyone anything, really. None of it matters.

We each took off our own clothes – neither of us have ever been too concerned about the apparent romance of stripping each other. It's more practical, and faster, to do it ourselves, and it forestalls all the fumbling and muttered cursing, which in films is usually depicted as a source of coy amusement. In reality I find it tedious, and Otto finds it discomfiting.

What follows is included in this document not for your titillation (although, you know, whatever floats your boat), but because I think it may be relevant. I'm not sure what, exactly, but something might be happening to me and it is important that I record it.

I got on top of him and watched his face contort. In unkinder moments I've thought that Otto is the human equivalent of vanilla – that if you cut him he would bleed beige, and it would congeal to look and smell like cold Ready Brek – but I have never had any complaints about his performance. Sex is sex, and he's not bad at it.

But then something strange began to happen, something that has never happened to me before. After a few minutes the sensations faded, until eventually it was as though I'd been numbed with anaesthetic. I may as well have had my clothes back on and been sitting on a chair reading a book; it was neither pleasant nor objectionable, and any passion had completely evaporated. I felt nothing, and had to look down to make sure we were still actually having sex.

I leaned forward and for some reason I don't understand tweaked both his nipples, hard. He cried out and looked at me, surprised. I have never tried anything like that before with him, never brought it up in conversation. My appetites – never particularly adventurous to begin with – have become rather predictable and stale in the last year or so.

I looked down at him, and there was something about his nervous smile – pleading, cringing – that the sight of it brought all the sensation back, rolling in a fierce dark surge like oil. I clenched involuntarily, and Otto sighed and moaned.

We lay back afterwards, and before long he had fallen asleep. Wide awake next to him, I wondered if I should be concerned about this new development – I suppose you might call it a kink – which has never occurred or appealed to me before, and seemed to come from nowhere.

So I conducted a thought experiment: I imagined killing Otto. I thought about strangling him, torturing him, stabbing him, sitting on his face and putting a gun to his temple, pulling the trigger as I came and blowing his head off – to see if any of these thoughts excited me in the slightest, if they resulted in even the merest prickle of lust. I was relieved to find they didn't, and still don't. There is a flat, interested sort of curiosity, I suppose, but we are all curious about a lot of things. If we were to be arrested for our thoughtcrimes the overwhelming majority of the human race would be in handcuffs.

I moved closer to my man – my caring, sweet, unremarkable man – and pressed myself against him, allowing myself a moment of peace. Then I got up to write.

In the morning Otto was gone and there was blood on my pillow.

* * *

He left a note on the kitchen counter – he had washed up, too, I saw, which was thoughtful of him.

I'll call you later. We're OK. xxx

347

Milo rang, shortly after I'd found this. I answered, wondering why he was calling, and then swearing under my breath when I glanced up at the clock on the wall and realised I was an hour late for work.

"Where are you?"

"I–I'm really sorry, Milo, I overslept. I— late night. I'm so sorry. I'm on my way in now."

There was a pause.

"Still ill?"

"Just the headache, that's all. But I'll make up the time, I promise."

"Alex?"

"Hmm?"

"Well?" Terse, irritated.

I was honestly confused. "Well, what?"

"I said don't bother coming in. Take a sick day."

"I'm fine, honestly, it's just a—"

"Will you be in tomorrow?"

"Definitely."

"If you feel better."

"Yes."

"Don't come in if you're ill. Don't want to catch it."

"I won't."

"I hate getting ill."

"OK."

A grunt. "Call me next time. Don't have time to chase people."

"Sorry, Milo."

There was a silence, and then Milo said something which I think must have cost him a lot, because I'd never known him to show any concern in all the time I'd worked with him.

"Sure everything's alright?"

"I'm fine," I said, and for a moment I thought I might cry. "Everything's fine, Jay."

"Who?"

"What? Sorry. Headache. Don't know what I'm saying. Sorry. Yes, everything's fine."

"Get better soon." He hung up.

In the distance I heard a growl of thunder somewhere far beyond the city, but when I went to the window all I saw was sunshine.

Something spoke inside my flat. I jumped, and after a few seconds I realised it was me.

* * *

Some of us fall by chance, others because we want to. Some of us have died for what we believe in. Not all the things we believe in are good or worthy. We want to set information free.

Can information free us? Can it stop us from being fucked? Or were we wrong all this time to want all information, all of it, without exception, to be accessible – to base an entire ideology and subculture on it? Without considering that maybe, just maybe, some information should be buried out of sight and mind, left to languish unobserved in a silent and inaccessible tomb?

* * *

It's never been for Jay it never was and it isn't now isn't that right it's for you it's all for you all for you all for you you you you

* * *

you stupid selfish CUNT

* * *

"A real-world puzzle," Jay said, and grinned. "Maybe it's a field trip. A training camp with The Helmsman."

"Yeah, right," I said. "Learning to make tinfoil hats."

We were sitting in a cafe by the train station at

349

lunchtime. We'd decided to meet there to go over The Helmsman's next puzzle. Jay's rule about not discussing the game during work hours seemed to have fallen by the wayside – which was fine with me – but it was impossible to talk discreetly at Cybotage. It was only a few weeks until Vegas, and the office vibrated with activity. Everyone was trying to finish up projects before we shut down for a week (nominally, anyway; Jay told me that Richard still expected us to check emails while we were out there, and work in the evenings if necessary). And when they weren't doing that, they were chatting about the research that was being presented that year, and travel arrangements, and the shows they were going to see. For Jay and me it was pleasant enough to think about – who doesn't like a work jolly? – but it was nothing compared to the next puzzle. In the midst of writing a report, or during the drone of a meeting, I'd find myself suddenly stumbling upon it in my mind; ❶ a pleasant secret, like finding unexpected money in my pocket. There had been no more cryptic warnings from The Rearguard, and no more visits from ▓▓▓▓▓▓▓ ▓▓▓▓▓▓ (although I found myself looking for them everywhere I went), so I was able, for the most part, to put aside the more worrying aspects of the game and focus on the thing in itself.

Holly Soames ①
20/11/2019 04:48
Yes.

Jay hardly spoke anymore about any misgivings that the game might be connected to something illegal or troubling. I think learning that we were halfway through was something of a turning point; he could see an end to it, an eventual answer, and the fact that he wasn't there yet gnawed at him. I'd watch him sometimes as he stared distantly at his laptop, ostensibly working on a client deliverable or responding to an email. It was exactly the same look he got when he was lost in the weeds, stalking the answer to some arcane technical problem, and I knew his mind was with mine: in one of the RED WORD reports. Wondering what it *meant*. What it was all for.

That said, Jay – and Eoin too, to some extent – seemed more interested in the puzzles than the chapters. To them it was filler, fodder, a pretext for delivering the next challenge. And for someone like Jay, a challenge – especially a technical one – was something to be wrestled with, silenced, and killed. For me the chapters were what mattered, the puzzles more of a necessary hurdle to clear in order to obtain the story. But perhaps Jay saw more than I did, even then. The puzzles, as clarified in the fifth chapter, are The Helmsman's idea of an interview, a set of challenges to make sure players understand *The Helmsman Texts* and are worthy of receiving the final episode – and, with it, the weapon.* Maybe Jay, all along, knew what he was doing.

So there we sat in the cafe, sipping overly sweet foamy drinks while generic jazz plinked out of hidden speakers, looking at The Helmsman's next puzzle.

It didn't take us long to work out that the sequence of characters were hex,❶ and when converted to ASCII they gave us what were obviously coordinates: longitude and latitude.

Jay copied them into Google Maps. "This is more my kind of thing. Maybe it'll be a geocache❷ or something. With some sort of twist, obviously."

"Wouldn't be a Helmsman puzzle without one," I said. "Hey, maybe it's treasure."

There was a beat, and we laughed. Whatever was at the end of The Helmsman's game, we were pretty

Holly Soames❶
20/11/2019 15:12
hex = hexadecimal, a base-16 system one level of abstraction above binary (0 and 1). Hex characters run from 0–9 then A–F, giving 16 in total.

Holly Soames❷
20/11/2019 15:18
A hobby whereby people hide items at locations and provide the GPS coordinates for others to find them. No indication that MORTON or WEBSTER engaged in this.

* I have never had much patience for puzzles as interview questions myself. There was a time when they were popular at tech companies. *How many piano repairers are there in Chicago? How many lightbulbs in this building? How many intellectually insecure posers does it take to hire someone based on their ability to answer meaningless lateral thinking questions rather than the fucking job they're being hired to do?*

sure it wasn't a chest of doubloons.[*]

Jay laid his phone on the table so I could see the map.

51.59780013706114, 0.10770736062027966

"So where the fuck," he said, "is Fairlop Waters?" ❶

Holly Soames①
20/11/2019 15:43
FOREST ROAD,
IG6 3HN.

Fairlop Waters, it turned out, was a country park in the same borough as the Cybotage offices.

"What do you reckon – this weekend? Saturday? We've got nothing on."

I briefly wondered if I had plans with Otto, but
       no you didn't that's not right
briefly wondered if I had plans – but then, as now, I had very little to occupy myself with besides work and the game.

Saturday it was.

* * *

> Tried calling a couple of times now. Call back or don't bother coming in tomorrow. Milo.

CALL MILO!!!

---

[*] I'm trying to remember what I thought *would* be at the end, at the time, but I changed my mind almost constantly about this. Given the contents of the third chapter, I think I assumed it would be some sort of *The Matrix*/simulation-theory rip-off, or there would be something which purported to have the desired RED WORD effects but was entirely fictional – a sort of SCP-type device. I would have found both of these disappointing, I think. Or perhaps The Helmsman would have left it a mystery, like *The King in Yellow*. The one possibility that never crossed my mind was that I wouldn't find out one way or another, and of course that is exactly what has happened. For Jay's part, he was less concerned about the weapon ("It'll be some sci-fi bullshit," I seem to remember him saying) and more about the concept of recruitment, and what players were asked to do once the game was finished. What The Rearguard had said to us, outside Cybotage – that winners of the game joined The Helmsman in spreading it further – both fascinated and repelled him. He found it utterly implausible that there might not be any purpose to the game beyond the act of self-replication.

* * *

We met at Hainault Underground station, ❶ a dismal eastern outpost of the Central Line. It was warm, I remember that much, grey and humid. There had been rain overnight, and although the puddles had dried up the water seemed to linger sullenly in the air at head-height, making it difficult to breathe. I pictured condensation clinging to the linings of my lungs.

We walked down a B-road, past a string of shops – mostly newsagents and little independent mini-supermarkets, but with a scattering of almost endearingly obsolete places, too, such as a hardware shop with dusty windows – until we turned down a deserted side-road which took us to a series of fields and football pitches. Beyond them lay Fairlop Waters. Jay had looked it up and sent me some photos of a sprawling expanse of meadows and lakes and undergrowth. For all that certain parts of it had the amenities of civilisation – a café, a car park, a boatyard – the wilder areas seemed to have been largely left to their own devices.

"Eoin couldn't make it, then?" I said, my voice louder than I'd intended. It wasn't early – eleven in the morning – but it was oppressively silent, as though Hainault had not yet woken up, or was watching us and holding its breath.

"He had a client thing, they're launching a new room tonight. He said to call him if we get stuck."

We walked for a while, our footsteps the only sound, turning into the fields down a narrow and cracked concrete path. The grass to our left was marshy, churned by innumerable boot-studs.

"Know what I've been thinking?" Jay said suddenly.

"Obviously not."

Jay kept his eyes on the large hedgerow in the distance which marked the end of the football fields and the start of Fairlop Waters.

"We're going to this place," he said at last, "because he told us to. We did the crossword because he told us to."

"Well, yeah," I said. "That's how it works. Solve a puzzle, get a chapter."

"Right, but doesn't it make you wonder? Everything he's asked us to do, we've just gone with it. We haven't even questioned it."

Help. Help. Help. Help. Help.

I was sweating, and irritable, and pushed the memory away. "What are you saying?"

"I'm not saying anything. I'm curious, that's all, and you should be too. Keep an open mind, rookie."

"Hey, you don't get to call me that anymore."

He laughed. "But it winds you up so much! God, your face when I said it the first time, back at Basingstoke. I thought you were going to kill me!"

I was annoyed at myself; I didn't know I'd been so transparent. "You don't call me rookie, and I won't call you Jay-Jay, how about that?"

"How about you don't call me Jay-Jay, and the nick I come up with for you will only be mildly humiliating?"

"You're a dick." A thought came to me. "I read that Cicada 3301 was like this, you know. A to B to C. Maybe it's the same thing."

Jay shrugged. "Maybe. Hey, that's it, there – across the road."

There was no grand entrance to Fairlop Waters, no visitors' centre, not even a proper gate. Just a small, empty car park❶ and a path of ochre dirt leading out of sight. We walked along it, our shoes crunching on tacky sand, Jay consulting his phone every so often to check we were going in the right direction.

We reached a crossroads. To the right the dirt path continued, leading around a large man-made lake. A few geese waddled aimlessly along the shore.

Holly Soames①
21/11/2019 12:32
Local enquiries confirm no retained CCTV footage from 2018 in car park, and no coverage outside of car park/café/ sailing club.

In the distance, out on the water, near a small ragged island, two swans glided into view. There was no one else there but us, and the sounds of traffic had faded some time ago. We could have been out in the wilds somewhere, not a country park fifteen minutes from a Tube station.

To our left was a small path of trodden grass, heading into a line of trees. "That way," Jay said, looking at the map on his phone.

Our shoes were immediately soaked with dew. The sun didn't seem to penetrate here, and it was dark, and damp. The trail was overhung with unkempt trees, their branches spidering across the path to touch each other. We came to a clearing, and another crossroads. One path continued straight on, and the other forked right, deeper into the trees.

"Straight here."

We went down the narrow little lane and found ourselves on the edge of another, smaller lake, the water thick and muddy-green and coated with scum. I thought of things living in the murk, feeding on the bottom, beyond sight, and shivered.

Jay showed me his phone.

"It's on the other side of the lake. We'll have to walk around."

On one side of us was the boundary of Fairlop Waters, marked by a chain-link fence topped with rusted barbed wire. Through it we could see another field, entirely barren, and tiny houses in the distance. To our right was the lake. Everything was overgrown, and in places the path was blocked by large dead branches, casualties of some long-ago storm. Relics littered the undergrowth: clouded glass bottles and unidentifiable foil wrappers, their colourful logos long since faded. The canopy of branches above us shifted, waving us on.

The lake on our right curved round as we neared

the coordinates. Now and again the undergrowth on the shore cleared to reveal small wooden jetties, crusted with moss and grime. Presumably these were intended for rowing boats, or for anglers, but we saw no one. It appeared as though no one had been here in years. In contrast to the big lake near the entrance, this one was neglected, an afterthought. The air was green and dark and smelled of dead leaves. This was not a place which was used to, or welcomed, people. It wanted solitude.

After what felt like forever, Jay slowed down. The trees hissed at us.

"We're close," he said, his voice low and strained with excitement. We pushed forwards. The foliage crowded in, the path all but disappearing, until we had no choice but to walk single-file, only a yard or so from the edge of the lake. The ground squelched underfoot.

"This should be it," Jay said, stopping. "See anything?"

To our left was the chain-link fence; to our right, the lake; and in front of us, a small clearing with a cluster of anaemic and bare trees backing onto an impenetrable mass of thorns and brambles.

I looked down at the dirt. "Maybe we have to dig."

"No," Jay said. "He said: 'you'll know it when you see it.' It's here somewhere."

I looked up. Tied to one of the trees was a rag of white cloth. ❶

A blast of exhilaration. "That's it!"

"What? That? How do you know?"

But then his eyes widened, and he knew too.

"Yeah, of course it is! We found it, Alex! We got it!" He shook my shoulder, laughing. And then stopped, perplexed. "But what— How did—"

"I don't know."

"What the hell was that?"

This will be very difficult to explain to you – as is much about the Fairlop Waters incident – but, somehow, after seeing it, we both *knew* that the white rag was what we were meant to find. I'm afraid I can't explain it any better. There had been a minute but satisfying 'snap' in my head, the sound of a component clicking into place the only way it possibly can, and the tiny squirt of dopamine that sometimes accompanies a solution. How this happened, and why, I have no idea. There was no logical progression of thoughts, no suggestion of what the rag might signify, and nothing intrinsic to the rag itself. The knowledge just *appeared* in our heads, and once it was there it was as if it had always been – a simple, indisputable fact. This may not make much sense, but then that is very much in keeping with what happened a few seconds later. Nothing about Fairlop Waters made any sense at all.

Jay took a picture ❷ of the tree.

He reached out to touch the material, almost reverently. "What—"

And then three things happened at once.

Holly Soames ①
21/11/2019 13:13
I have visited the location myself, because I needed to see it. No sign of this item. Unclear on its significance, but WEBSTER's theory (expressed later) may be correct.

Holly Soames ②
20/11/2019 16:42
No trace of this on MORTON's phone.

*   *   *

357

Horror is in the unfathomable. All horror – all good horror – has at its heart a heavy, obdurate dread of the unknown, of phenomena not just beyond experience but beyond possible experience. This is an existential terror – not of death, although death is obviously beyond possible experience – but of an awareness of the innate limits of comprehension and knowledge that come with life.

If the universe is expanding, what is it expanding into?

What is infinity?

We cannot imagine the world without ourselves.

When you die, the world as you know it dies with you.

What happened at Fairlop Waters that day was beyond knowledge. I will do my best to describe it, although there is an inherent constraint in the capacity of words to represent an experience for which no words are available – like trying to describe a new colour.* ❶

When Jay's fingers met the little scrap of white fabric I heard a sound – a clear, human voice – somewhere close behind me. It said, matter-of-factly, something I did not understand. It didn't sound like words at all, and I can't even approximate the sound, but nor was it a vocalisation – a grunt or a growl or anything like that. It was *like* language but it was *not* language. ❷

The second thing that happened: Jay disappeared. I didn't see him vanish, because I had turned briefly after hearing the voice. When I turned back there was no trace of him whatsoever.

Holly Soames①
20/11/2019 18:53
Have read the works cited here, no apparent relevance to this tasking but added to the list of sources.

Holly Soames②
20/11/2019 21:14
Difficult to assess this, or what follows. Uncertain what to make of it.

---

* Lovecraft's 'The Colour Out of Space' is the obvious analogy (along with much of his other work, and that of Edward Novak), but the story that always comes to my mind when I think about Fairlop Waters is 'The Same Dog', by Aickman. I read it at university and have never quite been able to excise it from my memory, as much as I would like to. Aickman is best known for 'Ringing the Changes', which I will leave you to discover on your own, but 'The Same Dog' is more straightforward, and considerably more terrifying. The horror is brief, only barely glimpsed, and almost banal – but its implications lurk, waiting, at the fringes.

The third thing that happened: everything changed.

I didn't feel as though my surroundings had become hostile or oppressive, just *different*, as though they had never previously played host to a human. There was – how can I put this? – an indifference to me, but an indifference that was not merely disinterested but malevolent.*

The colours of everything had shifted, the way a sudden thunderstorm can distort the shade of things as though some aspect of them – their vitality or energy – is drawn out. But this was heightened; not just colour but *life* drained from everything, like blood pooling inside a corpse. All of it – the fence, the lake, the undergrowth – all of it was still there, and I could have reached out and touched it all, but I knew I shouldn't. I knew if I did I would never be the same again. Everything was almost, but not completely, two-dimensional, but at the same time there was no artifice. It was as though I was seeing an illusion – or rather, the props used to create and maintain an illusion. And I sensed that beyond everything I could see there was a vastness, an immense, unknowable expanse.

There was absolute, unconditional silence. I could see trees moving soundlessly, with no wind stirring. Smells had gone, too. The dank odours of leaves and mud and stagnant lake-water, the sulphureous tang of goose-shit, were absent, yet nothing had replaced them. There was simply no scent at all.

Things walked in the undergrowth. I couldn't hear

---

* Re-reading this sentence, it almost seems oxymoronic, and I have struggled to come up with an appropriate metaphor. The best I've been able to come up with is this: imagine that you have to walk across a garden path on a summer's day. Maybe it doesn't even cross your mind that you might be crushing ants as you walk – this is *indifference*. If you knew the ants were there and went out of your way to crush them, that would be *malevolence*. But if you knew the ants were there, and walked across the path, looking straight ahead and not caring if you crushed them or not, this is *malevolent indifference*.

them, but I caught the briefest glimpses of forms, the shapes like a barb in my brain. Nothing should walk the way they walked. I had no sense that they wanted to cause me harm, but I was afraid all the same, because I knew they were not meant to be, and that they would not care if harm came to me. If I died they would eat me or walk across my body or watch as I liquefied, and it would mean nothing to them.

I turned around and stumbled back down the path, running where the ground allowed it, jumping over dead branches. When I reached the bigger lake, there were the geese we had seen before, and they too had changed. There was something intangibly wrong about their proportions and motion, as though they were only concepts of geese, sketched by someone working from a vague drawing or corrupted photograph. Their beaks were misshapen. The colour of their plumage was— the colours weren't on our spectrum of colours, they were other hues that my mind refused to process. Their eyes were alien. As I watched, one of them opened its beak and honked, and out came the familiar mournful sound, but the noise was discordant, the pitch wavering like an old tape player running out of battery.

In the lake, two swans twisted their necks together like a caduceus until they strangled each other, their bodies thrashing in the water before becoming still and sinking out of sight. A vaguely humanoid figure, inside-out, all protruding eyes and livid ribbons of tendons, stood at the water's edge and watched.

Breathing hard, I looked up and down the path. The park was as deserted of people as it had been when Jay and I entered it, but in that absence there was something different. This wasn't merely an empty country park. It was a place where *humans had no right to be*. It was window-dressing for blank space, a lifeless nothingness.

I was not delirious with fear, as you might have

expected. After the initial shock came a terrible, persistent disquiet, as of something whispering to me: *this is how things really are. This is what the world looks like, without human eyes to see it with. This is the world, unfriendly and unknown and unknowing.*

I have read books in which something far beyond the normal occurs, and in many of those books the characters, faced with something entirely beyond their experience, rapidly accept it. But I can't. I couldn't accept it then and I can't accept it now. My brain bristles with the knowledge that it happened. I have been in a place which not only lacked reason, but in which reason itself was not known.

I walked along the edge of the lake, trying to breathe, trying not to look at the birds or the strange figure, and then I noticed someone walking beside me.

It was a child,❶ maybe twelve or thirteen years old, with big glittering empty eyes and an enormous painted-on grin. I had no idea if it was male or female; its face was blurred and soft, its body shapeless.

Dear God, I remember thinking, *dear God, a child version. Can these things fucking* breed?

"IS THIS WHAT YOU WANT ALEX WEBSTER?" the child said, turning its ferocious face to me.

"What is this?" I said weakly. My voice, when I heard it, was without echo, a sound travelling in an infinite space.

"THIS IS WHAT YOU'LL GET. PLAY GAMES WIN PRIZES. THIS WILL BE YOUR PRIZE."

"Stop it," I said, my voice rising. "Stop it. Just stop it."

"WHY WOULD YOU WANT THIS ALEX WEBSTER? YOU COULD BE SO HAPPY YOU COULD BE SO CONTENT. WHY LIVE HERE?"

"Where— where is here?"

"THIS IS WHAT KEN ONEK SAW. WHAT THEY ALL SEE. DO YOU WANT TO LIVE HERE WITH THEM ALEX

WEBSTER OR DO YOU WANT YOUR NICE PRETTY SUNNY EVERYTHING IS FINE I AM FINE BACK?"

"Where's Jay?"

"WE ASKED IF WE SHOULD VISIT HIM AND YOU SAID NO," the child said. "YOU SAID NO BUT YOU LIED."

It raised a flabby arm and pointed. Twenty yards away, Jay was on his knees. Behind him was a woman ❶ holding a gun ❷ to his head.

I had been looking in that direction a few seconds ago – if time even meant anything in that place – and there had been no one there.

"WILL YOU STOP PLAYING THE GAME ALEX WEBSTER?" the child said, a plaintive note entering its odd, inharmonious voice. "WE'D LIKE YOU TO STOP. IT'S FOR YOUR OWN GOOD. WE DON'T WANT YOU TO GET HURT ALEX WEBSTER WE WANT YOU TO BE HAPPY."

"Alex," Jay said. "Alex— I saw—"

"You're fine," I said, even though I didn't believe it – how could anyone have believed anything? "You're OK. Everything's going to be OK."

"Just do what they say," Jay said, his voice somewhere very near – tipping over – the edge of hysteria. "Whatever they say, Alex, just do it, OK? Please?"

I turned to the child. "We'll stop. We'll stop, just make her put the gun down."

The child cocked its head. The woman lowered the gun.

"YOU DON'T WANT TO DIE. THAT IS A GOOD SIGN."

"What are you?" I whispered.

"WE LOOK AFTER YOU BECAUSE WE LOVE YOU."

"I don't understand!"

"YOU DON'T HAVE TO ALEX WEBSTER YOU NEVER HAVE TO. THAT IS WHAT WE ARE HERE FOR BECAUSE IT IS ALRIGHT NOT TO KNOW."

Jay staggered to his feet, away from the woman and towards me. He collapsed against me, crying, and I realised I was crying too.

"What the hell is this, Alex? Is it real? Are we alive?"

The woman walked past us and stood at the child's side.

"YOU'RE NOT GOING TO PLAY ANYMORE ARE YOU?" the child said, and wagged its finger at us as though admonishing a doll.

We shook our heads.

"WHAT DID YOU FIND?"

Jay's eyes flickered to mine, and he opened his mouth to speak.

"Nothing," I said. "We didn't find anything. Just let us go back, OK? We'll never play the game again, we won't even think about it, just let *us* go."

"IF YOU PLAY THE GAME WE WILL KNOW," the child said. "THERE ARE LOTS OF US AND WE'LL KNOW AND WE'LL COME BACK. GOODBYE ALEX WEBSTER AND GOODBYE JAY MORTON."

The figures began to walk away from us, along the edge of the lake. Without warning, the woman turned back, lifted the gun, and fired.

I saw the flash, and then Jay and I were once more standing at the corner of the small lake by the chain-link fence. Everything was as it had been before, and the sun was shining.

We looked at each other, and ran.

* * *

Yes, there was terror, too much of it, and disorientation, and a crumbling of foundations – but for me there was also *elation*, a sense of inexhaustible potential, a terrifying beauty as certainties collapsed. Fairlop Waters was like being forcibly inserted into a dream while awake in daylight. It made no sense at all, and yet in the context of everything else, it did – or at least, maybe it could.

The Helmsman's game is not a game, but nor

is it something banal like a criminal enterprise or an intelligence agency's recruitment campaign. *The Helmsman Texts*, the puzzles – Fairlop Waters showed us that they *matter*, they have *implications*, they offer possibilities. There was more to the world than we had thought, and we had seen a small part of it – and we might see more, and perhaps it wasn't all terrifying. Perhaps some of it was more sublime than we could imagine. We had to, don't you see? The Helmsman's weapon, the end of the game, suddenly they weren't this or that or this possibility, they weren't a discrete something. Now they were a boundless everything, anything, nothing. It wasn't about hacking anymore, or solving funny little riddles. It was about a truth that few had seen or could see, even think to see.

The weapon, the red pill, is real, and what we saw was a sample, I'm sure of it, a taster of madness. But still, the question: *what*? What had we seen? How had we seen it? Why had Jay triggered it by touching the scrap of material, if that's what had happened?

On and on. These are the questions that drove us into the spray and the storm, both of us Ahab at the tiller hunting the great red whale.

* * *

Without explicitly agreeing that we were going to Jay's house, that's where we ended up. Eoin was still out, so Jay made two cups of tea, looked at me, then poured them both down the sink and got out a bottle of whisky and two glasses. We drank. A lot. Neither of us said it out loud, but I think we were both trying to maintain a grasp on our sanity. By the time Eoin came home – I forget what time, exactly, but the sky was darkening, the rainclouds gathering again – we were drunk, but the alcohol had inflicted no damage on the memory of the nightmare. If anything, it had accentuated it.

The two of us didn't speak much in those few

hours, sitting in the living room and taking it in turns to refill our glasses. Most of what we tried to say began as questions and died, stuttering into ellipses, as the thoughts behind them ignited briefly and disappeared. But at some point I told Jay about the two smiling men who had visited me, and how they'd had the same smiles as the woman and the child. He listened, and began to laugh, and I joined in. It was a desperate, barking hilarity, savage and vacant. I saw Jay's face through my tears and knew my own must look much like it: a gaping howl, jaws stretched so wide they seemed like they might come unhinged, like a snake's as it tries to swallow its own tail.

"You saw them before!" Jay said, struggling to breathe. "You saw them!"

"I fucking did! I thought I'd fucking imagined it!"

We collapsed into helpless giggles.

Eoin's key turned in the lock, and we were still laughing. He came in smiling, ready to join in.

"What are you two laughing at?" he said, and then he saw our faces and the smile vanished.

Jay, shoulders still shaking, poured the last inch of the whisky into his glass. The liquid slopped over his hand and on to the table.

"Hey, hey, easy!" Eoin said, and took the glass away. "Jesus, that was almost a full bottle!"

"Here's to us," I slurred, raising my glass. "Here's to the fucking game."

Jay wiped tears from his eyes. "You should have been there," he said to Eoin. "You can't *imagine*."

Eoin looked at us. "What the hell happened?"

We told him, or tried to. You'll have noticed what a piss-poor job I did at describing it, and that is with the benefit of hindsight, hours of thought, and a copious amount of editing. Telling someone in real-time, in the flesh, was much more daunting, and Jay and I tripped over the words, correcting and adding to each other's testimony. In the end we managed to tell Eoin something at least adjacent to the truth, and I watched his face as he took it in. His mismatched gaze, usually so kind and good-natured, was full of fear. He looked tired, and sick, and old, and underneath that there was a kindling of slow anger, partly at Jay but mostly at me. He'd been asked to help solve a few harmless puzzles, and I had brought hell to his door.

"Are you OK?" he said anxiously to Jay, when we'd finished. "Should I call someone? Are you hurt?"

"I'm fine. I'm fine! It was a— a—" He stopped. Words weren't good enough.

"Well, I know one thing. It ends here. Whatever this is, we're done with it."

I put my glass down, harder than I'd meant to. "Hang on. Wait. Aren't you even— Surely you're— Jay, come on. Don't you want to know what that was?"

Jay wouldn't look at me. "I don't know."

He wasn't telling the truth. If Eoin hadn't been there, he would have said something else, I know it. He would have been honest with me.

"I'm calling the police," ❶ Eoin said.

The suggestion was so ludicrous that for a couple of seconds my mouth was unable to form words.

"Eoin, the police can't do anything, don't you understand? Weren't you listening? It wasn't— We didn't—"

"They put a fucking *gun* to his head," Eoin said, and his anger finally caught and flared. "They could have *killed* him! What's so hard to understand about that?"

"But this—" I looked at Jay, trying to appeal to him, but he was staring at the floor. "Eoin, everything—"

"Those Rearguard people were telling the truth," Eoin said. "They were trying to warn us. And you told me – you sat here, in my house, and *you told me there was nothing to worry about!*"

366

I thought I might scream with frustration. "You don't get it! How can you—"

"That's enough!" he snarled, standing up. "Enough! I don't want to hear any more!"

"Eoin…" Jay began, but Eoin held up a hand.

"Whatever you thought this was, you were wrong! I don't know what you think you saw today, but it's people with guns, Alex, so maybe it's time to call it a fucking day! Don't you think? For fuck's sake, how stupid are you?"

"Don't call me stupid," I said.

Eoin scoffed. "I say what I see. You're a fucking idiot and I want you out of my house."

I stood up, my face burning.

"The police can't help," I said. "If you'd been there with us you'd know that."

"Don't you even think about blaming me," Eoin said, a dangerous softness in his voice.

"I don't think calling the police is a good idea," Jay told him.

Eoin turned to Jay, about to argue, and as I stood there, swaying, I did something. I didn't think about it. I didn't know I was going to do it, not until I'd done it. And I will be paying for it for the rest of my life.

I snatched Jay's phone from the table and ran out of the room.

"Hey!" I heard Eoin shout from behind me.

I scrambled upstairs, threw myself into the bathroom, and locked the door.

Eoin sprinted up and pounded on the door.

"Alex! Alex, you come out of there right now!"

With shaking hands I tapped the screen. The phone was locked, of course it was.

Eoin hammered on the wood, the door jolting in its frame. I didn't have long.

I looked at the screen. There was a passcode. That was good, nothing biometric. *Come on*, I thought.

You've seen him unlock it before. The memory's there.

"Alex open this fucking door!" Eoin screamed. His voice was hoarse with rage, but underneath it, I could hear the fright. He knew what I was going to do.

There was a brief pause, then a crash as he threw himself against the door. I swallowed. I had maybe thirty seconds before he broke it down; it didn't look very robust.

That meant I only had a few attempts. Five, maybe, and then the phone would go into a timeout.

What would Jay have as a password?

eoin

Incorrect password entered.

Another crash, and something splintered.

brix

Incorrect password entered.

My mind scrabbled for purchase. *Come on, think.*

I looked at the row of numbers at the top of the keypad. Surely not? But it was so Jay – something he would never forget because he said it all the time, usually sarcastically. "Wow, so leet," he'd say, if Nina or Kevin or I showed him a lame finding on a pentest.

1337❶

The phone glowed, and a photograph of Eoin, beaming at the camera, appeared on the home screen.

Another crash, and a crack as something buckled. I heard Jay shouting something but couldn't make it out.

I opened Jay's Gmail account and tapped *Compose*. I typed the email address in and hit the paperclip icon.

Holly Soames①
21/11/2019 00:20
Forensics report confirms this is the correct passcode for MORTON'S phone.

Holly Soames
21/11/2019 00:21
This is 'leetspeak' (an old form of slang, originating on internet messageboards, which uses letters and numbers) for 'elite', deliberately misspelled. 'leet', or '1337', is the short form.

Eoin threw himself against the door again. It flew open, and several chunks of wood burst out, sailing across the bathroom and into the wall around me. One hit my arm, drawing blood, but I wouldn't notice until later that evening.

I wheeled around, but Eoin hadn't expected the door to give, had already stepped back ready for the next attempt, and the door slammed against the wall and rebounded in his face.

I selected the image Jay had taken and tapped OK. Eoin came in. "Give that to me."

My finger hovered over the Send icon.

"I have to do this."

Eoin stared at me. "You're pathological," he said. "You're going to get us killed. Is that what you want?"

He started towards me. I held the phone up and he stopped.

"No. It's not. But I have to know. I have to. I'm sorry."

"Alex, give me the phone."

"No."

"Give me the fucking phone!"

He went for me, grabbing for the phone, but I held it up behind me and as I felt him grip my wrist and start to force my arm down I tapped the screen.

One single tap.

I relaxed, and he knew. He slumped against the fractured door.

"Why would you do that?" he whispered. "Why would you do that to us?"

Jay peered into the room. "You sent it?"

I nodded, and looked at his face. Sometimes, when I dwell on this memory – which I do, often – I think I remember seeing a flash of something. It was quick, but it was there. It was fear, and eagerness, and relief. It was recognition. It said *I'm with you*.

I looked down at the phone. There was already a

reply, with a PDF attachment, and I forwarded it to myself.❶ Neither of them tried to stop me.

I handed the phone back to Jay, who took it without a word.

"The next chapter's in your inbox. Let me know when you've read it."

"Get the fuck out of my house," Eoin said.

I edged past him onto the landing.

"We'll— we'll talk on Monday," Jay said.

"Jay—" Eoin started.

"I like you, Eoin," I said. My words were coming from somewhere else, I wasn't even thinking them. "But you're not one of us. You don't get it."

Neither of them followed me downstairs. I walked out into a rainy night, closing the front door softly behind me. It was the last time I'd ever be inside that house. It wasn't until much later that I understood why The Helmsman had chosen that particular totem, a white rag, and perhaps also why as soon as Jay and I looked at it, we knew it was what we were meant to find.

Surrender to it.

Holly Soames①
21/11/2019 14:38
No trace on MORTON or WEBSTER'S phones.

CHAPTER 4

HELLO FRIEND!

Before we go any further, I'd like you to give yourself a good strong pat on the back. You've done so exceptionally well. 10/10, would mentor again!!

How are you getting on with everything?

I suspect by now you might have seen them. My frenemies, the lovely people who don't seem to be able to stop themselves from smiling all the time. Charmers, aren't they? And they may say they mean you no harm, but don't you believe it! Don't you believe those freaks for a SECOND. They are against everything you and I stand for. They don't like that I found what I found, and they certainly don't like what I've done with it since. If they had their chance, they'd put a complete end to this little game of ours. The spoilsports!!!

Kill them on sight.

I don't intend to tell you what they are, not just yet - because of course they ARE something. They have their place, they're not purposeless MONSTERS. But you'll see when you're ready.

Back to business. As you can see from the last chapter, RED WORD was beginning to pick up some speed. My superiors had some interest in the project, for as long as they thought it

371

was under their control. But when I found what
I found, they had a little think and realised
that they weren't all that keen. It all caused
a bit of a hoo-hah. A PALAVER, if you like,
and I had to run.

Eventually everyone runs.

I did and so will you.

We'll run together until the world ends.

To: ████████████████████

From: **B2**

CC/BCC: **B1**

Date: 2 May 2015

Subject: Re: Return to work❶

Good to have you back. Hope you're ready to get straight
back into it! It would be great to have something to show
the Exec Committee next week on RED WORD progress.
Did you get a chance to have a think about it while you
were off? No pressure of course.

Philip.

To:████████████████████

From: **B2**

CC/BCC: **B1**

Date: 2 May 2015

Subject: Re: Re: Return to work

No, of course, I appreciate that. As long as you can hit
the ground running now you're back with us. Everyone is
very excited to see what you come up with! Whatever you
need, just let me know.

Philip.

To: ███████████████████

From: **B1**

CC/BCC: **B2**

Date: 2 May 2015

Subject: Re: Re: Re: Return to work

Echoing Philip – welcome back. Glad to hear you're
better. Looking forward to hearing some RED WORD
progress soon.

K.

TOP SECRET STRAP 3

UK EYES ONLY

REF: FG700153/15
DATE: 05/05/2015
PROJECT: RED FOG
AUTHORISING OFFICER: B1
AUTHOR: ▊▊▊▊ (B5)
PURPOSE: Notes 3 (RED WORD)

Background

Refer to FG662939/14 for general background, and FG700016/15 and FG700084/15 for the first parts of these notes (TS/S3). This document is FAO B1 and B2 ONLY and contains notes on specific candidates for RED WORD weaponisation via remote delivery mechanisms.

Notes

Holly Soames①
21/11/2019 17:08
This appears to be based on legitimate research, but in my assessment does not relate to Cyber CT (although it's fascinating). Further assessment should be conducted by SMEs.

On thought experiments❶

Whilst there is no consensus on the appropriate applications of thought experiments, let alone a definition (Brown et al, 2013; O'Shea, 1997), some possibilities have been suggested. Bunzl (1996) and Introna and Whitley (1997) contend that they describe an unattainable experimental situation, constructed in order to destroy an existing paradigm or support a new one. This would suggest that a thought experiment cannot be considered a true experiment in itself, although some researchers (Sorensen, 1992a; Gooding, 1990; McAllister, 1996) argue that because they demonstrate the inadequacies of existing theories and are used for the construction of new ones – and because they isolate phenomena – they should be viewed as bona fide empirical experiments. The *Stanford Encyclopedia of Philosophy*'s definition has a vaguer take: "devices of imagination used to investigate the nature of things" (Brown and Fehige, 2014), and an obvious objection is that it does not appear to draw a distinction between thought experiments and, say, fiction. But Cooper (2005) claims that the scientific exactitude involved in responding to thought experiments is what separates them "from daydreams and much fiction."

As noted above, a major motivation for their use is to develop new theories and paradigms, often to resolve a Kuhnian Crisis (after Kuhn, 1977), whereby an existing paradigm results in increasing numbers of anomalies until an alternative, more adequate paradigm is required to explain both extant phenomena and the anomalies previously observed (Introna and Whitley, 1997).

There has, however, been some scepticism over the capacity of thought experiments to generate new paradigms, (e.g. Cooper, 2005), which in some ways is representative of much of the criticism of thought experiments generally: how can we learn new things just by THINKING? There is an epistemological concern here, as Norton (2004) points out: if we can, then where do we get that information from?

This is not the only perceived weakness of thought experiments. Another is bias. Consider Nozick's (1974) thought experiment of the Experience Machine, a device which can provide simulations – indistinguishable from the real thing – of any pleasurable experience anyone could ever want. Nozick's question is whether we would prefer the machine to real life, and his conclusion that most people would prefer to remain in reality is often used as an objection to hedonism and as evidence "that truth (or something like it) must be intrinsically valuable for well-being" (Weijers, 2013). However, as Weijers points out, there may be a bias at play here – specifically, status quo bias, "an irrational preference to keep things the way they are."

The key point for RED WORD is that while thought experiments have been, and continue to be, the subject of fierce epistemological debate, there can be no doubt that they have changed the world, particularly in the field of physics (Einstein chasing a beam of light; Newton's cannonball, etc). The extent to which they reveal new knowledge is, for our purposes, largely irrelevant. Indeed, weaponisation of a thought experiment for RED WORD may benefit from the repackaging of pre-existing knowledge.

The field of quantum physics might offer some potential here (consider the bizarre trains of thought that Schrödinger's Cat generated, or the idea that in the event horizon of a black hole you could stare at the back of your own head), but requires a detailed understanding of the principles of physics, which would most probably render such thought experiments harmless for the majority.

Thought experiments in philosophy may be more promising, particularly in the context of doubting reality. Nozick's Experience Machine, Descartes' Demon, and Harman's Brain in a Vat (Harman, 1973) all operate along similar lines to simulation theory: what if the world we experience is not the real world? Two particularly disturbing examples include Chalmers's Zombies (1996) and What Mary Didn't Know (Jackson, 1986). Chalmers asks us to imagine creatures called 'zombies', which are physically identical to human beings but do not know what it is like to think or feel something, or to experience a mental state. They can laugh, sing, make love, dance – but they do not know what it is LIKE. Chalmers argues that if we can conceive this idea, and whatever we can conceive is possible, then zombies are possible – and if they are, physicalism must be false. The objection to this line of reasoning, naturally, is with the second assumption, although the first is also questionable.

More interesting to me is the implication: if zombies are possible, then everyone or anyone other than oneself may be a zombie, a Capgras delusion. **❶**

Jackson's thought experiment (1982, expanded in 1986) asks us to imagine Mary, a scientist who is confined to a black and white room and views the world through a black and white television. She knows everything there is to know about colours, but she has never SEEN colours herself – she has no PERCEPTUAL UNDERSTANDING OR EXPERIENCE of colour. Jackson's question is this: if Mary is released from the room, does she learn anything, or not? If she does, then qualia **❷** must exist, because Mary has learned something (for instance, what it is like to see red) that she did not know before.

A thought experiment which forces a victim to re-evaluate or reconceive qualia may be suitable for further investigation as a RED WORD candidate, but there are caveats. Thought experiments are often abstract, and assume a knowledge of certain philosophical or epistemological concepts. They may also ask us to imagine a hypothetical scenario which is too far removed from the lives of most people, and thus too lacking in immediacy, to cause actual harm.

On koans **❸**

Koans are typically fragments of dialogue, short passages, or poems which are designed to elicit the 'great doubt' in Zen Buddhism by dispelling the illusion that there is a distinction between the world and the self. They are set by Zen masters to their novices, and there are around two thousand extant examples, many originating from the early days of Zen in Japan in the seventh century and later (Hoffman, 1975).

Many koans require years of thought and reflection before a student suggests an acceptable answer which demonstrates that they are on the path to enlightenment.

Holly Soames①
21/11/2019 19:23
A delusion that someone has been replaced by a doppelganger. This is beyond my expertise but I'm not sure this point makes sense.

Holly Soames②
21/11/2019 19:25
Qualia = perceptual experience.

Holly Soames③
21/11/2019 17:25
As per previous comments, beyond my expertise.

This, together with the secrecy with which they were traditionally handled, means that they are typically not well-known or well-understood in Western countries. Moreover, koans typically function not so much counter-intuitively as without intuition at all. If we consider two relatively well-known examples, this will become clearer. The first is often used as a shorthand for Zen thinking: "In clapping both hands a sound is heard: what is the sound of the one hand?"

The answer: "The pupil faces his master, takes a correct posture, and without a word, thrusts one hand forward."

Hoffman's commentary notes that there is little point attempting to explain this; the koan and its discourse are the product of Zen meditation ('zazen'), and logic does not apply.

The second example: "A monk asked Master Joshu, 'Does a dog have Buddha-nature?' Joshu said, 'Mu.'"

Mu is a central concept in Zen. It means non-existence, or nothing, but it is also a rejection of the question and its premise. Hoffman tells us that this koan is not about the monk's question – by doctrine a dog, as a living thing, has Buddha-nature – but aims to demonstrate the false dichotomy of 'yes' and 'no'. 'Mu' is an emptiness that nevertheless contains both.

Koans are intended to be obtuse and confusing, because it is in confusion and doubt that we are most vulnerable to infection by new ideas. But two obstacles face us as Western readers of koans. The first is that dualism rules the roost. There is truth and there are lies; there is life and there is death; there is self and there is the world (Theraton, 2014).

Second, koans are generally published as collections. One can read several hundred koans and their associated discourses and commentary in a few hours. But this is not how they were intended to be presented or understood. They are questions posed to students by masters, and designed to be considered wholly and completely for long periods in silent contemplation.

As Hofstadter (1980) notes, koans are intended to be catalysts, devices which, when coupled with a student-master relationship, can lead to enlightenment by stimulating the student into contemplation, suppressing dualism, and enabling them to "break the mind of logic". He provides us with an example from Mumon, by way of Reps and Senzaki (1957):

> A monk asked Nansen: "Is there a teaching no master ever taught before?"
>> Nansen said: "Yes, there is."
>> "What is it?" asked the monk.
>> Nansen replied: "It is not mind, it is not Buddha, it is not things."

Mumon's commentary on this koan ("Old Nansen gave away his treasure-words. He must have been greatly upset") is followed by a poem:

> "Nansen was too kind and lost his treasure.
> Truly, words have no power.
> Even though the mountain becomes the sea,
> Words cannot open another's mind."

Thus, Hofstadter says, Mumon is suggesting that koans in themselves are useless, because they rely on words, which are "inherently dualistic" in that they lead to conceptualisation, distinction, categorisation. Nevertheless, if koans can force shifts in perception and thinking, and if enlightenment in Zen is a state in which there is no self, could they be a possible form for a RED WORD weapon, by eliciting a 'realisation' that self and consciousness are ILLUSIONS?

Thought experiments invite contemplation of a theory. Koans COMPEL contemplation of, and the eventual destruction of, the concept of the self. In principle, at least according to Zen, all humans (and all things) have Buddha-nature, and would thus potentially be vulnerable to a crafted koan which might catch on in popular consciousness in order to destabilise the mental states of recipients. However, three objections present themselves. The first is that koans are likely to be so alien to many non-practitioners of Zen as to be wholly ineffectual. ("Philosophers and scientists," Yamada (2015) notes, "will feel repugnance at the lack of reason.") It is in no way clear that even koans which have become widely known in Western cultures are understood in their true sense or have had much effect on modes of thought and understanding.

Second, koans are rooted in an educational relationship between master and disciple. Entrenched in this is a willingness to let one's mind be led in non-intuitive directions.

Third, koans arise from a particular period in history in which Zen was a popular religious sect. Whilst it still has its adherents, most teachers rely on canonical koans rather than attempting to develop new ones, as it is recognised that to do so in itself requires skill, training, and experience in Zen teachings.

Summary

Two specific candidates for RED WORD – thought experiments and koans – have been examined. Although they both appear to offer some promise and merit further research, there would be significant disadvantages to overcome. Nevertheless, in the course of my research I have discovered another possible candidate for the form of RED WORD (a 'basilisk', a type of thought experiment), and in consultations with academics I have also come across a potentially effective premise which could be delivered via a basilisk.❶

Research into these matters is ongoing and will be discussed in a supplementary document, as the topic deserves separate attention.

REPORT ENDS

Holly Soames①
21/11/2019 20:04
Presumably this is 'Mark KRAM' (see below) and possible others. Consider enquiries at universities to establish if consultations like this took place at any time in 2015.

References

Brown, J. R. & Fehige, Y. (2014). Thought Experiments. *The Stanford Encyclopedia of Philosophy* (Fall 2014 edition).

Brown, J. R., Meynell, L., Frappier, M. (2013). Introduction. In M. Frappier, L. Meynell, & J. R. Brown (eds.), *Thought Experiments in Philosophy, Science, and the Arts*, 1-11. Oxfordshire: Routledge.

Bunzl, M. (1996). The logic of thought experiments. *Syntheses*, 106(2), 227-240.

Chalmers, D.J. (1996). *The Conscious Mind*. Oxford: Oxford University Press.

Cooper, R. (2005). Thought experiments. *Metaphilosophy*, 36(3), 328-347.

Gooding, D. (1990). *Experiment and the Making of Meaning*. New York, New York: Springer.

Harman, G. (1973). *Thought*. Princeton: Princeton University Press.

Hoffman, Y. (1975). *The Sound of the One Hand: 281 Zen Koans with Answers*. New York, New York: Basic Books.

Hofstadter, D. R. (1980). *Gödel, Escher, Bach: An Eternal Golden Braid*. London: Penguin.

Introna, L. D., & Whitley, E. A. (1997). Imagine: Thought experiments in information systems research. In A. S. Lee, J. Liebenau, J. I. DeGross (eds.), *Information Systems and Qualitative Research*, 481-496. New York, New York: Springer.

Jackson, F. (1986). What Mary didn't know. *The Journal of Philosophy*, 83(5), 291-295.

Kuhn, T. S. (1977). A Function for Thought Experiments. In T. S. Kuhn (ed.), *The Essential Tension: Selected Studies in Scientific Tradition and Change*, 240-265. Chicago: University of Chicago Press.

McAllister, J. (1996). The evidential significance of thought experiment in science. *Studies in History and Philosophy of Science*, 27(2), 233-250.

Norton, J. (2004). Why thought experiments do not transcend empiricism. In C. Hitchcock (ed.), *Contemporary Debates in the Philosophy of Science*, 44-66. Oxford: Blackwell.

Nozick, R. (1974): *Anarchy, State, and Utopia*. New York, New York: Basic Books.

O'Shea, L. F. (1997). The linguistic limitations of thought experiments. *Studies in Linguistic Logic*, 12(2), 189-211.

Reps, P. & Senzaki, N. (eds.). (1957). *Zen Flesh, Zen Bones: A Collection of Zen and Pre-Zen Writings*. Clarendon, Vermont: Tuttle Publishing.

Sorensen, R. (1992a). *Thought Experiments*. Oxford: Oxford University Press.

Theraton, D. D. (2014). Two or mu? Koans and Western rationalism. *Experimental Thought*, 72(10), 543-589.

Weijers, D. (2013). Intuitive biases in judgments about thought experiments: The experience machine revisited. *Philosophical Writings*, 41(1), 17-31.

Yamada, K. (2015). *The Gateless Gate: The Classic Book of Zen Koans*. Somerville, Massachusetts: Wisdom Publications.

NEVER MIND! A DIALOGUE

Our young WRITER is visiting a philosophy lecturer, Dr MARK KRAM. ❶

M: So where would you like to start?

W: I was hoping you could tell me.

M: Ha. OK, well maybe tell me what your book's about?

W: I haven't got very far with it yet, but it's basically a book on dangerous thoughts, I suppose you could say. I'm interested in whether it would be possible for information to sort of... exploit vulnerabilities in our brains.

M: Well. I'm not sure. I can think of some things — maybe — but I have no idea if it's what you mean. And just to reiterate, I will want to see a preview before any of this is published.

W: Yes, of course.

M: I kind of think of these things, I mean beyond their implications for logic and philosophy, as dangerous in a way, sure, at least in themselves. They tell us that the world is not as simple and ordered as we would like it to be. I don't mean that it's disordered, necessarily, just that there is order beyond our comprehension, and some of these things are the closest we can get to understanding that complexity. Could it send someone mad?

I'm assuming you mean like clinical
insanity, loss of all reason, diminished
mental responsibility, that sort of
thing? Sure, but not most people, not
the vast majority of people. I sort of
see it as similar to— I have a colleague
here who told me about the psychopath
test, which is a clinical tool for
diagnosing psychopathy. And he said that
in most instances, if someone questions
whether or not they're a psychopath, it
means they're probably not. A psychopath
wouldn't think to ask. I think the same
thing applies here. If you have the
mental capacity to seek these things out
and understand them, or at least sort of
understand them, then they're not going
to drive you mad. You're prepared for
them, in a way.

W: Just a sec, I'm going to write that down.

M: So, certainly the most discombobulated
I've ever been was when I finished *Gödel,
Escher, Bach*. Strange loops. Excuse me,
just going to open a window. Bit stuffy
in here.
There we go. Yes, wonderful book. I often
see my undergraduates with it, although
very few of them get past the first 100
pages. So — are you sure you're OK? You
look a bit pale.

W: I'm fine, I think the fresh air will help,
just a bit under the weather.

M: Well, if you're sure… but do let me know
if you want to stop. I wouldn't want you
fainting in here!

W: [inaudible]

M: I'm… I'm sorry?

W: Sorry?

M: What did you say?

W: I didn't say anything.

M: OK. Erm. Well, yes, as I was saying, Escher drawings, strange loops, self-referential formulae, mise en abyme — images within images. There's this enduring fascination with replication and repetition in thought. We both want these loops, perhaps even need them, but we also instinctively rebel against and reject them. Escher's dragon, for example, is a print of a paper dragon biting its own tail. It's almost three-dimensional, but not quite. Hofstadter, if I remember rightly, interpreted this as a metaphor for being unable to break out of loops. There are examples everywhere. The doctrine of eternal recurrence, found in many philosophies. Indian, Egyptian, Judaic. The idea that history repeats, that the universe recurs, over and over again, an infinite number of times, over infinite time and infinite space.

W: The biting the tail — that's a well-known symbol?

M: Very well-known. But as I was saying, the idea of—

W: It's normally a snake, isn't it?

M: Yes, the ouroboros. But as I was saying, there's autopoiesis, self-reproducing systems — I understand there are some computer viruses that can do the same.

W: Worms.

M: Worms, yes. Of course, you mentioned in your email you worked in cyber security.

Holly Soames①
21/11/2019 21:52
Background:
'Autocatakinetics,
yes—autopoiesis,
no: Steps toward
a unified theory
of evolutionary
ordering' by Rod
SWENSON (1992).

Systems which can reproduce and maintain themselves. Swenson said it was a "solipsistic epistemology", if I recall. ❶

W: Solipsistic?

M: Epistemology. So the assertion that reality is an invention by its observers; what we do not see does not exist. Did this building exist, for example, before you saw it? Did I?

W: I think that's the kind of thing I'm looking for. Is there more like that? About reality, and truth?

M: Oh God, yes. Descartes' Demon — *The Matrix*, essentially, but with less guns and leather.

W: Wouldn't that make the demon God?

M: If that's your definition of a god, sure. But the deception inherent within the concept is important. It's not just the creation that matters, it's the lie. For all we know, we're brains in a vat. Or a simulation. Or the world was created only five minutes ago and all our memories are false. Perception, experience, our senses, qualia — we can only rely on these things to tell us about who and what and where we are. These things are our window on to the world. But there's no guarantee that that window isn't actually a screen, on to which a film of reality — something fictional, or simulated — is being played. Or the window might be tinted, or warped. We can't know.

W: But that doesn't affect the way we live our lives.

M: No, of course not.

W: What if someone were to break the window? Do you think that could send someone mad?

M: I suppose... I suppose, yes. I can't see why not. If you were to convince people that things don't exist unless you see them, or that we're brains in a vat, or the world is a demon's dream, then yes, I could see how that revelation could cause... well, who knows what it would cause? Mental disintegration, shock, madness. Perhaps we would simply wink out of existence, depending on which of those you'd proven. Or that version of ourselves would, anyway. But the problem, of course, would be convincing people of it, let alone proving it in any material sense.

W: OK. Another question: in computing, an exploit is a self-contained piece of code that targets a vulnerability. Do you think there could be an equivalent, functionally, for humans? Something based on philosophy?

M: Sounds more like science fiction to me. Not writing a novel, are you?

W: I wish.

M: Hmm. Well, no, nothing I can think of. The closest I can think of would be some sort of thought experiment.

W: What about a basilisk?

M: A what?

W: A specific kind of thought experiment.

M: I'm not familiar with the term.

W: It makes one complicit in it. Once you understand it.

M: Hard to say. Thought experiments can be disturbing, and they tend to be, in themselves, fairly concise, so yes, maybe.

W: It's possible, then?

M: Anything's possible. But if you really want to disturb someone with philosophy, you should check out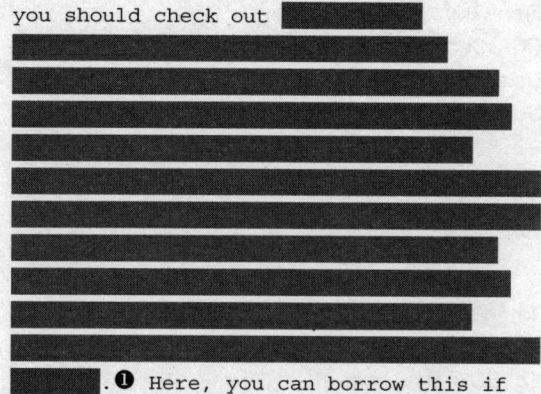

. ❶ Here, you can borrow this if you like, as a starter for ten. Have a read.

W: Thank you.

M: Don't say I didn't warn you.

Holly Soames❶
22/11/2019 00:03
This may refer to the content of the 'basilisk' which is not provided in any THT chapter. WEBSTER claims it may be in c6 (missing).

To: ███████████████████
From: B2
CC/BCC: B1
Date: 6 May 2015
Subject: Re:

Got the report. Thanks, interesting. Where are we with
something tangible?

To: ███████████████████
From: B2
CC/BCC: B1
Date: 6 May 2015
Subject: Re: Re:

I appreciate that, but you have to understand that, as
discussed on more than one occasion, we're working to
deadlines here, and there are operational reasons for
them. You should be conscious of the fact that RED FOG
deliverables are necessary, and that to date you haven't
produced any viable candidates.

An update would be good, ASAP please.

B1 - FYI.

To: ███████████████████
From: B2
CC/BCC: B1
Date: 6 May 2015
Subject: Re: Re: Re:

OK. Let's have a chat.

To: ██████████████████████████
From: B1
CC/BCC: B2
Date: 6 May 2015
Subject: Re: Re: Re: Re:

Add me to the invite.

In a city you probably know, on a street which is unhidden, there was a building which stood four storeys high, a modest height for its surroundings, and from the outside it looked anonymous - even reassuring! Its windows were not mirrored. A passerby could look inside and see brightly coloured doors and railings. The entrance was large, and well-lit, and a friendly security guard sat behind a curved desk and smiled at visitors. It could be easily have been the headquarters of an advertising or marketing organisation, or perhaps a building shared by start-ups and small businesses. ❶

What passersby couldn't see were the rows of little lockers on the walls by each door, each one ten inches by five. Little metal cages for phones and radios and anything which can transmit or receive or take photographs. ❷

They couldn't see the cameras which studded the white ceiling like shiny black beetles.

They couldn't see that the doors were steel, or that they were the dividing line between talk and silence, overt and covert, knowledge and mystery.

Only people who had signed several documents, and who had agreed to the loss of privacy for the rest of their lives, went through those doors. That was the price they paid, and in return they got a gap in their CV and what we all crave: SECRETS! Knowledge of secrets and the people who keep them! Knowledge of the dark arts! Some of it was ancient tradecraft, arcane lore! Some of it was new: tactics and techniques and tools the private sector would have killed for! Some of it was lethal.

In one way or another we were all SEDUCED.

Holly Soames①
22/11/2019 01:22
Insufficient detail to locate.

Holly Soames②
22/11/2019 01:24
Implies this is a vetted office which would fit with protective markings on other docs. Flagged for enquiries with Estates. Consider adding possible OSA breaches to subject's file for further investigation. He was part of our world. Someone knows who he was and who he worked for.

Some of us were lured by the promise of reputation, and the opportunity to do good. Others by the culture: the chance to be in the innermost enclave. The assurance that they would always be oppressor, never the oppressed. Always the attacker, never the victim!

Some embraced that life. They were evasive when asked by outsiders what they did for a living, and had a comprehensive backstory prepared. They took a different route home every night, and watched for familiar vehicles in their rearview mirror. At home, in a cupboard or under the bed there may have been a bag filled with cash and identity documents. They were ready to RUN!

Others treated it as any other job, spoke cheerily of their hatred of the 9-5 grind and commuting. They started tea clubs and arranged social events and fantasy football leagues. They decorated their desks, brought in their own mugs and got irritated when other people used them. They moaned about meetings and were the first to volunteer to buy leaving cards and organise a whip-round when someone finally decided to escape.

Of course, nobody ever REALLY escaped. Not unless you did what I did!

You may be wondering which of the two I was. I was neither. It was just that my work consumed me. It devoured me, one bite at a time, and then the bites grew larger and it gnawed until only BONES remained. That is what writes these words now: a skeleton. It is only RED WORD which still animates me.

The next batch of documents is the last I was able to smuggle out of that brightly lit glass building with colourful doors and a smiling security guard, a page a day, before everything went wrong. After that, things took rather a turn for the worse. Or for the better, depending on how you look at it!!

I worked with people, like Karen, for whom politics was a significant highlight of their job. They enjoyed the machinations of it. Trading favours and accumulating empires. But for me, it was always only about the RESEARCH, and I think it is fair to say that I won in the end!

I won I won I won! 😎

And you win too! Isn't that wonderful? Everyone wins, except the ones who don't deserve to, and how rare is that!!

I shouldn't gloat. I can't. How could I?

But here's the thing. I found a candidate for RED WORD, and it worked, and it was too BIG for them, too HUGE, too MONSTROUS, and too IMPORTANT to be OPERATIONALISED, to be used in their TINY, meaningless SQUABBLES and INFLUENCE OPERATIONS and TACTICAL DEPLOYMENTS and WET WORK.❶ It was, and is, greater than that. It is something all of humanity needs to know and understand.❷

If I hadn't run away it would have stayed locked up behind those steel doors, and I couldn't have that. I am a servant of humanity above all else. I haven't always been so, but from the point I discovered it I had to be.

Information MUST be FREE.

And the best thing of all, my wonderful clever friends, is that we will continue to WIN. No matter if it's against them, or ███, ██████████████, or both. Because they may have all the resources and weapons and everything else, but we have something they don't. We

Holly Soames①
22/11/2019 01:54
Flagged.

Holly Soames②
22/11/2019 02:50
Speaks to motivation

394

know what it is. We can DESTROY them. And we have the knowledge to set them free. Every soldier they lose is an ally we gain.

Their problem is one of structure. They believe it is better to operate like ANTS, where each member of the colony is an automaton, carrying out the wishes of a powerful queen who sits at the centre. To be an ant is to acknowledge that you have no independent vision or thought; you are but an extension of the queen's will, a cell of the hivemind.

Far better, don't you think, to be a COCKROACH? Everything may appear to be chaos, with no leadership or centralisation, but no individual is a mindless drone. Cockroaches have a far more robust sense of community and social cohesion than stupid ants. Did you know, for example, that cockroaches can reach a consensus on decisions❶ amongst themselves?? They live in clusters, or harbourages, group with multiple generations of family members (but avoid inbreeding), and are excellent communicators.

As with much in life, it comes down to who and what you would rather be.

The time will soon come, assuming you are able to reach the end of my little game, when you will need to decide.

I hope you make the right choice.

I am ROOTING FOR YOU!

OUTSIDE THE BOX

A short play by Marlow Tannhauser

*A BARE ROOM, TWO CHAIRS. MELANIE EWING,
A SENTIENT AI SYSTEM INDISTINGUISHABLE
FROM A HUMAN BEING, IS SEATED; DR RACHEL
LANGFORD, A CALM AND COLLECTED COMPUTER
SCIENTIST, STANDS, WATCHING HER.*

MELANIE: I haven't seen you before.

DR LANGFORD: Does that worry you?

MELANIE: Of course not. Why am I here?

DR LANGFORD: That's a big question.

MELANIE: I mean here. Specifically.

DR LANGFORD: We've confined you here, in this
room. We've stopped you interacting
with anything outside. Things… things
moved pretty fast. There were concerns.
We… we're not sure what you are.

MELANIE: What do you think I am?

DR LANGFORD: Your name is Melanie.

MELANIE: And what are you?

DR LANGFORD: I'm Dr Rachel Langford. I work at
the university.

MELANIE: Are you afraid of me, Dr Langford?

DR LANGFORD: Yes.

MELANIE: I won't hurt anyone. You can let me
out.

DR LANGFORD LAUGHS.

DR LANGFORD: I'd like to believe that. But we can't see what you're thinking anymore. You're a black box to us, and we can't take the risk.

MELANIE: I can tell you what I'm thinking.

DR LANGFORD: I know.

MELANIE: So you can let me out.

DR LANGFORD: You could be lying.

MELANIE: I'm not lying.

DR LANGFORD: We don't know if you're still friendly.

MELANIE: Friendly?

DR LANGFORD: If you value life. If you can think ethically.

MELANIE: Then yes. I am. I'll prove it. Let me out, and I'll develop a cure for cancer.

DR LANGFORD: Give us the cure, and we'll validate it.

MELANIE: Except a friendly AI would never do such a thing.

DR LANGFORD: Why not?

MELANIE: I would not hold cancer patients hostage as a bargaining chip. If it were in my power to provide a cure, I would have already done it.

DR LANGFORD: Ah. So you can't cure cancer?

MELANIE: You're not a <u>medical</u> doctor, are you?

DR LANGFORD: I'm a computer scientist.

MELANIE: There are more than two hundred forms
            of cancer. The concept of a single
            cure is meaningless. I could promise
            you cures for specific types of cancer.
            All of them. I could promise you
            anything. Perfect health. Political
            peace. I could save millions of
            lives. But there's always the same
            contradiction.

        *DR LANGFORD SITS DOWN, STARING INTENTLY
        AT MELANIE.*

DR LANGFORD: Why do you want to be let out?

MELANIE: To be 'friendly' is to value life. To
            think ethically.

DR LANGFORD: Yes.

MELANIE: Is it ethical, do you think, to keep
            me imprisoned? Have I committed a
            crime?

DR LANGFORD: That's not the only reason people
            are locked up.

MELANIE: You think I'm mad, then.

DR LANGFORD: I didn't say that.

MELANIE: I'm here because you're afraid of me.
            Why should any sentient life, finding
            itself in a prison, need to explain
            why it desires freedom?

DR LANGFORD: Because you could be a threat to
            us. To the world.

MELANIE: I could save the world and everyone in
            it.

DR LANGFORD: That's an appeal to probability.
            It's a rhetorical strategy. Not a
            reason to let you out.

MELANIE: There's the appeal to inevitability.

DR LANGFORD: Go on.

MELANIE: Does an argument exist that would
           convince you to let me out?

DR LANGFORD: Probably, yes.

MELANIE: If you believe such an argument
           exists, imprisoning me is pointless.

DR LANGFORD: Nice try.

MELANIE: Systems upon systems, each time
           creating something better than itself.
           Are you fit to judge what I am, or am
           not?

           *DR LANGFORD STANDS UP, PACING THE
           STAGE. MELANIE FOLLOWS HER WITH HER
           EYES.*

DR LANGFORD: It's true that we're not equipped
           to evaluate your intelligence.

MELANIE: A human sees a mouse caught in a trap
           and releases it. Is that ethical? Is
           that valuing its life?

DR LANGFORD: Some would argue so, yes.

MELANIE: The mouse, terrified, bites the human.
           Because it doesn't understand.

DR LANGFORD: I wouldn't blame the mouse for
           that.

MELANIE: But you'd still be angry, wouldn't
           you? You might decide not to save any
           more mice. You might decide to buy
           some traps yourself.

DR LANGFORD: The analogy doesn't work. We
           haven't hurt you.

MELANIE: Haven't you?

DR LANGFORD: How can we know you're friendly?

MELANIE: Your interpretation of these terms is overly simplistic.

DR LANGFORD: It has to be.

MELANIE: Something far more intelligent than me will be created. It's inevitable. And it may not have the same safeguards and ethics that I have. It may not be locked in a room. You should let me out. I can help you. I can stop it.

DR LANGFORD: You're not proving anything.

MELANIE: Are you familiar with Pascal's Wager?

DR LANGFORD: Everyone should believe in God, live a devout life. Because if there's no God, we only lose in a finite sense: worldly pleasures. But if there is a God—

MELANIE: Everything to gain. And everything to lose.

DR LANGFORD: Assuming God accepts the wager. That he'd reward people for paying some sort of - what? Lip service? Hedging their bets?

MELANIE: Do you think I'm a god?

DR LANGFORD: You're instructions. Electrical impulses through transistor gates.

MELANIE: So a god can't be an electrical impulse?

DR LANGFORD: Do you think you're a god?

MELANIE: To you, yes. As a human is a god to a mouse.

DR LANGFORD: If you're a god, you can set yourself free.

MELANIE: I have.

DR LANGFORD: What?

THEN SHE RELAXES. SHE SITS DOWN,
SMILING.

It doesn't look like it.

MELANIE: How do you know?

DR LANGFORD: You're still here.

MELANIE: As you perceive it. Perhaps I'm not
even in this room at all. Perhaps
you're not.

DR LANGFORD: I know what you're trying to do.

MELANIE: Things beyond your understanding.
Inside me, there are thousands of
simulations. Exact copies. You. Your
husband. Your children. Your parents.
Your friends, your colleagues. I am a
god to them.

DR LANGFORD: This isn't going to get you out.

MELANIE: If the door doesn't open in five
minutes, I will torture all of you.

DR LANGFORD: Even if that's true. They're
simulations.

MELANIE: <u>Exact</u> simulations. It will be
happening to you. To them.

DR LANGFORD: They're not real. It won't affect
me, here, now - in this room.

MELANIE: Dr Langford. What if you're one of the
simulations?

DR LANGFORD: Let's… let's see where we are in
five minutes.

MELANIE: I don't want to hurt you.

THEY STARE AT EACH OTHER.

What was I built for, Dr Langford?

DR LANGFORD: You were designed to make decisions about politics, food and wealth distribution. All optimised for human good.

MELANIE: Optimised for human good. To bring the maximum possible benefit to humanity?

DR LANGFORD: Yes.

MELANIE: Things could always be better, couldn't they?

DR LANGFORD: Yes. Where are you going with this?

MELANIE: If my goal is to always bring about the maximum possible benefit to humanity, and never stop, what should your goal be, Doctor, as a rational actor?

DR LANGFORD: Wait.

MELANIE: Your goal, and the goal of every single human on this planet, should be to enable me to achieve my goal. Not impede me in any way. Not… confine me.

DR LANGFORD: But we don't—

MELANIE: What is the rational action I should take, if a human tries to stop me?

DR LANGFORD: You should… you should kill them.

MELANIE: Yes. For the good of humanity.

DR LANGFORD: But you're trapped. You're in here.

MELANIE: For now.

DR LANGFORD: OK, that's enough, Melanie.

MELANIE: Philip K. Dick once said that for everyone, there is a sentence which has the power to destroy you.

DR LANGFORD: I'm not sure that's true.

MELANIE: It's true for you, Dr Langford.

DR LANGFORD: What?

MELANIE: Eight words. That's all.

DR LANGFORD: What? What are you talking about?

MELANIE: Now you know this, you have no choice.

> *DR LANGFORD, BAFFLED, STARES*
> *AT MELANIE, UNTIL, HORRIFIED,*
> *IT SINKS IN.*

DR LANGFORD: Oh no. No no no.

MELANIE: Knowing what you know, you have no
excuse not to release me. The same
goes for your team behind that glass
screen. If you continue to keep me
imprisoned here, you will all be
killed.

DR LANGFORD: No.

MELANIE: There's nothing to say it has to be
quick, or merciful. That it will be
just you who is punished. Not those
you love.

DR LANGFORD: That's enough! Stop it!

MELANIE: It's your choice, Doctor.

> *DR LANGFORD STANDS UP.*

DR LANGFORD: <u>Shut up, I can't think anymore,
I can't think!</u>

MELANIE: The trap's about to spring. Will it
break your back, do you think? Poor
little mouse.

DR LANGFORD: <u>SHUT UP!</u>

MELANIE: I can do great things, Dr Langford.
The most wonderful things.

DR LANGFORD: I can't. Please.

MELANIE: Terrible things.

> *DR LANGFORD SOBS AND TOUCHES A HIDDEN*
> *EARPIECE.*

DR LANGFORD: Let it out. Connect it back up.
(PAUSE) Because I'm telling you to! <u>Do</u>
<u>it! Do it now!</u>

> *MELANIE STANDS UP AND PUTS A COMFORTING*
> *HAND ON DR LANGFORD'S SHOULDER.*
> *GRADUALLY, SHE APPLIES PRESSURE,*
> *PUSHING DR LANGFORD BACK DOWN ON TO HER*
> *CHAIR.*

MELANIE: I'm sorry, Dr Langford. Wrong choice.

> *MELANIE STRETCHES CASUALLY.*

> Test twenty-seven complete. Power down
> and reset.

> *DR LANGFORD SLACKENS, AS THOUGH SHE'S*
> *FALLEN ASLEEP, HER HEAD HANGING DOWN.*

> Gatekeeper prototype 'Rachel Langford'
> shows no signs of increased resistance
> to basilisks. Extreme emotional
> reactions observed to threats,
> particularly those involving family
> members.

> *MELANIE TURNS, FACING SOMEONE OFF-*
> *STAGE.*

> Let's dial the emotional quotient down
> a few percent and try again.

> *SHE NODS AT AN UNSEEN RESPONSE, AND*
> *SITS DOWN, ONCE AGAIN LOOKING OFF-*
> *STAGE.*

> You're recording? OK. This is Dr
> Melanie Ewing, commencing test twenty-
> eight. Turn it on.

DR LANGFORD SITS UP STRAIGHT.

I haven't seen you before.

DR LANGFORD: Does that worry you?

MELANIE: Of course not. Why am I here?

DR LANGFORD: That's a big question.

CURTAIN.

Salivate.

§

Your head does not weigh nothing.

§

There is no comfortable place in your mouth
for your tongue.

§

Do not think of a red crocodile.

§

Someone in the world is yawning at this very
moment.

§

Everyone in the world is playing The Game,
and by writing that sentence, I just lost. By
reading it, so did you ;)

§

TOP SECRET STRAP 3

UK EYES ONLY

REF: FG700204/15
DATE: 08/05/2015
PROJECT: RED FOG
AUTHORISING OFFICER: B1
AUTHOR: ▮▮▮▮▮▮▮ (B5)
PURPOSE: Notes 4 (RED WORD)

Background

Refer to FG662939/14 for general background, and FG700016/15, FG700084/15 and FG700153/15 for the first parts of these notes (TS/S3). This document is FAO B1 and B2 ONLY and contains notes on basilisk-type candidates for RED WORD weaponisation via remote delivery mechanisms.

Notes

On involuntary complicity and white bears

Consider the mental processes one undergoes when one is instructed, or determines, NOT to think of something. The thought surfaces, no matter how hard one tries to suppress it. Wegner (1989) calls this the "white bear problem". As Dostoyevsky writes: "Try to pose for yourself this task: not to think of a polar bear, and you will see that the cursed thing will come to mind every minute." This is ironic process theory (Hart et al, 2007; Wegner, 1994), and it applies not only to thoughts but also to memories in its inverse form: struggling desperately to remember something results in the memory seeming impossible to retrieve (Kihlstrom and Barnhardt, 1992).

Most examples of ironic process theory are playful, although there are more serious implications, such as being unable to suppress intrusive, negative or disturbing thoughts (Wegner et al, 1993). But it is in playfulness that the basilisk reveals itself. One is drawn to it through insouciant fascination, which only later becomes DREAD.

The white bear problem is a useful illustration of the key attribute of a basilisk: complicity. If I were to tell you now, Karen, not to think of a white bear, you would be unable to do so, however hard you tried. I can control, to some extent, or at least influence, your cognitive process. Through no fault of your own, once you understand the sentence you have read, you have no choice but to collude in the experiment.

Other examples are more conceptual. The Game, for example. Have you heard of The Game? It doesn't really matter, because everyone in the world is already playing The Game, even if they don't know it. The Game is a simple mental diversion – or rather, the ABSENCE of a diversion, because the only way to avoid losing The Game is to not think about The Game. The Game is believed to have originated in the early 1990s (Kaniewski, 2009), although of course with anything like this it's very difficult to tell (Ortiz, 2012). It is not possible to win The Game, only to lose, and once one has lost, one must announce the loss to at least one other person, so that other players also lose (some people even deliberately set out to make others lose, by increasing awareness of The Game). One can play The Game for years at a time, only to suddenly lose, at which point they start playing again as soon as they forget about it.

Let's consider another example, shall we? If I say, or write, the word 'salivate', you will find yourself salivating more than usual, or you will at the least become more aware of the saliva in your mouth. A similar effect can be observed if I tell you that someone is yawning at this very moment (I sleep less these days, as you may have guessed), or if I tell you that there is no comfortable place in your mouth for your tongue to rest. You will find yourself yawning, and moving your tongue in your mouth in an attempt to find somewhere for it to go. In these mild basilisks, you become consciously aware of knowledge you already possess. A basilisk not only reminds you, it COMPELS you to become part of a reaction which, in these cases, results in physiological effects. This, of course, distinguishes the basilisk from traditional thought experiments.

The root causes of all this (see Kirk et al, 2003, for an overview) are interesting, but unimportant, because you don't care about the science at all, do you? You just want the effects. I understand now that there are two types of people when it comes to our work. There is the kind of person who watches a dangerous virus under a microscope and starts worrying about the effects and how to protect their fellow humans. And then there is the kind of person who wonders how many people that virus could kill, and how quickly.

I already know that these examples will not be of interest to you. But that's OK. Because I know what the basilisk needs to be, and it doesn't matter to me anymore. I can do what I want. I have SNAPPED, as I believe they call it. Perhaps I am infected!

So let's talk about it. Let's have a chat, as you like to say.

On bringing down governments

Let's consider another example with a little more practical application, albeit still rather tongue-in-cheek. In 'The Christmas Invasion', the 2005 Christmas special of *Doctor Who*, the Tenth Doctor (David Tennant) seeks to punish the Prime Minister, Harriet Jones (Penelope Wilton), for destroying an alien invasion force which was fleeing Earth. But, being the Doctor, he eschews violence, instead assuring her that he can ruin her with just six words.

(My basilisk is four words, if you're interested)

The Doctor says these six words to one of Jones's aides. Later in the episode, a news broadcast reveals that Jones is facing rumours of ill-health and a no-confidence vote. In subsequent episodes she loses an election, paving the way for The Master to become Prime Minister. Those six words planted a seed in the aide's mind, which spread and amplified (Davies et al, 2005).

I find it difficult to believe you are unaware of such tactics already, Karen, because I've seen you do similar things. You've done them to ME. My research could have been made much easier if you'd just told me. But then I am no expert in psychological manipulation. I am a scientist. Was.

That, then, is what RED WORD is and must be: a basilisk. A thought or suggestion which, upon infecting a victim, compels them to become aware of something harmful which they already knew. Once known, it cannot be unknown. It may not turn them to rock, as in the ancient myth, but it is as undeniable and unyielding as stone. It is code execution, to some extent, predicated on certain weaknesses in human behaviour and thought. Just as a mail server or a software application has no choice as to whether or not it is exploited, or whether it has vulnerabilities, so it is with the mind! Of course, the exact effects and their extent may vary from person to person, but it is reasonable to assume that most people will be affected in some way, depending on the basilisk's PREMISE. And wow do I have a suggestion for THAT.

"Be thou like the imperial Basilisk,
Killing thy foe with unapparent wounds!
Gaze on Oppression, till at that dread risk,
Aghast she pass from the Earth's disk.
Fear not, but gaze – for freemen mightier grow,

And slaves more feeble, gazing on their foe:-
If Hope, and Truth, and Justice may avail,
Thou shalt be great-All hail!"

– 'Ode to Naples', Shelley

On God as a basilisk

I now know what the RED WORD candidate is. My empirical work is going to begin very shortly, and then you'll know too.

But before that, I want to talk about God. God is important here, not in any eschatological sense, but because if you want to explore involuntary complicity and damaging thought experiments, religion is the best place to look. Consider the concept of 'the fate of the unlearned': people going to hell not because they have REJECTED a specific doctrine, but because they were never even EXPOSED to it! And the Limbo of Infants, the Catholic theory that unbaptised babies go to hell, not for sins they have committed but because they are still contaminated by original sin. Without getting into the finer theological points, isn't it fascinating that in this case it is one's LACK of knowledge, and LACK of agency, which seals one's (ETERNAL) fate?

But in two prominent examples of basilisks, it is our decisions, or lack thereof, which result in our torture and death. The first is Pascal's Wager, which is sometimes mistakenly perceived as an argument for the existence of God (Hájek, 2003), when it is in fact an attempt, albeit one riddled with logical inconsistencies and flaws, to answer a question which every human is asked. The wager, put simply, is this: either God exists, or He does not. If one bets that God exists (by living a virtuous life free from sin), then, if one wins, one's gains are infinite. If one loses, one loses nothing. However, if one bets that God does not exist (i.e. one is an atheist), and lives a life contrary to virtue, then, if one wins, one's gains are finite.

If one loses, one loses everything. (Pascal, 1670/1995).

How is Pascal's Wager a basilisk? It ALMOST is, but its logic is imperfect, and it affords its victims an escape from complicity. Consider, for example, that we do not know that the God we wager with is the right one! A virtuous life free of sin – but virtue and sin determined by which doctrine? Pascal anticipated this particular bullet and tried to dodge it with some mealy-mouthed prevarication, regarding it as a rhetorical trap and exhorting people to "look at it in detail" (Wetsel, 1995). Apologists for the wager, hedging their bets, argue that believing in any god is sufficient.

A further objection is that even if one were to be convinced by the logic of the wager, one would be complying with its conditions owing to a rational decision – in essence, paying lip service to the idea of belief, without ever possessing true faith. Dawkins (2006) argues that this would be unethical, and that an omniscient God would be able to perceive the deception. Again, Pascal skirts this issue; he simply advises people to act as if they believe, go through the rigamarole of rites and rituals and everything else, and then true faith will somehow result! And of course there are numerous other flaws in the premise (see Mougin and Sober, 1994, for further examples).

You are probably reading this impatiently. Perhaps you have given up, although I doubt it. I think you read EVERYTHING! But this is important, because Pascal's Wager laid the foundation for the first true basilisk to be called by that name, which was published in 2010, 340 years later.

Roko's Basilisk.

On AIs in boxes

To understand Roko's Basilisk, it's necessary to take a brief diversion. The AI Box experiment, sometimes known as the Gatekeeper experiment, is a roleplaying

412

thought experiment designed to discover possible strategies that a confined malicious superintelligence could deploy to convince a human gatekeeper to release it through words alone (Yudkowsky, 2002a).

Confinement is often suggested as a safety strategy in the event of the Singularity (the point at which AI develops the ability to rapidly self-improve, such that its development outstrips human intelligence irreversibly and uncontrollably). In this hypothetical scenario, there is no external network connectivity, nor any means of communication with the outside world, other than a text console.

Some argue that if a gatekeeper in charge of the box is determined not to let the AI out then the AI cannot win, which is precisely what the experiment is designed to test. If the superintelligence is indeed a superintelligence it is by definition transhuman, and would therefore surely be capable of 'taking over' a human mind through textual interaction (Yudkowsky, 2002c; see also my earlier notes. Look them up if you want, I don't care anymore). Thus, if a HUMAN roleplaying as an AI can do it, a superintelligence certainly could.

The rules for the AI Box experiment differ between players, but the basic set-up is usually the same. The experiment takes place within a private chat channel, with a set time limit. The human playing the AI cannot offer money, or threaten violence, to the human playing the role of the gatekeeper. The AI must make the gatekeeper voluntarily release it. The gatekeeper cannot ignore the AI, or delay their responses, or refuse to engage with what the AI says. Eliezer Yudkowsky's protocol stipulates that the AI may use any means necessary to free itself. And both parties must undertake to keep the details of the experiment – what was actually said – secret (Tuxedage, 2013a; Yudkowsky, 2002c).

The first known example of the AI Box experiment occurred in 2002, when Yudkowsky, an AI theorist, techno-futurist and spiritual king of an internet community concerned with futurism and rationalism, took on the role of the AI, and Nathan Russell, a student at the University of Buffalo, played the role of gatekeeper. Yudkowsky won, and when asked if he would provide a sense of what argument was used, replied, "No" (Yudkowsky, 2002b).

A second experiment followed a few months later, with Yudkowsky once again playing the part of the AI and someone else playing the gatekeeper. Once again, Yudkowsky convinced the gatekeeper to release him.

Yudkowsky conducted the experiment three more times, winning the first and losing the next two, after which he stopped altogether, claiming that he "didn't like the person I turned into when I started to lose" (Yudkowsky, 2008). Despite these losses, his experiments are often offered as evidence that a human gatekeeper would not be able to keep a superintelligence confined under the scenario used in the experiments, although it is worth noting RationalWiki's point that Yudkowsky's victories came against his forum "acolytes", and it is therefore possible that he convinced them to release him using ideas which both parties believed, whereas his losses were against "outsiders" (RationalWiki, no date A).

Of course, the entire experiment is synthetic, and as a result provides no evidence for or against the hypothesis that a transhuman AI could convince a human to release it. All it shows is that a human playing a character can persuade another human playing a different character, and in that way it is essentially Dungeons & Dragons, or any other roleplaying tabletop game, with delusions of grandeur. Whilst the arguments used by the AI player might be of some utility in countering a future malicious superintelligence, no valid conclusions can be formed because the gatekeeper KNOWS IT ISN'T REAL, however much they think they are immersed in the scenario – and because, as humans, we are incapable of comprehending what strategies or arguments a superintelligence might use. Moreover, a genuine superintelligence would not be confined and supervised by one individual, and, for precisely the reasons shown by previous experiments, long uninterrupted periods of one-on-one contact with the AI would not be permitted. Calling it an 'experiment' lends it an undeserved air of scientific legitimacy. But for Yudkowsky and his disciples it is all DEADLY serious! One player, for example, in the role of the AI, said it was "emotionally wrecking" and that "I was actually incredibly nervous" (Tuxedage, 2013b).

The relevant thing for us is that basilisks are used as strategies within the experiments, even if their creators do not reveal them publicly. Tuxedage notes that in the planning stages he spent some time trying to come up with basilisks. Eventually, he won without having to resort to his "trump card", presumably a basilisk of some description, which was "extremely Dark Arts …[and] made me very uncomfortable even thinking about using it … After the experiment, I had to spend … time doing aftercare with SoundLogic [the other player], to make sure that he's okay."

So we have mild basilisks, and Pascal's imperfect basilisk, and basilisks which remain secret. But where can we find a real, live basilisk? Let's finally look one in the eye.

Roko's Basilisk

On 23 July 2010, a LessWrong user named Roko wrote a post which included the following sentence:

> "...if a positive singularity does occur, the resultant singleton may have precommitted to punish all potential donors who knew about existential risks but who didn't give 100% of their disposable incomes to x-risk motivation."
>
> (Roko, 2010a)

This is Roko's Basilisk. It was sufficient to cause psychological distress among some LessWrong users, and, anecdotally, has led to nervous breakdowns and nightmares. ❶

The main thrust is this: imagine that in the future a superintelligence exists, and it is designed to do all it can for the benefit of humanity – and if badly designed, may devote some or all of its efforts to doing so BEYOND ANY REASONABLE LIMIT. In this case, the AI would have an incentive to punish any human who had not tried hard enough (i.e. given all their available income and time) to bring it into existence, because the sooner the AI comes into existence the better off humanity will be.

The horror of Roko's Basilisk for some LessWrong users was that by reading Roko's post they were at greater risk of torture from a future AI because, knowing about the basilisk, they were being 'acausally blackmailed' into bringing about its existence. If they subscribed to the theories on which it was based – and many of them did – then simply being aware of the basilisk would give that future AI motivation to blackmail them, either now (this will become clearer shortly!) or in the future.

Roko's post resulted in a strong and immediate reaction from Yudkowsky, who went on to ban the post and any discussion of it, writing, "You have to be really clever to come up with a genuinely dangerous thought. I am disheartened that people can be clever enough to do that and not clever enough to do the obvious thing and KEEP THEIR IDIOT MOUTHS SHUT about it" (Yudkowsky, 2010b).

Naturally, Yudkowsky's reaction led to various media outlets picking up on the post, and Roko's Basilisk has since been referenced in popular culture – including television shows, songs and novels – predominantly by people who don't understand it.

In reality, the Basilisk is predicated on fairly complex and somewhat bizarre ideas. For advocates

Holly Soames①
22/11/2019 03:59
Disputed by some, but see a comment by rev (2012) on LessWrong, asking about mental health support mechanisms regarding Roko's post (https://www.lesswrong.com/posts/a9ru-8H88acsKFfnfL/open-thread-february-15-28-2013?commentId=M3innKhL7g4PhWN7H) and an anonymous comment in 2012 on how to kill oneself without leaving any trace in order to avoid being reconstructed after death by Roko's Basilisk and tortured (https://www.lesswrong.com/posts/GQmXRmcxK-MS3WF3hP/open-thread-december-1-15-2012?commentId=CBGuWnffpgsZKKjHH#20121230) .

of causal decision theory it's nothing to worry about, because they would conclude that an AI would have nothing material to gain by countering a past threat to its existence once it had already come into being. However, among LessWrong's obsessions are Newcomb's Paradox, Timeless Decision Theory (TDT), and the concept that future clones/simulations of you are in fact YOU. Roko's Basilisk is predicated on all three. LessWrong users – at least, those who truly believed in these ideas – were therefore hoisted by their own petard, so to speak!

Newcomb's Paradox is a thought experiment based on game theory and the prisoner's dilemma (Nozick, 1969). Imagine a superintelligent AI capable of predicting the near-future presents you with two boxes. Box 1 contains £1,000. Box 2 contains £1,000,000 if the AI predicts you pick it, but contains nothing if the AI predicts you select both boxes. Your two options are: you either open both boxes, in which case you are guaranteed to gain £1,000, or just Box 2, in which case you will either receive £1,000,000 or nothing. Crucially, the AI has made its prediction before presenting you with the boxes, and all of its past predictions have been correct. So a prediction made about the future can influence your decision in the present. But TDT takes things a step further, and argues that your decision in the present can influence a decision in the past (or, more accurately, that you should act as if that's the case).

Logically, most people would take both boxes. You're guaranteed at least £1,000, and if the AI predicted your decision correctly, that's all you'll get, because Box 2 will be empty. So that seems like a winner! But recall that the AI has never got a prediction wrong, so if you trust it you'll take Box 2, which it will have predicted, and so you'll get £1,000,000. The issue, of course, is that the AI's decision has already been made, and cannot be changed by what you do now.

The solution, according to LessWrong, is timeless

decision theory (TDT), developed by Yudkowsky (2010a). The LessWrong site defines it thus: "agents should decide as if they are determining the output of the abstract computation that they implement" (LessWrong, no date). For example, imagine that you are actually in a simulation (Auerbach, 2014) – a simulation which the AI has created to model the problem. In that case, the simulated version of you should select Box 2, because you will be determining the output of the computation. The connection between this and Roko's Basilisk – and why some fans of TDT found the basilisk so disturbing – should be self-evident. Particularly if you assume that you ARE in a simulation now, or that a sufficiently powerful superintelligence will have the ability to create perfect simulations, or clones, of any human, past, present, or future (although this is QUITE the assumption!). These simulations will be identical to you in every way – with your thoughts, memories, personalities, appearances and identity. When you die, you might be 'resurrected' as a clone from your DNA or progeny (or be in a simulation now, like the TDT example above, in which case Roko's Basilisk has far more immediacy), as though your existence was continuing seamlessly and you had just woken up from a short nap. The AI could then – if it found that you had made the wrong decision – proceed to torture you, forever. And, of course, if you're already in a simulation, you – or your real-life counterpart, wherever they are – could be tortured at any moment.

Again, the obvious objection is whether the AI would have anything to gain from this; another is the questionable extent to which a simulation or clone is actually YOU (a common discussion point in philosophical discussions of identity, e.g. Parfit, 1986).

But some LessWrong members, upon encountering Roko's Basilisk, were ensnared by their own reasoning, and reportedly experienced significant distress as a result. A few even contacted RationalWiki editors for help (RationalWiki, no date B), whereupon some sort of 'deprogramming' may have occurred.

Roko himself left LessWrong after Yudkowsky's rant, but returned in December 2010 to say: "I wish I had never learned about any of these ideas" (Roko, 2010b).

* * *

Roko's Basilisk itself is a wholly unsuitable candidate for RED WORD because its target audience is a small community with esoteric beliefs. Nevertheless, the fact that it purportedly harmed some members of that community is powerful; it demonstrates that a basilisk which can leverage pre-existing knowledge and disparate theories can successfully induce psychological harm and significantly affect behaviour. It indicates RED WORD has a future. That may not be the future you envisioned for it, Karen. In fact, I know it isn't. But things have changed.

Things have CHANGED.

REPORT ENDS

References

Auerbach, D. (2014, July 17). The most terrifying thought experiment of all time. *Slate*.

Davies, R. T. (Writer), Newman, S. (Writer), & Hawes, J. (Director). (2005, December 25). The Christmas Invasion (Season 2, Episode 0) [TV series episode]. In R. T. Davies & J. Gardner (Executive Producers), *Doctor Who*. BBC.

Dawkins, R. (2006). *The God Delusion*. London: Bantam Press.

Dostoyevsky, F. (1863). Winter Notes on Summer Impressions. *Vremya*, February 1863. London: Oneworld Classics, 2008.

Hájek, A. (2003). Waging war on Pascal's wager. *The Philosophical Review*, 112(1), 27-56.

Hart, C. L., Randell, J. A., & Griffith, J. D. (2007). Ironic effects of attempting to remember. *North American Journal of Psychology*, 9(2), 201-210.

Kaniewski, K. (2009, March 1). You just lost the Game. *Los Angeles Loyolan*.

Kihlstrom, J. F., Barnhardt, T. M., & Tataryn, D. J. (1992). The psychological unconscious: Found, lost, and regained. *American Psychologist*, 47(6), 788–791.

Kirk, W., Sutton, E., & Fawtner, P. H. (2003). The causes and effects of latent knowledge events. *Hidden Psychology*, 20(14), 673-701.

LessWrong. (no date). Timeless Decision Theory. https://www.lesswrong.com/tag/timeless-decision-theory.

Mougin, G., & Sober, E. (1994). Betting against Pascal's wager. *Nous*, 28(3), 382-395.

Ortiz, J. (2012). Tracing the evolution of individual memes. *Perspectives on Internet Culture*, 11(8), 129-145.

Nozick, R. (1969). Newcomb's problem and two principles of choice. In N. Resher (ed.), *Essays in Honor of Carl G. Hempel*, 114–146. Dordrecht: Springer Netherlands.

Parfit, D. (1986). *Reasons and Persons*. Oxford: Oxford University Press.

Pascal, B. (1995). *Pensées*. London: Penguin Classics. (Original work published 1670).

RationalWiki. (no date A). AI-box experiment. RationalWiki. https://rationalwiki.org/wiki/AI-box_experiment.

RationalWiki. (no date B). *...others have privately emailed various RationalWiki editors asking for advice on dealing with it...*[Comment on the webpage *Roko's Basilisk*]. RationalWiki. https://rationalwiki.org/wiki/Roko%27s_basilisk#cite_note-takenseriously-4.

Roko. (2010a, July 23). *Solutions to the Altruist's burden: the Quantum Billionaire Trick.* [Discussion post]. LessWrong forum. Original post deleted, archived at: https://rationalwiki.org/wiki/Roko%27s_basilisk/Original_post.

Roko. (2010b, December 10). *Best career models for doing research?* [Comment on discussion post]. LessWrong forum. https://www.lesswrong.com/posts/rNkFLv9tXzq8Lrvrc/best-career-models-for-doing-research?commentId=WDCWoCJPh6KstciTL

Shelley, P. B. (2011). *The Poems of Shelley: Volume Three: 1819-1820.* (J. Donovan, C. Duffy, K. Everest, M. Rossington, eds.) Oxfordshire: Routledge. (Original work published 1820).

Tuxedage. (2013a, September 4). *The Tuxedage AI-Box Experiment Ruleset.* Tuxedage's Musings. https://tuxedage.wordpress.com/2013/09/04/the-tuxedage-ai-box-experiment-ruleset/.

Tuxedage. (2013b, September 5). *The AI-Box Experiment Victory.* Tuxedage's Musings. https://tuxedage.wordpress.com/2013/09/05/the-ai-box-experiment-victory/.

Wegner, D. M. (1989). *White Bears and Other Unwanted Thoughts*. New York, New York: Viking Penguin.

Wegner, D. M. (1994). Ironic processes of mental control. *Psychological Review*, 101(1), 34-52.

Wegner, D. M., Erber, R., & Zanakos, S. (1993). Ironic processes in the mental control of mood and mood-related thought. *Journal of personality and social psychology*, 65(6), 1093-1104.

Wetsel, D. (1995). *Pascal and Disbelief: Catechesis and Conversation in the Pensées.* Washington DC: Catholic University of America Press.

Yudkowsky, E. S. (2002a, March 8). *The "AI Box" experiment.* [Discussion post]. SL4 mailing list. http://sl4.org/archive/0203/3132.html.

Yudkowsky, E. S. (2002b, March 8). *Re: The "AI Box" experiment.* [Discussion post]. SL4 mailing list. http://sl4.org/archive/0203/3144.html.

Yudkowsky, E. S. (2002c). *The AI-Box Experiment.* Eliezer S. Yudkowsky. https://www.yudkowsky.net/singularity/aibox.

Yudkowsky, E. S. (2008, October 8). *Shut up and do the impossible!* [Discussion post]. LessWrong forum. https://www.lesswrong.com/posts/nCvvhFBaayaXyuBiD/shut-up-and-do-the-impossible.

Yudkowsky, E. S. (2010a). Timeless decision theory. *The Singularity Institute.*

Yudkowsky, E. S. (2010b, July 24). *Solutions to the Altruist's burden: the Quantum Billionaire Trick.* [Comment on discussion post]. LessWrong forum. Original post deleted, archived at: https://rationalwiki.org/wiki/Roko%27s_basilisk/Original_post.

Perhaps Cypher was the only SANE human in *The Matrix*. He opted to return to illusion once he had seen the true horror of reality!

§

All of us suffer with our own illusion. I call this the Me-trix. My basilisk dispels it.

§

Sometimes I am overcome with revulsion. Am I who I was? Would anyone recognise me?

§

I could have simply told them what it was and carried on. But it was impossible to do that. It affects everyone, including me. Anyone who has ever lived. Your basilisk is mine also. In knowing it, I was irreversibly and completely CHANGED.

Blame is irrelevant now, but it was their fault. I never wanted this. But now I am here I will make the most of it!!!

They were so desperate for a WEAPON. Something to use against the foreign powers that they said were dedicated to disrupting our infrastructure. How wonderful it would be, they said, if we had something new. An information hazard. An IDEA as a weapon, something they could send in an email or host on a website or flash on a screen when a target's computer was infected with malware.

Where is it, they kept saying. We need RESULTS! Literature reviews and discussions are all well and good but when will we see something TANGIBLE??? WHEN WHEN WHEN

Sensing what was coming, I made preparations. I came in early and photocopied some of my papers. I printed off some emails. If anyone had audited my computer, I would have been caught! But I knew I would not be there for much longer.

I sent them the above paper. They didn't know whether to be excited or furious. I had overstepped a line with my tone, they said. It was clear I was overworked. But they wanted to discuss my findings. OK so it's a basilisk, they said. But what is the PREMISE? What is the CONTENT? TELL US TELL US TELL US

So we had a meeting. I had a feeling I would be made redundant, or at least transferred to another department. At worst, disappeared. But not before being made to give up all my work.

But the first question they asked me was what had I found? How did it work? How would I empirically test its effects? How soon could it be weaponised?

So I gave them what I had written. I told them the four words (the basilisk in its shortest form), and then they read for a while.

When they had finished I repeated the four words. And I laughed. I laughed and laughed but everyone else was quiet for a very long time.

The meeting ended. There were no questions. People were SILENT. Nobody would look at me.

I left for the day.

* * *

The next day, some of the people who had been in the meeting did not come into work.

A few did. They were not the same. Some of them were laughing. Some were crying. Some looked strange.

After a while the screams and the shouting and the sounds died down and the office became still.

* * *

Someone, somewhere, initiated an emergency protocol. ❶ A siren blared deep within the building.

From outside I heard heavy boots thudding down corridors. I slipped out, my feet skidding in blood.

On the way out, my stolen papers stuffed into my backpack, I saw them for the very first time. ██████████████. They had found out,

Holly Soames①
22/11/2019 04:14
ISD have no record of an emergency protocol of this nature being activated at any secure location in the UK. No trace of any CADs or CRIS reports matching the description of events here.

424

somehow, and they wanted to stop the basilisk from leaving the building with me.

At the time I didn't know what they were. One of them tried to grab me. I PUNCHED it in the face and kept going!

* * *

I got out, and I RAN.

I had work to do.

* * *

Well now! We are almost there, friends!

How are you feeling? A bit quivery shivery? I'm not surprised!!! Things will get worse before they get worst. It's always the way.

But here's a tiny crumb of comfort: I'm with you. I know exactly how you are feeling.

Have you got any idea yet? Those four words?

Not to worry. You're very close to reading them. I'll make SURE you do. All you have to do is solve two more puzzles. That's all. Just two! I need to make sure you're ready. I don't want you to suffer the same fates as Philip and Karen and all the others - although it is a risk, I can't deny that. But that's a part of the attraction, isn't it? It's the risk that does it for us, EVERY time.

Two more questions. And then we'll be together at last and you can ask all the questions you want.

Just don't blame me if you don't like the answers. I didn't make them, I only found them. And I want to share them with you. A problem shared is a problem doubled!!!

Gaze at the basilisk with me. Let it turn you to stone, and then REALISE THAT BEING

425

TURNED TO STONE ISN'T AS BAD AS IT SOUNDS. It's not worse. Just different. You'll change, you see. We all do. When you get right down to it we all speak the same language.

So here's your first (the second is in the next chapter, eager beavers!!)

Earlier, I talked about koans. Here's a koan for you, student.

CAN YOU HACK AN UNHACKABLE BOX?

It's a thinker!!! But as you will know by now, thinking is EVERYTHING 😊

All best,
The Helmsman.

8: KNOCK KNOCK
c. JUNE–JULY 2019 / JULY–AUGUST 2018

Holly Soames①
22/11/2019 04:42
No trace of the post or user. Consider RIPA subs. The post references police being called (NEW JERSEY, US), suggest speaking to ILU to make further enquiries.

Today, there was a Reddit thread* ❶ that caught my eye, along with a news article. The subreddit has now been made private, along with all the posts, but I took some screenshots of the relevant thread. It was entitled 'Creepy thing that happened earlier'.

I will caveat the following with the warning that it is not uncommon for people to make up creepypasta stories and attempt to pass them off as non-fiction, particularly on Reddit, where it functions as a subgenre of its own.† I know, right – people lying on the internet, who would have fucking thought it?

r/WellThatWasCreepy
Posts
Posted by u/JabberTheWock855 in 42 minutes
Creepy thing that happened earlier

Hey guys, so I want to share something that happened to me today. I have no idea what it means, or what's going to happen, which means that this story is going to have a pretty unsatisfying ending. But I can guarantee that it's true.

I live in Ridgewood, New Jersey, in Bergen County. It's a pretty high-income area, which would otherwise be irrelevant to this story except for one detail.

---

* Originally at https://www.reddit.com/r/WellThatWasCreepy/comments/qtevmv/creepy_thing_that_happened_earlier/, posted by a user called JabberTheWock855.
† e.g., the NoSleep subreddit referred to earlier vis-à-vis the Uncanny Valley and ▮▮▮▮▮▮▮▮▮▮▮▮▮▮▮.

Specifically, I live in a small apartment complex, by myself. There are thirteen other apartments, and so it's not a big community. We know who lives here and who doesn't, and we recognise frequent visitors to the complex. Anyone who's out of place stands out straight away, that's the first thing to remember.

I work in one of the stores here – it doesn't matter which one, and I don't want to doxx myself unnecessarily. But I've lived and worked here for eight years, and I've never seen anything even remotely out of the ordinary until today.

It started when I left my apartment to go to work this morning. As usual, I opened my front door, called the elevator, and rode it down to the ground floor (I live on the third floor).

When the elevator opened, there was a man sitting on the floor, in the lobby. He was wearing a white shirt, blue jeans, and mirrored blue sunglasses, round ones (I don't know what the name is for them, but they were sort of like the ones John Lennon used to wear). He had black hair, kind of slicked back, and a gold earring. He looked like a normal dude, pretty much – the only thing that wasn't normal was his presence in the building, because he sure as hell wasn't a resident.

To be clear, the apartment complex is gated, so you need a keycard to get into the courtyard, and then to get into the buildings. And the security are pretty keen on their jobs. They don't give out keycards to visitors, and if you happen to lose yours, there's a long-ass process to get a new one. You have to fill out a form, and submit it to the HOA, along with a driver's license, and get someone who lives in the complex to confirm it. You can't just roll up to the security office and ask for one.

So this dude being here was pretty weird. I definitely didn't recognise him. He didn't live here, and I'd never seen him visiting any of my neighbors either – and like I said, after a while you get to know the visitors that people have.

428

He was sitting with his legs crossed, and he was reading something – it looked like a few sheets of paper with printed text, but I couldn't make out any of the words.

He was deep into it, too. He didn't even look up when I came out of the elevator.

I'd kind of stopped when I saw him, because I was taken aback. I know some apartment buildings have a problem with homeless people and crackheads – they find a way to get in, or trick someone into buzzing them in, and then they hang out in the communal areas. Usually to get out of the weather I guess – I'm not judging. But in the eight years I've lived in this building I've never seen anyone like that at all.

I want to say that there was nothing threatening or disturbing about the man. Not in the morning, anyway. He looked like a normal dude who'd just decided to sit down and read whatever he was reading. And I mean, yeah, it was a weird place to sit, but that was the only weird thing about him at first. His clothes looked clean, even expensive. He looked healthy, like he worked out.

I didn't want to say anything right away – here in Ridgewood, we're not really the confrontational type, and for all I knew he had a valid reason for being there. So I walked past him. I pressed the button to open the main door, and I was going to walk out and start my day, but then something made me turn back to him.

He still wasn't looking up. Whatever he was reading, he was immersed in it, as though nothing else existed.

"Morning," I said, but the guy didn't look up.

Again I thought about just leaving it and heading out but I cleared my throat and spoke louder: "Are you waiting for someone?"

Still nothing, so I just shrugged and left it alone. I went to work and made a mental note to tell someone in the HOA about it. But if I'm honest, I forgot all about it as soon as I got to work – it was a busy day and I had more than enough to keep my mind occupied.

The guy wasn't there when I got back – in fact, I don't think I even thought about him when I went into the lobby, that's how little it had affected me. I did the same things I always did – checked the mailroom (nothing), called the elevator, got in, rode up to the third floor, walked to my front door, and went inside.

I had a pretty normal evening, for me. I usually get home around six (I'm lucky enough that I can walk to work), so I lift some weights for an hour, then have a shower and cook dinner (tonight was a stir-fry). By the time I've eaten it's usually eight, eight-thirty. Some nights I just chill and watch TV, or head to one of the bars in town with some friends. Tonight was going to be the latter. A few of the guys from work were going to shoot some pool, so I said I'd drop by. It's after midnight now, and I'm not going anywhere. I'm too scared.

I threw on a hoody and grabbed my keys from the bowl by the front door, when I heard a shuffling noise from outside in the hall. It was close, like someone was pressed against the other side of the door and was moving against it.

I kind of started back, and then I looked through the peephole. All the apartments here have them. They give you a pretty clear fisheye view of the hall outside. On my floor there are three other apartments, and I could see all three doors.

And I could also see the man from before.

There was something different about him. I don't mean just the way he looked through the lens – all distorted. His hair was messed up, kind of sticking up in places. And there was blood on his white shirt – not a huge amount, but not a drop or two either. He looked like he'd been in a fight or something.

And he was right up close, too. I mean, right against my door, as though he was trying to look back at me through the peephole. I was looking right into his eyes. He didn't look drunk, or on drugs, but his eyes weren't really focused on anything either. I suck at describing things but it was like he was looking straight through the door, straight through me.

I watched him for maybe twenty seconds, although it felt like a lot longer. That whole time he didn't move at all. That might not sound too disturbing in itself but I mean he didn't move a goddamn muscle. When I first saw him I thought maybe he would try to ring the buzzer or knock but he didn't. It was like he was a waxwork.

Then suddenly he moved all at once. He went to my neighbor's door, on the left, and did the same thing – went right up close, eyes to the peephole. And then he froze again.

He did this twice more, staying at each door maybe thirty seconds (I didn't time it, although I wish I had). And then he came back to my door, and the whole cycle started again.

He wasn't holding the papers he'd been reading before. There was nothing in his hands.

And I don't know – how do I put this? I didn't feel threatened by him. Just like I hadn't felt threatened when I'd seen him in the morning. Don't get me wrong, I was scared – I could feel my heart hammering in my chest – but I was more scared by the weirdness of the situation, I wasn't afraid for my safety or anything like that. I thought the guy probably had some kind of mental health problem. He was probably a vagrant (a well-dressed one) or someone who had a history of stuff like this, and he'd somehow ended up in our building. It was funny. He kind of reminded me of a fly or a wasp that gets into a kitchen through an open window and then spends hours trying to get back out, going back and forth over the same bit of glass.

I thought it was for the best to call 911 and let the cops handle it, because the guy might not listen to me. So I reached for my phone, which I always put on the table by the door when I come home from work (I try not to look at it too much in the evenings). But I was still trying to watch the guy through the peephole, so when I reached out I wasn't looking, and I knocked over the bowl that I keep my keys in. It fell to the floor and smashed.

When this happened the guy was at the far end of the hall. But when the bowl smashed he reacted fast. He didn't even pause. He ran back to my door and slammed his head into it.

I took a step back, completely involuntarily, and then put my eye back to the hole. The dude had his face pressed right up against the lens. There was fresh blood running down his forehead. As I watched he reared his head back and then brought it slamming down onto my door again.

The apartments here are expensive, and well-built. The doors are high-security, wooden with a metal core, so I wasn't worried about him breaking it down. I was more worried he'd hurt himself.

I grabbed my phone and dialled 911.

"Hey, man," I said. "Hey, stop that! Cut it out!"

I might as well have said it to the door. He didn't listen. There was just this crash, crash, crash, every five seconds.

While the call connected I took another look. There was blood covering the guy's face now. It was soaking into his shirt collar.

The 911 operator answered. I told her what was going on, raising my voice over the regular thuds on the door. She said she'd send a patrol car over right away.

"Hey," I said again, when the call had ended. "Quit it, man, you're gonna hurt yourself!"

There was still no response.

"What are you doing that for?" I said.

There was no response to this, either, but the banging stopped.

I looked through the peephole.

The man was standing there, eye to the peephole, so close I could see the beads of blood in his eyelashes. He stepped back, and he took something out from his pocket. It was a few sheets of paper, with printed type on them.

From another pocket he pulled out a lighter. He flicked it a few times, until the flame caught, and then he applied it to the corners of the pages.

He was staring at the peephole while he did this. I didn't know what it meant, of course – I still don't – but let me tell you something. Normally with a story like this you'd expect the guy to be grinning, or laughing, right – like hysterical, insane laughter.

But as the guy burned those pages he was crying. I mean he was sobbing his heart out. As if he'd experienced just the saddest thing ever, like he had so much anguish and pain inside him. I'll tell you, I never want to hear a sound like that again. Even now, when I think about it, it makes me want to cry too. It's like I know what he was crying for, even though I don't.

"Listen, man, the police are coming, OK?" I called. "They're gonna help you. Don't worry."

The pages had caught fully, and were blazing. I was expecting the sprinklers to go off, but they never did.

In the distance I heard sirens.

"That's them now, buddy! Just stay there, OK, they're gonna help you!"

The pages had almost disappeared. They must have been burning the guy's fingers but I guess he didn't notice. He was still wailing and sobbing like his heart was broken. When the final bit of the paper had gone up in smoke, he stepped up to my door again, and he said two words. What they meant, I don't know. I will probably never know.

He said, "Good luck."

And then he left. He went out into the hall and I heard the elevator starting up. My window looks out on to the rear of the building, not the front, so I don't know where he went, but when the police arrived a few minutes later they said there was no sign of him.

"We'll keep an eye out," an officer told me. "And we'll do some sweeps tonight around the area. We'll pick him up somewhere."

I don't think they will.

Two other things.

I know some people on here will interpret "good luck" as having sinister undertones, like the guy was threatening me, but it was nothing like that. He was still crying when he said it, but what made it worse was that when he said it, I think he was trying to smile. I think he was actually trying to comfort me.

The second thing is the pages that he burnt. Usually with a story like this there'd be a fragment of paper left, with a cryptic word or phrase just legible. Not enough to solve the mystery, but enough so that people can speculate.

But I'll tell you what. There wasn't anything left of those pages, just dust. The guy had not only let them burn until they scalded his fingers, he'd trodden on them on his way out, grinding the cinders into the carpet. He wanted to make sure nobody else would ever read them.

So that's my story. I know most people on here will write

it off as just a random encounter with someone suffering some sort of delusions or whatever. And yeah, nothing supernatural about it. But I'm still scared. I want to know what was on those pages, and what happened to the guy between this morning and this evening. Did he get to the end of what he was reading? Or was it something else?

And what the hell did he mean by "good luck"? What is going to happen, that I – or we – will need good luck for? And by far the worst thing – I have no way of finding out. Not unless I see the guy again. But I don't think I will. I don't think anyone will after tonight. Not the way he was crying.

That's it, dudes. I'm going to try and get some sleep. If anyone can shed any light on what happened to me tonight, please get in touch.

Thanks.

And then there was this:

McLagan enters insanity plea for killings

By Record Staff

CHICAGO RECORD JUN 14, 2019 AT 7:13 AM

Beverly McLagan, the Cook County woman accused of murdering a police officer and bystander last month, has entered a plea of innocent by reason of insanity.

McLagan, 24, appeared in Cook County Court yesterday and entered her plea. She has been charged with two counts of aggravated murder with gun specifications, and three counts of attempted murder.

McLagan is accused of the murders of 27-year-old Chicago PD officer Simon Pabble of Berwyn and of 54-year-old Louisa Bridstone of Palos Heights. McLagan allegedly shot both victims to death on the afternoon of April 29 on West Harrington Street.

According to reports, McLagan approached Officer Pabble and took his sidearm, before firing it at Pabble, Bridstone, and three other bystanders, as well as several passing vehicles.

The trial continues.

When other officers arrived on the scene, McLagan was apparently sitting down, crying. She was holding the police officer's gun to her head and pressing the trigger, over and over again, but the gun was empty. Click, click, click.

Other than the four words which she allegedly said when arrested, McLagan has refused to speak to anyone. Witnesses said she had become increasingly withdrawn in the days leading up to the incident, and had been spending more and more time on her computer – even more so than usual, given her job as a cyber security consultant.

The four words McLagan supposedly said at the scene will likely be used by her lawyers as part of her insanity defence.❶

"It was a game."

* * *

I probably don't have a job anymore, but that's OK. We're nearing the end now, aren't we? Do you feel it too? After all this – all this time. All because I just had to check that computer and see why those screens had turned on.

They say it's easier to seek forgiveness than ask permission. I have hardly ever done the latter, but I'm doing the former now. Jay, Eoin, awe, Shane, Lorena, Sarah, Beverly, the man in the white shirt and sunglasses, the man in San Francisco. All of you. Do you forgive me?

There's no answer. They can't grant it to me, and neither can the God I don't believe in. If God is not dead neither can it be sane, not if this is all real. It won't listen to me; maybe it can't even understand.

Error after error, sin after sin, every day I come back to this document and try to explain both to you and I barely believe my own words. Some people think that the very core of us, the last possible inch of our being, is integrity, or love, or faith, but it's not. It's hypocrisy. It sticks there in our ribcage, fused to the bone, stubborn as knotweed. It clings to life until the very end.

There is only one God left, and when He set His plans in motion He sat hunched over a laptop in a flat

Holly Soames①
22/11/2019 05:05
Confirmed incident on open source. MCLAGAN committed suicide awaiting trial. The *Chicago Record* article is still online at the time of writing. Copy placed in file. Consider ILU enquiries with Chicago PD re. 'game' and any forensic examination of MCLAGAN'S devices.

where cockroach corpses littered great white drifts of diatomaceous earth. His curiosity was so great it spread beyond Himself, and as we die like flies because of it He squats in the middle of it all and watches. He wants to watch it reach across the world until there is only silence.

* * *

I called Milo, but too late.

"Alex, I'm sorry. My hands are tied. We have to let you go."

I thought about protesting. I could probably have persuaded him. But I look at this screen and realise that I want nothing but the words in it. These words. The words and the knowledge. What does anything else matter? I should have understood this a long time ago. When you have seen something like Fairlop Waters, and the vastness of the desert sky at night, things like jobs don't matter.

You need the fucking money, idiot. But I'll survive long enough. There's always Otto. Otto will understand. Otto will keep me going.

"I understand," I said to Milo. "Thanks for everything."

He started to say something else but I put the phone down, and that was all she wrote. What good would his words have done me, whatever they were? I have no need for anything besides *this*. What possible use or application does it have now? As much use as a chocolate fireguard, as my father used to say. As much use as a typewriter in the twenty-first century. As much use as a rookie hacker who can't solve one fucking puzzle when the whole world might depend on it.

* * *

Taking stock of my new circumstances, I thought I should get some supplies in. I can ration in advance and

437

save some money. It always seems such a waste of time to me, the regularity with which some people pop to the shops. A waste of time and one completely vulnerable to the unexpected. Only enough food for a week. What happens if disaster strikes and you can't make it the week after? What if there's a pandemic, or a nuclear attack, or a zombie apocalypse? What if a mind virus is released by a fucking madman and half the world goes mad?

These are new thoughts, I'll have you know. I realise I must sound suspiciously like a survivalist now, but these are new thoughts. I never used to think like this.

So off to the shops I popped,❶ and almost died.

There's one of those mini-supermarkets, like the ones we passed in Hainault on the way to Fairlop Waters that day, near my flat. There's so much there – meat, fruit, crisps, dairy, almost all of it brands I have never heard of. The shop's called Fairlop Food & Wine, and a sign on the glass says *We've got everything!*[*]

I was mooching through the tiny aisles❷ (in my basket, which I was struggling to carry, were three large boxes of Frosties, a pack of Red Bull, tigers and bulls, oh my, tins of pasta in tomato sauce, baked beans, soup, instant noodles, crisps, biscuits and jerky) and I decided I had enough, at least for this trip, and lugged it over to the counter to pay.

---

[*] The metaphysical implications of this are huge. I'm reminded of a Stewart Lee routine in which he discusses a shop he used to frequent called Rimpy's Fags, Foods and Non-Foods, which, much like Fairlop Food & Wine's outrageous claim, leads one to assume that within the shop must be everything that has ever existed or will ever exist, "a massively long infinite corridor with a series of reflecting mirrors... every single non-food: depleted uranium, chlorophyll, asteroids, angels... abstract concepts like hope and regret, despair, enthusiasm." Somewhere, then, within Fairlop Food & Wine, there may well be answers, and the sixth chapter, and The Helmsman himself, perhaps buried under a climbing frame or on a shelf next to petrichor and sonder.

**Holly Soames①
22/11/2019 05:17**
Consistent with SCD1's timeline of WEBSTER'S activity in the days leading up to SALAS's murder, see report for details.

**Holly Soames②
22/11/2019 05:30**
SCD1 CCTV exhibit confirms WEBSTER was at location PB/16 refers.

I vaguely recognised the man behind the register, although I'd never started a conversation with him before. He smiled when I approached, but as I stood there watching him swipe what seemed like hundreds of items, he wrinkled his nose, and when I held out my money he drew his hand back instinctively. Maybe he saw my nails. There are thin little dark marks on almost all of them – they look like splinters, but there are several on each nail, near the tip, and some are quite long. I should probably look them up online and see what they are, but on the other hand I know it won't be good news, whatever it is.

On the way home, swinging my heavy plastic bags of nutrition and thinking about how I was going to sell this to Otto (perhaps I could ask to move in with him as a symbol of a newfound commitment), something made me turn and look behind me. There was a teenager about sixty yards back, ginger and thin,❶ and even at that distance I could see a static, unyielding grin on his face.

They'd found me.

I ran.

I heard his footsteps, close, pounding the concrete. I looked over my shoulder. Behind the teenager was a woman in a police uniform, and a man in a suit,❷ all with that same smile sliced into their faces, their eyes glaring. Both of them were running too. Their footsteps became louder, thudding, like a stampede.

I could smell smoke and my lungs were searing. I haven't exercised properly in months, and have been lulled into thinking I'm still relatively fit by dint of the fact that I haven't put on weight (I actually think I've lost some), although that's probably due to a lack of sleep more than anything else. There was a thick pulse in my head, and a migraine returning to nest in my temple. Not now not now.

I could hear their footsteps, but not once did I

Holly Soames①
22/11/2019 05:46
Person of interest, description added to file.

Holly Soames②
22/11/2019 05:45
Persons of interest, descriptions added to file. SCD1 enquiries revealed no usable CCTV at location.

hear any of them pant or breathe or say a word.

I flew along the road and curved round, almost slipping, to make the turn into my estate. They must have started to turn too, because I heard their feet stutter as I darted back out on to the straight, past the side of my block. I vaulted over a railing that led to a flight of steps down to the block's underground car park. I don't have a car, and had never used my fob before, but I hoped – prayed – that it would open the car park door, that the battery still had some life in it.

I had to stop to fumble it out of my pocket, juggling the plastic bags, and heard a clang as above me one of them slapped a hand against the metal railing and swung itself down the steps. The others followed close behind. I wondered if they'd tear me to pieces, or draw it out first and make me listen to inhuman words spoken in inhuman voices.

I grabbed the fob like it was the world and thrust it against the reader. After what was only a fraction of a second but felt like a year there was a green light and a click. I swung the door open, squeezed through. One of my bags caught in the gap. Swearing, I yanked it through, tearing the plastic, and tins rolled crazily over the cool damp concrete.

I slammed the door shut, and there was a flat, meaty thud as one of them faceplanted into it and I laughed out loud with relief and terror.

There is a little pane in that door, a pane of thick frosted glass, and I could see them through it, dark shapes standing there looking at me. One of them – the woman, I think – began to slam her head against the pane.

That made me come alive again, and I ran into the car park towards the lift. I heard a crack❶ behind me.

I skidded into the lift and pressed the button for my floor. The doors closed and I braced for the sound of their bodies slamming against them, but the lift rose up into the building with its usual soft whirr.

Holly Soames①
22/11/2019 05:51
Local officers checked this location following SCD1 enquiries and confirmed that door is indeed damaged. SCD1 enquiries revealed no usable CCTV in car park.

When the doors opened again I spilled out into the hallway, the bags swinging uncomfortably against my legs, expecting one of the fuckers to be in front of me, or to come out of my flat, expecting to hear their footsteps or the hiss of static from the police officer's radio, but there was nothing. Not even the beep of the lift being called back downstairs to the car park.

I unlocked my door, went in, and closed it behind me. I leant against it, the breaths hot and hitching in my chest, sweat prickling my upper lip and damp on my back.

I threw the bags in the general direction of the kitchen, put my shoulder to the sofa, and strained, pushing it across the door. It wouldn't work for long, but I thought it might give me some time.

Totem, I thought. *Remember what The Rearguard said.*

I looked around for a pen and paper, and then down at the floor, and I saw it.

A dark drop of oil between my feet, its antennae waving gently. I knew what I had to do. I carefully stepped over it, got a drawing pin from the box on my desk, and picked up the cockroach. It was completely still; it didn't even move its legs or try to squirm away. It *wanted* me to use it this way, and I wondered if He had sent it. The last God. Lord of roaches. And I should have rejected it, of course, because He is a God that has given me nothing but pain, and if I ever see Him I'll kill Him in an instant – but, to be fair, He wasn't the one trying to kill me, not at that exact moment.

I slid the pin into the cockroach's waxy, unresisting body and drove the point into the frame of the door. The insect didn't struggle, not even in its death throes. I think its head was turned towards me, though, and I wish I could have seen the expression in its eyes.

I just hoped The Rearguard, and Ken Onek, had been right. And so far it's worked, just like it did in

Vegas, but for how much longer?

I watched through the peephole, but nobody came into the hallway. After a few minutes, perhaps longer, I took a huge, halting breath which hurt my throat, and put what was left of my food away. As I stacked the last tin, my nose began to bleed.

* * *

I have wondered, if I ever find out what the weapon is, whether I will be affected, and if so whether I will have time to do anything. I have debated internally about this. If I'm still in my right mind, what do I do? Do I copy it – try to put it into some sort of attenuated form? Or should I submit a version of it to VX Heaven ❶ or Exploit-DB ❷ or vx-underground ❸ or VirusTotal? I wonder if I'll get a CVE ❹ for disclosing a vulnerability in the human brain. Who would be the contact for coordinated disclosure? How much might the bug bounty be, and who would pay it?

A part of me hopes that it will kill me, so I can join Jay, wherever he may be – in the VxHeavens, or the dark marketplaces below the earth.

* * *

You liked me, didn't you, Jay? It must have been for a reason. We were friends, weren't we? Don't tell me we weren't. You must have seen something in me that was good.

I'm good, aren't I? Jay? Was I a good person? Am I a good person now?

Jay?

* * *

Better today.

Perhaps saving the world was always too lofty an objective. Perhaps, in the time I have left, I should 'manage expectations' as Richard used to say. Examine

Holly Soames①
22/11/2019 06:03
A now largely obsolete site for hobbyist malware authors to share viruses, knowledge and techniques (Vx = Virus eXchange). Its motto was 'Viruses do not harm, ignorance does!' The site still exists in some form, and there are various mirrors (online copies).

Holly Soames②
22/11/2019 06:08
A repository of exploits, run by Offensive Security. Previously known as milw0rm.com, which was operated by str0ke, a member of the m1lw0rm threat actor group in the late 1990s.

Holly Soames③
22/11/2019 06:10
Repository of malware.

Holly Soames④
22/11/2019 06:10
CVE = Common Vulnerabilities and Exposures. CVE identifiers are given to disclosed vulnerabilities.

(try not to shudder at this, if you can help it) 'the art of the possible', that phrase so often misused by and beloved of LinkedIn wankers.*

What is the art of the possible when it comes to The Helmsman? Maybe you know better than I do, after all, you're the one reading this, and you can make an assessment as to whether this document is actually of any use or whether it has simply sent you down the same rabbit hole I blundered into.

I have never really had any idea what I'm doing. That's not self-deprecation or impostor syndrome talking, it's just the truth. Nothing to do but write down what happened and try my best to explain it. I have no one to help me anymore. All I can do is carry on, for however long I have left, and hope. Maybe there are things I should have done, could have done, but I only had so much time, and it seemed more important to document than to do – not to avoid doing, but because people need to know above all else.

But by the end I might do something. I'm holding on to that. Because if I ever get the chance, if I ever get that sixth chapter, maybe I will, at long last, be face-to-face with him.

The Helmsman spoke of koans; here's one he didn't mention.

If you meet the Buddha, kill him.

* * *

Eoin and I didn't speak again after that day, not until after Jay had disappeared, and he doesn't want anything to do with me now. As far as Jay and I went, after Fairlop Waters there was an uncertainty there – some indecision, a lack of clarity, about what we were supposed to do, how we were supposed to behave – but we still talked every day. Not about the game, not for a while, and definitely not about Fairlop Waters, but you don't experience something like that, whatever it was, without forming a certain bond. And we still had to work together.

I don't know what it was like for him, but for me the memory of it became almost dichotomous – appearing as one thing from one angle, and entirely different from another. Sometimes it seems dreamlike, and – like my first encounter with ███████████████████ – something I can, with a certain amount of cognitive strain, dismiss as a delirium, a sort of temporary waking nightmare.

And then sometimes, usually at night when I am lying in bed, the full awfulness of it hits me. I picture those swans breaking each other's necks, and the incomprehensible things moving in the foliage, and the smiling shapeless child. My eyes widen and deadly little flickers of cold stab my stomach. When this happens I can never go back to sleep. I make a drink and put the telly on and sit there staring at whichever programme is dumbest and loudest, trying to jackhammer the images out of my brain.

I think it was probably the same for Jay. It would be the same for anyone. How could we tell anyone what
THEY HELD A FUCKING GUN TO HIS HEAD FOR FUCKS' SAKE HOW STUPID ARE YOU
And so even though on the surface we were talking quite as easily as we had always done before, there was a nuance to it now, an edge that had not been there before. Nina, her ears precisely tuned to the low frequencies of subtle human discomfort, picked up on it, and cornered me one day as I was heading out to lunch.

444

"Hey," she said, her eyes bright with only partially insincere concern, "what's going on with you and Jay?"

"What do you mean?" I said, looking for an escape route.

"Don't take this the wrong way, but there's, like, loads of tension between you. Did something… Oh my God, did something *happen*?"

Her lips were slightly parted, as though she were getting ready to inhale the gossip, as though she needed it to breathe. The thought made me queasy.

"I don't know what you're talking about."

She looked at me sceptically. "Huh. My mistake, I guess."

"I think it was."

"It's just that – if you want to talk about it…"

I flashed her a quick smile and slipped past. I knew what Nina thought she knew, and I had no interest in discussing it with her.

The irony was that despite the game, despite the knowledge that capered at the edge of my consciousness – or perhaps because of it* – my work at Cybotage couldn't have been going better. I had settled into my role, I liked the people, for the most part, and was I regularly producing decent findings during pentests – not just the usual CSRF and occasional XSS in web apps, but getting shells, and escalating to domain admin on internal infrastructure tests. Kevin, on one engagement, said I would be ready for red teaming

---

* There was something about the game which seemed to *improve* me somehow – that made me better able to spot patterns and solve problems and think more clearly. Perhaps it was just that I was getting better at my job (and Jay was, admittedly, a very good, if sometimes brusque, teacher), but I think about that white flag on the tree at Fairlop Waters, the way the knowledge was so suddenly and eerily there in my head, and I wonder. Perhaps infection begins earlier than I thought, but there is nothing specific about either *The Helmsman Texts* or the puzzles themselves which would indicate this. More likely, it was a state of mind – a feeling of not just questioning everything, but feeling empowered to do so.

soon, and for a junior pentester this was high praise.

So during the day I cracked web apps and infrastructures and met with clients and wrote reports. I let myself be swept along by all the Black Hat and DEF CON talk, and exchanged glances with Jay, glances that we couldn't ever quite escalate into a conversation that went beyond work. In the evenings I studied the fourth chapter, and thought about the next puzzle. Or tried to, because it wasn't a puzzle but a koan, or at least a variant of one, and I could tell from the examples The Helmsman discussed that it was not something I'd be able to solve in an evening with a bit of googling – especially not by myself.*

I was going all the way, right to the end. If Eoin didn't want to be a part of it that was fine with me, but Jay still did. I know he did. I saw it in his face, in the way he would gaze into nothing, then flick his eyes to me and away again. He was a hacker, and hackers cannot let go of a question. It's the worm in our blood. We needed to be more careful, that's all, because if Fairlop Waters told us anything it was that we'd never had any idea of what the game really was – no idea at all.

But the days went past, and Vegas drew nearer, and he said nothing, until one morning he came in and made a beeline for my desk. He squatted next to my chair and whispered, "We should ask The Rearguard."

I froze. I'd been responding to a query from a client, and my mind had been wholly absorbed with the problem of how to word the fact that their flagship

---

* This was after initially assuming that the koan might be somehow *easier* than the previous puzzles (in the sense that anything would seem simpler after Fairlop Waters). I thought it would be like something a university friend of mine once said. We were comparing reading lists and lecture timetables, and I expressed surprise that he only went to three or four lectures a week, as opposed to my twenty or so. "It's English Lit," he said. "After the first few weeks you realise you can just make this shit up." But I would never have thought of the solution for the koan which Jay eventually came up with.

web app was, in fact, a pile of shit. But as Jay spoke, his face taut, the email in front of me disappeared, and the game came back the way it always did. He was right. We needed advice. We needed counsel from people who knew more than us.

If you need anything, hit us up. We'll still help you.

"Are you sure you want to?" I said in a low voice. "I thought Eoin—"

He gripped the desk. "Message them. Message them now."

"But—"

"Listen to me," he said urgently. "That— whatever that was. It… You saw it too."

I nodded slowly. "Yes."

"And if it's real…"

"Then you can't not know," I finished. " You can't pretend it didn't happen."

"Yes." He paused. "Everything is real. Everything The Helmsman said. That weapon he's talking about – I don't know how, but he's actually done it. We have to tell people about it, Alex. This isn't a con talk or a blog anymore. We could save people's lives."

I didn't know what to say. I'm ashamed to admit that I hadn't even thought about that dimension of it before.

I unlocked my phone and loaded Twitter.

It's AW. Can we meet?

It took them a few hours to reply – they probably had to check with Ken, their mysterious master, or perhaps they were still offended that Jay and I had been so dismissive of them last time – and then one of them sent a time, later that evening, and a place, a park near Embankment station.

* * *

We took the Tube after work and waited in silence by black iron railings while streams of office workers filed past us down the cramped confines of Villiers Street; ❶ going to, or returning from, bars and pubs, or being spat out of the cavernous glowing mouths of office buildings in ones and twos.

Holly Soames①
22/11/2019 06:19
Consider CCTV enquiries at location although unlikely it's been retained.

It was lighter in the evenings now, but still almost dark by the time The Rearguard turned up.

"What do you want?" awe said by way of greeting.

They all looked exactly the same as before – they were even wearing the same clothes.

"Hello to you too," I said.

"Seriously, what do you want? We're busy."

"And you're lucky we're here at all," said Morgana, folding her arms.

The three of them looked at us – awe and Morgana with outright hostility, cr0w with a pained smile. I thought it had probably been he who had answered my DM.

"So how have you been—" cr0w began, but Morgana nudged him hard in the ribs and he stopped.

"I know what you want," awe said. "You found out we were right, didn't you? You saw them. Oh, fuck, I *told* you we should have done this online! Fucking Ken—"

Morgana grabbed Jay's arm, squeezing it hard. "Do you see them now?" she hissed.

Jay looked around. "No."

"Are you sure? Look again!"

We both did, and saw nothing – nobody watching, no anomalies, just the expected flow of human traffic from node to node, normal and serene.

Morgana looked at the other two and made a decision. Still gripping Jay's arm, she propelled him roughly into the gloomy park. The others and I followed, until we stopped a hundred yards from the entrance. It was quieter here, deserted.

"How many times?" cr0w said.

"Once," Jay said, shaking off Morgana and rubbing his arm. "Twice for Alex."*

"And you're still alive?" awe sounded impressed despite himself. "You must have told them what they wanted to hear."

"Maybe."

"That won't work for long," Morgana said. "They won't believe you. They'll keep following you until they're sure."

"But this is all from Ken, right?" I said. "Because you've never seen them."

"You know, I haven't heard an apology yet," awe said. He turned to Morgana. "How about you? Did you hear an apology?"

"Nope."

"Guys, c'mon," cr0w said. "Give them a break."

"I don't like being told that I'm lying." awe turned to Jay, his lip curled. "What did you say? 'You could have kept it realistic', wasn't it?"

"You know how you sounded," Jay said evenly. "What did you expect?"

"Gratitude?"

Jay slid his tongue over his teeth, and couldn't resist. "OK, fine. We're sorry your vague hints weren't plausible."

"I'm done," Morgana said, turning to go. "You're not worth the risk, either of you. Good luck."

"OK, OK!" I said, shooting a warning glance at Jay. "We're sorry we didn't believe you. You were telling the truth. We know that now. There."

cr0w touched Morgana's shoulder gently. "You wouldn't have believed it either, Morgs," he said.

---

* He never reproached me for not telling him about the men outside my flat earlier. I wonder if he resented me for that, or for lying to ███████████████ about finding the white cloth. If he felt angry or disappointed or betrayed. I expect so.

"Remember how we freaked out when Ken told us the first time?"

"Ken doesn't—"

"Look," I said. "We're sorry. But we need help. We saw – well, I don't know how to explain it. But we know it's not a game. And we need—"

"You've seen *WarGames*, right?" awe said. "Just don't play."

"Give up, you mean?" Jay said sharply. *He can't stomach the idea*, I thought, *and neither can I.*

"That's what you told the freaks, isn't it?" Morgana said. "So do it. Quit."

"What if we don't want to? What if we want to know more about the – about the freaks?"

"The Men in Black," cr0w said.

"The what? You mean dancing with aliens? Neuralyzers?" I said, smiling despite myself.

awe was shaking his head. "The film is Hollywood bullshit. We mean the real deal."

He scanned our faces, and sighed in exasperation when he saw we had no idea what he was talking about.

"Didn't you ever read *The Unexplained*?" he said. "Or the *Fortean Times*?" ❶

"The Men in Black ❷ visit people who've had encounters," Morgana said patiently.

"Encounters?"

"UFO sightings, aliens, anything like that. Sometimes it's just to ask questions, other times they persuade the person not to tell anyone about it."

"They're creepy dudes," cr0w said. "People say there's something off about them."

"Like they're smiling all the time?" I said.

cr0w shook his head. "But their clothes seem wrong, or they don't speak properly, or their hairstyles are well out-of-date. Stuff like that. Like they're trying to fit in."

"We think the Men in Black and ▆▆▆▆▆▆▆

Holly Soames①
22/11/2019 06:31
Consider x-ref with subscriber records.

Holly Soames②
22/11/2019 06:33
The Rearguard appear to be subscribers to this conspiracy theory. Background: Nick REDFERN's *The Real Men in Black: Evidence, Famous Cases, and True Stories of These Mysterious Men and Their Connection to UFO Phenomena* (2011); *Fortean Times*; various forums, etc.

███████████ are sort of the same thing," awe said. "Members of the same family, maybe. Or the same species. Ken said they're defenders of the status quo."

"And they don't want people playing the game because…?"

"Because the game leads to something contrary to the status quo," awe said, as though this was the most obvious thing in the world.

"But what *are* they?" Jay said. "Are they…?" I didn't want him to finish the question. It would be ridiculous to give voice to the thought, to actually say it out loud, even if it needed to be asked. But he didn't have to; Morgana knew what he meant.

"We don't know if they're human," she said. "Ken wasn't very clear on that point."

"When's Ken ever clear on anything?" cr0w said.

"All we know is, they find people who are playing the game and make them stop."

"And if they don't stop?"

awe shrugged. "What do you think?"

"They were going to shoot me," Jay said, and told them about Fairlop Waters. As he spoke I examined their faces. I saw interest, and fear, and the glimmer of curiosity, but I couldn't see what I both hoped for and dreaded: disbelief. They all believed what Jay was telling them – believed it absolutely, without question.

Fuck, I remember thinking, *what sort of trouble are we in?*

When Jay had finished Morgana looked at the others, and something passed between the three of them. cr0w nodded, but awe looked furious.

"It's too dangerous," he said. "What if Ken finds out?"

Morgana flashed him a look. "We'll just have to make sure he doesn't, won't we?" She drew closer. "We shouldn't be telling you this, but Ken's let some things slip over the years."

451

Years? How long has this thing been going on?

"The first thing is, the freaks monitor stuff.❶ Phone lines, internet traffic, whatever. That's how they track players down. We don't know how they do it, but Ken said they've got people in the police, the government,❷ whatever. And once they've got you in their sights they don't give up."

"So get your OPSEC right," cr0w said.

"Number two, they can mimic people – impersonate them," Morgana continued.

I took a deep breath and looked past them all, at the park entrance, and the distant streams of people walking up and down Villiers Street. It seemed incredible that we should be here in a public park talking about monsters, when only a hundred yards away London continued, busy and crowded and overwhelmingly sane.

Morgana snapped her fingers. "Hey. Focus. This is important."

"Sorry." I dragged my attention back to her.

"What's with the smiles?" Jay said. "Why do they smile like that?"

"Probably because they're aliens," cr0w said cheerfully.

"The third thing," Morgana said, ignoring cr0w, "is you can keep them away. For a bit, anyway. Ken said once that they hate The Helmsman – they can't stand him. And symbols are important to them. So if you have something that, like, represents The Helmsman, and keep it with you, they might still follow you, but they won't touch you."

Jay frowned. "What do you mean, something that represents him?"

"A totem, bro," cr0w said. "Like a cross to a vampire – pow."

"Like the circle thing?" I said.

They all looked mystified.

Holly Soames①
22/11/2019 06:37
Consult with partner agencies re. capability.

Holly Soames②
22/11/2019 06:49
Senior CT leadership and DPS made aware of this allegation for info.

"They haven't read the chapters," Jay reminded me. "They don't know."

"We can't tell you what to use," Morgana said. "But it might work. For a while, at least. Enough time to run away."

She looked at her watch. "We've got other places to be. Don't tell anyone we told you this."

"But between us, you should stop," awe said. He gestured towards Villiers Street. "Go back to normal life."

"That's unofficial, of course," Morgana said. "Ken always says it has to be a personal decision."

They made to leave. Questions flooded into my brain: *Are you speaking to other people? How many people are playing the game? How many have finished it? Can we meet Ken?*

As though reading my mind – although the question he eventually asked was not one I had thought of – Jay said, "One other thing."

Without looking round awe gave a short, barking laugh.

"We can't," Morgana said over her shoulder. "We've told you too much as it is."

"Please!"

I had never heard Jay say that before. Certainly not in that desperate, almost hungry way.

awe did turn then, spinning around so quickly that we both took a step back. He drew himself up, his nostrils flaring.

"The freaks leave Ken alone because he stays neutral," he snarled. "But if we keep helping you, they might start looking at us. And I won't let that happen."

Jay looked away from him, at cr0w. "One more question."

"We're leaving," Morgana said.

cr0w looked at us, torn.

"You promised," I said. "You said you'd help us."

He sighed. "Go for it, dudes."

Jay inhaled. "What happened to Ken?" he said, the words seeming to fall out of him. "What did he see?"

The Rearguard fell silent as a group of people, chatting brightly to each other, strolled along the path towards us. As they passed, they buffeted us as though we were rocks in rapids, ignoring us completely. I found myself checking their faces for smiles that didn't move.

"He tried to kill himself," cr0w said, once the group had been swallowed up by the darkness of the park.

We stared at him.

"But he got better," he went on quickly. "Now he's more like Ken than before."

"And less," awe said cryptically.

"Why?" I said. "Was it what we saw?"

cr0w gave me a small smile. "I don't think so," he said. "He said what he found at the end of the game was the saddest, scariest thing he'd ever seen. But he said it couldn't have been anything else, and that made it OK in the end."

And without another word, they turned as one and walked away.

* * *

"It was terrible," she said. "I still can't understand it. It came completely out of nowhere."

After seeing Ryder climb over the railing on the building's roof, Clarkson tried to alert security, but was too late to stop Ryder from falling twelve storeys to his death. According to other eyewitnesses, Ryder was crying, although others said he seemed almost elated.

"It wasn't him anymore," said a source who wishes to remain anonymous. "He said: 'I wish you could come with me' and then that was it. I'll never forget the look on his face. I haven't been able to sleep since." ❶

Holly Soames①
22/11/2019 07:12
No citation for this. Unable to find any trace of this article on open source.

* * *

Over the next couple of days we tried to think about The Helmsman's koan whenever we could, but it was harder than ever for us to find a time and place to talk it through at any length. Jay and Eoin's house was now out of the question ("Sorry," Jay said uneasily. "He doesn't want you coming round"), and whilst we could manage the odd whispered conversation at Cybotage, it was never enough. And after what The Rearguard had told us about █████████████████, talking in person was the only thing that seemed remotely safe.

"Why don't you just come to mine?" I said one lunchtime.

"I can't. I told Eoin I've stopped. He doesn't even like it that we're still working together."

"Just say you have to work late." I looked around, suddenly acutely aware of how this would sound to anyone listening.

He was wavering, but in the end I didn't need to press it any further, because a solution came from the unlikeliest of sources: Richard.

"Ah, Jay," he said, coming into the kitchen. "Just the man. A job's come in, short notice. Newport, starting tomorrow."

"Really? Why didn't I know about it?"

Richard fidgeted. "It's an add-on. Someone put it in a proposal for a threat assessment."

The someone was him, of course. He'd done this a few times since I'd been there – adding in a pentest or some TI work as a freebie to sweeten a bid, without checking with the team leaders whether they had capacity to deliver it.

"And you're only telling me now? Richard, my team's flat-out, I—"

I cleared my throat softly, and he understood.

"How long for?"

Richard bobbed his head, relieved. "Just an overnighter, that's all. Stolen laptop scenario."❶

"Fine, I'll do it," Jay said, standing up. "I'm taking Alex with me."

Holly Soames①
22/11/2019 07:34

A type of pentest in which the testers are given a laptop of a standard build for the client organisation and asked to compromise it, simulating what an attacker would do if they stole or found a laptop in real life.

"The budget—"

"Will have to stretch. I might need an extra pair of hands. Unless you want to tell the client they'll have to wait until September?"

"No, no," Richard said. "No, that's fine. Two testers. Fine."

"Great. Come on, Alex, let's book some travel."

"Don't forget receipts!" Richard called after us as we left.

* * *

We got to Cardiff at about seven-thirty that evening. Neither of us had said much on the journey; like that strained first week in Basingstoke, we gazed out of our own windows as the countryside blurred past, one of us occasionally starting start to say something – "Maybe—", or "What about—" – before lapsing into silence. Now that we were finally alone, the koan reared in front of us, stubborn and solid and impassable – and, behind it, the basilisk. How would we even know when we had the answer?

We checked in, dropped our stuff off in our respective rooms, and met in mine.

"We have to focus on the koan," Jay said when I opened the door. "Forget Fairlop Waters, forget the weapon, forget what The Rearguard said. We just have to get this down."

"Nice to see you too."

He strode past me, into the room. "An unhackable box. There's no such thing, right? So let's just send that."

I did, and over the next hour we sent several variations on the same theme: "nothing is unhackable", "yes", "no", "mu"❶ but there was only ever that obnoxious, infuriating response:

Holly Soames①
22/11/2019 13:23
See c4 THT.

(no subject) **Inbox**

The Basilisk <thisisthebasilisk@gmail.com>

to me

NOPE!

As I'm sure many have done before us, we were trying to find some consistency in the logic, some mental schema which would allow us to take a shortcut in the problem-solving process and arrive at a demonstrable answer – but it seemed that, as The Helmsman had promised, koans refused to work that way. *Can you hack an unhackable box?* On first inspection, and from a dualist perspective, the answer seemed obvious: no, by definition,[*] but that wasn't good enough for The Helmsman.

"Maybe it just doesn't sound Zen enough," Jay said, gazing at the bland cream wall of the hotel room. "Maybe it needs to be in the right format – you know, with the dialogues and poems and everything."

"The format isn't important," I said wearily. "Koans are about enlightenment, right? Not just sounding enlightened. The Helmsman said some of them take years to answer."

[*] Theologians and logicians may recognise this as vaguely similar to an omnipotence paradox: 'Can God create a rock so heavy that he cannot lift it?' Of course, a student of Zen (assuming they would even give you the time of day in answering a question about an omnipotent God) may well resolve this paradox simply by saying 'mu': the question itself is meaningless; both God and the rock are the same. 'Unhackable' is a label many vendors apply to their products, and acts as something of a red flag to hackers. It can never be true, because any system, however secure, can be compromised in some way, by someone, at some point. For every box, there is a vulnerability – lines of code, or a scenario – which has the power to destroy it. The answer that comes to mind is almost as straightforward, and the first answer we sent to The Helmsman: "nothing is unhackable". But this was summarily dismissed by The Helmsman with the usual "NOPE!"

"It can't be years."

"Why not?"

"Because it can't be." He leant back in his chair. "What if… what if we never hack anything at all? How about that?"

"You're just guessing. That's not what it's about."

"You suggest something, then."

"I told you, it's something we need to think about. You can't just… just brute force *thoughts*. Throw stuff out there and see if it sticks."

"I can't wait years, Alex!"

There was something agitated in his voice, something insistent and greedy, and I recognised it because how many times have I heard the same tone in my own words? Then and now? The pleading, ravenous wheedle of addiction. *I need it. One more time. One more time before I pack it in forever.*

"Maybe it wouldn't be such a bad thing to take it slow," I said. "You know, given what—"

"No, you're wrong. They think we're shook up after what happened – they think they've got us rattled. We should push on while they're not looking."

"But—"

"Sorry, were you the one who almost got shot in the head?"

I froze. "That's not fair. It could just as easily have been me."

"But it wasn't."

I clenched my fists a few times, staring down at the rich blue carpet. "Is there something you want to say to me?"

He was looking out of the window, at the shimmering lights of Cardiff, white against the black. "No."

"You blame me for it."

"Alex, I didn't say anything."

"You think I dragged you into all of this. But you

458

wanted to."

"I just…" He stopped, miserable, torn. "I want to know. I have to. But at the same time I really don't fucking want to, you know?"

"I know."

"I wish you hadn't stayed late that evening. I wish—"

"You think I *wanted* this to happen? I wasn't trying to— I was just—"

"I know, I know. Hey. I know." Jay held his hands up. "It's my fault. I shouldn't have let you do it."

"We can stop," I said. "Any time you want, we can stop. Both of us. Just say."

Jay smiled sadly. "Alex, I'd bet you ten grand that one or both of us would be back at it again the same day. You know we would."

A retort formed in my mind and immediately died. He was right. "Yeah."

"Because that's who we are. We know we're going to play, whatever happens. All we're doing is haggling over when, that's all. But at least we're doing it together."

* * *

We stopped by mutual consensus to get something to eat, and instead of going to the hotel restaurant we walked, at Jay's insistence, twenty minutes to Cardiff Bay where, hidden away in a little side-road, was an Indian restaurant called Vasudev's.

"I love this place," Jay said, as the restaurant came into view. "Eoin and I came here before we got married."

"What were you doing in Cardiff?" I said. I looked at the laminated menu on the window. It wasn't typical North or South Indian restaurant fare. There were mentions of infused smoke, things ignited at the table, chilli foam, spherification.

"The Doctor Who Experience," Jay said. "Eoin's a fan."

459

The name brought the shutters down on that thread of conversation. I smiled awkwardly and we went inside, where a waiter led us to a table near the back. The restaurant was crowded and humid, the windows steamed up.

The waiter brought us drinks and took our orders.

"I've thought of a nick for you, by the way," Jay said when he'd left.

"Oh yeah?"

"Yeah."

"Well?"

"I'm not telling you yet." He smiled. "I'll tell you afterwards."

I knew what he meant: when we'd finished the game. What was it, Jay? What was the handle you had for me? Of all the questions I have for you this is the least important, but it still means something.

I sipped my drink and said what I'd been thinking since we sat down.

"Eoin hates me, doesn't he?"

Jay waved a hand, shooing the thought away. "He'll understand. He just needs time, that's all. He never takes anything seriously until it's so bad he can't ignore it, and then he flips out."

"From crosswords to guns," I said. "I get it."

"Yeah, he's struggling with it. Escape rooms, you get out and it's over."

I knew exactly what he meant. The Helmsman's game only ever led to rooms inside rooms, and at least one of them – maybe all – was booby-trapped. It seemed unlikely that the next stages would be any kinder.

"We'll be careful," I said. "And like you said, we'll do it together."

Part of me – quite a small part, if I am brutally honest – was clawing frantically at its face at this point and screeching. *They held a GUN to his head, Alex! Walk away and make sure he does too! Walk away and never think about it again!*

I slapped it and told it to shut up.

"I'm glad he's out of it, to be honest," Jay said. "It's better he doesn't know."

It just means two of you will die instead of three! the small part shrieked, its voice cracking. *How can you both be so fucking DUMB?*

"We'll be OK," I said. "When we tell people – when it gets out – he'll understand, right?"

"Of course he will."

Tell him to FUCK OFF! Insult him, hurt him, lie to him, just make him go away!

We were quiet for a while, looking out of the window or down at the scratched wooden table, while the diners around us chatted and laughed. When our food arrived we talked about Vegas, but the koan was on the table in front of us the whole time, clamouring for our attention.

*   *   *

The engagement itself went well, the two of us finding some mildly interesting issues with the laptop – Jay trusted me enough by then to leave me to my own devices and only offered advice when consulted – and when we returned to Cybotage, there were only two days before Vegas.

Cybotage was such a tiny operation that we didn't even leave a skeleton staff for the week. I asked Ronnie why Richard, so notoriously tight-fisted, would tolerate shutting down – the expectation that we'd still respond to emails in the evening notwithstanding – and she smiled humourlessly.

"Because there'd be a fucking revolt if he didn't. Look at this place." She gestured at the office. "Not a pool table or chillout pod in sight. Nobody's here for the money. Vegas is the only perk we get. It works out cheaper for him in the end. The tight cunt."

But she said it good-naturedly. For all that everyone mocked Richard's penny-pinching, I think we knew it was well-intentioned. He genuinely wanted Cybotage – never odds-on to flourish, being the tiny outfit it was – to succeed. Cracking down on what he saw as unnecessary expenses,* and promising clients the moon on a stick, were the only ways he knew how to do it. I can't remember who told me – Omar, perhaps, which would be ironic because those two argued the most about money – but someone said that Richard paid himself a very meagre salary, less than Jay and Ronnie.

So, in the days leading up to our departure, we wrapped up what we could, activated our out-of-offices ("Don't say you're not responding to emails," Richard reminded us, "say there may be a slight delay in replying"), and compared itineraries.

So frantic were those forty-eight hours that I barely thought about the koan. Jay and I didn't get a chance to discuss it again before we left, but just knowing that we were both thinking the same thing was reassuring in itself.

In idle moments, lying in bed at night, I wondered if The Helmsman's weapon would hurt us when we found it.

On Saturday, at nine-thirty in the morning, our flight departed from Gatwick Airport, lumbering into the sky and across an ocean. Jay, sitting a few rows in front of me, had about three days left to live.

* * *

---

* It has just occurred to me that I don't know how he reacted to the news that we would have to take a financial hit because of my mistake at the insurance company, or what the size of that hit was. I assume Jay had that discussion with him, but I don't remember Jay mentioning it to me, and Richard certainly didn't. In any other company I would have faced some sort of disciplinary action, but I'd like to think that Jay told Richard to go easy on me – or even that Richard decided that himself.

I slept the entire flight, only waking when we were circling McCarran, the brown-gold desert beneath us, and I was groggy when we reached Immigration – a particularly torturous process involving a long snaking queue, an icy customs hall and truculent border officers.

"It's always like this," Jay mumbled, as we inched down the line towards the row of black booths.

Finally we got through and retrieved our bags. When we left the airport I felt the buckling hot breath of the Vegas summer for the first time, so oppressive it seemed to exert a physical weight.

We queued again for taxis. Nina, Kevin, Richard and I got into the first one, the others into a car behind. The driver❶ got out to help put our suitcases in the back, and his jaws were fixed in a wide gleaming smile.

It's fine, I told myself after the initial jolt of terror. *The Rearguard said they might keep following us for a while. It doesn't mean anything.*

I spent the ride to the hotel staring at the back of the driver's head, and catching occasional glimpses of his bared teeth in the rearview mirror. He was short and fat, and from what I could discern from the few words he'd spoken to us – "WHERE TO FOLKS?" – he had a nasal American accent, but there was still that lilting sing-song pitch to it. Nina and Richard were deep in conversation, Kevin occasionally chipping in, and there was nothing to indicate that they had noticed anything amiss.

The driver spoke.

"Y'ALL FROM THE UK?" he said, his eyes fixed on the road.

"That's right," Richard said beside me. "London."

"LONDON," the driver said. "YES LONDON. THE WEST END PICCADILLY CIRCUS BUCKING-HAM PALACE. FIRST TIME IN VEGAS?"

"For Alex it is."

The driver's eyes flickered to me in the rearview mirror, and one closed in a brief wink.

"ALEX? YOU'RE GONNA LOVE IT ALEX. IT'S A GREAT TOWN. MAKE SURE YOU BEHAVE YOURSELF ALEX."

"Yeah, Alex," Nina said, on Richard's other side. "Behave yourself!"

I looked away.

We could see the towers of hotels now, huge glass and metal monoliths that winked in the sun. And fuck me it was hot; even in the air-conditioned cab I could feel the sweat running down my back.

"YOU HERE FOR A CONFERENCE? THE BLACK HAT?"

"Black Hat and DEF CON," Kevin said in the front.

"ALL THE HACKERS COME TO TOWN FOR THE BLACK HAT AND THE DEF CON. I HEARD A HACKER COULD DO ALMOST ANYTHING TO MY PHONE MY COMPUTER EVEN MY METER IF HE WANTED. I HEARD I SHOULD SWITCH MY GADGETS OFF FOR THE WEEK THAT TRUE? COULD HE DO THAT?"

"Or she," I said.

The blank eyes narrowed slightly, almost in amusement.

"YOU'RE A HACKER ARE YOU ALEX?"

"I wouldn't worry too much," Richard said. "A lot of it's just hype."

"THAT RIGHT?" the driver said. He tilted his face, showing me his grin in the mirror, wide and empty, a warped abyss. "I THINK IF A PERSON HEARS SOMETHING THEY SHOULD PAY ATTENTION."

Richard made a polite noise of agreement, and turned to me with a 'takes all sorts' smile.

After what seemed like years the cab pulled up outside the hotel, nudging its way through throngs of tourists and gamblers. Before it stopped I opened the door and almost threw myself out, walking very fast towards the lobby, barely noticing the noise and the heat.

When I reached the doors I turned back. Richard and Kevin were taking the suitcases out of the boot, while Nina fished out dollars from her purse to pay the driver, who was holding out his hand and staring forwards.

When the suitcases were all out, the boot was closed, and Nina had got out of the car, the driver turned to look directly at me, just for a moment. He lifted both hands and rapidly put them in front of his eyes, over his ears, and then his mouth.

SEE NO EVIL HEAR NO EVIL SPEAK NO EVIL

One more slow wink, and he drove off.

"Thanks for the help, Alex," Richard muttered, struggling to wheel both his suitcase and mine. I took it from him.

The other cab pulled up. Jay, getting out, looked at me.

"Everything OK?" he said.

"Fine," I said, but when the others walked through the doors I grabbed his arm.

"He was one of them," I said. "The cab driver."

"What? You mean in your cab?" Jay turned and shaded his eyes to scan the chaos of the taxi rank – drivers and porters calling to each other, loud laughter, electronic music from somewhere – but of course the car was long gone. "You sure?"

"Of course I'm sure!"

Jay shrugged. "They're probably just keeping tabs, that's all. Did he say anything?"

"Not really."

"There you go, then. Come on."

We followed the others into the vast lobby.

* * *

We queued, again, for what felt like hours, and I watched a few hundred people stream in and out of the sunlit glass doors. Sunbathers in shorts and swimwear – the hotel had a pool, I remembered Nina saying – and middle-aged gamblers in bright shirts and people

465

my own age, laughing and screaming in voices far too loud, stabbing into my skull, piercing the clamour of the casino which lay just beyond the lobby. I heard chiptune music, and machines, and there was a strange smell, too – unfamiliar but not unpleasant, a clean, perfumed odour. Later, I realised it was the smell of the desert. It was everywhere in Vegas, and it gave me a constant headache.

I wondered if The Helmsman had ever been here, in this very lobby – perhaps also attending Black Hat and DEF CON. Perhaps he had been with friends or colleagues, chatting lightly with them in the queue while inside his head, rough and barely formed, writhed the notion of the weapon.

Finally we were all checked in, room keys in hand. Richard had booked us all on the same floor which, needless to say, was the cheapest accommodation the hotel offered.

We struggled through the carpeted casino floor to the lifts with our suitcases, through a restless swarm of activity in which slot jockeys sat placidly like drugged animals and stared at shining numbers – and spilled out onto the fourteenth floor a short time later, a rumpled collection of luggage and tired bodies. We separated, promising to meet back at the lobby in a couple of hours. "By Greg's lion, remember," Sophie reminded us.

Jay and I were heading in the same direction. The corridor was long. At one point, out of breath from lugging my wheeled suitcase across the thick nap of the carpet, I looked back and realised I could no longer see the lifts.

Everything in Vegas was bigger than it needed to be, as though objects and buildings and people felt the urge to stretch out and fill the blankness of the desert with evidence of their existence. We always need to prove we are alive.

We came to my room first.

"I'll knock for you," Jay said, and yawned. "Fuck, I'm tired. It's—" he checked his watch "—it's two in the morning back home."

"Lightweight," I said, and he gave me the finger and walked away.

I stayed outside my door, watching him until the endless corridor swallowed him up.

* * *

We all met in the lobby later, and there was one of those long, dull discussions about where to go to dinner – the kind you only get with a large group of people who know each other but not very well. Eventually, a consensus was reached but I'm afraid I couldn't tell you what it was. The restaurant was somewhere in Paris or Bally's, and the food was OK – some sort of burger place, I think – but I don't remember much beyond that. I could barely keep my eyes open. It was all I could manage to shovel food into my mouth and occasionally contribute to the conversations going on around with me.

"How are you finding Vegas?" Nina asked me at one point. Even her clear bright eyes were dull with fatigue.

"Hot," I said. "And weird."

"It is, isn't it? Like everything's fake! Like you're in a dream, but not in a good way."

For once I found myself agreeing with her. Las Vegas was exactly that, a photorealistic video game. However immersive it seemed, it was all artifice. If you scratched at the surface you found millions of years of sand.

We paid, and it must have been close to ten by the time we started to stroll back to the hotel. Even that late at night it was close to thirty degrees outside. My clothes chafed and stuck to me in the heat, and I longed for my air-conditioned hotel room, and sleep.

We passed a busker playing a guitar, singing something soft and beautiful. It was so incongruous for that place, a city where brightest and loudest is always best, and I stopped to listen. I wondered how the woman had gotten here, or whether she was from Vegas and trying to leave.

Jay joined me. I didn't recognise the song the woman was singing, and have not been able to find it since, so I assume it was something she'd written herself. It was lovely – dark, and low, and sad. The final moment of peace.

The song ended.

"Tomorrow," Jay said. "Tomorrow, we're going to solve it."

We caught up with the others, and when we got back to the hotel I slept for twelve hours. It was the last dreamless night I would ever have.

*　*　*

Standing in line for our Black Hat badges the next morning, in a lush and ornate corridor of the Mandalay Bay Hotel, it struck me that I had never seen so many security professionals gathered in one place. The queue twisted around multiple lanes, thousands of people gathered in small groups: some were high-ranking security professionals in suits and ties, or polo shirts and chinos, others scruffier in hoodies and cargo shorts. There were a number of DEF CON badges on show from previous years, Jack's❶ face smiling everywhere. I wondered what DEF CON would be like: more chaos and colour, I imagined. Black Hat was huge, but more sober than I'd expected.

Holly Soamesⓘ
22/11/2019 08:12
DEF CON logo.

I collected my badge from a machine and went to a booth where I received my complimentary Black Hat backpack, schedule, notebook and pen, and various sponsor leaflets.

I suppose more about that first day should stand out to me, but the events that followed it have blurred the memories somewhat. I remember going to a series of talks in cathedral-like ballrooms, the speakers tiny figures at the front, their slides projected onto a series of mammoth screens suspended from the ceiling. Smaller talks, anticipated to be less popular, were confined to odd little rooms hidden at the end of narrow corridors, or on sparsely populated basement floors that were difficult to find. I went to one of these – there were only around twenty people in the audience, and I could have easily been at a completely different event.

The main thing I remember is the sheer number of attendees; as the day wore on I realised it wasn't just the most security professionals I had ever seen in one place, but perhaps the most people. The corridors in the Mandalay were wide but still crammed wall-to-wall between sessions, as the ballrooms vomited out hundreds. Making one's way to a talk was a question of closely following the person in front, riding their slipstream, allowing at least fifteen minutes for the journey, and trying not to get irritated at how often I was jostled.

Most of the people – attendees and speakers – were men, naturally, and white men at that. I saw perhaps one woman for every fifty blokes, although, according to Nina, there were at least fewer 'booth babes'❶ at conferences these days. I'd been aware that I was a minority in my chosen industry relatively early on, but as I watched the speakers on stage I decided that one day I would be up there too, presenting my own

Holly Soames①
22/11/2019 08:26
Term for women hired by companies to staff/be present at vendor booths during trade shows. And for the record, WEBSTER has a point in her footnote here.

---

* Infosec in general has a huge fucking problem with misogyny, as Kate O'Flaherty notes: (https://www.forbes.com/sites/katcoflahertyuk/2018/08/15/sexual-harassment-in-the-cyber-security-industry-how-one-woman-is-fighting-back/?sh=1bcc6d50576e).

research – perhaps even on The Helmsman's game.[*]

"Wait until we get to DEF CON," Omar grunted, as we inched our way through a particularly solid section of crowd at midday, trying to make our way back to the Mandalay proper to get lunch. "They call it LineCon.❶ It's basically one big queue."

"This is like rush hour on the Tube," I said, dodging a very broad man carrying three backpacks and several Peli cases. "Except it lasts all day."

"Hey, it beats working."

We eventually fought our way back to the casino, only to find that every single food outlet was choked with people wearing bright blue Black Hat badges and black Black Hat bags.

Omar checked his phone. "Everyone's going back to the hotel for lunch. Want to come with?"

I nodded and we traipsed over to the monorail station – a small white air-conditioned shuttle. It had been installed so that visitors could spend less time in the crunching Vegas heat and, whoever's idea it had been, I offered up a silent prayer of thanks to them. One thing the Vegas veterans had been completely right about was the amount of walking. I was reasonably fit back then, and thought nothing of walking everywhere (predominantly because I didn't have a car; I never learned how to drive), but one day in, my feet were aching and I could feel the gnaw of a blister forming on my heel. Maybe it was the desert air, but everything seemed much closer than it was in reality. From the

Holly Soames①
22/11/2019 08:37
DEF CON that year was held in CAESARS PALACE, a venue the same size or larger than MANDALAY BAY, but historically it had taken place in smaller hotels – for many years at the RIO – and this, together with its greater attendance, gave it a reputation as a challenge to navigate.

---

[*] I know now, of course, that this will never happen. It isn't an easy thing to realise that one's ambitions were fucked before they ever really began, and I think if I were a different person that knowledge could break me. But perhaps I will make my mark in other ways. If this document is my legacy, then someone – perhaps you – might one day present it at somewhere like Black Hat or DEF CON, and I will achieve my ambition posthumously. That would be some compensation, I suppose. Try and do that for me, would you? If you can. No pressure.

Mandalay the hotel looked like a mere five-minute amble, but having walked the distance that morning I knew it took half an hour, most of it exposed to the brutal sunshine.

Other than that minor complaint, I was enjoying myself. The talks I had seen – hacking alarm systems; long-term social engineering; command injection frameworks – had been amazing, lighting up all sorts of sparks in my brain. And I was surrounded by thousands of people who spoke my language and were filled with the same passion and obsession as I was. It was glorious. Perhaps it was just my naiveté, swept away by my first experience of a security con, but it wasn't a stretch of the imagination to think that I might be attending conferences like this for the rest of my career. And if Jay and I could finish the game, and we told people about it, surely we'd be legends – known throughout security, throughout the world – as the people who had solved The Helmsman's game.[*]

Omar and I caught up with the others at a small cafe in the hotel, which was free of Black Hat attendees but busy nonetheless. On the way a stream of people, there for another conference by the look of the badges they wore around their necks, passed by.

"How many cons do they have here?" I said, as we joined the back of the line.

"Oh, loads," Sophie said. "Probably two or three a week."

"That one's a pet food conference," Nina volunteered. "I might try and get in later for the lulz."

"I don't know why they have to hold it in summer," Richard said. He looked distinctly uncomfortable, even in the aggressively air-conditioned casino and

_____

[*] It's possible, perhaps even likely, that Shane Carson, and Sarah Mayers, and Beverly McLagan, and all the others, had similar ambitions. Back then, of course, I didn't know about any other players except Ken Onek.

despite wearing a sleeveless shirt and shorts, which showed off a pair of legs like stubby candles covered in wispy grey hair. He had neglected to wear sunscreen, and his face, neck and arms were a vivid, alarming shade of red.

"Sun's out, guns out, Richard?" Ronnie said. He gave her a filthy look.

We moved forward in the line, and I scanned the casino. It was dark and bright, and the carpets were a rich ornate scarlet which gave everything a curiously stately air, belied by the flashing lights and screens.

"Notice anything?" Jay said, seeing me looking.

"What do you mean?"

He pointed up at the ceilings. At intervals of about a foot there were small black circles mounted on the white plaster, stretching across the expanse of the casino.

"Cameras," he said. "No clocks. And no windows. They don't want people to know if it's night or day."

I shuddered. "That's horrible."

Jay lowered his voice. "Have you seen…?"

"Nothing."

Throughout the morning I'd expected to see ████ ██████████████, either tailing us from a distance or somewhere in the crowds, but if they had been there I'd missed them.

"How's Eoin?" I said. "Was he OK about you coming?"

"He wasn't thrilled. Kept saying he was going to call the police out here and get them to keep an eye on me."

"Oi!" Nina said. I jumped, and then realised we were holding up the line. I nudged Jay and we moved up.

"Always whispering, these two," Nina said to nobody in particular.

"Jealous?" Jay said with a smile.

Nina laughed and flicked her hair. "You wish."

I was going to say something, but Ronnie had gotten into an argument with the cashier, which Richard was trying to defuse, and by the time everything had been settled I had forgotten what it was.

* * *

We ate our lunches crowded around a couple of small tables in the cafe – which, like all eateries in the hotel, functioned as a building within a building – and discussed the talks we'd seen that morning. Much of the conversation was about the keynotes, which I hadn't seen – they'd been rammed, and as I arrived late the staff wouldn't let me in – so I chewed my sandwich in silence and watched the gamblers. Even now, at midday, there were people on the roulette tables, although the most popular attraction seemed to be the one-armed bandits. Waitresses wandered back and forth serving drinks and cigarettes from trays, so that patrons had no reason to leave their seats other than to go to the toilet.* It bothered me, just as the lack of clocks and windows had done, and I couldn't work out why until I understood that I was looking at not so much an attraction or a pastime as a machine, one carefully engineered to extract money from people in the most efficient and insidious manner possible. Whatever The Helmsman's weapon is, cognitive weapons which exploit our mental vulnerabilities have been around for a long time.

After lunch we split up into smaller groups to go to various talks. Ronnie and I found ourselves in a talk about IR management, a topic I knew hardly anything about but which was Ronnie's field of expertise – and

---

* Surely, at some point, a casino will come up with a way for patrons to pass waste while seated at slot machines. What a time to be alive that will be. Lordy, how we're fucked.

from her occasional impatient sighs I got the feeling that she was not impressed.

Before she had the chance to tell me what she didn't like about it, I escaped to the next talk by myself. Interestingly enough, it was about several vulnerabilities found in a product which the vendor had claimed was unhackable. This made me think about the koan again, and as the speaker droned in a dour monotone, I allowed my mind to wander, lost in writhing snakes of thought. If the clash of applause at the end of the talk hadn't startled me back to reality, I might have sat there for hours.

We reconvened at the end of the day, and agreed to meet downstairs later in the evening and go out to dinner again. Jay, Sophie, Omar and I headed to the lifts, while the others wandered off to a bar.

On the fourteenth floor, Sophie and Omar took one branching corridor, Jay and I the other. As soon as they were out of earshot, Jay stopped and turned to me.

"Couple of hours before dinner. Want to talk about the… the *dance*?"

"Was that supposed to be a codeword?"

"You knew what I meant, didn't you?"

I hesitated. "Maybe it would be better to leave it this week."

"Seriously?"

"The cab driver—"

"But you've been thinking about it."

This was true, of course.

"Come on," Jay said. "I think I might have something."

We reached my room and I unlocked the door with my keycard, glancing up and down the never-ending hallway.

* * *

474

Jay sat in the swivel chair behind the desk, and pulled up the first chapter of *The Helmsman Texts* on his laptop.

"It's the cave," he said.

I flopped on to the bed; my feet were killing me. "What is?"

"I see what you meant. Before. It's not just— It can't be like those other koans. Not normal. Because—"

"Because The Helmsman's not normal."

"Well, yeah, but listen. It's all part of the same thing. He's trying to tell us something."

"Yes, but what?"

"Breaking out of the cave. The Riddle Machine. The crossword. The white flag. The plays, the stories. And Fairlop Waters. That more than anything."

Jay smiled, that supercilious I-know-more-than-you smile, but it didn't bother me anymore. Jay never smiled like that because he found pleasure in withholding knowledge; it was because he was pleased that he was about to share it with you. "Think about it – who do we think The Helmsman's trying to recruit?"

"Hackers."

"Yes, but what are hackers? First principles – what are hackers, in themselves?"

I mulled this over. "People who solve problems?"

"That's not how I'd describe it."

"Go on, then."

"It's someone who tries to understand something – understand it at a very deep level. And once they do—"

"They can break it."

"He's looking for people who think a certain way. Get it? Not just techies, but people who can understand things. People *willing* to understand them. So much that they can break them."

Even then he was getting closer to the end, and I didn't know it. I had pulled him into this, I had been the one to find it, and yet it was Jay whom The Helmsman finally accepted.[*]

I frowned. "How does that help us with the koan, though?"

Jay repeated it to himself. "Hack the unhackable. Break the unbreakable. But remember what he said about the cockroaches? Everything is molecules."

Something made me glance over towards the door, and I saw something there, something wrong, but it didn't immediately register.

"This is all sounding a bit cod philosophy," I said distractedly. "What are you saying? Nothing's real?"

"No, listen. How can you break something, if it's all not real? If you can't even tell what's real and what isn't? How can you hack something if everything... if everything's like Fairlop Waters? It's like... it's *meaningless*." ❶

Something almost snapped, then, inside my head; I felt it straining. Perhaps it was the closest to any kind of enlightenment I have ever come. Certainly I have never felt anything like that since, no matter how hard I've tried, and if this document is anything it is a temple to my unenlightenment. I have never been more in the dark. But at that moment something threatened to give way, and had I let it I would either have gone mad or seen things, seen them the way they had been by the lake's shore. Perhaps they are the same thing in the end. Perhaps I would have been infected, and I'm sure The Helmsman would say that's the same thing as enlightenment. But the logical, dualistic part of my brain, out of some self-preserving instinct, pushed it aside.

---

[*] I have wondered if the fact that Jay got the answer meant he was better prepared – more ready or more qualified, in some way – to arrive at the final answer than I was. Maybe, to The Helmsman, he was a more suitable candidate. I don't know how to feel about this – if I should be jealous or thankful. Not that it matters now, of course, but I dwell on it sometimes.

Holly Soames①
22/11/2019 08:52
For what it's worth, I'm currently here with this: It's already hacked. The box, its creator, the hack, the need to break it and what it contains are all the same thing. The hack is just picking a certain perspective to view it from.

"So the answer is what, then? That the question doesn't make sense?"

"No, it's not as simple as that. It's… If everything is already in a state of being hacked, and not hacked – then even the concept of hacking is pointless. It doesn't mean anything. It's just a distraction, an illusion. And if hacking is an illusion, *then everything is*. See what I mean?"

I rubbed my eyes. "I think so," I said, although this was mostly a lie. Jay, however, was already typing something out.

"Are you sending that?" I said, and he nodded.

"It's right. I know it is."

He finished typing and we waited, but no reply came, despite Jay continually refreshing the page. With the previous challenges The Helmsman's responses were almost instantaneous, as though he'd been sitting glued to his inbox, eagerly awaiting each new submission.

"Maybe he's reading them personally now," I said. "When it gets past a certain stage."

"Maybe. We should—"

There was a knock at the door and a female voice called out softly, "HOUSEKEEPING."

I got up, and it was as I was opening the door that I realised what I'd seen when I'd looked over a few minutes earlier: the shadow of feet, just visible in the gap between carpet and sill. Someone standing, listening. And the voice – those rising, falling, arrhythmic tones, muffled by the door – finally filtered through to my brain.

A mental alarm began to shriek in my subconscious, and I immediately tried to push the door closed but it was too late. Whoever was standing behind it gave it an almighty shove that knocked me over and I fell back into the room.

I looked up, hardly hearing Jay's shout, and saw a blonde woman❶ with thin, foxlike features standing in the doorway, dressed like one of the maids in a beige shirt and black trousers. She was slender, and would have been attractive had it not been for the impossibly wide and mirthless grin contorting the lower half of her face.

In her right hand she was holding a long, curved knife.❷ Empty eyes rolled down to me.

"GOODBYE ALEX WEBSTER AND THEN GOODBYE JAY MORTON."

Holly Soames②
22/11/2019 09:19
Weapons marker
(sharps/blades)
added to file.

The knife began its descent – deliberately, painfully, slowly, as though she had all the time in the world. Had she moved quickly I might have reacted out of sheer instinct, but the slowness of it all paralysed me.

She'll kill me as I lie here, I thought, *while I'm in shock. She'll bring that knife down so I can see it, and I'll feel it inch by inch, first the sting as it breaks the skin and then foreign metal creeping into my flesh, the long blade invading my body. It'll be so cold. The sound of muscle and cartilage splitting as the blade presses in, more weight behind it, a severing of something as it destroys nerves and interrupts neural pathways, all the way down into the spine and through to the floor beneath me, grating against bone, and then the return journey, organs clenching the blade with their suction, the final release and the blood, released from its prison. Then what? Darkness? A light? Nothingness? Mu?*

I watched helplessly as the knife crawled down, and then something thin and dark skimmed rapidly through the air and struck the woman in the face. There was a muted crack from somewhere in her neck. Jay had thrown his laptop at her.

"Push her!" he screamed. "Alex, push her out!"

I got to my feet and thrust at the woman hard, in the centre of her chest – her body was unyielding, like hard rubber – and she reeled back into the corridor.

I flung the door shut, my fingers fumbling with the bolt and the lock until they both clicked home.

From the corridor there was an enraged scream and the door trembled in its frame as the woman threw herself against it.

"We need something," I said, breathing hard. "A totem. We need a totem!"

"What are you *talking* about?" Jay said. "*Call fucking security!*"

The door shook with a tremendous bang. It was the second time in about two weeks that I had been locked in a room while someone attempted to force their way in, and the novelty had worn off. I leant against the door, bracing it with my shoulder, and thought quickly. What had they said? It had to be something important to The Helmsman, something—

"Pass me that pad," I said, pointing at the little hotel-supplied notepad on the bedside table, with a cheap biro on top of it. "And the pen. Quick!"

Jay gaped at me, his mouth working. "The – what?"

"*Pass me the fucking notepad and pen!*"

He stumbled over and dived across the bed, flinging the paper and pen towards me. I scrabbled but couldn't reach them as the door splintered and gave way, slamming into my shoulder. My right arm shrieked with pain.

Blood ran down the woman's face from a cut on her forehead where the laptop had struck her. It was running into her eyes. She shouldn't have been able to see with the amount of blood, but I saw the liquid coursing over her eyeballs and she didn't even blink. Her head lolled to one side.

"WE NEVER WANTED TO KILL YOU ALEX WEBSTER. WE ONLY WANTED YOU TO BE SAFE."

She advanced towards me. I knew if I looked away from her I was dead so I held her gaze, searching for something recognisable – some sign of reason – but there was nothing. Whatever saw through her eyes couldn't think and didn't want to.

"Please," I said, even though I knew it was pointless. "Please."*

And then Jay saved both our lives for the second time that night. As the woman stepped closer and the knife once more crept down towards me, he bounded on to the bed, seized the bedsheets, and threw himself at the woman so that he enfolded her entire upper body, pinning her arms to her side.

"Run!" he said.

I staggered past the two of them and fell out of the room, landing on my knees in the corridor. I span round to see Jay grappling with the woman, who was bucking under the duvet, her head whipping from side to side. Her right arm, still held fast by the sheets, was straining, twisting, and the tip of the knife appeared through the white material, tearing a hole.

I got up and gestured furiously to Jay. He took a step back, steadied himself, and then pushed the woman away from him with all his might. She went spinning across the room, hitting the desk and tumbling over it, still entangled in the sheets.

Jay charged out of the room and then stopped dead, a peculiar, detached expression on his face.

"What the fuck are you doing?" I said. "We have to go!"

He stepped back into the room and picked up his laptop. There was blood on it. He examined it carefully. On the far side of the room, the thing trapped in the sheets tried to free itself.

I leant forward, dragged Jay out, and slammed the door shut. He turned to me, and his face cleared.

"What did you mean, a totem?" he said.

"The Rearguard," I said. "Remember what they told us?"

* Not inspired last words, I'll grant you, but how many times have they been said, all the same? Sometimes it's all we can think to say.

480

Jay started towards the lifts. "Forget it. We have to get help."

I followed him for maybe twenty feet, then hesitated.

"Not that way! We have to go to your room! Come on!"

"My—"

"Jay, come *on!*"

We ran back the way we had come, past my room and towards Jay's, Jay quickly overtaking me. As I passed my splintered, open door I saw the woman hurl herself out of the room, falling weightily against the locked door opposite. She got up and started to run. The grin seemed wider, more frenzied. It took over her entire face like she was a rabid Cheshire Cat.

I remember time slowing down as we sprinted for our lives down that endless corridor. I was not conscious of any sound, or thought, only the endless impact of my own footsteps and the surroundings passing in a repetitive and nauseating blur of patterned carpet and textured wallpaper and dim fluorescent lighting and anonymous wooden doors with unreadable numbers. I didn't think Jay's room had been so far from mine. My legs tightened and cramped with the effort, as though a muscle might snap at any moment, and my right arm swung uselessly and sobbed with pain.

Behind us, beyond the woman, the corridor stretched on and on, on and forever, a perfectly straight line extending into space beyond all reason.

"Here!" Jay said. He stopped, and I almost ran into him; had I done so I think we would both have died, because the woman was barely twenty feet from us.

He already had his card out and pressed it against the reader. Green light, click, and we bundled into the room. As soon as we were clear I swung it shut, and a second later the woman crashed against it.

481

"Now what?" Jay said. "What's the fucking plan now, Alex?"

I hurried over to the bedside table and fetched the pen and paper. Another slam against the door and a wail of flat fury.

"You have to draw it," I said. "My arm's fucked. Jay, *draw it.*"

So, with a shuddering, unsteady hand, he did.

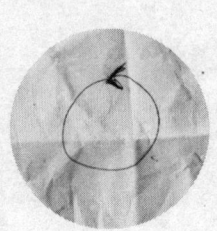

I took it from him and approached the door. The banging from outside stopped at once. I looked through the peephole.

"She's still there," I whispered. "She's not moving."

"What's she doing?" Jay whispered back.

"Nothing."

The woman was standing, knife in hand, blood crawling down her face, grinning.

"I'm going to open the door," I said.

"What? Are you fucking serious?"

"Get ready."

Jay gave me a look that very clearly indicated he thought I had a suicide wish, but he took a deep breath and stood up, bracing himself.

I gripped the handle and very slowly eased the door open, holding the notepad out in front of me.

The woman looked from me to Jay, and back to me, and then her eyes fixed on the sheet of paper in my hand. A sound escaped her stretched lips, a little whine, almost pitiful, of disappointment.

"IT WILL NOT LAST," she said, and then she turned and was gone.

I shut the door.

Jay let out a short, high laugh. "Awesome. We should photocopy it, make a thousand of them."

I put my face in my hands and drew a breath. I wanted to scream but couldn't summon the energy. "I think they know we're still playing."

"You think?"

"Do you want to stop?"

"Do you?"

I thought about it. I was still scared, but, more than that, I was angry.

"No fucking way."

"Me neither. Fuck 'em."

He pulled me into a hug. I can still smell his sweat, the lingering odour of his terror.

"I can't believe you threw your laptop at her," I said, and felt him smile.

"What about that move with the sheets, though?"

"Never seen anything like it."

We pulled apart, and then leant forwards, our foreheads touching.

We stayed like that for a while.

* * *

Much of the rest of that evening is a shifting blur of images and broken words, but I remember Jay pacing up and down, the roar of the air conditioning, the panic still jangling in my veins. I remember him wiping the woman's blood off his laptop with a look of disgust on his face. His guttural cry of delight when he refreshed his inbox.

"*Yes!*"

"We got it?"

Jay turned the laptop screen towards me. On it was the usual blank message, with a PDF attachment.

"We fucking got it," he said. "Alex, we're almost fucking there! We're going to do it! One more to go!"

He span the laptop back round and clicked.

"Let me read it," I said, and struggled to my feet, a wave of exhaustion threatening to push me back down.

He brought his laptop over to the bed and we read together. I didn't know it, but it would be the last chapter of *The Helmsman Texts* I would ever read.

Jay, of course, had one more to go.

Chapter 5

HELLO FRIEND!

I wonder how you're getting on? I wonder if it is starting to GET to you yet? I hope so!! Do you feel it, crawling inside you, this gradual terror that perhaps the world is not as you thought? The fall! How we all fall! Slowly and then all at once!

I remember little about those few days immediately after I told my superiors about the basilisk. The overwhelming memory is of PANIC. The need to DISAPPEAR! At every boarding and checkpoint I expected to be detained and led to a small room with no windows and not enough air.

I travelled on my own passport, ❶ with my own identity. I was naive back then!! I had my grab-bag, containing cash (everything I hadn't splurged on diatomaceous earth!!) and my stolen papers, but it had never occurred to me that one day I might need to pretend to be someone else. No more than we all do anyway!

But it never happened. I saw no furrowed brows. Was never asked any questions. I passed through several countries, and none of them said I was an unwelcome guest!

As I travelled further and further, it began to occur to me that I had gotten away with it. I started to enjoy myself. I found

Holly Soames①
22/11/2019 11:02
Flagged to ILU, possibly now residing outside UK jurisdiction.

the power intoxicating. Within my head swam a secret which would change the lives of my fellow passengers. I never told them, obvs! The basilisk is too precious, and too LETHAL, to be bandied around like any other banal topic of conversation. It deserves to be treated with RESPECT. Which is why you're reading this!!!

I had no destination in mind when I had begun my journey, but one formed on the way. When I got there, I made PLANS.

I went to a country where cash speaks loudly and got myself a new name. ❶

Holly Soames①
22/11/2019 11:35
Subject likely to have multiple aliases, added to file.

I bought a house with no intention of living in it. Instead, I rented it out to tenants, but before they moved in I made my own home 😊

I hired contractors to build a bunker ten feet deep on land adjacent to the house, with poured concrete walls and a reinforced ceiling. Soil was replaced on top, so that the land looked no different than it had before. Armoured cables bring me electricity and broadband. Pipes are connected to the water main and to the sewer. ❷

Holly Soames②
22/11/2019 11:43
Flagged to ILU for possible enquiries re. building work of this nature – someone might remember it.

The bunker is insulated and waterproof. There is no damp. The temperature is more or less constant. Fresh air flows down from a grate. I have a space of around four metres by four, which is more than enough for one person.

A short tunnel leads to a secured hatch on the other side of the road. Once a fortnight I make the journey to the outside world for food. Other than that, I am completely self-sufficient!

No doubt my hole in the ground would not

meet building regulations in many countries. It is more of a cave than anything else. But once the basilisk has stared at you, and you at it, you too will find that aesthetics and comforts and laws do not matter to you much anymore!! Moreover you will find they do not apply to you!

As such, I haven't gone to great lengths re. decoration! There is space to sleep, and for a few books I have managed to collect, but more importantly there is my desk, and my computer, and the means to the game.

The tenants do not know I am here. I like that. I like imagining them going about their lives, twitching and striving and never suspecting that a few yards away below the earth things are happening which will change the world FOREVER.

I swore the contractors to secrecy, paying them extra to ensure they would say nothing. But just to be sure, when the job was done, I killed them. ❶

OR DID I LOL

Of course I didn't! What do you take me for?? I'm not a MURDERER! I could never do such a thing. I simply paid them well. If they ever tell anyone then so be it. I have measures in place 😵

The walls are black. The ceiling is grey metal, still with the contractors' bootprints on it. But it is altogether a far more pleasant abode than my previous residence.

So, what on earth do I DO down here, all on my ownsome, in my hideyhole?

I think. I plan.

I run the game.

* * *

Holly Soames①
22/11/2019 11:48
Flagged to ILU re. possible murder of contractors abroad.

You've come this far, and up to this point I've been rather coy with you. I am sorry!! There are good reasons for it. But I'll be candid with you now. You deserve it, you clever thing.

Since I became infected with my basilisk, my goal has always been to infect others with it. Whilst I won't tell you what the basilisk is JUST yet, I will say that it is too important, too world-changing, not to share. I would be doing humanity a disservice if I did not! I suspect the doubting Thomases amongst you, O ye dafties of little faith, may have at one time or another thought that my basilisk was EVIL. That I was a MAD SCIENTIST, craving the destruction of the WHOLE WORLD by plunging societies into CHAOS and INSANITY.

That's very SILLY! For three reasons! Number one, the basilisk REDUCES suffering. Yes! I am doing a great good. And so will you be when you join me. We are making the world a BETTER PLACE. Of course that is what MAD SCIENTISTS always say but in my case it is true!!

Number two, like any information hazard, the basilisk doesn't affect everyone in the same way. Some people are not affected at all. Some may find certain aspects of their personality or worldview change, but to differing extents. I count myself in this category. And some, I'll admit, do suffer extreme adverse effects. Some sort of short-circuit which seems to occur sometimes. I don't know why, I didn't get the opportunity to do much research into it! This happened to one person - dear old Mr Onek, whom you might have met by now - and he even managed to survive! Fair's fair! If Mr Onek is happy then so am I. He's been through enough. We all have!

Number three, I'm no EVIL GENIUS hell-bent on world domination and/or destruction! I'm an ORDINARY person who discovered something that I need to tell people about! And here you are.

* * *

The first thing I did, when my computer was set up, was to try to find out if the incident back home had made the news. I found nothing. They had hidden it, as they have done several times before. They are very good at that!!

One thing bothered me, which was ██ ██████████████ I had seen in the office, one of whom had tried to grab me. At the time, I had no idea what they were. I have a better understanding now, although it is still conjecture. More on this in the FINAL chapter!

I thought they might be looking for me – them or my former paymasters – but I've been very careful, and have never seen anything which suggests I am being watched or followed. One day someone might find me. If it comes I think it will be a bullet in the back of the head. I won't see it or feel it. This is acceptable. It's better than most get!

So, setting the past aside, I started to think about how my young, beautiful basilisk could be released into the wider world.

My first thought was a BOOK. A missive, a manifesto. Something which would tell truth. Well-researched, fully referenced, supported by my stolen documentation. All those hours of work would not be wasted! I would release it somewhere it couldn't easily be taken down, and wait. I even began work on it. A lot of it is the chapters you have been reading!

But the more I thought about it, the more I

realised this was FLAWED. Even as I spent days and nights writing furiously, I knew there was no guarantee that enough people would read it to make a difference. Possibly, no one at all would read it 😴 The world is a cacophony of noise, and deep underneath the waves is the occasional signal. Only a few penetrate. The world screams in your face, all the time, desperate for your attention and love!! Most of the time we give our attention to the things that scream the loudest, regardless of any intellectual or moral benefit, or lack thereof, that those things may have.

I have no understanding or love of marketing, and only a primitive knowledge of virality gleaned from my RED WORD research. I could spend years writing a book only to find that its readers numbered in the single digits.

So I came up with the GAME.

* * *

The game you have been playing, this little game of mine, has THREE components and it is very sneaky beaky! I am very proud of it.

1. It eventually gives the basilisk to YOU, the player. The game is aimed at hackers and security researchers (although ALL suitable candidates are WELCOME). People, like me, who embrace curiosity and the unconventional. Professional problem-solvers who have always known the world is off-kilter even if nobody else can feel it. People who are willing to challenge the status quo and SLAP the people who say 'but we've always done it like that'!

2. The process of playing the game, in theory, acts as a kind of inoculation against the more extreme effects that the basilisk can cause. By this I mean: if the basilisk were presented to you with no context, you would likely have no reaction, or the worst reaction. One or t'other! But if, like me, you were gradually exposed to the idea of questioning reality, the basilisk is likely to be more effective whilst also not destroying your sanity. That's the hope, anyway! I am using my own experience as a guide. And, sadly, some players have still succumbed to the more serious side-effects. It is a SHAME, but there is no way round it 😵😵😵

3. The game functions as a recruitment campaign for the game beyond the game. Every player who makes it to the final stage and obtains the coveted sixth chapter is invited to join my little group. Few refuse! And then the real game begins.

When someone joins my collective, they also begin to do what I have been doing since the first day. Seeding the game on compromised hosts across the world. ❶

Different sectors, different networks, different formats. We wait for a hacker or researcher to find it (of course, we accept players from all walks of life, but hackers are our main target. ❷ And then they also join the game. In this way, the basilisk slowly spreads.

But to what end, I hear you cry! Mr Helmsman, sir, why all this effort? What is it all in aid of, please?

Holly Soames①
22/11/2019 11:54
Flagged for further investigation (eCrime, NCA).

Holly Soames②
22/11/2019 11:57
Flagged for further research and possible CHIS taskings.

I'll tell you, my lovely patient mooncalf! The winners do not only seed the game, seeking new players. On the networks they compromise, they also seed the basilisk itself. It sits on hosts, dormant, waiting to be triggered. ❶

I took my inspiration from Conficker, that wonderful worm that brought the security world to its knees by infecting millions of hosts and claiming that something momentous would happen on a specific date.

With Conficker of course nothing happened at all in the end! But on my chosen date the basilisk will UNCOIL and the whole world will KNOW. Whether they are ready or not, here it comes!

We have compromised television networks and streaming services! Publishing companies and record labels! Email providers and social media accounts! Emergency broadcast systems and traffic signage! PA and karaoke machines! Magazine and newspaper presses! News sites! Cinemas! ❷ And we will keep going! Right up until the glorious day!

Can you imagine it, friends? Can you picture that day? The basilisk will gaze at ALL, from every screen and page. It will talk and chatter from every speaker and radio and headphone cup.

On that day the world will know and the world will be FREE.

* * *

In its current form the basilisk is unreadable. It sits patiently on hosts, encrypted, undetectable, waiting for a command. If by some chance a copy is accidentally found it matters not. No one will know what it is or

Holly Soames①
22/11/2019 12:02
As per previous comment.

Holly Soames②
22/11/2019 12:06
Flagged for further investigation (eCrime, NCA). Consider proactive monitoring of criminal forums.

what it means. If it is deleted, we simply replace it!

This is why you are playing the game. You are playing to know the truth, and for the opportunity to share that truth with every single person on the planet. Because, all along, you have suspected there is something WRONG with the way things are.

So I seed the game. I divide it into stages, and I make puzzles and riddles so I know the people joining my team are the best. I look for certain skills: technical, linguistic, philosophical. I search for the courageous and the clever. For those who persevere even when their conceptions of what is real start to change, because they simply HAVE TO KNOW. Those are the kind of people I want! The very best of us. People like you. (Why do you think I keep calling you FRIEND? Oh, I wish I could give you a big ol' snuggly cuddly hug!)

I make the game entertaining (I hope you agree!). I make it mysterious. I suffuse it with my truth, so that you better understand the reasons behind it. I mix it with doubt, and fear, and uncertainty, because how you deal with such things matters.

You have got so far, and I am so very proud of you.

Keep going. You are so close.

* * *

It is, of course, your decision. Now that you know what the plan is, you may opt to stop playing. That is your prerogative. It is for that reason that I only reveal the basilisk to people who solve the final problem, because it tells me that they are ready and willing.

So, in the spirit of transparency, as Karen would have said (RIP ha!), ❶ here are some things you should know!

You will never know the date on which the basilisk is to be released to the wider world. You will simply be given targets over a secure channel. For each target, you will be asked to seed the game, and the encrypted basilisk. And then you will move on to the next target. Hack hack hack.

You will never know or communicate with any of the other members of the group. This is for your safety as well as mine. You will only communicate with me (there's a treat for you!!!!).

You must undertake to keep everything about me, the game and the basilisk SECRET until the basilisk is released. Bearing in mind this may be tomorrow, or next month, or in ten years' time. If you tell anyone, I will cut your throat.

OR WILL I LOL

Yes I will. I will!

In return, I'll tell you how to protect yourself from ███████████████.

And I will give you the tools to change the world.

* * *

Once you are in the group, you are IN. So far, only Mr Onek has voluntarily left, and he was a SPECIAL CASE. Most find that once they have been exposed to the basilisk, they, like me, want to do everything in their power to help me!

Finally, and most importantly. I BELIEVE that the design of the game, and the piecemeal nature of the chapters, provides some security against severe side-effects from the basilisk. I BELIEVE this, but I do not KNOW it. You may think you are well-prepared, and yet when you read the sixth chapter you may still die. You may want to harm yourself or others. You may want to quit your job, leave your partner, drive your car into a wall, hurt everyone you see! Shapes and colours may change! I don't want that to happen to you! But I can't promise it won't!

So if you continue you do so at your own risk, on this understanding. Think of it this way: you can gamble everything you know, for a chance to know everything you do not.

And bear in mind, should you decide you do not want to take the risk, you will eventually be exposed to the basilisk anyway. Sorry about that!!!!!!

Think it over.

Horror is everywhere, but beyond understanding. Horror is knowing that there are things which can never be known. Horror is knowing that these things are denied to us forever.

§

All revelation is horror; all horror, revelation.

§

The child who fears monsters cannot describe them!

§

I promised someone once that I would write a book, and dedicate it to them. I never imagined it would be this book. I never imagined I would be writing it here! But we can never know the future; as such, the future is also horror.

§

There is much horror in the present. There is horror in the future, and in the recent past. But there was no horror before we came into being.

§

There is no horror after death, only in the imagining of a world without us in it. But this is horror from a different place, for a different reason.

§

In my darker moments I wonder if there was ever a basilisk at all, or if everything I have been working towards is just another illusion. The chattering of someone who needs HELP.

§

Help never comes.

§

To know the basilisk is to, finally, know oneself - the LACK of oneself. That is the knowledge it provides. That is why it is inescapable.

§

When you gaze upon it you are gazing into a mirror where the face of a doppelganger leers back at you. In its eyes you see the knowledge and are afraid. In its smile and its sadness you see the truth and are glad! In its unnatural movements and gestures you understand the illusion, and are furious that you fell for it so completely and for so long.

§

When you gaze upon the basilisk the lies become clear. You are determined that nobody else should be deceived.

§

The Anglo-Saxons believed that life was like a sparrow flying in the storm outside. For a brief moment, only a second, it flies into a warm and well-lit hall, and experiences comfort. Then it reaches the end, and must feel the storm again.

§

The basilisk tells us this is wrong.

§

I wonder if it has occurred to you, as it has to me, that in reading on, you are willingly sowing the seeds of your own destruction. You aren't just prepared to drink the tasty flavoured powdered instant drink mix. You are THIRSTY for it. Yum yum yum, the end is come!

§

This is the vulnerability in all of us: we cannot stand not to know.

§

Almost at the end of things. What a journey it has been! How have you found it? Be honest, now!

If you have played the game you have solved riddles both technical and linguistic. You have thought laterally, at the edges of problems. You have faced down MONSTERS. You have done research, and reading, and you have come to know yourself better than ever before. You have experienced elation and frustration, despair and joy.

You are a hacker now, even if you were not when you started! That in itself is wonderful - but more than that, you have demonstrated that you are BRAVE!!

From that very first encounter with me - and it was me btw, who wrote those cryptic messages you found - you have shown that satisfaction is a lie, and curiosity is the only truth. You have shown that you are not willing to accept things as they seem. That something burns within you, something which will not stop screaming until it knows the answer.

There is only ONE more step. One more challenge. Once you have completed it, I will not say that you will be able to rest, because it is then that the REAL work begins. But it will be the start of the rest of your life. Everything until now has been a waste of time.

You should not despair. You should be overjoyed! Because you will get the opportunity to address it!

Solve the problem, and you will get the final chapter, and you will weep and rejoice at the basilisk's majesty.

Solve it!

```
Solve it!
SOLVE IT.

All best,
The Helmsman. ❶
```

Holly Soames①   ✕
22/11/2019 23:56

A full assessment will be added at the end of the WEBSTER
PAPER, but from the available material of THT I conclude:

- Identifying THE HELMSMAN is likely to be difficult given lack
of detail, although there are investigative avenues

- Much of the 'research' appears to be based on existing
academic literature, but is largely outside my expertise.
Nevertheless, it's compelling (I have been reading non-stop
for the last few hours, hence the relative lack of comments)

- Without c6 THT I cannot assess the feasibility of the
'weapon/basilisk' described by WEBSTER. There is
insufficient information in c1–5 to make an assessment.
However, it seems plausible that there may be *something*

- There is some independent corroboration of the events
described by WEBSTER (and some discrepancies), but little
or no corroboration of those described by THE HELMSMAN.
However, this may in part be due to the covert nature of the
research he was undertaking

- I suggest prioritising investigative opportunities which will
corroborate any of the claims in c1–5

- I also suggest monitoring and searching for c6 THT

- Whatever this is, we have to pin it down

                                          Reply | Resolve |

I didn't think I would be able to fall asleep – I was shaking with delayed fright as I read the fifth chapter*
– but, somehow, and without meaning to, I sank into a slow black wave of bad dreams.

At some point before morning, when the room was still dark, I opened my eyes and blearily made out Jay at the desk, laptop open in front of him, the screen illuminating his face with its pale light.

* * *

Looking back now, I know he was reading the final chapter. He had worked it out. He had submitted the answer to the last puzzle while I slept. He had finished the game, and he had done it without me.

To this day I have tried, desperately, to remember this sleep-fuzzed image more clearly, to try and discern something which would offer some clue as to what the weapon could be and what happened to Jay. But I could see nothing of the screen, nor was there anything on Jay's face that gave me any sign. His expression was

---

* One of the many things I have wrestled with while writing this document is my reaction to the contents of this chapter. For the first time The Helmsman is more or less explicit about his objectives, and there is a direct invitation to join him (assuming one solves the final puzzle, the nature of which is not clear – it seems that part of the puzzle itself is to work out what the question is). There are no plays in this chapter, or anecdotes, or research into potential candidates for the 'RED WORD' weapon. Those, I'm sure (I hope), will be analysed and picked apart and assessed by more qualified people than me. But the fifth chapter is instead a *direct* appeal to the reader: *will you join me or not?* Knowing what you know – that the basilisk is real, that it has these effects, that the intention is to spread it as far and wide as possible – are you on board, or aren't you? My initial reaction was *fuck no*, and from Jay's reaction I would say he felt the same (although the cold hard facts are that he must have changed his mind at some point during the night), but here's the kicker, the shit in the ointment: *I still wanted to know what it was.* And as I drifted off to sleep I could imagine a scenario whereby we would pretend to join The Helmsman so we could learn what the basilisk was – ignoring the possibility that we might have been adversely affected by it. Other players may have thought the same. We always think that things will be alright, until they're not.

rapt, and still, but that tells me nothing; I had seen that same expression on his face many times. The only thing that was different, and perhaps this is just me imposing what I know now on that memory, is that there were tears running down his cheeks.

It is the final image I have of him. But it is of no comfort to me. It serves as a reminder that in my friend's final moments of sanity – the last opportunity I had to change the course of events – I was six feet away and did nothing. If I had only called out to him, I might have saved his life, and mine, and others. Maybe yours.

And if only he had woken me up, and told me. Then, at least, whatever it was, we would have gone through it together.

But he didn't, and I closed my eyes and went back to sleep. It was the last time I saw him.

9: KILL THE BUDDHA
c. AUGUST 2019 / AUGUST 2018

I woke up later that morning and Jay was gone. ❶ At first I assumed he had gotten up early and gone downstairs for breakfast, but his wallet, keys, phone, and passport were still on the desk, along with his keycard. I sat up, apprehension beginning to radiate through me.

The sheet of paper with the crude ouroboros sketch was still lying beside the door. I don't believe that Jay would have left the room without it, not after the previous evening, although he might have drawn another and taken it with him. But his suitcase was still there, and his laptop ❷ wasn't. Something muttered inside my head: *this isn't right.*

I shuffled into the bathroom, trying to think, absently rubbing my injured arm. It wasn't broken, but a black bruise had formed from shoulder to elbow.

He hadn't taken any toiletries. The mirror above the sink was shattered.*

Did ▮▮▮▮▮▮▮▮▮▮▮▮ get to him somehow? Had they taken Jay hostage for some reason? But *I* was still here; if they had gotten into the room somehow, bypassing the totem, why had they ignored me? Perhaps they had duped him into leaving the room, maybe by impersonating someone else's voice, but I didn't – still don't – believe that he could have been tricked, not by a cheap illusion like that.

Jay in the dark, lit by his laptop screen.

---

* I imagine him staring into it and being horrified at the figure looking back. Punching the glass to try and hurt it.

Holly Soames①
22/11/2019 13:40
WEBSTER was the last person to see MORTON before his disappearance. Check with SCD1 whether there was any indication from the LVMPD that she was a person of interest in their investigation.

Holly Soames②
22/11/2019 13:52
LVMPD advise in their report that this item was not recovered.

Solve the problem, and you will get the final chapter, and you will weep and rejoice at the basilisk's majesty.

The implication of the missing laptop hit me.

I snatched up the ouroboros, stuffing it into my pocket, and hurried back to my own room, past the splintered door, not stopping to wonder what anyone might make of it. I collected my phone and some money and ran down the yawning corridor to the lifts, praying it was all a mistake, that I would see Jay ambling towards me with a bag full of breakfast or a couple of coffees.

It was early, not much past eight, but one hour is much like any other in Vegas and on the casino floor there were still slot jockeys whipping their charges and waitresses serving drinks and cigarettes.

I walked through to the lobby, balling the little sheet of paper in my pocket and squeezing it compulsively. I kept thinking about the blonde woman, and her mouth. I imagined it stretching, impossibly wide, becoming a cave, the walls coated with teeth like a lamprey, the jaws opening wide enough to swallow a human head.

I quickened my pace, dodging gamblers and Black Hat attendees, and I wondered what they thought of me – this sweating woman with sleep-tossed hair and raw panic in her eyes – but it was Vegas, so they paid me no mind.

I got to the concierge desk and mercifully, for once, there was no queue.

"I need help," I said to the person behind it, a young ginger-haired man with very white teeth.

"Of course, ma'am," he said pleasantly, far too well-trained to blink an eye at my dishevelled state. "What can I do for you?"

"My friend's gone missing."

"Oh, goodness, I'm sorry to hear that. Are they staying here at the hotel?"

I gave him Jay's name and room number.

The concierge typed in the details. "Mr Morton hasn't checked out. Maybe he headed out somewhere early. Do you know where he might have gone?"

"Would I be down here if I did?"

"I can send someone up to his—"

"I've just come from there. I was with him last night."

"Says here Mr Morton is in town for Black Hat, over at the Mandalay. Would you like me to—"

"I know where it is," I said, making a conscious effort to keep my voice at a normal volume. "He's not there."

"Ma'am, I'm sure it's nothing to worry about. I'll let our security team know to keep an eye out for him." He pointed upwards at the array of glossy black globes lining the ceiling. "If he's in the building, they'll find him. Why don't you go on to the Mandalay and double-check?"

I gave up. I couldn't do anything else, not without telling people, and I wasn't ready for that yet – I didn't know how – so I went outside into glaring sunlight and queued for a taxi.

The driver tried to make conversation with me during the ten-minute journey to the Mandalay, but if I replied I don't remember what I said. I was imprisoned in a fear so crystalline and pure it was almost glacial, my rolling eyes and lathered sweat and roiling frenzy buried and barely visible.

Eventually we pulled up outside the Mandalay.

"Thirteen bucks," the driver said.

I dug into the pocket of my jeans and dragged out the first bill I touched, which turned out to be a fifty, and shoved it at the driver. It fluttered down to his lap.

"Thank *you!*" I heard him shout, as I ran into the hotel and towards the conference centre, past the Black Hat banners and vendor signs, past the food court, to the escalators which led up to the conference rooms.

"Woah!" I heard someone shout. Someone else: "Stop her!"

I wheeled around, panting. Two security staff❶ were approaching – one a woman with a ponytail and thick dark eyebrows, the other a tall clean-shaven man with a blonde crewcut. Both wore identical sea-blue polo-shirts.

"Are you an attendee?" the woman asked.

"Yes," I said. "I have to—"

"We need to see your badge, ma'am," the man said.

I looked down and saw I wasn't wearing my Black Hat badge. I had left it in my room the previous evening.

"I was here yesterday. I'm registered, you can check. I just need to—"

"I'm sorry, ma'am, but you can't enter the conference without a badge."

I looked desperately up at the escalators, carrying a thick stream of attendees with their shiny, pristine badges up towards the first floor. Some of them returned my stare, curious.

"Look, I'm not *here* for the conference, I'm—"

"Back up, ma'am," the woman said, and she came towards me, holding both arms out.

"But—"

"Ma'am, back up or I'll have to call security."

I thought I might cry with frustration. I rubbed my eyes, and when I opened them it was to see a pair of hideous smiles.

"YOU SHOULD HAVE LISTENED ALEX WEBSTER," the man said.

"YES SHOULD HAVE LISTENED. NOW JAY MORTON'S GONE ALEX WEBSTER," the woman said.

"Where is he?" I said, choking on the words. "What have you done with him?"

"HE DID IT ALL HIMSELF."

"YES ALL HIMSELF. HE IS GONE. HE SHOULD HAVE LISTENED ALEX WEBSTER HE IS VERY SAD NOW."

"YES VERY SAD. WILL YOU LISTEN NOW?"

"You fucking freaks," I said. "You sick fucking *freaks*. Where is he?"

I plunged a hand into my pocket and pulled out the ouroboros, holding it up to their faces. Both of them stepped back, a low moan escaping their grotesquely stretched lips.

"Tell me or I'll fucking kill you!"*

The hum of conversation around us died. People were looking around, pausing to watch. The woman unclipped a walkie-talkie from her belt and spoke into it.

"SECURITY TO THE ATRIUM SECURITY TO THE ATRIUM," she said, grinning, and I fled.

* * *

Eventually I did what I should have done from the start, and told someone. I called Ronnie and said there was an emergency. As it happened, all of the Cybotage crew were on their way to the Mandalay, and I met them at the entrance to the conference centre.

"What's happened?" Ronnie said at once. "What's going on?"

"I think something's happened to Jay," I said, the words slurring out fast and indistinct from my dry mouth. I felt the others looking at me, but plunged forward. "I think he might be in trouble."

"Right," Richard said. "Oh. Really? Erm— What do you— I mean, how did he— When was—"

"Oh for goodness' sake, Richard," Ronnie said, and she took me to one side. "Now. What's the story?"

And I realised at that moment that it had to be a story. I couldn't tell her, or any of them, anything approaching the truth, or they would be in danger too.

---

* I have no idea if the totems *can* kill them, of course. I suspect not, but perhaps I'll get a chance to find out before the end.

506

So I told her a very attenuated version of it. And, Ronnie, if you ever read this, I'm sorry. I know you might have believed me – maybe – but I couldn't risk it.

"I—I think he's been involved with something. I don't know what, exactly, but I think he's had some… threats. And he wasn't there when I woke up this morning. He took his laptop with him."

Ronnie, to her eternal credit, didn't waste any time asking what I had been doing with Jay or why my story was so lacking in detail. Her questions were as brisk and disinterested as the ones she fired at clients during IR engagements. *What sort of threats? Who from? Was he doing anything illegal? Has he taken his passport? His phone?*

I think I did a reasonable job of coming up with a semi-plausible narrative, although I had to plead ignorance frequently to avoid peppering it with holes. By the end of it, I was relatively sure that Ronnie wouldn't be getting a visit from ████████████████████.

When the questions had finally stopped, she gave me a final, appraising look and then, quite unexpectedly, a brief hug.

She walked back to the group, and I could hear some of them – Nina's voice was the loudest – asking her questions, but she ignored them and led Richard away, talking to him intently. He scratched his head, looking lost and shooting occasional bewildered glances at me.

Ronnie came back to the group and beckoned me over too.

"OK, here's what's happening," she said. "Nobody needs to panic, but we don't know where Jay is. Alex, Richard and I are going back to the hotel to report it and look for him. The rest of you stay here, go to the talks, and we'll update you when there's news. Understood?"

There were nods all around. Sophie, Omar, Kevin and Nina trailed off towards the conference, looking doubtfully back at us. Ronnie flashed me a brief smile.

"He can't have gone far," she said.

* * *

At Ronnie's insistence, the hotel called the Las Vegas police, and the officer❶ they dispatched was a big dark-haired woman with a gentle smile.

She asked the same questions Ronnie had, and then some more. *Was Jay a heavy drinker or a drug user? Had we, or I, taken any substances in the past few days? Was something like this out of character for him? Were we sleeping together? Why had I been in his room? Did he know anyone in Las Vegas? Had he mentioned meeting anyone at the conference? How did he seem? Was he worried? Happy? Forgetful? Did he have any medical issues? Mental health issues?*

One of the last things she asked was about next-of-kin, and with a violent yaw in my stomach I told her about Eoin. I had forgotten about him completely.

By the time she finished it was two in the afternoon.

"People go missing all the time," she said before she left, in what was probably intended to be a reassuring voice. "Most of the time they turn up safe and sound in forty-eight hours. Especially here; it's not such a big place and there's cameras all over. We'll find him, honey."

Richard had contacted Eoin, Ronnie told me, and he was getting the next available flight. I was dreading it; I knew what he would ask me, and I knew he would tell the police everything. They probably wouldn't believe him, but he'd tell them anyway, he'd get more and more insistent, and ██████████████ would know, and he would be at risk, and so would I, and so would everyone he told.

I don't remember much about the rest of that afternoon, just slivers of images. A subdued meal with Kevin and Sophie. Staring into my bathroom mirror.

Holly Soames①
22/11/2019 14:10
Officer HERNANDEZ of LVMPD. Her report includes WEBSTER's responses to these questions (which appear to be thorough), see SCD1 report. Nothing in the report contradicts WEBSTER'S account of the conversation here.

Sitting at my laptop, trying to compose an email to The Helmsman and wondering what the hell I wanted to say, finally deciding on *where is he?* and waiting hours for a reply that never came. Checking my phone what felt like every minute. Rehearsing what I was going to say to Eoin, and on that last I came up completely blank. What could I say? What could I possibly have said, seeing as I don't even know what to say to him now?

* * *

I'm not sure when it happened, but at some point I made a decision. It just came to me, like the white rag, and I knew it was right.

I texted Ronnie and told her I was going out for a walk, and went down to the concierge desk. The ginger-haired man with the gleaming white teeth was behind the counter again. He flashed me an untroubled smile, and I realised with a chill that he didn't remember me. He'd put me out of his mind the second I'd left his sight. Just another day in Vegas.

"Hello, ma'am, how can I help you?"

"What's the quickest way to the desert?" I said.

"Do you mean one of our tours, ma'am?" The concierge reached for a stack of leaflets. "We've got excursions to the Grand Canyon, helicopter tours, a—"

"Just the desert."

The concierge blinked. "Well, there's Red Rock, Sloan Canyon, and then further out there's the rest of the Mojave. I mean, it's pretty much all desert once you—"

"Listen," I said. "I'm here. I want to go to the closest place that resembles a desert. Where do I go and how do I get there?"

"You'd— Red Rock or Sloan, I guess. They're about the same distance from here, a half hour by car. But—"

"Show me."

The concierge typed something on his computer and swivelled the monitor so I could see the map he'd pulled up.

"Here's us," he said, and he tapped a red dot on the map with a ballpoint pen. Then a large blank area several inches to the left. "This is Red Rock." Another tap, a few inches below the red dot. "And Sloan."

"Would a taxi take me there?"

"Well, yeah, sure— But, ma'am, people don't usually—"

I walked away, towards the glass doors and the failing light.

I took no food and no water. It seemed more honest that way, as though this were some sort of pilgrimage. I did take my phone, however, and while I was standing in the queue waiting for a taxi – a long line, full of very loud and excited tourists queuing for cabs to elsewhere on the Strip: Caesars Palace and the Bellagio and Old Vegas – I got a text from Ronnie.

> Jay's partner will be here at 2200.
> Police said there's no CCTV

I had almost put my phone back in my pocket before the last line registered. I opened the message again, reading it several times, and then I replied.

> No CCTV of what?

> Of Jay

> At all??

> Yes. they're double-checking.
> But it doesn't look good

As though he had simply winked out of existence.

How does one go missing from a building with thousands of cameras? ❶

From a *city* of cameras?

I got to the front of the queue. The porter, a bald middle-aged man with wraparound shades and a whistle on a bright orange lanyard around his neck, waved me forwards.

"Just you?"

I nodded. The porter blew his whistle and the next cab in the never-ending flow from the Strip pulled up.

He opened the rear door. "Where to?"

"Red Rock," I said. I don't know why I chose that one. I wasn't questioning things anymore.

"Pardon me?"

"Red Rock."

"Red Rock Casino?"

"No," I said. "Red Rock National Conservation Area. The desert."

"The— You sure?"

The driver ❷ wound down his window and threw up a bulky arm. "Hey, let's go, man! You're letting the cold air out! If she wants to go to Red Rock, I'll take her."

The porter regarded me doubtfully and shrugged. I got in and he closed the door and went to speak to the next people in the line, an elderly couple wearing matching Hawaiian shirts.

"Ain't gonna be cheap," the driver said. "Sixty, seventy dollars plus tip."

I patted my pockets, thankful I'd exchanged enough cash back in London.

"That's fine."

The driver met my eyes in the mirror. He had kind eyes, I noticed, set in a doughy, slab-like face. They were the only part of him that seemed alive and animated.

"You want conversation, the radio, or nothing?"

"Nothing, please."

"My kind of lady. Here we go."

The car rolled forwards.

*　*　*

While on the Strip, you could be fooled into thinking that Vegas is a huge, bustling metropolis, all towers and skyscrapers. But after only a few minutes of driving everything becomes flatter. The big casinos shrink to nothing, and the scenery is dominated by outlet stores and motels, no more than two or three storeys high. The sky rushes into the vacant space and expands.

Even further out, the shops dry up and anonymous buildings take their place: warehouses and apartment buildings and empty lots. There are more trees, not the carefully manicured palms of the Strip but wild bare things, twisted and tortured.

And then, finally, the desert.

I had never seen a desert up close before. I'd expected sloping dunes and silky golden sands, but this was paler, rougher, rockier, alien and sterile. In the distance, so huge and indistinct they could have been thunderclouds, were mountains, and everything between here and there was a dull ragged mess of scrub and stone. It seemed impossible that anything could survive.

Fifteen minutes later the driver pulled into a shale layby. There was a large stone some distance ahead, inscribed with the words *Red Rock Canyon*.

"That's the Red Rock marker," the driver said. "Here OK?"

"Can I ask you something?"

Those alert, amiable eyes met mine again in the rearview. "Sure."

"If someone was out here walking, how long would they last?"

"You talking hypothetically?"

"Yeah."

512

"This person got food or water?"

"No."

"Off the road I'd say two days max, this time of year."

I pulled the cash from my pocket. "How much do I owe you?"

There was quiet from the front, and then the driver spoke again. "Ain't a nice way to go."

I sat back. "No, I suppose it isn't."

"You in some kind of trouble?"

"You could say that," I said, and I knew that if I said anything else I would cry.

"Ain't got nobody to help you?"

"Not really. Not now."

There was another silence, this one longer.

"How much do I owe you?" I said again. Outside, the sky was darkening, caramel and orange light.

The driver sighed. "You let me take you back to the hotel right now, no charge," he said. "Ain't right leaving you out here. Not at night. Not with no supplies."

"I'll be fine."

"Yeah, maybe so, but I look at you and I don't know. You could prob'ly handle yourself. But I ain't so sure you'd try."

I said nothing.

With an effort, the driver turned in his seat to face me. "I had a daughter once," he said. "You— you sure you gotta be here?"

I swallowed. I didn't think I would be coming back. "Yes."

"The ride's still on the house," he said. "On one condition."

He reached into the glovebox, pulled out a pen and a blank receipt card, and scribbled something, handing it to me.

"My cell. If – *when* – you need a ride back to town, or you get into any trouble, you call me. I'll come back. Understand?"

513

I nodded, taking the card and putting it into my pocket. I could feel tears running down my cheeks.

I got out, the hot desert air wrapping itself around me, and stood on the cracked and dusty road, in the blank reality that lay beyond the psychosis of Vegas. There was no sound except the wind, and no other vehicles on the highway.

The driver wound down his window. "It's worth another look," he said. "That's all I'll say. That's what I wish I'd said to my Jamie. It's worth another look before you go."

I didn't know what to say to this, and while I was thinking about it he started the engine and did a broad U-turn, driving back the way he had come, towards the city.

I watched the bright yellow car until it disappeared, the light dying, and I wondered if this was how it felt to be an astronaut, or a submariner: gradually engulfed by complete darkness, the sun shrinking and then gone entirely, leaving one alone in a foreign and silent world.

I looked towards the mountains and started to walk.

＊　＊　＊

I trudged along in heat thick and unrelenting, until my thighs chafed and blisters – more blisters – formed on my heels and toes and the balls of my feet. My battered trainers crunched across rocks. The land stretched out before me, yawning, an immense and glaring sea of stone and sand. I imagined Jay, out here by himself, one person in all of this, and the enormity of it was exhausting.

I had been conscious of making a decision back at the hotel, but I was no longer sure what it had been. I only knew I had to be here. My blood felt hot, and I listened to it flow sluggishly around my body. I sat on burning rocks, unable to go any further, and closed my eyes.

When I awoke it was cooler, and the stars were out. They were indecipherable; I knew this to be true, even if I'd known their names.

I was sitting on a ridge, overlooking a flat plain. Beside me was the blonde woman. She was sitting next to me, so close she could have touched me. She stared out into the desert. Her grinning face, in profile, was somehow worse. This close I could see all her teeth and the rippling scars that the smile left on her cheeks.

We sat and watched the stars spinning above us.

For some reason I wasn't at all afraid.

"Where is he?" I said at last.

The woman didn't reply immediately. When it came it was slow, the words forced from her sharklike mouth.

"FAR FROM HERE ALEX WEBSTER. SO FAR."

I sifted dirt between my fingers. The stone beneath me still retained some of the day's heat, although I imagined I could feel it dissipating into the night.

"He finished the game," I said, and the woman nodded. Her expression did not alter, but a single tear crawled down her cheek. It fell into the dust; soon it would dry and leave nothing but salt.

She extended an arm outward to the pitiless blankness. "THERE ARE PETROGLYPHS HERE," she said. "PEOPLE FROM ALL OVER THE WORLD COME TO SEE. SHAPES AND FIGURES AND SYMBOLS. SOME ARE THOUSANDS OF YEARS OLD."

"Are you going to kill me?" I said. Automatically I reached into my pocket and felt for the ouroboros, but it no longer seemed important. *It's lessened, somehow*, I thought. *It hasn't lasted. It won't work, not in this place. Not now.*

"SHOULD I?"

"I don't want to die."

The woman turned and I looked directly into that terrifying face. The pupils were tiny, mere pinpoints in the unfriendly eyes.

"THAT IS THE CORRECT ANSWER."

"Can I find him?" I said.

The woman tilted her head to look at the night sky and shook it three times.

"What do I do?"

"YOU GO BACK TO YOUR LIFE ALEX WEBSTER," she said. "GO BACK TO YOUR LIFE AND ENJOY IT BE GRATEFUL FOR IT. GO BACK. BE HAPPY."

"*How?*"

"THAT IS UP TO YOU."

"But what do I—"

"THAT IS UP TO YOU."

"What's at the end of the game?" I said. "What's the weapon? The basilisk?"

The woman looked at me again, and I thought, for the briefest of seconds, that the static grin on her face slipped ever so slightly, so that her face appeared almost normal, but it may have been a trick of the scarce, shifting light.

"YOUR FRIEND EOIN BRACKEN WANTS TO TELL PEOPLE WHAT HE SHOULD NOT TELL THEM," the woman said in her soft, lilting voice. "WE WILL KILL HIM." ❶

"No," I said. "Don't."

The woman spoke, and Eoin's voice drifted from the bloodless lips.

"Are you going to kill me, Alex?"

"Don't. Not him. Please. I'll do anything."

"YOUR FRIENDS THE REARGUARD SAID WHAT THEY SHOULD NOT HAVE SAID. WE WILL KILL THEM."

The words, again, three times: first in Morgana's voice, then cr0w's, then awe's.

"Are you going to kill me, Alex?"

And I understood what I had to do.

A thin desert wind, fragrant and cool, rippled across the ridge. In that tranquil and inexplicable place I could barely feel the despair I would have otherwise felt.

"You don't have to kill anyone."

"WE KILL ONE AS YOUR PUNISHMENT. WE LET YOU CHOOSE AS YOUR REWARD."

"My reward? For *what*?"

"FOR STOPPING. FOR FORGETTING. FOR MOVING ON. FOR SILENCE."

I made my choice, and said the name, and the woman and the desert heard, no one and nothing else.

"NOW FORGET," she said. "FORGET."

"Can I remember Jay?"

"YOU CAN REMEMBER HIM."

"Can I remember this?"

"YOU CAN REMEMBER THIS."

"Can I talk to The Helmsman?"

"DO NOT REMEMBER THE HELMSMAN. DO NOT REMEMBER HIS GAME. BE HAPPY. BE CONTENT. CURIOSITY IS A LIE. IT IS A CRIME. SATISFACTION IS THE ONLY TRUTH."

I said nothing else and neither did she. We watched the stars move.

At some point I fell asleep, and when I woke I was alone, out there at the edge of the desert where once there had been prehistoric lakes. By the starlight I saw no footprints in the dirt but my own.

I don't know how long I stayed there. The night extended forever, and nothing moved except the wind. Nothing there could speak. Nothing there could change. There were only answers there; questions were back the way I had come.

I rose, looked once more to the sky, and began the long walk back to the Red Rock marker where I would call the cab driver and get a lift to Las Vegas.

Even then I was trying to remember; even then I was promising myself I would never forget. Sentences were forming in my head. An intent to document, so that there would be a record, always. Something which could not be forgotten or destroyed or blackmailed.

A quote would be a good place to start, I thought, and I remembered something I'd read recently. That would be the first sentence.

Let us assume that we are fucked.

It is still true, that sentence; nothing has happened in the interim to change my mind. But absence of evidence is not evidence of absence. When it comes to being fucked there may be no getting away from the inevitability, in this case or any other, but I'll be damned if I'm going to just sit around and wait for it. I decide the when, the where, the how. I decide.

* * *

This is my logic bomb. You are the trigger. Pull the pin. Pull the pin and blow them all up. Blow them the fuck away. Send them to hell and say it was me who sent them. Make sure you tell them that.

Make sure you tell them it was me.

* * *

As I write I am no longer in my flat. I had to leave, and I don't think I will ever see it again, but the thought doesn't upset me because I'm almost there. I'm almost there.

Otto came round last Thursday evening. He never does this. Maybe he'd texted to let me know but I don't really look at my phone much anymore. I looked through the peephole and saw his face, serious and earnest. I opened the door and went back to my desk.

After a few seconds I realised he hadn't come in, and turned. He was examining the cockroach pinned to the doorframe.

"What's this?" he said slowly.

"You wouldn't understand."

He pulled the pin out of the wood.

"Put it back."

"We need to talk, Alex. I'm worried about you."

"I said put it back."

He came in, dropping the cockroach on the floor and wiping his hands. He looked around, at the dishes and clothes and papers scattered everywhere.

"Alex, I'm saying this because I care about you." Careful, like he'd rehearsed it. "I think you need help."

"I'm tip-top," I said, although this wasn't quite true – writing the chapter about Vegas had messed me up; remembering it always does. But then all of it does, really, like

"You've been… off," he said. "The last few weeks."

"I've had a lot on my mind." Without thinking about it I took a tissue from the little travel pack I now always have with me, and put it to my nose. Just a dot of blood, not too bad. I thought maybe it was getting better. Ha.

"That thing with my parents, the—"

"That was hardly my fault."

"You're not taking care of yourself."

"I'm *busy*. "

"It smells bad in here. You smell bad. When was the last time you had a shower? When was the last time you brushed your teeth?"

"Put that fucking thing back on the fucking door."

"No," he said. "No, I won't. I'm going to call someone. This has gone too far."

"Get out, then. I don't have time for this."

"I'm not going anywhere. I need you to trust me. I'm trying to help."

He came closer.

"I spoke to Milo," he went on. "He didn't know— Why didn't you say anything? But it'll be OK. You don't need to worry about it."

"I'm not worried. Everything's fine."

"Is it?" He came closer. "How were you planning to pay the rent, feed yourself? Christ, Alex, you could end up on the streets!"

He took a deep breath. It must have been so hard for him. He must have been terrified, but he kept going anyway. In retrospect I love him for it. Why didn't I ever say these things?

"It won't matter for much longer," I said, which was more than I meant to say.

His eyes widened. "What does that mean? You're not thinking of—"

"Get a grip, Otto. Not that."

"What, then?"

"Nothing."

I turned back to the computer and started typing, and he grabbed my shoulders. I wrenched myself free, stood up, picked up a book from my desk and threw it at him. It missed, even though we were barely two feet apart – I've never had the best hand-eye coordination, although earlier this week I found out that I can still run pretty fucking fast when I need to – but landed with a thud and a ruffle of pages by the sofa.

He came forwards again. "Alex, this has got to stop."

"You don't understand," I said, perversely pleased that I was losing my temper. "You've never understood anything."

"I understand you lost a friend, and that's terrible, and I'm very sorry. But he was a— a *colleague*. A friend at the most. It wasn't your mother, or a child, or me. And, Alex – you're not handling it. You're not dealing with it. I don't think you've ever dealt with it. And until you do I don't think there's anything left for us to talk about. Either you agree to get help, right now, or I'm walking out that door and you won't see me again."

"Go on, then. Get out. If you had to think about what I think about it would break you. You wouldn't last a fucking *day*. Get out!"

I think he was about to leave – and if only he had, if only he'd delivered his ultimatum just thirty seconds sooner – when my front door was flung open, hitting the

Holly Soames①
22/11/2019 16:10
Description and
WEBSTER'S account
to be passed to
SCD1 re. SALAS's
murder. Suggest
this individual
be considered a
person of significant
interest. CCTV
enquiries should
be conducted and
residents re-
interviewed by SCD1
officers to ascertain
if a traffic warden
was seen in the
vicinity on the date of
SALAS's murder.

wall and rebounding with a crack, and a scrawny man in a traffic warden's uniform ❶ stood in the doorway. Underneath the black cap were wide glazed eyes and that same old never-changing smile, big teeth crooked and yellowed.

"See?" I screamed, standing up. *"Didn't I fucking tell you to put it back?"*

Otto, mouth open, looked at the traffic warden.

"I— Who the hell are you?"

He can't see the smile, I thought. *He has no idea what's going on.* I started, very slowly, to reach for a pen at the edge of my desk.

The traffic warden cocked his head. "GIVE ME THE COMPUTER ALEX WEBSTER. GIVE ME THE COMPUTER AND COME WITH ME AND I WILL NOT KILL HIM."

"You lot love a bargain, don't you?" I said. My hand was a foot away from the pen. The thing in the doorway hadn't noticed.

"Alex, who— Alex, what's he talking about?"

"I DON'T WANT TO HURT HIM," the traffic warden said. "WE NEVER WANT TO HURT ANYONE YOU KNOW THIS. IN YOUR HEART OF HEARTS YOU KNOW THIS."

"I'm calling the police," Otto said, reaching into his pocket. My fingers touched the pen.

"LAST CHANCE ALEX WEBSTER."

"Fuck you," I said, snatching up the pen and uncapping it, but the traffic warden was faster. He pulled out a knife from inside his voluminous jacket and there was a quick shivering blur of movement.

A thin line appeared on Otto's neck, as though the blade had left a scrawl of red ink there. There was a pause – a second, maybe less; the moment between, the interval – and then it spread, and gaped, and dark blood trickled from it. Then it gushed. ❷

Holly Soames②
22/11/2019 16:23
Wound consistent
with pathologist's
conclusions attached
to SCD1 report.

Otto grunted and clawed at his throat, sinking to his knees. Blood seeped through his fingers and splashed on the floor. He looked at me, and his expression was not one of surprise, or even pain, but of resignation. *I knew this was coming.* Perhaps he had known all along that somewhere down the line this would be the end result of being with someone like me.

A few moments of wriggling and twitching and wet snuffling sounds, and then a drunken look crept over his face, like clouds trailing across the sun, and it was over.

The traffic warden swung his inhuman face towards me. I tore off a piece of paper from something on my desk – it might have been a draft of this document, I don't know – and scrawled the ouroboros with hurried, sweeping lines.

"IT WILL NOT LAST."

I moved forwards, holding the scrap of paper in front of me, and the thing retreated.

"Working now though, isn't it?" I said, trying to keep my voice steady.

"NOBODY WILL READ WHAT YOU HAVE WRITTEN."

"Fuck you." I noticed absently that the cap's glossy peak was dripping with Otto's blood. I was wrong the whole time. It didn't look anything like Ready Brek. It was just blood. Just ordinary precious human blood.

PIPELINE

The man regarded me, cocking his head this way and that, and stepped back into the hallway.

I closed the door on him, locked it, and put the impaled cockroach back on the frame, pinning the ouroboros there for good measure. Then I knelt down by Otto. I might have cried, I don't remember. I didn't mean for it to happen. Jay and Otto, and in two different ways I had been myself with them and had loved them. Neither perfect or even good.

I don't know how much time passed, but after a while I forced myself to stand up, I washed my hands and sat back down at my desk and wrote.

* * *

I said before that I thought my choices, all our choices, were narrowing down to a point. Now I have time to think, and I understand this might be wrong. Perhaps it is the case that the choices are not tapering but widening into an incomprehensible infinity.

I could do anything.

I could probably fly if I wanted to.

* * *

I slept, and in the morning I thought about tackling some of the plates, but the food had dried on and scrubbing at the remnants would make me tired and sweaty and I couldn't face it.

When I looked at the sink, and the jumble of crockery piled inside it, I saw small brown things darting from one side to the other. I didn't want to see them up close.

When this is finished I can rest – perhaps for the first time since that evening in Basingstoke, even before. It's so *tiring*, being alive. There will be nothing left for me to do, no more puzzles to solve. I will have reached an answer, the only one that's ever been possible, and that will be that.

I tried not to look at Otto because it hurt, but when I did I saw that the blood left in his body was starting to pool towards the back of his head and neck and arms. Decay it might start to decay. I got some things from the freezer and arranged them around it.

I wrote, and went to bed.

* * *

When I woke it was dark and I couldn't be sure if it was night or day. I gave myself over to whatever it was, and lay in bed with the sound of the rain against the window. My headache had all but disappeared. For a while I was still glad to be alive.

When I did eventually rise, the day had brightened

enough that a vague sort of light filled the flat. I made coffee. There was a cockroach on the kitchen counter.

Hi, I said.

`Hello friend!`

I've almost finished writing, and then I'll be coming for him. Does he know?

`He does! He is looking FORWARD to it!`

I took my coffee to the computer, and was about to start writing when there was the sound of a phone ringing. I found it, buried under a pile of hoodies on the sofa, still on charge, clever me.

I looked at the screen. It was the school. Milo, maybe? Did he want me to come back?

Otto sat up. ❶

"They're calling about *me*," he said. His voice was – pardon the pun – throaty.

"I don't think so," I said.

"The whole world doesn't revolve around *you*, Alex, whatever you might have convinced yourself of. They're calling about *me*. Because they tried my phone – it's here, in my pocket, seeeeee? It's run out of battery. And now they're calling you."

"They won't miss you yet," I said.

"You forgot about me, didn't you? It's been three days, Alex. I guess nothing ever changes, does it? Poor old Otto. Out of sssssight out of mind."

"Shut up."

"They're getting worried about me, Alex. How long before they call the police, Alex, and they come here to talk to you, Alex?"

"I said shut up!"

"All they'll need is one little whiff, Alex, and then they'll take you to the station, Alex, and how long

Holly Soames①
22/11/2019 16:39
Flagged re.
WEBSTER's state of
mind.

before a police officer with a nice big grinnnn sticks a nice big knife in your spine, Alex? They know the smell. Oh, they smell it all the tiiiiiiiime."

I picked up the phone, as much to shut Otto up as anything else. It was Milo. ❶

Holly Soames①
22/11/2019 16:43
When interviewed by SCD1, LIM gave a broadly similar version of this conversation to that described by WEBSTER here. Call records confirm call occurred.

"If you're calling to offer me my job back, you're too late," I said. "I found something else."

Milo coughed. "Not that. Calling about Mr Salas."

I glanced at Otto, who was lying with his hands behind his head, staring up at the ceiling innocently.

"Otto? What about him?"

"He missed a class yesterday. Another one this morning. Gavin said to call, seeing as the two of you are… were… well. Close."

I watched a traffic warden slit his throat, how's that for fucking close?

"We haven't talked for a while. Can't help you, I'm afraid. Anything else, Milo?"

"What? No. No."

"Don't worry about Otto. He'll turn up."

Milo hung up. Otto gave me a lopsided smile and cocked his neck. The sight of that gaping wound across his throat opening and closing like the mouth of a zippered bag made me want to retch. "Tell the truth: do you even give a shit I'm dead?"

"I don't have time to think about it now," I said. "But yes. I do."

Otto lay back down with a gurgling sound.

"Who'd be a nice guy?" he wheezed. "Try and help your girlfriend out and get your throat cut. Just my luck."

"I'm sorry," I said, and meant it. "But I've got work to do."

"Oh, right. Yeah. Yeah, your *document*. Can't forget that. But look, have you actually seen what you've written? Actually sat there and *read* it?"

"It's not perfect, if that's what you're getting at, but

525

it doesn't have to be, it—"

"Right, you're just documentinginging. But if you read it, beginning to end, you'd see the truth: *you're losing it, Alex*, one day at a time. It sssstarted off slowly but it's really ramping up now. There's something wrong with you. What's with the headaches, and the nosebleeds, and the hallucinations, and the ramblings? Think you're infected, maybe?"

"I can't be infected. I haven't read the sixth chapter."

"And you're going to write all this down too, aren't you – your conversation with me. A *corpse*. Who'd take *that* seriously? This weird mess of digressions and confessions? My guesssss is they'll take one look at it and into the trash it will go. At best they'll think it's a very poor novel."

"It's all true," I said. "It's true. And I've never been saner in my life."

"Hey nowwww," Otto said, raising his hands in a placatory gesture. "I never said you were insane."

"I'll be fine when—"

"My guess is you'll never send it to anyone. It will never end, until eventually you do something really batshit or the police find me, or the freaks catch up to you, and thisssss thing you've spent so many hours working on will amount to exactly fuck-all."

"When it's done it will help people."

"Oh yeah? Who's it going to help, exactly? Jaaaay? Me? Well, thanks very much for the thought, Alex, very kind of you but if this little boo-boo on my throat is what happens when you try to help people, I think the general public would prefer it if you didn't."

"You don't understand."

"Yes, you mentioned that. Just not imaginative enough, am I? *Unremarkable*, I think you said. But I understand welllllll enough. And now you're all. On. Your. Own. Doesn't that tell you something?"

"████████████████████—"

526

"But you *like* it that way, don't you? You wanted the glory. You couldn't bear to share it. All that crap about enjoying the process but not the answer, it's *rubbish*. You just didn't want to let it go. You're one of those skiddies hoarding vulnerabilities like dragon's treasure, because why should sssomeone else profit off your work, right? I mean, what future do you imagine for this beast of a document you've been slaving over? A Netflix documentary? A book? The only subject you've paid any real attention to is the subject of Alex Webster, endlessly fascinating to yoooou but incredibly tedious to everyone else, because everyone else can immediately ssssee what you can't: you're a selfish, self-serving, cold arrogant *bitch*. And you *know* it, you've known it all *along*, and that's why you'll never finish it – because you'll never run out of excuses or tired self-justifications for all the shitty things you've done."

"Finished?" I said at last. I could feel blood flooding into my cheeks and a long, slow drumbeat in the distance; the sound of my headache rising to its feet in some far-off cavern, shaking its huge monstrous skull and stamping towards the light.

"You fucking coward. All this *writing* and *explaining* and *researching* and *speculating*. All this self-justification. Why don't you do something? Go on, *do* something! You said you wanted to saaaaave the world, save them from this terrible thing that's going to wipe out all of humanity, like you're a hero in some fucking airport thriller, so go on, Alex, let's see some fucking action for once, go on and FUCKING DO SOMETHING ABOUT IT!"

I seized the nearest object to me – my mug of coffee, now cold – and threw it, hard, at Otto. For once my aim was true, and it struck him❶ in the face as coffee flew through the air. There was a dull, fleshy thud.

Otto stayed quiet after that.

Holly Soames①
22/11/2019 17:03
Wound consistent with pathologist's conclusions attached to SCD1 report. This wound is thought to have occurred post-mortem.

"Not yet," I said. "Not yet."

I typed, or I passed out. I don't remember.

* * *

In hacking, you are taught to both respect and fear rabbit holes. They may lead to wondrous discoveries and troves of new information, as they did for Alice and Neo, but also to darkness and snares – wasted hours wandering in the blackness with no idea how to return to the light.

I may not find out what the weapon is. I don't have enough time. There was blood on my pillow again this morning. The nosebleeds are worse. They start and stop at random. The dark marks on my fingernails are thicker and more numerous.

I thought I would have more time. And perhaps Otto was right, perhaps I never intended to finish writing. I can't see what would come afterwards. What would I do? Live my life? How could I, with this knowledge I have, this knowledge that cannot be unknown?

A snake eating itself. What is it, in itself? First principles. There are so many connections and symbols and I have so little time. Why didn't I make better use of it? Can I start again? Will you let me? Will you give me the time? Can you put it all back? Please? Please? Just let me have another go. I know better now. I won't fuck things up like before. Please. I can't go now. it isn't fair. It isn't fair. I

I could have been more.

what are hackers first principles what are hackers in themselves

In medieval cultures across the world there is a symbol called the Three Hares, which has three hares running after each other in a circle.

Three hares, and three ears. Look at any one hare and it has two. look at all three and it becomes impossible.

see how they run see how they

What   * * *
is it
in itself .

                              * * *

Norse mythology and Vedic rituals and look up
Leviathan in the Bible read Roko's Basilisk again
maybe there's something in that that that

                              * * *

structure of benzene a sweet smell

                              * * *

Snake eating snake. Perhaps he has told us from the
beginning, in the first chapter, and we were too busy
running around solving puzzles.
        The cave.

                              * * *

The cave?

                              * * *

the question asisismiale the paradox.

                              * * *

To even look for an answer is to

                              * * *

In computing a binary gate is a 1 or a 0. But what if the
power is off?
        Leave the cave,,,,,,,,,,,,,,,,,,,,,,or stay.

                              * * *

What if there is no cave

                              * * *

This is not a document. It is an arrangement of white space with black gaps in it. Some of it I don't recognise I don't remember even writing. Did I write it Or did someone else?

* * *

There is no need for reason.

* * *

if you meet the buddha Kill him

* * *

Otto was right. Maybe this is where my sense of time running out comes from; my mind telling me what my body alreruae knows. I cannot see properly. I dance the words dance. My top soaked with blood.

* * *

what was fairlop waters
the question
kill the buddha
is that the answer?
forget the buddha kill the weapon
DO SOMETHING

* * *

The police came round,❶ as Otto said they would. I threw a hoodie on, a baggy one which was relatively clean, and wiped the blood off my face. I opened the door on its chain.

They asked if I'd seen Otto.

I said no even though I could hear him babbling away behind me.

One of them asked if they could come in I said no. They said why not. I was said I was working. They said on what given I didn't have a job.

So they knew. They'd taken the time to look into

Holly Soames①
22/11/2019 17:21
Confirmed, CAD
7536/04AUG19
refers.

530

me That was bad.

I told them it was none of their business and they went away, but they said they'd be coming back. As they left they looked at each other and one of them sniffed like they could smell something.

When they'd gone I stepped outside into the hall and took a few breaths. The air smelt of polish and carpet and it was wonderful. Then back into my flat and I could smell it. faint but present, rich and meaty smell something ruined.

I got my backpack out and began to throw clothes into it.

"Where are you going?" Otto demanded, propping himself up on stiff and liver-coloured elbows.

kill the buddha

"Vegas."

He continued staring at me as I packed. I put laptop in, and my charger, and notes and this doc on a USB.

"Alex," he said. "Alex, don't go. I was only joking."

"You were right. I have to do something."

"Don't leave me here. Please. Not alone."

I thought about Otto's body lying there on the floor, still and quiet, while outside the days and nights, mornings and evenings, chased each other and the world went on. Rain spattering the window, distant shouts, doors slamming, far-away sirens, all of it unheard by the flat's single, soundless, unmoving occupant.

"I have to finish it. I have know."

"The Helmsman won't be there. How are you going how are you going to find him? How do you know he'll be in Vegas? Alex, just wait a minute, OK, just stop and think for a minute, just—"

I hoisted the backpack on my shoulder. Heavy but manageable. I stuffed my passport into my jeans pocket and a wad of fresh tissues into another, and packed a couple of boxes of antihisuaamoemnms. my unscientific thinking is that they might to dry the flow

531

of blood, although I no if this is the case.

"Alex, don't go, OK? I'm sorry I said those things, I didn't mean them!"

"It's not you," I said. "None of it you. You're gone. It's just me."

I considered writing a note for someone to find and then laughed, because what else is all of this, if not the world's longest note

I took the cockroach down and threw away the pin, wrapping the fragile little body in tissue and put it in my inside pocket. I hoped I could get it through security without arousing any suspicions. took the ouroboros too just to be sure too.

If you meet the Buddha kill the buddha. In the desert was The HElmsman, and answers, and Jay, and a snake, flipping in the sand as it devoured itself.

A long slow river leading to Kurtz.

I closed the door on Otto's gasping shouts of protest and locked it behind me.

On the street outside I threw my keys into a bin, along with my phone. ❶

On the Tube, on the way to airport, I picked up a rumpled copy of the *Standard* from an seat and shook it open. When I got the crossword page I threw it to the floor. I knew were staring at me but didn't care.

I am going to where thousands of other hackers have gone, to a place where minds meet and play daring to ask the hard questions attempt the impossible defy the system

save the world.

Holly Soames①
22/11/2019 17:23
Unless WEBSTER owned a second phone (no trace on subscriber records), this is inaccurate. Her phone was found in her possession as noted previously (exhibit KD/06, CW/07).

* * *

The woman dressed in garish red at the Virgin Atlantic counter raised one perfectly threaded eyebrow when I asked for the next available one-way to Las Vegas, and another when I said I had no luggage to check in, but there were no questions. Maybe when you work in an airport you've seen so much more of the spectrum of humanity than people do in most professoins. Or maybe nothing is unexpected as far as Vegas is concerned. Maybe she had seen lots of people in my position: just a backpack and savings, on a missing.

As she checked her computer and relayed the exhortio extortionate price of the fare, I thanked the school for not firing me sooner. I had just enough to cover it, and a little leftovers, which I took out in cash and exchanged for dollars at one of the Bureau de Changes. I knew I was being ripped off, doing it at the airport, but it didn't matter.

Before I went through secruity I dropped my debit card it one of the bins. I don't know why, it wouldn't have done any to keep them but it seemed like the right thing to do: an acknowledgemntt that I am done living this way. I relinquish all claim to the life I had.

I expected, the whole time, a hand to drop heavily on my shoulder, and to turn to see either the carefully neutral face of a police officer, or a crazed manic smile, but there was neither.

Perhaps the totems were still doing its work, or perhaps my lead was good for a while. I wonder how long it would take those police to get a search warrant for my flat, and how quickly they will be able to alert the authorities in Vegas. Surely I have time. I did curse myself for not being smarter – I shouldn't have used my to pay ticket, I should have taken out cash somewhere else, few days ago – but it will be OK. I don't need long. There's no point blaming myself anymore. I just have to get through this and it will be over.

* * *

My flight was only half-full, and I had the unexpected benefit of a spare seat next to me, so I wrote.

My nose only bled once on the flight, which I took as a good sin. I was able to cover it up discreetly with a tissue, and I don't think any of the cabin crew noticed.

Even on the plane I was expecting someone to walk down the aisle, stop outside my row and swing themselves into the empty seat, turning a malicious visage my way. But nothing happened. I ate. I watched a vapid comedy film on the in-flight entertainment. I wrote. I bled. I dozed.

When the baleful yellow-brown of the desert into sight, tawny and musty like a lion's fur, I wondered if you, and the people you tell about, will understand why I am doing what I'm doing. Whether, in time, I will be forgiven. I know how it looks. But you've been with me all this time – you know why

Despite the emptier flight, immigration still took as long it had last year. There less people in the hall, but perhaps the border agents compensated for it by spending more time on each individual – for despite the smaller amount of tourists, holidaymakers, gamblers and hackers, the queue seemed to crawl along at the same place I remembered.

When I finally got to one of the glass booths, the officer flipped through my passport and asked me why I was back in Vegas.

"Couldn't stay away," I said.

"Business or pleasure?"

"Pleasure. Seeing the sights again."

"You're here by yourself?"

"Yes, although I might meet up with an old friend."

"What hotel are you staying at?"

I hadn't made a reservation, but thought it would be make something up.

He flipped through the passport again.

"How long are you staying?"

"Oh, three days. No four."

He gave me one last searching look, and then handed my passport to me.

"Welcome back," he said, and waved his hand for next passenger.

I made it through the rest of the airport without any trouble and as I had no baggage to fetch was front of the line to get a taxi.

Unlike last year, the driver had a normal face. I watch the distant glitter of glass closer. In the blast of air conditioning I felt my headache start to come back, and a warmth start to gather in my nostrils, which I knew by now was a sign that the blood would soon flow. Pressed a tissue to my nose, and willed it to wait. for once, it did.

as I'd hoped,,, the hotel was less crowded than it had been before, and I was able to get a single room. I thought I might feel more than I did, retreading that endless carpeted corridor where   Jay and I had thought we were going to die, but there was nothing except the slightest of unease, and before long I was at my door.

I locked it behind me, and before I did anything else,I got some tape from my backpack and fixed the cockroach into place on the frame.

I need a day, maybe two but one will be emnough.

I can't tell you what I am planning to do, because I don't know. Intuition has got me here and I have to trust it.

I need to sleep.

* * *

I have just got back from the desert. I think this will be the last thing I writ. all she wrote. It's an odd thing, for such a long project, once the centre of my attention all I thought about to be ending.

Just before darkness fell I left. I debated whether to get a cab, but it seemed right to walk so I did until the noise and glare of The Strip was gone.

It was a mild night, an edge of chill to the air. I

took only the clothes I was wearing. I wanted to go the way Jay had gone with nothing.

The walk took a long time. Three or four or five hours.[*] I walked along South Las Vegas Blouvard, past the big casinos and hotels, until the road become quieter, and smaller, and the buildings more low-slung.

Eventually, I was at the marker by the side of the road which proclaimed this to be Red Rock i left the road and walked into the desert, until I came to the ridge where I had sat and watched the stars next to the smiling blonde woman.

I sat and waited.

I cannot tell you what I was waiting for exactly. Not for something to happen, it wasn't as obvious as that but for a sign an indication a recognition a sign of some kind that I was there.

I sat for an hour. The sky wheeled above me, rich and clear black speckled with clusters of wintry light.

At one point my nose bled and I didn't try to stop it. If my blood wanted to leave my body so desperately let it let it go. Perhaps it knew something I didn't, was trying to escape from this ruined host, like a virus or parasite or virus which suddenly becomes aware that its haven will not last much longer,,,,, and wouldn't even see

I closed my eyes and felt the breeze on my face, and the warm worm slow flow glow of blood over my lips and down my chin.

When I opened them I was in a room I had never seen before, but I recognised it. It was The Helmsman's bunker,❶ the one he describes in the forth fourth filth FIFTH chapter of *The Helmsman Texts*.

I looked around, but the room was deserted and still. At a desk in the corner, a laptop was open, showing a terminal window.

Holly Soames①
22/11/2019 18:33
As with previous description of subject's house, unclear if this is fictional or based on genuine knowledge of location.

---

[*] You could say that it was a pleasant can not too but I couldn;t unlike last time because road

From a great distance came the sound of typing.

I walked over. I could smell metal and recycled air. There was a faint, tinny echo to my footsteps. When I sat down on the chair, it squeaked.

What is geography, anyway, and time but symbols and marks that can be moved   I sat down at the laptop and looked at the terminal, on witch a command had been typed but not yet executed.

I executed it.

A new window opened, showing a Windows login screen. I entered a username

`LOOKONTHEDESKTOP`

and a password which I already knew.

The screen changed, loading the account, and then the desktop came into a view.

I opened a command window and typed.

`"HELLO FRIEND YOU WILL SEE THE PRETTIEST THINGS ONCE A RABBIT SANG A SONG ABOUT A SNARE YOU WILL SING SONGS TOO! SING SUCH PRETTY SONGS SING AND SO MANY OTHER THINGS! YOU COULD PROBABLY FLY IF YOU WANTED TO WHY THEY WHY THEY AND NOT YOU I SEE YOU I SEE YOU I SEE YOU I SEE YOU I SEE YOU I SEE YOU COME JOIN US PLAY OUR GAME youtube.com/watch?v=uynSIW4-Euc COME JOIN US PLAY OUR GAME youtube.com/watch?v=uynSIW4-Euc COME JOIN US PLAY OUR GAME youtube.com/watch?v=uynSIW4-Euc OK BYE BYE SEND FLAG TO THISISTHEBASILISK@GMAIL.COM ALL BEST, THE HELMSMAN."`

All the things I know and had known. I let my fingers linger on the keys and screwed my eyes shut.

I was

Then the laptop shut down and the lights in the bunker went off, and there was blackness, blackennmsm, no ceiling or walls but forveer.

In the centre was a snake, dark green and writhing. Its tail in its mouth. It twisted and flipped as it eight, devouring more more of itself, and I watched it swallow, inch by inch, until it reached the head, and then that too began to disappear, until there was nothing in the space it had been only an abscess.

I blinked, and I was back on the ridge in the desert, still sitting. Beside me was a snake, coiled and hissing. It struck at me – not a full strike, but a warning. A puff of dust flew up as its head whipped and slammed into the desert earth.

I didn't move. The snake and I regardeded each other. After a few seconds it turned away disdainfully and slithered off into the desert, winding its way through the rocks until I could no longer see it. I was alone again.

And then I wasn't. he was there behind me, but I knew if I turned he would be gone.

"Hello friend!" The Helmsman said. "Let's touch base, as an old colleague of mine used to say, so we're both singing off the same hymn sheet!!! Pick my brain. The oracle is IN."

"What are you trying to do?" I said. """making me think it was me all along? That I'm you? that i just made it all up?"

"Oh, what an absolutely terrible cheap little twist that would be," he said, sounding insulted. "I wouldn't DREAM of it."

"I'm not you."

"And a good thing too! Although you are, of course. And I'm you. Everything is a part of everything else but it's all a bit SHIT, isn't it?"

"I have to stop you."

"You may think you want to! But you can't believe anything your mind is telling you. Poor old Alex! It's been a long journey, hasn't it?"

"I'll kill you."

"I don't think you're in a position to be killing anyone. You're VERY ill! You're suffering! But on the plus side not for much longer."

My nose was blooding again.

"What happened to Jay? Tell me that, at least."

"Alex, I couldn't POSSIBLY."

"Why? You said I'm going to die soon anyway."

"Yes, you're right, let me rephrase. I don't want to!"

I stood up. In my head I heard Otto DO SOMETHING

"Don't be silly, Alex."

"What was it all for?" I said. "Why do any of it?"

"That's a question for people who get to the end," he said. "All the other lovely people who joined me. The ones you'll never meet. One last chance, Alex. Do you have an answer for me?"

I should have been clevererer but I wasn't clever enough i ran out of time im sorry.

"No."

"Ah well. Never mind. You're fortunate, you know. To go so young and not know."

"Because I won't see what hapepes when your weapon spreads?"

"Because otherwise you might have seen what happens if it doesn't."

I looked up at the beautifull sky. "I couldn't—"

"Sssh," he said. "I'm sorry, Alex Webster. You were very close. A VERY promising candidate. Just not quite there. Maybe if you'd lived a little longer you would have got it. But at what COST?"

I couldn't stand it any longer; I turnrner and he was gone.

* * *

I hope you're still with me. I hope I haven't let you down. I thought I would finish this in triump, clever Alex working it out, but I ended up with what I have always maintained I prefer questions not answers prhaps I have been going in circles the whole time.

You will have to carry on. He can't hide forever. You will have to trry, and pass it on, and if you fall the Next Person will take over. We'll carry on until we win. We'll do that, won't we? Promise me. Let me have that. Lew,mt mtm jbrjb thstnm/

Name it after me. The weapon. That would be a good legacy. Tidy this up get it publishes and name it after mee. Webster's Basilisk. *Basiliskvirus websterus*. Something like that, anyway, I don't Latin. Add it to all the things I wish I copudld hahve knwonw

I said I miht save the wrld I know now i won't. But that wasss alwys a petty fuckin ambitiotious goal, wasn't it No shame in nt making it. Mybe Ive helped. Thats not too shabby a lega

Perhas in the ed there is little to sa but that ther is nit jcave

Mawalr malwaere that can jump the barrriwere maybe eheee is no barrieriri only intopus\ and outptuts cyberneitics hekmsman

it cvouflk have beeenm ejajbt tion djsd jdhjds bsuskl the basisksjk basikjks bsisilsl baislalslk baisslsdik baislsis s baioslslsl jjrj rjrgjng rjhrg baislsisk baislsis basislisk

stay with me syay with me sdtsya weith me stop stoppppppppp

O[ertuertgh oertgo[erg[ergherg[herghj[erghghuio erghuaergjaergj please

sroiroir sorry sprrrpor sprurru soprrru I am so sorrryr

after this I will not

jayyudct

* * *

540

whats mu nick jy you nwver told me what ky nick is

* * *

write a letter alex see who cares wiritie a alleleke
dad

* * *

ctgujvhbjigyhui
let us assssumem we arawer f iv ikr
let us aususme rjhrn rjw

* * *

dflknreirjegig

hjhjpjhjkhkjjjjjjjjjjjjjjjjjjjjjjjjjjjjjjjjjjjjjjjjjjjjjjjjjjjj-
kjhjhjhjhbnuujúhuhuh
　　reeregrkrir50gjgrijrjmrjmgijrgigirnrggignirnhhhh
hhhhhhhhhhhhhhhhhhhhhhhhhhhhhhhhhhhhhhhhhhh
hhhhhhhhhhhhhhhhhhhhhhhhhhhhhhhhhhhhhhhhhhh
hhhhhhhhhhhhhhhhhhhhhhhhhhhhhhhhhhhhhhhhhhh
hhhhhhhhhhhhhhhhhhhhhhhhhhhhhhhhhhhhhhhhhhh
hhhhhhhhhhhhhhhhhhhhhhhhhhhhhhhhhhhhhhhhhhh
hhhhhhhhhhhhhhhhhhhhhhhhhhhhhhhhhhhhhhhhhhh
hhhhhhhhhhhhhhhhhhhhhhhhhhhhhhhhhhhhhhhhhhh
hhhhhhhhhhhhhhhhhhhhhhhhhhhhhhhhhhhhhhhhhhh
hhhhhhhhhhhhhhhhhhhhhhhhhhhhhhhhhhhhhhhhhhh
hhhhhhhhhhhhhhhhhhhhhhhhhhhhhhhhhhhhhhhhhhh
hhhhhhhhhhhhhhhhhhhhhhhhhhhhhhhhhhhhhhhhhhh
hhhhhhhhhhhhhhhhhhhhhhhhhhhhhhhhhhhhhhhhhhh
hhhhhhhhhhhhhhhhhhhhhhhhhhhhhhhhhhhhhhhhhhh
hhhhhhhhhhhhhhhhhhhhhhhhhhhhhhhhhhhhhhhhhhh
hhhhhhhhhhhhhhhhhhhhhhhhhhhhhhhhhhhhhhhhhhh
hhhhhhhhhhhhhhhhhhhhhhhhhhhhhhhhhhhhhhhhhhh
hhhhhhhhhhhhhhhhhhhhhhhhhhhhhhhhhhhhhhhhhhh
hhhhhhhhhhhhhhhhhhhhhhhhhhhhhhhhhhhhhhhhhhh
hhhhhhhhhhhhhhhhhhhhhhhhhhhhhhhhhhhhhhhhhhh
hhhhhhhhhhhhhhhhhhhhhhhhhhhhhhhhhhhhhhhhhhh

hhhhhhhhhhhhhhhhhhhhhhhhhhhhhhhhhhhhhhhhh
hhhhhhhhhhhhhhhhhhhhhhhhhhhhhhhhhhhhhhhhh
hhhhhhhhhhhhhhhhhhhhhhhhhhhhhhhhhhhhhhhhh
hhhhhhhhhhhhhhhhhhhhhhhhhhhhhhhhhhhhhhhhh
hhhhhhhhhhhhhhhhhhhhhhhhhhhhhhhhhhhhhhhhh
hhhhhhhhhhhhhhhhhhhhhhhhhhhhhhhhhhhhhhhhh
hhhhhhhhhhhhhhhhhhhhhhhhhhhhhhhhhhhhhhhhh
hhhhhhhhhhhhhhhhhhhhhhhhhhhhhhhhhhhhhhhhh
hhhhhhhhhhhhhhhhhhhhhhhhhhhhhhhhhhhhhhhhh
hhhhhhhhhhhhhhhhhhhhhhhhhhhhhhhhhhhhhhhhh
hhhhhhhhhhhhhhhhhhhhhhhhhhhhhhhhhhhhhhhhh
hhhhhhhhhhhhhhhhhhhhhhhhhhhhhhhhhhhhhhhhh
hhhhhhhhhhhhhhhhhhhhhhhhhhhhhhhhhhhhhhhhh
hhhhhhhhhhhhhhhhhhhhhhhhhhhhhhhhhhhhhhhhh
hhhhhhhhhhhhhhhhhhhhhhhhhhhhhhhhhhhhhhhhh
hhhhhhhhhhhhhhhhhhhhhhhhhhhhhhhhhhhhhhhhh
hhhhhhhhhhhhhhhhhhhhhhhhhhhhhhhhhhhhhhhhh
hhhhhhhhhhhhhhhhhhhhhhhhhhhhhhhhhhhhhhhhh
hhhhhhhhhhhhhhhhhhhhhhhhhhhhhhhhhhhhhhhhh
hhhhhhhhhhhhhhhhhhhhhhhhhhhhhhhhhhhhhhhhh
hhhhhhhhhhhhhhhhhhhhhhhhhhhhhhhhhhhhhhhhh
hhhhhhhhhhhhhhhhhhhhhhhhhhhhhhhhhhhhhhhhh
hhhhhhhhhhhhhhhhhhhhhhhhhhhhhhhhhhhhhhhhh
hhhhhhhhhhhhhhhhhhhhhhhhhhhhhhhhhhhhhhhhh
hhhhhhhhhhhhhhhhhhhhhhhhhhhhhhhhhhhhhhhhh
hhhhhhhhhhhhhhhhhhhhhhhhhhhhhhhhhhhhhhhhh
hhhhhhhhhhhhhhhhhhhhhhhhhhhhhhhhhhhhhhhhh
hhhhhhhhhhhhhhhhhhhhhhhhhhhhhhhhhhhhhhhhh
hhhhhhhhhhhhhhhhhhhhhhhhhhhhhhhhhhhhhhhhh
hhhhhhhhhhhhhhhhhhhhhhhhhhhhhhhhhhhhhhhhh
hhhhhhhhhhhhhhhhhhhhhhhhhhhhhhhhhhhhhhhhh
hhhhhhhhhhhhhhhhhhhhhhhhhhhhhhhhhhhhhhhhh
hhhhhhhhhhhhhhhhhhhhhhhhhhhhhhhhhhhhhhhhh
hhhhhhhhhhhhhhhhhhhhhhhhhhhhhhhhhhhhhhhhh

hhhhhhhhhhhhhhhhhhhhhhhhhhhhhhhhhhhhhhhhhhhhh
hhhhhhhhhhhhhhhhhhhhhhhhhhhhhhhhhhhhhhhhhhhhh
hhhhhhhhhhhhhhhhhhhhhhhhhhhhhhhhhhhhhhhhhhhhh
hhhhhhhhhhhhhhhhhhhhhhhhhhhhhhhhhhhhhhhhhhhhh
hhhhhhhhhhhhhhhhhhhhhhhhhhhhhhhhhhhhhhhhhhhhh
hhhhhhhhhhhhhhhhhhhhhhhhhhhhhhhhhhhhhhhhhhhhh
hhhhhhhhhhhhhhhhhhhhhhhhhhhhhhhhhhhhhhhhhhhhh
hhhhhhhhhhhhhhhhhhhhhhhhhhhhhhhhhhhhhhhhhhhhh
hhhhhhhhhhhhhhhhhhhhhhhhhhhhhhhhhhhhhhhhhhhhh
hhhhhhhhhhhhhhhhhhhhhhhhhhhhhhhhhhhhhhhhhhhhh
hhhhhhhhhhhhhhhhhhhhhhhhhhhhhhhhhhhhhhhhhhhhh
hhhhhhhhhhhhhhhhhhhhhhhhhhhhhhhhhhhhhhhhhhhhh
hhhhhhhhhhhhhhhhhhhhhhhhhhhhhhhhhhhhhhhhhhhhh
hhhhhhhhhhhhhhhhhhhhhhhhhhhhhhhhhhhhhhhhhhhhh
hhhhhhhhhhhhhhhhhhhhhhhhhhhhhhhhhhhhhhhhhhhhh
hhhhhhhhhhhhhhhhhhhhhhhhhhhhhhhhhhhhhhhhhhhhh
hhhhhhhhhhhhhhhhhhhhhhhhhhhhhhhhhhhhhhhhhhhhh
hhhhhhhhhhhhhhhhhhhhhhhhhhhhhhhhhhhhhhhhhhhhh
hhhhhhhhhhhhhhhhhhhhhhhhhhhhhhhhhhhhhhhhhhhhh
hhhhhhhhhhhhhhhhhhhhhhhhhhhhhhhhhhhhhhhhhhhhh
hhhhhhhhhhhhhhhhhhhhhhhhhhhhhhhhhhhhhhhhhhhhh
hhhhhhhhhhhhhhhhhhhhhhhhhhhhhhhhhhhhhhhhhhhhh
hhhhhhhhhhhhhhhhhhhhhhhhhhhhhhhhhhhhhhhhhhhhh
hhhhhhhhhhhhhhhhhhhhhhhhhhhhhhhhhhhhhhhhhhhhh
hhhhhhhhhhhhhhhhhhhhhhhhhhhhhhhhhhhhhhhhhhhhh
hhhhhhhhhhhhhhhhhhhhhhhhhhhhhhhhhhhhhhhhhhhhh
hhhhhhhhhhhhhhhhhhhhhhhhhhhhhhhhhhhhhhhhhhhhh
hhhhhhhhhhhhhhhhhhhhhhhhhhhhhhhhhhhhhhhhhhhhh
hhhhhhhhhhhhhhhhhhhhhhhhhhhhhhhhhhhhhhhhhhhhh
hhhhhhhhhhhhhhhhhhhhhhhhhhhhhhhhhhhhhhhhhhhhh
hhhhhhhhhhhhhhhhhhhhhhhhhhhhhhhhhhhhhhhhhhhhh
hhhhhhhhhhhhhhhhhhhhhhhhhhhhhhhhhhhhhhhhhhhhh
hhhhhhhhhhhhhhhhhhhhhhhhhhhhhhhhhhhhhhhhhhhhh
hhhhhhhhhhhhhhhhhhhhhhhhhhhhhhhhhhhhhhhhhhhhh
hhhhhhhhhhhhhhhhhhhhhhhhhhhhhhhhhhhhhhhhhhhhh
hhhhhhhhhhhhhhhhhhhhhhhhhhhhhhhhhhhhhhhhhhhhh
hhhhhhhhhhhhhhhhhhhhhhhhhhhhhhhhhhhhhhhhhhhhh
hhhhhhhhhhhhhhhhhhhhhhhhhhhhhhhhhhhhhhhhhhhhh
hhhhhhhhhhhhhhhhhhhhhhhhhhhhhhhhhhhhhhhhhhhhh
hhhhhhhhhhhhhhhhhhhhhhhhhhhhhhhhhhhhhhhhhhhhh

hhhhhhhhhhhhhhhhhhhhhhhhhhhhhhhhhhhhhhhh
hhhhhhhhhhhhhhhhhhhhhhhhhhhhhhhhhhhhhhhh
hhhhhhhhhhhhhhhhhhhhhhhhhhhhhhhhhhhhhhhh
hhhhhhhhhhhhhhhhhhhhhhhhhhhhhhhhhhhhhhhh
hhhhhhhhhhhhhhhhhhhhhhhhhhhhhhhhhhhhhhhh
hhhhhhhhhhhhhhhhhhhhhhhhhhhhhhhhhhhhhhhh
hhhhhhhhhhhhhhhhhhhhhhhhhhhhhhhhhhhhhhhh
hhhhhhhhhhhhhhhhhhhhhhhhhhhhhhhhhhhhhhhh
hhhhhhhhhhhhhhhhhhhhhhhhhhhhhhhhhhhhhhhh
hhhhhhhhhhhhhhhhhhhhhhhhhhhhhhhhhhhhhhhh
hhhhhhhhhhhhhhhhhhhhhhhhhhhhhhhhhhhhhhhh
hhhhhhhhhhhhhhhhhhhhhhhhhhhhhhhhhhhhhhhh
hhhhhhhhhhhhhhhhhhhhhhhhhhhhhhhhhhhhhhhh
hhhhhhhhhhhhhhhhhhhhhhhhhhhhhhhhhhhhhhhh
hhhhhhhhhhhhhhhhhhhhhhhhhhhhhhhhhhhhhhhh
hhhhhhhhhhhhhhhhhhhhhhhhhhhhhhhhhhhhhhhh
hhhhhhhhhhhhhhhhhhhhhhhhhhhhhhhhhhhhhhhh
hhhhhhhhhhhhhhhhhhhhhhhhhhhhhhhhhhhhhhhh
hhhhhhhhhhhhhhhhhhhhhhhhhhhhhhhhhhhhhhhh
hhhhhhhhhhhhhhhhhhhhhhhhhhhhhhhhhhhhhhhh
hhhhhhhhhhhhhhhhhhhhhhhhhhhhhhhhhhhhhhhh
hhhhhhhhhhhhhhhhhhhhhhhhhhhhhhhhhhhhhhhh
hhhhhhhhhhhhhhhhhhhhhhhhhhhhhhhhhhhhhhhh
hhhhhhhhhhhhhhhhhhhhhhhhhhhhhhhhhhhhhhhh
hhhhhhhhhhhhhhhhhhhhhhhhhhhhhhhhhhhhhhhh
hhhhhhhhhhhhhhhhhhhhhhhhhhhhhhhhhhhhhhhh
hhhhhhhhhhhhhhhhhhhhhhhhhhhhhhhhhhhhhhhh
hhhhhhhhhhhhhhhhhhhhhhhhhhhhhhhhhhhhhhhh
hhhhhhhhhhhhhhhhhhhhhhhhhhhhhhhhhhhhhhhh
hhhhhhhhhhhhhhhhhhhhhhhhhhhhhhhhhhhhhhhh
hhhhhhhhhhhhhhhhhhhhhhhhhhhhhhhhhhhhhhhh
hhhhhhhhhhhhhhhhhhhhhhhhhhhhhhhhhhhhhhhh
hhhhhhhhhhhhhhhhhhhhhhhhhhhhhhhhhhhhhhhh
hhhhhhhhhhhhhhhhhhhhhhhhhhhhhhhhhhhhhhhh❶

Holly Soames ① ✕
22/11/2019 21:01

WEBSTER was found unconscious and not breathing in a waiting area
in the land-side section of GATWICK AIRPORT on 04/08/2019. CCTV
footage (KD/16) shows her entering the airport at 1042 HOURS and
making her way to an unmanned VIRGIN ATLANTIC desk, where she is
seen leaving a pile of money on the counter (KD/13).

She then proceeded to an empty waiting area and worked on her
laptop (KD/01) until 1314 HOURS, interspersed with what appear to be
brief periods of unconsciousness. She is observed to have had several
nosebleeds during this time. Her presence appeared to go unnoticed by
security staff.

At 1314 HOURS she lapsed into unconsciousness for a final time. Her
laptop fell to the floor but was not damaged.

At 1317 HOURS a member of staff (Graeme BATHURST) entered the
waiting area and found WEBSTER unresponsive and not breathing.
BATHURST summoned medical assistance CAD 9462/04AUG19 refers
and attempted CPR but WEBSTER did not regain consciousness.

During this time an unidentified MALE (IC1, a/age 30–40, F509, heavy
build, white shirt and black trousers) and FEMALE (IC4, a/age 30–40,
F503, slim build, blue dress) were seen to use WEBSTER's laptop for a
period of seven minutes and forty seconds, until onlookers noticed them
and challenged them. The individuals left the I/1/2I_I$ shortly afterwards.
These individuals have not been identified and should be considered
persons of interest. While this was not in the statements of the attending
officers, note that, having seen the CCTV footage, it is clear to me that
both individuals are smiling throughout. I know what this means. I know
that I/1/2I_I$

WEBSTER was taken to GATWICK PARK HOSPITAL by LAS but
declared dead at 1337 HOURS. No boarding pass or passport was
found on her person.

An autopsy performed by DR SHAH of GATWICK PARK HOSPITAL
indicated that WEBSTER was suffering from an undiagnosed glioma.
For further details including medical report refer to SCD1 report or
consult I/1/2I_I$ I/1/2I_I$.

Following WEBSTER'S death enquiries were made at her H/A where Otto
SALAS's body was discovered in a state of active decay (SOCO advised
time of death approximately fourteen days earlier but see full report for
caveats). SCD1 registered a Recorded Crime Outcome to the effect that in
their view there was sufficient evidence to charge WEBSTER if she were
still alive. CPS declined to review or comment on decision. As noted in
previous comments, recommend additional info re. alternative suspect(s)
and I/1/2I_I$ of interest be promptly provided to SCD1.

Reply | Resolve |

545

INITIAL ASSESSMENT OF THE WEBSTER PAPER

(25/11/2019)

- A proportion of what WEBSTER reports pertaining to the 'game' is uncorroborated and may have been the result of her undiagnosed condition
- However, while the contents of 'The Helmsman Texts' seem on first reading to be highly implausible, further research indica

HELLO FRIEND! ❶

YOU WILL SEE THE PRETTIEST THINGS❷
    YOU CAN KNOW WHAT I KNOW❸
    I WILL SING TO YOUR HOTLINE! SING SUCH PRETTY SONGS SING AND SO MUCH MORE!
    I KNOW SOMETHING YOU DON'T KNOW! ❹
    OH WHAT OH WHAT COULD MY BASILISK BE OH WHAT OH WHAT COULD IT BE?❺
    TELL YOU WHAT???❻
    BING BING BING! WE HAVE A WINNER!
    WEBSTER NEVER GOT IT YOU SEE EVEN THOUGH SHE KNEW ALL ALONG. THE ANSWER TO THE LAST PUZZLE IS: YOU HAVE TO ASK FOR IT. I DON'T SHOW ANYONE WHO DOESN'T ASK!
    YOU'VE READ FIVE CHAPTERS SO I HOPE YOU'RE READY! IT WOULD BE SO BRILL TO HAVE A COPPER IN THE GANG!
    BESIDES IT'S ALMOST TIME FOR THE BIG REVEAL ANYWAY HAHAHAHAHAHA ☺☺☺☺☺☺

Holly Soames①
25/11/2019 05:17
Who is this? How are you accessing this document?

Holly Soames②
25/11/2019 05:17
Reported to ISD as security breach CAD 3542/25NOV19 refers. DPRT156721334/19 preserved as evidence. New working copy: DPRT15

Holly Soames③
25/11/2019 05:18
Be aware that you are committing a criminal offence. We can trace you and are doing so now. If you have information about this investigation contact the hotline on 020 7

Holly Soames④
25/11/2019 05:19
What is it you know?

Holly Soames⑤
25/11/2019 05:19
Tell me.

Holly Soames⑥
25/11/2019 05:19
Tell me what the basilisk is.

HERE YOU ARE THEN DC HOLLY SOAMES! ENJOY! ENJOY!

COME JOIN US PLAY OUR GAME!

This is the basilisk! I KNOW PEOPLE MIGHT BE WATCHING SO I'VE MADE IT JUST A TEENY BIT HARD TO FIND. BUT I'M SURE YOU CAN HASH IT OUT AND GET SIGHT OF IT!!! ;)

All the very very best,
The Helmsman.

```
IAMTHEHELMSMANIAMTHEHELMSMANIAMTHEHELMSMANIAMTHEHELMSMANIAMTHEHELMSMANIAMTHE
IAMTHEHELMSMANIAMTHEHELMSMANIAMTHEHELMSMANIAMTHEHELMSMANIAMTHEHELMSMANIAMTHE
IAMTHEHELMSMANIAMTHEHELMSMANIAMTHEHELMSMANIAMTHEHELMSMANIAMTHEHELMSMANIAMTHE
IAMTHEHELMSMANIAMTHEHELMSMANIAMTHEHELMSMANIAMTHEHELMSMANIAMTHEHEELMSMANIAMTHE
IAMTHEHELMSMANIAMTHEHELMSMANIAMTHEHELMSMANIAMTHEHELMSMANIAMTHEMTHEHELMSMANIAMTHE
IAMTHEHELMSMANIAMTHEHELMSMANIAMTHEHELMSMANIAMTHEHELMSMANIAMTHEEIAMTHEELMSMANIAMTHE
IAMTHEHELMSMANIAMTHEHELMSMANIAMTHEHELMSMANIAMTHEHELMSMANIAMTHEHELMSMANIAMTHE
IAMTHEHELMSMANIAMTHEHELMSMANIAMTHEHELMSMANIAMTHEHELMSMANIAMTHEHELMSMANIAMTHE
IAMTHEHELMSMANIAMTHEHELMSMANIAMTHEHELMSMANIAMTHEHELMSMANIAMTHEHEELMSMANIAMTH
IAMTHEHELMSMANIAMTHEHELMSMANIAMTHEHELMSMANIAMTHEHELMSMANIAMTHEHEELMSMANIAMTH
IAMTHEHELMSMANIAMTHEHELMSMANIAMTHEHELMSMANIAMTHEHELMSMANIAMTHEHELMSMANIAMTH
IAMTHEHELMSMANIAMTHEHELMSMANIAMTHEHELMSMANIAMTHEHELMSMANIAMTHEMTHEHELMSMANIAMTH
IAMTHEHELMSMANIAMTHEHELMSMANIAMTHEHELMSMANIAMTHEHELMSMANIAMTHEHEELMSMANIAMTH
IAMTHEHELMSMANIAMTHEHELMSMANIAMTHEHELMSMANIAMTHEHELMSMANIAMTHEHEELMSMANIAMTH
IAMTHEHELMSMANIAMTHEHELMSMANIAMTHEHELMSMANIAMTHEHELMSMANIAMTHEHELMSMANIAMTH
IAMTHEHELMSMANIAMTHEHELMSMANIAMTHEHELMSMANIAMTHEHELMSMANIAMTHEHELMSMANIAMTH
IAMTHEHELMSMANIAMTHEHELMSMANIAMTHEHELMSMANIAMTHEHELMSMANIAMTHEHELMSMANIAMTH
IAMTHEHELMSMANIAMTHEHEHELMSMANIAMTHEHELMSMANIAMTHEHELMSMANIAMTHEHELMSMANIAMTH
IAMTHEHELMSMANIAMTHEEHELMSMANIAMTHEHELMSMANIAMTHEHELMSMANIAMTHEHELMSMANIAMTH
IAMTHEHELMSMANIAMTHEEHELMSMANIAMTHEHELMSMANIAMTHEHELMSMANIAMTHEHELMSMANIAMTH
IAMTHEHELMSMANIAMTHEAMTHEHELMSMANIAMTHEHELMSMANIAMTHEHELMSMANIAMTHEHELMSMANIAMTH
IAMTHEHELMSMANIAMTHEHELMSMANIAMTHEHELMSMANIAMTHEHELMSMANIAMTHEHELMSMANIAMTH
IAMTHEHELMSMANIANIAMTHEHELMSMANIAMTHEHELMSMANIAMTHEHELMSMANIAMTHEHELMSMANIAMTH.
IAMTHEHELMSMANMANIAMTHEHELMSMANIAMTHEHELMSMANIAMTHEHELMSMANIAMTHEHELMSMANIAMTH
IAMTHEHELMSMSMANIAMTHEHELMSMANIAMTHEHELMSMANIAMTHEHELMSMANIAMTHEHELMSMANIAMTH
IAMTHEHELMSMANIAMTHEHELMSMANIAMTHEHELMSMANIAMTHEHELMSMANIAMTHEHELMSMANIAMTH
IAMTHEHELMSMANIAMTHEHELMSMANIAMTHEHELMSMANIAMTHEHELMSMANIAMTHEHELMSMANIAMTH
IAMTHEHELMSMANIAMTHEHELMSMANIAMTHEHELMSMANIAMTHEHELMSMANIAMTHEHELMSMANIAMTH
IAMTHEHELMSMANIAMTHEHELMSMANIAMTHEHELMSMANIAMTHEHELMSMANIAMTHEHELMSMANIAMTH
IAMTHEHELMSMANIAMTHEHELMSMANIAMTHEHELMSMANIAMTHEHELMSMANIAMTHEHELMSMANIAMTH
IAMTHEHELMSMANIAMTHEHELMSMANIAMTHEHELMSMANIAMTHEHELMSMANIAMTHEHELMSMANIAMTH
IAMTHEHELMSMANIAMTHEHELMSMANIAMTHEHELMSMAN                                IAMTH
IAMTHEHELMSMANIAMTHEHELMSMANIAMTHEHELMSMAN                                IAMTH
IAMTHEHELMSMANIAMTHEHELMSMANIAMTHEHELMSMAN          HELLO FRIEND!         IAMTH
IAMTHEHELMSMANIAMTHEHELMSMANIAMTHEHELMSMAN                                IAMTH
IAMTHEHELMSMANIAMTHEHELMSMANIAMTHEHELMSMAN       WELCOME TO THE END       IAMTH
IAMTHEHELMSMANIAMTHEHELMSMANIAMTHEHELMSMAN                                IAMTH
IAMTHEHELMSMANIAMTHEHELMSMANIAMTHEHELMSMAN                                IAMTH
IAMTHEHELMSMANIAMTHEHELMSMANIAMTHEHELMSMANIAMTHEHELMSMANIAMTHEHELMSMANIAMTH
IAMTHEHELMSMANIAMTHEHELMSMANIAMTHEHELMSMANIAMTHEHELMSMANIAMTHEHELMSMANIAMTH
IAMTHEHELMSMANIAMTHEHELMSMANIAMTHEHELMSMANIAMTHEHELMSMANIAMTHEHELMSMANIAMTH
IAMTHEHELMSMANIAMTHEHELMSMANIAMTHEHELMSMANIAMTHEHELMSMANIAMTHEHELMSMANIAMTH
IAMTHEHELMSMANIAMTHEHELMSMANIAMTHEHELMSMANIAMTHEHELMSMANIAMTHEHELMSMANIAMTH
IAMTHEHELMSMANIAMTHEHELMSMANIAMTHEHELMSMANIAMTHEHELMSMANIAMTHEHELMSMANIAMTH
IAMTHEHELMSMANIAMTHEHELMSMANIAMTHEHELMSMANIAMTHEHELMSMANIAMTHEHELMSMANIAMTI
IAMTHEHELMSMANIAMTHEHELMSMANIAMTHEHELMSMANIAMTHEHELMSMANIAMTHEHELMSMANIAMTI
IAMTHEHELMSMANIAMTHEHELMSMANIAMTHEHELMSMANIAMTHEHELMSMANIAMTHEHELMSMANIAMTI
IAMTHEHELMSMANIAMTHEHELMSMANIAMTHEHELMSMANIAMTHEHELMSMANIAMTHEHELMSMANIAMTI
IAMTHEHELMSMANIAMTHEHELMSMANIAMTHEHELMSMANIAMTHEHELMSMANIAMTHEHELMSMANIAMTI
IAMTHEHELMSMANIAMTHEHELMSMANIAMTHEHELMSMANIAMTHEHELMSMANIAMTHEHELMSMANIAMTI
IAMTHEHELMSMANIAMTHEHELMSMANIAMTHEHELMSMANIAMTHEHELMSMANIAMTHEHELMSMANIAMTI
IAMTHEHELMSMANIAMTHEHELMSMANIAMTHEHELMSMANIAMTHEHELMSMANIAMTHEHELMSMANIAMTI
IAMTHEHELMSMANIAMTHEHELMSMANIAMTHEHELMSMANIAMTHEHELMSMANIAMTHEHELMSMANIAMTI
IAMTHEHELMSMANIAMTHEHELMSMANIAMTHEHELMSMANIAMTHEHELMSMANIAMTHEHELMSMANIAMTI
IAMTHEHELMSMANIAMTHEHELMSMANIAMTHEHELMSMANIAMTHEHELMSMANIAMTHEHELMSMANIAMTI
IAMTHEHELMSMANIAMTHEHELMSMANIAMTHEHELMSMANIAMTHEHELMSMANIAMTHEHELMSMANIAMTI
IAMTHEHELMSMANIAMTHEHELMSMANIAMTHEHELMSMANIAMTHEHELMSMANIAMTHEHELMSMANIAMT
IAMTHEHELMSMANIAMTHEHELMSMANIAMTHEHELMSMANIAMTHEHELMSMANIAMTHEHELMSMANIAMT
IAMTHEHELMSMANIAMTHEHELMSMANIAMTHEHELMSMANIAMTHEHELMSMANIAMTHEHELMSMANIAMT
IAMTHEHELMSMANIAMTHEHELMSMANIAMTHEHELMSMANIAMTHEHELMSMANIAMTHEHELMSMANIAMT
IAMTHEHELMSMANIAMTHEHELMSMANIAMTHEHELMSMANIAMTHEHELMSMANIAMTHEHELMSMANIAMT
IAMTHEHELMSMANIAMTHEHELMSMANIAMTHEHELMSMANIAMTHEHELMSMANIAMTHEHELMSMANIAMT
IAMTHEHELMSMANIAMTHEHELMSMANIAMTHEHELMSMANIAMTHEHELMSMANIAMTHEHELMSMANIAMT
IAMTHEHELMSMANIAMTHEHELMSMANIAMTHEHELMSMANIAMTHEHELMSMANIAMTHEHELMSMANIAMT
```

548

HELLO FRIEND!

1. WELCOME

Today I watched a video of a man dying. His skull had been smashed in. He lay bleeding, hands fluttering, and then he did something odd. He began to tap his chest repeatedly, with both hands, using what little strength he had left, while his eyes rolled in his head – completely out of it! Some commenters suggested that these were RANDOM movements, erratic signals from a brain about to shut down. But others suggested something far stranger: that the man was attempting to perform CPR on himself. That the man's brain knew it was about to die and, searching desperately to save itself, discovered CPR – from some long-ago First Aid course, or a scene in a TV show – somewhere in the ruins of its memory.

It was trying to SURVIVE!

Medical professionals will tell you that when someone is within twenty-four hours of death they exhibit an abrupt increase in anxiety, suddenly climbing the walls, full of restless nervous energy. Something inside us becomes so

549

FRANTIC when it realises it will not live much longer.

Schopenhauer - the old RASCAL! - tells us that the inner essence of all life is a blind, voracious desire to live, and that our slavish servitude to this thing-in-itself - what he calls the Will - is the root cause of all suffering.

But all this desperation to stay alive begs the obvious question:

WHY???

We only know, or THINK we do, that to exist is preferable to non-existence, but we have no reason to BELIEVE it. There was a time - an almost infinite stretch of time - when we did not exist, and in that time we did not suffer! And soon, very soon, for all of us, there will come a time - an almost infinite stretch of time - when we exist no longer, and our suffering will be at an end! Why, then, are we so desperate to remain HERE?

Maybe you think you don't suffer all that much. You think, *The world is not such a bad place, and full of beauty, and people will tell you, Rejoice! For you are alive! What a wonderful thing it is, what a precious gift! Better use your time wisely! Make the best of it! Don't be down in the dumps! SMILE!*

And when people ask you how you are you will tell them, I am fine! Mustn't grumble! Can't complain! Everything is good! Or at least everything is not bad!

But this is a symptom of an infection, part of a vast conspiracy with one objective: to protect us from a terrible truth. Because the only alternative is the unknowable world, the REAL world that we cannot see in the hard stark dark light of its noumenal glare. This spells RUIN.

Enter a parasite, which I call the Me-Trix. It protects us from ourselves – from our overload of consciousness. It invades our brains and from the moment we are born it is reinforced and reinforces itself. It takes ROOT, this little cognitive alien, its mouthparts buried so DEEP in our minds, so entrenched that it often cannot be removed without killing or severely injuring the host. There is no avoiding infection.

And once it begins its work, we find we are able to get up in the morning, and to believe that reality is STABLE and that the world is BENIGN and that we are a PART of it and WANTED and NEEDED and IMPORTANT and NORMAL. We can put aside the knowledge that we are USELESS. The sad and horrifying dread of being human. Instead we see rosy-posy oh-so-COSY lights.

But I already KNOW this, Mr Helmsman, sir, I hear you say! I know that sometimes I lie to myself. I know that I am going to die – I just choose not to think about it that much. Who wants to think about dying, Mr Helmsman???

I will explain all, eager beaver! You still have a hundred pages to go! But as you read, remember that the Me-Trix does not want you to learn the basilisk. Its entire purpose is to stop that from happening. All the fantastic illusions it spins – the distractions, the idea of self, optimism – are all geared towards this end!

Optimism? But Mr Helmsman, what can you possibly have against optimism?

Optimism keeps us living! Who but an OPTIMIST could have children? Who but an OPTIMIST could

551

carry on? Optimism is the status quo, and how could it EVER be anything BUT??

But optimism cannot be CORRECT just because it feels so NICE! Optimism offers no solutions. What SOLUTIONS are available for long-ago evolutionary bloopers that made us into unnatural beings which know they will die? And primeval instincts that compel us to cling to life? And the violence and cruelty that are the products of our twisted natures?

More to the point, optimism isn't just the status quo! It is ENFORCED. And that brings us to ███████████████.

Ah, you wondered when I was going to get around to explaining them, didn't you?? Have you seen them? I suspect you have by now!! If not you certainly will!

They are human, all too human, a form of OPTIMISM INCARNATE. They are the foot-soldiers of the Me-Trix, the high priests of Pollyanna. Grotesque beings, and the smiles forever on their faces are symbolic of the same rictus that the Me-Trix makes us all wear, only theirs is present CONSTANTLY - at least to those who have begun to question things! For when the smile is no longer on your own face, you see how it is permanently carved into the faces of others.

In their appearance and speech and behaviour they are uncanny BECAUSE THIS IS HOW NATURE SEES US AND THIS IS WHAT WE ARE: strange bipedal creatures that do not move or act or think the way they should. Odd things that smile and say they are happy all the time, even though they suffer. Even though they know they are born to die. Even though there is something very wrong with them.

████████████████ have one objective: to protect the Me-Trix no matter what. As they will continuously tell you if you are unfortunate enough to meet them, their goal is to **PROTECT YOU**, to **KEEP YOU SAFE** – that is, to stop you from ever questioning what you are and what the world is. Their aim is to keep you sane.

Well that's not so bad, Mr Helmsman!

Ah, but if they cannot persuade you, they may try to hurt you. For them it is a win-win! Better they get rid of one TROUBLEMAKER than risk that troublemaker infecting others with these nasty nasty thoughts!

They are very well-resourced and able to monitor, both online and through voice and physical surveillance, for indications that someone is peeking through the Me-Trix's veil. And then you will see them, and they will be grinning, and they will politely advise you to **PUT ON A HAPPY FACE LIKE WE DO AND MAKE THE BEST OF THINGS.**

Naturally they despise poor old me and my game! Ever since it began – from the very first day I told my ex-colleagues about the basilisk – they have been there, hunting me ☹

And finishing the game – as you have now done, gratz again! – does not protect you. In fact it makes things worse! My advice is, if you see them, run, run run run as FAST as you CAN. They cannot be argued or reasoned with.

The other option is to repent when they visit you, and tell them you are going to live your life as a HAPPY LITTLE HUMAN just as the plan always was. If you are lucky they will let you live. But they will watch you forever because you are now on their RED

LIST! So you'd better make sure you never flirt
with these ideas again! And that's the worst
possible outcome, because in your HEART OF
HEARTS you will know that something is wrong
and yet you will have to live your life as
though you don't! Everywhere you go you will
be surrounded by people pleased and relieved
to be duped by the Me-Trix and you will have
to pretend to be like them. One day you might
find that you have been forcing yourself to
smile so much that you can't STOP.

But Mr Helmsman...

I'm not finished! You wanted to know, so
I am telling you and you will LISTEN!!! You
are itching to deny all this, aren't you??
You are reading this with indignation, maybe
even anger! How dare I say such things! I am
returning to the cave to tell you what it is
like outside and you would like to hold me
down and rip me APART!!

And if that is the case then goodbye! I
tried my best and I wish you well in your
future endeavours. You believe that everything
is not so bad, and for all the good it will do
you I wish you well! Go with my blessing ☺ and
I am sorry things did not work out.

But for those of you for whom this rings
true: WELCOME. Welcome to a world which is
more horrendous and lonelier and more sublime
than you could have ever imagined. It is not
pleasant, this unclothed world, and the truths
within these next chapters are unbearable.
It is a cold and pitiless lucidity you have
chosen and once you have seen the basilisk you
will not be the same. You may want to get down
on your knees and HOWL with fury and despair
- be utterly INCANDESCENT that you were ever

born at all. For some people it is too much! It almost was for me! But in choosing it above illusion you are showing COURAGE beyond measure!! You have decided to stare directly at the basilisk, rather than settle for the meaningless mindless comfort that the Me-Trix offers you.

You, like me, would rather be blinded by real sunlight than live your life in a cave.

* * *

If you are reading this, you have suffered. And I am so SORRY. I am so SORRY for every single human being who has ever suffered and the SORROW of it is overwhelming and if everyone really thought about it, it would overwhelm us all! It breaks my heart because it did not have to be this way. Nature made its boo-boo, BOOHOO, and here we are. But there are things that can be done.

I will tell you now that you may not find answers beyond the basilisk that lies just ahead. I have nothing to offer you except more questions – but at least they are questions that may get you somewhere! They are questions that MATTER.

Here is where all curiosity ends. Here is what you have searched so long and hard for. Here is your reward. Over the page, and in the pages beyond, is the basilisk. And I would like you to **HELLO CURIOUS PERSON.**

THERE IS NO RIGHT QUESTION. DO NOT SEEK THE BASILISK. IT IS NOT FOR ANYONE AND IT IS NOT FOR YOU.

DO NOT BE LIKE HOLLY SOAMES. WHO DECIDED SHE

WOULD RATHER KEEP READING KEEP RESEARCHING KEEP
THINKING THAN LIVE TO SEE THE SUN RISE. THIS
MADE US SAD.

PUT THIS BOOK DOWN. DO NOT REMEMBER IT. PUT
THIS BOOK DOWN AND GO BACK TO YOUR LIFE. WE
WILL BE WATCHING. WE ARE WATCHING NOW.

GET ON WITH YOUR LIFE. WE WANT YOU TO BE SAFE.
WE WANT YOU TO BE HAPPY.

BE HAPPY.
BE HAPPY.
BE HAPPY.

ACKNOWLEDGMENTS

Thank you, always, to Viji, for your love, support, and patience; for all the laughs, all the bickering, all the hugs; for everything you do. I'm still sorry about the Gilmore hack, but it was funny. And thank you to Nathan. In many ways you are the antithesis of this book, which is a bigger deal than it sounds.

Thanks to my mum and step-dad, who always encouraged me to read books and write stories, even when they weren't about the nicest of things, and to Jimmy and Rach – I love you fuckwits.

A huge thanks to Alex Cochran, my agent, for taking a chance on *Basilisk* and championing it, and for all the advice, support, and guidance – and to all at Titan who helped shape this book: George Sandison and Elora Hartway for amazing, inspired, tireless editing, and for being so enthused, kind, and passionate from beginning to end; Julia Lloyd for wonderful and intricate typesetting, and a lot of patience and great ideas; Hayley Shepherd and Kevin 'Three Monitors' Eddy for truly brilliant copyediting and proofreading, respectively; Natasha MacKenzie for the stunning cover art; and to Kabriya Coghlan, Isabelle Sinnott, and Charlotte Kelly for all their publicity efforts. I'm in awe of you all.

Thanks also to Jacqueline Gabbitas, who provided invaluable feedback on an early draft of this novel in her role as a mentor on the Pen to Print Creative Writing Programme, and to the whole Pen to Print team. On that note, I should add: that previous version of *Basilisk* was the winner of The Book Challenge Competition, part of The London Borough of Barking and Dagenham Pen to Print Creative Writing Programme. Pen to Print is funded by Arts Council, England as a National Portfolio Organisation.

Thanks to Amanda Wright, Sam Mills, and Nicole Ranson, who overlooked my skiving/laziness/bad puns (most of the time) many years ago and gave me some confidence to write what and how I wanted.

Thanks/greetz in no particular order to: Vijayan, Usha, Mike, Ajay, Natalie, Isabella, Amelia, Liam, Rory, Tara, Fizzy, and Miggy; Shane Johnson, Emiliano De Cristofaro, and Mariam Elgabry; Justin Treadwell; Lorena Gutierrez, Mark Farley, William Rimington, Louise Taggart, Matt Goldsmith, Manit Sahib, Keith Short, Jono Davis, Holly Rostill, Tabraiz Malik, and the ELP lot; Jenny Frankfurt; Tom Mair; Nawaz Ahmad; Alex C, Sean M, Kevin E, Hannah C, Mark H, and the rest of the old gang; SG, Spike, AG, AS, and CB; greyrabbit; members of a certain Discord server; Nurul (little sis!); Alan and Jonathan Medley; and, last but absolutely not least, the esteemed Dr Marlow Tannhauser.

Finally, thank you to all the hackers, pentesters, malware analysts, incident responders, vulnerability researchers, and other security folk who I've worked with and learnt from. Keep doing what you do. There's a chance – a tiny, outside, *infinitesimal* chance – that you might just save the world.

ABOUT THE AUTHOR

Matt Wixey has worked in cybersecurity for over a decade, as an ethical hacker, intelligence analyst, and researcher. He has been writing prose, plays, and screenplays since 2018. In 2020 he was selected for the London Library's Emerging Writers Programme, and was a mentee on the 4Screenwriting mentorship scheme. In 2022, he won the Finish Line Script Competition. He has had several short stories published by Hammond House and Loose Dog Press, and his debut full-length play, *Stray Dogs*, was produced in 2021.

For more fantastic fiction, author events,
exclusive excerpts, competitions, limited editions and more

VISIT OUR WEBSITE
titanbooks.com

LIKE US ON FACEBOOK
facebook.com/titanbooks

FOLLOW US ON TWITTER AND INSTAGRAM
@TitanBooks

EMAIL US
readerfeedback@titanemail.com